The Lost Girl

The Lost Girl

Liz Harris

Where heroes are like chocolate – irresistible!

Copyright © 2016 Liz Harris

Published 2016 by Choc Lit Limited
Penrose House, Crawley Drive, Camberley, Surrey GU15 2AB, UK
www.choc-lit.com

A CIP catalogue record for this book is available
from the British Library

ISBN 978-1-78189-301-2

P... .... Group UK Ltd, Croydon, ...0 4YY

*To my husband, Richard, with love and
gratitude for his unfailing support*

Acknowledgements

I should like to begin by thanking Choc Lit and
my lovely editor. I feel privileged to be published
by such a great team of people, and to be part of
a group of authors who are so unstinting in their
support for each other and in their friendship.

Before I began *The Lost Girl*, I was already familiar
with the history of the American West, and of Wyoming
in particular, having visited Wyoming and also having
read a wide range of books prior to writing my first
two historical novels set in Wyoming, *A Bargain Struck*
and *A Western Heart*. However, *The Lost Girl* was
the first novel I'd set in the south west of Wyoming,
and it called for research into the tensions that
developed between the white miners and the Chinese
in that area during the 1870s and early 1880s.

I'm extremely grateful for the tremendous help given
me by Janice Brown, The Rock Springs Historical
Museum, Wyoming. Amongst the literature given to me
by Janice was the invaluable 'The Chinese Story and
Rock Springs, Wyoming', written by Henry F. Chadey,
Director of Sweetwater County Historical Museum.

There are many articles on the tensions prevalent
during this period and it's difficult to single out any
one article from the many sources I found, but I should
like to say how greatly indebted I was to 'Marriage and
the Family Among Chinese Immigrants to America,

1850–1960' (*Phylon: The Atlanta University Review of Race and Culture*, Vol. 29, no. 4, 1968, p. 322).

Once again, I have to thank my Friend in the North, Stella, who reads every word I write, and who never fails to tell me the truth. Such honesty is the sign of a true friend, and I very much appreciate Stella's friendship and support.

Thank you, too, to the members of the Choc Lit Tasting Panel – Isabelle, Helen D., Sarah C., Jenny K., Lee, Tina and Bruce – who took the story of Charity and Joe to their hearts and recommended its publication.

A writer's life may be a solitary one, but it is never a lonely one if the writer belongs to the Romantic Novelists' Association. A source of help, support and, above all, friendship, the RNA continues to play a large part in my life. In addition, I derive a great deal of pleasure from my membership of the Oxford Writers' Group and of the Historical Novel Society.

Finally, my two sons have fled the nest and are unaffected by the many hours a day that I hide myself away in my study, writing. My husband, however, is not so lucky, and I'm extremely grateful to Richard for keeping our real world running so smoothly while I create a fictional world.

Chapter One

Carter Town, Wyoming Territory
May, 1868

The cry hung in the air, then slowly died away.

Joe looked up sharply. That sounded like it came from a person, he thought. He gripped his metal pan tightly, sat back on his heels and listened hard. But all he could hear was the familiar thumping of the mine pump, the chirping of birds and the rasping scream of a red-tailed hawk as it soared above his head.

Shrugging his shoulders dismissively, he turned back to the river and tilted the pan to let the last of the water trickle over the metal lip and fall back into the river, just like he'd seen his pa do in the days when they'd gone panning for gold together. Gold was heavier than sand and gravel, his pa had told him as they'd knelt side by side at the water's edge, and flakes of gold would be left on the bottom of the pan when everything else had been washed away.

But there'd never been any flakes of gold; only mud and stones.

And finally his ma had made his pa give up prospecting and go and work down the mine that had opened after the railroad had been built, and now he, Joe, was the only person left who was able to go out in the day and look for gold.

He'd have liked Sam to come out with him, but Sam was twelve, five years older than he was, and had to go to school. He could've come out on the days when he wasn't in school, but Sam just laughed at him whenever he suggested it. He said looking for gold was a waste of time, and he was going to be a miner. Sam went into Carter Town whenever he could and did any job they'd pay him to do, until he was old enough to go down the mine with his pa and the other men. And when there wasn't any work, he'd hang around the town with his friends.

So it wasn't going to be Sam or his pa who found the gold; it was going to be him.

Joe gave the pan a final shake, changed its angle so that the sunlight fell on the sand and gravel that lay at the bottom, and stared hopefully at what was left.

Yet again, his hope faded. That was all it was – sand and gravel. There was no glint of gold.

In despair, he stood up and tossed the silt as far as he could into the creek. There was gold somewhere in the mud at the bottom of the river, he thought, scowling into the clouding water, and he was going to look for it until he found it. His pa was never wrong about things.

And when he did find it – when he struck gold, as Pa used to say – everything would be all right again, just like it had been when he was very little and they'd lived on the ranch. It would be his gold because he'd found it, but he'd share it with Ma, Pa and Sam. His ma would stop being angry all of the time, and she'd smile again in the way she used to. His pa would be proud of him and thankful he no longer had to go down the mine every day, and Sam would want them to play together. Maybe Sam would even ask him to go into Carter with him and his friends. He'd like that.

So he just had to find that gold.

He knelt down again, dipped the pan back into the water and vigorously swirled it.

And then he heard the crying noise again. He stopped, raised his head, and listened intently.

Gravel rattled to his right. Startled, he glanced over his shoulder up the gully slope behind him.

A grey-headed sagebrush sparrow was darting between the pebbles, its tail raised in the air. It saw him, stopped abruptly and stared back, its eyes unwinking and bright. Then it chirruped, flapped its wings and flew off.

Silence fell again, broken only by the occasional cry of a bird and the muffled noise that came from the mine further down the river.

It must have been a bird each time, he thought, or a lone prairie dog; it couldn't have been a person. But he was ready to go home – he'd done enough panning for the day. He'd check the silt that was left behind, and then he'd go back to his ma. He angled the metal pan more sharply to speed up the water draining away.

As soon as the last of the water had trickled out, he peered closely at the mud in the pan, and he heard the sound again.

It was louder this time, and closer. And it came from a person, not a bird; he was certain of that.

His hair prickled on the back of his neck and his forearms.

And it wasn't just a cry he could hear – there were footsteps, too. But it didn't sound like people usually sounded when they were walking. The steps were hesitant, as if someone kept on stopping, waiting a moment, and then started to walk again.

And that someone seemed to be coming towards him.

In sudden panic, he clambered to his feet and stared up at the wide blue sky, his pan hanging from his hand, its muddy contents sliding to the ground.

The sun was almost at its height so it wouldn't be Pa coming for him – Pa would be in the mine. And it wouldn't be Sam – he'd still be in town. And it wouldn't be his ma – she'd have started on the cooking as soon as she'd finished the washing, and she knew he'd come home when he was hungry so she wouldn't waste time going out looking for him. And it wouldn't be Indians – everyone said they were long gone.

The footsteps stopped, and he heard the person cry out again, a cry of pain. Then the walking started again.

His heart beating fast, he threw the pan to the ground and scrambled up the short distance to the top of the gully. Shielding his eyes from a sun hazed by the grey mist of ash from the mine, he scanned the expanse of dusty white ground, broken in places by sparse clumps of yellow and green sagebrush, anxiously searching for the person whose footsteps he'd heard.

But there was no one to be seen.

Biting his lip, he turned right and stared past the row of miners' houses where he lived to the town that lay beyond. Squinting, he studied the sparse grey wooden shacks and the buildings belonging to the mine; then he turned towards the jagged hills of rock that rose up on the opposite side of the river from the town, peaks grey-white against a blue sky.

He gave a sudden start and took a step forward. A figure was making its way down the side of one of the hills, heading in the direction of the plank bridge that stretched across the gully, linking the hills with the town.

Relief washed through him – it wasn't someone coming towards him after all. It was someone who wanted to cross the river to get to Carter Town.

He stood still and stared at the figure, amazement growing. The man didn't look at all like his pa or the other men in Carter. He was wearing baggy trousers – not jeans

– and his shirt was hanging loose outside his trousers. Also, he was wearing a yellow hat with a wide brim that sloped up to a point. He'd never seen anyone in a hat like that before. And he was carrying a bundle of clothes in his arms, or maybe dirty washing. But that was the sort of thing his ma would carry, not his pa.

Maybe he'd come from the Overland Trail, and his horse and wagon had run off so he was heading into Carter to buy another set. Or maybe he was making for the railroad to get on a train. If he'd been walking for a long time, his feet would be hurting because of the hard ground, and that could be why he kept crying out.

The man reached the bridge and started to cross to the other side, walking slowly, one hand on the wooden rail, the other clutching the bundle of clothes. Halfway across, he stumbled and leaned heavily against the railing, as if trying not to fall.

Instinctively, Joe started to run towards the man, wanting to help him. Then he suddenly stopped in his tracks, and his hand flew to his mouth. Ma had told him there were bad men around, men who did terrible things like robbing banks and shooting guns at people. The man in the pointed hat might be a bad man, and the bundle he was carrying might be full of things he'd stolen. Maybe he'd even got a gun tucked into his trousers.

Joe put his thumb in his mouth, and stared hard at the man, wondering what to do. He didn't look like a bad man, even if his clothes were funny. But he'd never seen a bad man so he might be wrong.

As he stood hesitating, the man straightened up and started walking again. A few steps from the Carter end of the bridge, he paused, gave a loud cry and bent low over the clothes he was carrying. Hugging the bundle to his stomach, he crumpled on to the wooden planks. Before Joe could move, he'd rolled under the railing, slipped over the edge of the bridge and had disappeared from sight.

Flinging himself forward, Joe sped across the ground as fast as he could.

Reaching the bridge he saw the man lying halfway down the gully, face down on his stomach. The parcel of clothes had rolled further down the slope and had stopped at the water's edge.

He crouched on the edge of the bridge, jumped down and ran to the side of the man. As he neared him, he saw that the man's bare feet were red and swollen, and had been cut on the rock-strewn ground.

'Mister,' he said, leaning over him and shaking him. 'You okay, Mister?'

The man didn't move.

'You okay, Mister?' he repeated more loudly.

Still the man didn't move.

He pulled off the man's hat, and his eyes opened wide at the sight of the long plait of black hair that had been wound up inside it. His hands hovered momentarily above the man's left shoulder, then he caught hold of the shoulder, pulled hard to roll him on to his back, and stared at the man's face.

Only it wasn't a man's face – it was a woman's.

And a woman who looked ill, with her skin a yellowy colour and scratched from the gravel, and with her eyes open wide, staring at him. He frowned; he was sure he'd seen people before with eyes a funny shape like the woman's, but he couldn't remember when or where.

'I'm Joe, ma'am,' he said, and he shook her hard. 'Say somethin'.'

But the woman remained silent, and she didn't move.

Glancing down the length of her, he saw that the front of her trousers was drenched in blood.

Panic welled up.

'Ma!' he screamed. 'Ma!'

He stood up, spun round and started to clamber up the side of the gully at speed.

A faint cry from behind stopped him.

He looked back at the woman in surprise. He'd thought she might be dead. He stared hard at her – she sure looked dead, being that colour, and he was certain she hadn't moved. Yet he'd definitely heard her cry.

The cry came again, stronger this time, more insistent. But it didn't come from the woman – it came from the bottom of the gully. It was the cry of a baby.

His eyes flew to the bundle she'd been carrying.

His feet slipping from under him, he slid down the gravelly slope to the edge of the river, the crying loud in his ears. Reaching the pile of rags, he tore the outer dirty white shirt from around the bundle. A smaller bundle, wrapped in a tightly wound shawl, lay inside. A tiny wooden animal, painted the colour of gold, with black stripes drawn across its back, was pinned to the front of the shawl, holding it closed.

Pricking his fingers in his haste, he undid the pin, unwound the shawl, and drew in his breath in a gasp: a baby stared up at him.

It was the littlest baby he'd ever seen, with eyes the same shape as its mother's.

Crying loudly, the baby kicked its legs in the air. Then its cries died away and it made a funny noise in its throat, a whimpering sound. Joe stared at it in amazement.

The piece of cloth wrapped around the baby's tummy looked wet, and it smelt. He wrinkled his nose. 'I'm gonna take you home to Ma,' he said, nodding reassuringly at the baby. 'She'll look after you 'cos your ma's real sick.'

He slipped the animal clasp into the pocket of his jeans, wrapped the shawl back round the baby as best he could, and stood up, holding the baby tightly in his arms.

'I'm gonna go for my ma,' he told the woman when he reached the place where she lay. 'She'll know what to do.' And he continued climbing slowly towards the bridge, the baby in his arms.

Reaching the bridge, he carefully placed the baby on the wooden plank closest to him and pulled himself up by his arms. Then he picked up the baby again.

It gave a slight sigh.

'Don't be afraid baby,' he said, smiling down at it. 'I'm takin' you home.'

Chapter Two

'She's mine. I found her so she's mine.' Joe tightened his grip on the side of the wooden box sitting in the centre of the table. 'I'm gonna keep her.'

The baby whimpered. He glanced quickly into the box and patted her cheek.

Standing with her back to the store-closet, her arms folded in front of her, Martha Walker stared at her son in irritation. 'You're not thinkin' clearly, Joe. You're seven years old. You can't look after a newborn baby – or any baby, for that matter.'

'I can.'

'You can't. You can't even look after yourself yet! And sure as a black winter brings a full graveyard, I don't want another baby. I've already too much to do as it is, what with lookin' after you, Sam and your pa. I've cleaned her up, but that's all I'm gonna do for her. Your pa must take her into town now.' She set her mouth in a thin line.

Joe's eyes filled with tears. 'But *I* found the baby, so she's mine. Pa said you get to keep what you find. Isn't that so, Pa?'

Hiram Walker leaned forward in his wooden chair. 'You're right, son, I did, but I was talkin' about gold, not babies. Like your ma said, you can't keep her, and that's that. Best thing is I take her to the railroad office and they can decide what to do with her. Her ma's dead so we can't ask her where she came from, or where she was goin'. I'm guessin' she walked from one of the railroad camps down South Pass way. I reckon she'd have been the only China woman in her camp, and they wouldn't've wanted—'

'What's a China woman?' Joe interrupted.

'A woman who comes from a country called China. You

can always tell them – they've got yellow skins and they speak a different language. China's a mighty long way away so they come here by boat. You won't recall, but we met a few Chinamen last year when I was prospectin' up in South Pass.'

'D'you think she went for a walk one day and got lost?' Joe asked.

'Nope. I reckon the people in the camp where she worked didn't want her and her baby. Like we don't want a baby here, and certainly not a China woman's baby. The railroad can decide what to do with the gal. She's nothin' to us.' Hiram rose from his chair and made a move towards the box. 'When we've dealt with the gal, I'll bury the mother. Sam can help if he's back by then.'

'No!' Joe shouted, and he flung himself over the box.

Martha moved quickly to Joe's side. She caught hold of his shoulders, pulled him back, slid her arms around his chest and hugged him to her. 'Your pa's right, Joe. The baby's gotta go.'

'No, it hasn't; it's mine. Please, Pa.' Breaking free of his mother's grip, Joe flung himself at his father. 'Please let me keep her,' he cried, winding his arms around his father's legs. 'I'll help Ma look after her. I promise I will.' He broke out into loud sobs.

Hiram stared down at his son, then he lifted his eyes to his wife's face, and raised his eyebrows questioningly.

She tightened her lips and shook her head.

He glanced back down at Joe, and at the wet patch of denim beneath Joe's face. Then he looked at his wife again. 'Maybe we should think this through some, Martha,' he said slowly.

Joe clutched his father's legs more tightly.

Martha glanced towards the baby, hesitated a moment, then picked up two dirty mugs from the table and turned towards the sink and bowl. 'There's nothin' to think about,' she said bluntly. 'I don't want another baby, and that's my last word on it. Havin' all that work all over again.' She shook her head. 'I sure as anythin' don't want that. You take it into town, Hiram,' she added, nodding over her shoulder towards the baby.

Hiram didn't move. 'But you did want one, and not so long ago, either,' he said. 'And so did I.'

She turned and stared at him. 'What're you sayin'?'

'We lost two babies between Sam and Joe, and we lost two since Joe. I reckon there ain't gonna be any more for us, gal. This could be our last chance for that daughter you wanted. For the daughter we both wanted.'

She gestured dismissively with her shoulders, and gave a dry laugh. 'But she wouldn't be like my daughter, would she? She won't look like us – she'll look like a China woman. She'd never feel like family.'

'I guess that's true.' Hiram paused. 'But does it matter?'

'It sure does. I wanted a daughter of my own, not someone else's. The railroad man can decide what to do with her; she's not for us.'

'But we know what he'll decide, don't we?' Hiram said quietly.

Their eyes met, then she looked away. 'Maybe; maybe not. Anyway,' she added briskly, moving to the sink. 'I can't stand here all evenin'. I've got a meal to put on the table.' She put the mugs on the draining board, pulled open one of the drawers and took out a handful of knives and forks.

His hand ruffling Joe's hair, Hiram gazed around the living room of the two-bedroomed wood-frame shack they rented from the mining company.

The last rays of dusty sunlight were trickling through the small-paned windows on either side of the front door, bringing light to the kitchen area in the front of the house, and casting in shadow the back of the room.

Three unlit kerosene lamps hung from hooks on the wall behind him, alongside his mining tools, miner's hat and an assortment of ropes. A large wooden tub stood on either side of the opening in the wall that led to the corridor running between the two bedrooms to the rear. One of the tubs was full of clothes needing ironing and the other already half-full with clothes for washing on the following Monday.

In the opposite corner stood an iron stove, its stovepipe running up to the ceiling and out of the roof through a circle of tin. The smell from the cabbage cooking inside the cast-iron pot on the stove was slowly filling the room.

Glancing up, Hiram saw that the strip of sticky paper that hung down from the ceiling was thick with black flies.

He looked back at his wife's face, at the lines of tiredness and disappointment etched around her eyes – eyes that had once sparkled with life.

'Somethin' else to think about, gal,' he said. 'You're always sayin' how much work you've got, that there's never a time when everythin's done. If you had someone to help in the house, you'd get through it all a bit faster. Sure, havin' a baby would mean extra work for the next three years, but after that … And Joe will help out. He don't start school for several months, and when he does, he can do chores before and after. And I'm sure the Oaklands next door would give a hand, too. They're right neighbourly people.' He looked down at Joe. 'You'd help your ma with the baby and do whatever she asked, wouldn't you, son?'

Nodding vigorously, Joe turned to his mother. 'Can we keep her, Ma?' he begged. Leaning back against his father's legs, he gazed up at his mother, his eyes full of hope.

'Think about it, Martha,' Hiram urged. 'The gal won't be a baby for long. In no time at all she'll be able to help you with the chores. Your day would be a mite bit easier if you had someone doin' the preservin' with you, and the washin', ironin' and mendin', and all the other things you do.'

Martha glanced towards the baby, and then back at Hiram. 'And just where d'you suggest she sleeps?'

He shrugged. 'Same place as if we'd had a gal of our own, like we wanted – she'll be in with us while I build a room on the back of the house. It'd be easy enough to fit it between the house and vegetable patch, opposite the privy. The company's got no problem with it. Lots of folk've done it.'

Martha stared across the room towards the bedrooms, and then she turned back to Joe, her expression thoughtful.

'And you reckon you'd really help some more about the house, Joe?' she asked after a short pause. 'You wouldn't start wantin' to be doin' somethin' more interestin' and keep on disappearin', leavin' me to do everythin'? And you'll go out to work as soon as you're old enough to help us pay for her?'

'I promise I'll help you,' he said solemnly. 'And when I'm older, I'll work hard and give you all the money I get. I promise.'

She wiped her hands down the front of her pinafore. 'Well, I guess that's settled then.'

Joe's face broke out into a wide smile. He gazed up at his father, then at his mother, his eyes shining.

'Thanks, Ma,' he said, beaming.

'You may not be thankin' me for long,' she said sharply. 'Babies need a lot of lookin' after, so you're gonna take over some of my chores. One of the things you can do is help with the vegetable patch, and I don't wanna hear you complain it's a woman's work.'

He shook his head. 'I won't.'

'And you'll need to get the neighbours' help to build the room, Hiram, or its roof won't last the first flurry of snow,' she added, the trace of a smile flickering across her lips.

'That I will,' he said.

Turning away, she leaned over the table and picked up the box with the baby in it. 'OK, Charity; let's put you in the bedroom. While I'm puttin' her down, Joe, get me any shirts you've outgrown. I'll make her some clothes out of them and I'll use the cut-off strips as diapers.'

'What's that you called her?' Hiram asked.

'You heard me – Charity. For all your fancy talk, that's what takin' her in is, isn't it? It's an act of charity. And when you've given me the shirt, Joe,' she went on, 'you can run into town and get some cans of milk. Your pa will give you the money since he's so keen on keepin' the baby. And while you're there, find Sam and tell him he should've been home a while ago, and he's to come back now.'

Joe ran along the short corridor to his bedroom door, and flung it open.

Hiram watched him go into his room, and then turned back to his wife. 'Thanks, Martha,' he said. 'It's a kind thing you're doin'; it means a lot to the boy.'

'You're soft, Hiram Walker; that's what you are. But *I'm* not. Don't think I'm gonna love this baby, just 'cos I've had a moment of weakness, 'cos I'm not. I've taken it in as much for me as for Joe. You happened on the right words when you pointed out the help she could be. Back on the ranch, we always had help in the house, so I'll only be gettin' what I was used to, and what I thought you'd be able to give me, but couldn't. This baby's not gonna be a daughter, and she's not gonna be a sister for Sam and Joe. She'll never be part of our family – she's here to help me in the house, and that's the way she's gonna be treated.'

Her lips tightening, she went through to her bedroom, holding Charity at a slight distance.

Chapter Three

Four years later
June, 1872

Charity picked up the first of Sam's heavy work boots, its dark brown leather deeply engrained with black coal-dust, and passed it to Joe. Joe handed the boot to Sam, and without looking at Charity, held out his empty hand towards her again. Giggling, she put the second of the boots into his hand, and he passed that one, too, to Sam.

When he'd pulled his boots on, Sam sat back in his chair, stretched out his legs, ran his hand over his chin, and stared thoughtfully at Joe.

Sam's face, Joe suddenly noticed, was ageing beyond his years.

'You know, Joe,' Sam said. 'Instead of doin' whatever it is you do all day, you're old enough now to be out workin'. After all, you're eleven now. You could be earnin' fifty or sixty cents a day, and Ma could use the money. With a second mine openin', they'll need lads to work in the breakers. All you'd have to do is pick out pieces of slate from the coal that goes by you on the chute, and at the end of your shift, they'd pay you.'

'Oh, yeah – bein' under the ground all day would be grand. What could be better than bein' in the dark for ten hours, with coal dust all around, listenin' to loud machinery and the sound of blastin'? And never seein' the sun? I'm not gonna do it and you can't make me.' Joe's mouth set in a stubborn line.

Sam shrugged. 'You'd get used to it. Me, I wouldn't

wanna work out in the sun all day. At least down the mine, you're workin' in your own room, you and your partner, and you're with a group of men you know. And you can bend an elbow with the boys at night. It's a good life for a man.'

'And how good would my life be if I cut my hands on the slate so bad that I couldn't hold the reins of my horse?'

'You haven't got a horse.'

'When I have one.'

'You wouldn't have to stay in the breakers for long. In a year or so, you'll be old enough to be one of the boys who control the air in the mines. Every right-thinkin' lad in Carter wants to be a door tender. Or a trap boy. You'd just have to open the doors for the mules. If you were already workin' in the mines, you'd be top of the heap when those plum jobs came up.'

'Right-thinkin'!' Joe laughed scornfully. 'You think it's right-thinkin' to wanna go even further down the stinkin' mines than the breakers go? To be alone in a dark passage for maybe fourteen hours, with no one around for company 'cept rats? To stand in muddy water, hour after hour, waitin' for the mules and their loaded cars, openin' and shuttin' the door for them, and then standin' and waitin' again? I've talked to some of the other miners, and I know what the work is, and you ain't gettin' me down there.'

'Too good for the work, are you?' Sam sneered. 'So what you gonna do then? 'Cos you gotta do somethin' at your age. I did, didn't I? And no brother of mine's gonna sit around a coffee pot all day and do nothin'.'

'And I won't – I'll get work. I dunno what yet, but whatever it is, it'll be on the ground, not under it. I want fresh air and green grass all around me, and I wanna hear birds sing, and not blastin'.'

'You seen much grass around here, Joe?' Sam asked, standing up, "Cos I ain't. There's bits here and there, but the sun dries it all up, and even if it starts out green, it sure ain't green when it finishes. As for fresh air, there'll not be much of that when the second mine opens. We live on top of coal and we've gotta get it outa the ground if we want money for food and fuel for the trains to run on. And that means dirt, steam and smoke. And I reckon it's time you accepted it.'

'Mornin', boys,' Hiram said, coming from the corridor into the room.

Sam glanced at him. 'Mornin', Pa. I've just bin tellin' Joe there's work to be had in the mines.'

'There is today, son, but there may not be for much longer,' Hiram said flatly, going across to Martha, who was dividing cake between two metal lunch buckets.

Sam stared at his father, alarm on his face. 'What're you sayin'?'

Hiram picked up one of the bucket lids, and glanced at him. 'Just that the Union Pacific seems to have got the taste for what it did last year when they cut the price of coal and the men went on strike.'

'You mean firin' the strikers and bringin' in the Swedes and Irish?'

'Yup. that's it.'

'But like you said, that was last year.' Sam's brow furrowed. 'What's it gotta do with now?'

'Just that havin' done it once, they can do it again. Now the railroad's built, they no longer need the Chinamen for that. But it seems they're good at blastin', and the company's started puttin' them in mines hereabouts. Carter's could easily be the next. They pay Chinamen less than the whites, and there's talk of them takin' jobs from the whites. If that happens, we'll soon be the ones who look out of place, not Charity.'

Sam shook his head. 'I can't see that happenin'. No, sir; I can't.'

Hiram started pressing the lid down on the bucket. 'I sure hope you're right, Sam.'

Martha tapped Hiram on the back of the hand. 'Here, I'll do that.'

'I'll do the cups, then,' he said, and he picked up one of two metal teacups next to the buckets and started tying it to one of the handles. He looked across at Joe. 'So you thinkin' of askin' at the mine office for work, Joe?'

'You leave Joe be, Hiram,' Martha interrupted. 'He's like me. He liked it on the ranch, and he'll look for ranch work one day. Aren't I right, Joe?'

'You're too soft on Joe, Ma,' Sam said sharply. 'I don't hear you tellin' him how hard it is to make ends meet, but you sure tell me often enough. Well, I'm doin' my bit, and it's time he helped out, too. There's work goin', and he's old enough to get a job.'

'Maybe I'll be a cowboy,' Joe mused. 'I'd get to see a fair few places if I was a cowboy. Or maybe I'll get me a homestead. Truth is, I don't yet know what I wanna do most of all, but whatever it is, it won't be minin'.'

'Sam's right about there bein' work in the mines, Joe,' Hiram said, glancing at him.

A bolt of alarm shot through Joe. 'I—'

'Charity's four now,' his father cut in, 'and she's an extra mouth to feed. But she ain't yet big enough to help your ma and pay her way. You wanted us to take her in, so it's only right you help us pay for her keep, so go and get yourself a job. By the time you're old enough to do whatever it is you decide to do, Charity will be old enough to help your ma in the house and bring in some money.'

Joe glanced at Charity, who was staring up at them, her

thumb in her mouth, her gaze moving from him to Hiram, and back to him again. 'I can't go down the mines – I've gotta help Ma,' he said, a note of pleading creeping into his voice. 'I promised I would.'

'Now Charity's grown I don't need as much help in the house, Joe, so you can go for that job,' Martha said, going across to Sam, a lunch bucket in each hand. 'That's your lunch, Sam, and here's yours, Hiram.' She handed them each a bucket.

'Thanks, Ma,' Sam said.

Turning away, Sam gave Joe a sly grin, and then he and Hiram reached up and took their wide brimmed hard-leather hats from the hooks on the back wall. They crossed to the front door and Hiram pulled it open and went out. A triumphant smile on his face, Sam followed his father. The door clicked shut behind them.

Martha turned to Joe. 'I know you don't want to, Joe, but you're gonna have to take a job in the mines. Not the full ten hour shift, but for a few hours each day. With both your pa and Sam workin' for the company, I reckon they'd give you a couple of hours after school, and a few more hours on the days when you're not in school. The mine doesn't have to be forever – I want you to get away from here almost as much as you do – but you promised to help out, and a promise is a promise.'

'I'm tired,' Charity said. She stopped walking and raised her arms to Joe. 'Carry me, Joe.'

He smiled sympathetically, leaned down, put his hands under her armpits and lifted her up. 'I guess it's a long way for little legs,' he said, hoisting her on to his hip, and he continued up the narrow track that led to the top of the rocky outcrop on the opposite side of the river from the town.

'Phew, you're gettin' heavy,' he said as they neared the top. 'Ma must be feedin' you too much.'

She giggled.

They reached the crest of the rock, and he let her slip down to the ground. Standing side by side, they stared down at the river while he gathered his breath. Then he gently turned her by the shoulders to face the plain that lay to the left of the town, stretching back to the far horizon.

'Look at that,' he said, taking her hand in his.

Together they stared across an endless flatland of violet-grey stone, broken in places by sandy white patches and grey-white pebbles. Here and there, clumps of short grass, seared yellow by the summer sun, broke through the hard ground, and with the intermittent clusters of yellow and green sagebrush, brought colour to the seemingly barren desert.

'And now look this way,' he said, after they'd stared at the plain for a few minutes, and he turned her slightly to the right to look towards the town. 'You can see how much bigger Carter's gotten now, with all those new shacks the company's put up, and the shops. It sure is lookin' ugly. And sounding noisy. The pumps never seem to stop. It was bad enough with one mine, but now there's gonna be another.' He shook his head. 'Yup, it's an ugly place to live.'

'Sure is, Joe,' Charity said solemnly. Sucking her thumb, she leaned against his leg and stared towards the town.

His eyes followed the straggle of weathering miners' houses lying on the outskirts of the town, set well back from the river.

'That big house belongs to the mine superintendent,' he said, pointing to the house closest to the outbuildings of the mine. He moved his hand slightly to the left. 'And that's our house,' he said, pointing to one of the small wooden houses in the middle of the row.

She nodded.

He raised his gaze above the roofs of the miners' houses and the stovepipes that jutted from them, to the backs of the wood-framed shops that lined the street that ran the length of the town until it came to a stop at the point where the narrow-gauge spur of the main railroad crossed from one side of the town to the other. A small railway depot stood on the opposite side of the track from the end of the main street. Behind the depot sprawled the mine and the outlying buildings and chimneys, from which a dense cloud of black smoke and steam arose.

He shook his head. 'Nope, it's not pretty.'

She nodded again.

His eyes fixed on the tapering frame that housed the twin shafts, the steam-run compressor that pumped air through a hose to the bottom of the shaft and the steel cable that hoisted the cages up and down. Then his gaze moved to the blackened chutes along which coal fell into the flat cars that were lined up beneath, waiting to be pulled by the train to the main railroad when full.

'Whatever they say, I'm never gonna work in there,' he repeated.

'No, Joe,' she echoed. Wriggling her hand free of his, she bent down and straightened her cotton dress over her black lace-up boots.

'Like I told them today,' he went on, his eyes still on the town, 'I'm not stayin' in Carter. Soon as I'm old enough, I'm leavin'. But I'll see you're all right, Charity,' he added, and he smiled down at her. 'I found you and I feel kind of responsible for you, so you're not to worry about anythin'.'

She stopped fiddling with the hem of her petticoat and

gazed up at him, her almond-shaped eyes shining with happiness. 'Sure, Joe,' she said.

He nodded. 'Just so's you know.' He turned again to face the view.

She straightened up, slipped her hand back into his and stared towards the town, hopping from one foot to the other.

'But I reckon some things are gonna have to change right now,' he went on after a few minutes, his voice full of regret.

She stared up at him, her forehead wrinkling in dismay.

'I'm gonna take that job in Mr Culpepper's livery stable. For a while now he's been askin' me to do a few hours a week, but I've always said no 'cos of helpin' Ma. But Ma says she can manage now. I'll like the work and I'll learn a heap of things I'll need to know for when I'm a cowboy or a ranch hand. And I'll be able to give Ma and Pa some money.'

He saw that her eyes were filling with tears, and he knelt down and put his arm around her shoulders. 'You're not to worry, Charity. I'll still take you for walks when I can.'

'I wanna be a cowboy, too,' she said, a sob in her voice.

Laughing, he hugged her. 'I'm sure you'd make a grand cowboy – or rather, cowgirl. But drivin' cattle all the way up from Texas to the Kansas City railhead is a man's job. It's a long way to go, and it's hard work. I know 'cos I've listened to the drovers talkin' when they're passin' through Carter.'

She was silent for a moment, then her face suddenly brightened. 'I work in livery stable, too.'

He laughed again, and shook his head. Her face fell. 'Mr Culpepper wouldn't like it. You can get hurt by horses. Nope, you'll have to stay at home with Ma. Besides, you're a big girl now and you'll soon be able to help her around the house. She'll like that, and you will, too. You'll learn the sort of things a woman needs to know.'

'Don't wanna. Wanna go with you,' she said stubbornly. She stuck her lower lip out.

'I'm sorry, but that just ain't possible. Tell you what, though, as soon as I get my first wages, I'll buy you somethin' nice. You'd like that, wouldn't you?'

Pursing her lips, she stared down at her boots. Then she suddenly looked into his face, anxiety in her eyes. 'Will you still learn me my letters before I go to school?'

'Sure, I will. I can tell you're real smart for a gal, Charity. I won't be workin' at Culpepper's every evenin', so I'll start teachin' you soon. Just like I said I would. Nothin's gonna stop that. Okay?'

'Okay, Joe.'

He stood up and turned to look across the plain. 'It's Carter for me for a few more years, but not forever. Definitely not forever. That's the way out of Carter, Charity,' he said, pointing towards the white pebble-strewn plain, 'and one day I'm gonna be takin' it.'

Chapter Four

Charity tightened her hold on Joe's hand as they went out of the back door of the house, past her bedroom and the vegetable patch, and across the stretch of dust-covered open ground that led to Second Street. In her free hand, she clutched a small tin lunch pail covered with a blue and white gingham cloth. Joe carried the bag that held her slate, slate pencil and school book.

'You look a proper seven-year-old in your new pinafore and dress,' Joe said, smiling down at her as they walked along. 'You look good in green.'

Beaming, she glanced down at her dress. She slipped her hand from Joe's, smoothed the creases from the pinafore that covered most of her skirt, and then tucked her hand back into his.

'You're gonna like bein' in school,' he went on, swinging her hand as they walked along. 'You'll make friends with the other children in town and play games with them.'

'No, I won't,' she said, her voice taking on a sullen note. 'They won't wanna play with me. They never talk to me when I see them in town. I smile at them, like you said I must, but they never smile back.'

He glanced at her nervous face. 'You'll find them real friendly once they get to know you,' he said reassuringly. 'And Miss O'Brien will be pleased with you 'cos you already know your letters and numbers. Not all the kids startin' today will know them.'

She stopped walking and stared up at him, her face suddenly serious. 'I wish *you* could be my teacher, Joe. The other kids don't like me, and Miss O'Brien don't like me. I seen the way she looks at me when I've been waitin' for you outside the livery stable.'

'She don't know you. She's gonna like you when she does. Everyone will like you 'cos you're nice. They've probably not been friendly yet 'cos you look a bit different. Nice different,' he added with a grin, 'but different. When you've got to know them, you won't look so different to them, and then they'll like you and you'll like school. So come on.' He squeezed her hand encouragingly and they started walking again.

Glancing down at her when they reached the corner where Second Street crossed Main Street, dividing the town into two, he saw that she was still worried. 'It's gonna be okay, Charity; you'll see.' She looked up at him, her face clouded with anxiety. 'You'll see,' he repeated.

'I'm scared, Joe.'

He gave her a warm smile. 'Don't be; I won't be far away. Look, that's where I'll be when you're in school.' He pointed to the stable on the corner to his left. 'Now I'm not in school any more, I'm gonna work at Culpepper's every day till I'm old enough to leave Carter. I'll walk you all the way to school today as it's your first day, but in future I'll leave you here and you must go the rest of the way by yourself. It's not far – you can almost see the schoolhouse from here. That'll be okay, won't it?'

She moved closer to him, but didn't answer.

He looked anxiously down at her. 'That's all right, isn't it?' he repeated.

Her eyes on the boardwalk, she kicked the thick layer of charcoal-grey dust that coated the weathered planks. It swirled in a dense cloud around her legs, and then settled slowly on to her black leather boots and on the cover protecting her lunch pail. 'I don't like bein' in town on my own,' she said.

He smiled at the top of her head. 'You don't know that 'cos you've you never been in town on your own. You and me, we're always together. But you're a big girl now, and you'll soon get used to bein' here by yourself. And when you make friends, you'll wanna talk to them without me bein' around. And if there's somethin' you simply just gotta tell me, you can stop by at the stable on your way home. Unless I'm busy, that is.'

'Whatever you say, people won't like me,' she said, her eyes on her boots as she tried to wipe the dust from the toe of one boot with the heel of the other.

He frowned slightly. 'Like I said, they don't know you yet so they've not got feelin's about you.'

'Sam knows me and he don't like me.'

He gave an awkward laugh. 'You're not talkin' sense, gal. Why would you think that?'

She looked up at him. 'He don't like me, and you know he don't.'

He released her hand, knelt down, put his arms around her and hugged her. Then he stood up again. 'It's not you he doesn't like – it's what he's afear'd about. He looks at you and he sees the things that are worryin' him.'

'What's worryin' him?' She put her thumb in her mouth and stared up at him.

'You're still real young, Charity. Too young to understand minin' things. But it's about what happened earlier this year.'

'What happened?'

He gave a sigh, glanced towards the school, and then

looked back at her face. 'You remember Pa telling us that Union Pacific had cut the price of coal and were payin' the miners a dollar a ton, not a dollar twenty-five, don't you? And he and Sam were angry 'cos it meant they'd be bringin' home less money?'

She nodded.

'And then the men stopped workin', didn't they, and no one dug up any coal? They went on strike – that's what it's called. Well, a coupla weeks after that, the company brought in some Chinamen to break the strike, and the mines opened again. The Carter miners didn't wanna lose their jobs, so they went back to work, even though it meant takin' home less. D'you remember that?'

Sucking her thumb, she nodded again.

'Well, you've seen that more Chinamen have come to Carter since then, and 'cos they'll work for whatever the company pays, the price of coal is still droppin', and the white miners are takin' home less. It's not you that Sam doesn't like: it's Chinese people 'cos of what the Chinamen are doin' to the price of coal. D'you understand that, Charity?'

She bit her lip.

'And the Chinamen aren't just down the mines now – they're everywhere. They're workin' on the railroad, they're openin' shops ...' He pointed towards the right-hand side of Main Street. 'It's more Chinese down there than white now. At first it was just the laundry and the barber's, but look at all the other Chinese stores that've started up. The latest is the general mercantile, but I wager it won't be the last. People aren't happy about havin' so many Chinese here.'

'I don't wanna go to school, Joe.'

He looked back at her. 'Now, you hear me good, Charity. After what you said about Miss O'Brien, I figured you should understand why some people think like they do. But it's nothin' to do with the school. If you give school a chance, you'll like bein' there and you'll make friends. You need to make friends with other gals your age.'

'But you've not got friends your age, Joe,' she said, her face stubborn.

He hesitated. 'That's 'cos I was too busy lookin' after you. And if I'm honest, although I sometimes played with the other boys in town in the days before I found you, I'm not like Sam and I didn't really like bein' in town and was keener on findin' gold, so I didn't make any real good friends. But Mr Culpepper's a sort of friend now. I know he's old, but he's okay. And the Marshal that's just come to Carter seems nice, too.'

'Maybe the children in school have got folks like Sam and your pa. Maybe they don't like Chinamen, either, and that's why they don't smile at me.'

'You didn't know what happened in the mines till I just told you. And there's no reason why the other kids will know about minin' problems. I only told you 'cos of the colour your skin.' He paused. 'Anyway, you're not Chinese. Sure you look a bit different with your eyes and your skin, and you've got black braids like a Chinaman's got – well, you've got two and they've only got one – but you're American like me. You talk like me, wear the sort of clothes American girls wear, and you think like me. Yup, you're American, Charity.'

Her face broke into a smile. 'Am I, Joe?'

He knelt down and hugged her tightly again. 'You sure are,' he said. 'And everyone's gonna think you're a swell gal like I do. Now, let's go to school.' He stood up and held out his hand to her. 'You don't wanna be late the first day, do you?'

They continued slowly down the short path leading to the red-painted schoolhouse with a pine flagpole above the entrance, the sound of the chattering children inside the wooden building becoming louder and louder as they got closer.

Just before they reached the door, Joe stopped and turned to Charity. 'I'd better leave you here,' he said with a smile. 'I'll see you tonight. Just this once, you can come by the stable on your way home and tell me what you learnt.'

Her face pale, she nodded.

They stood back to let a couple of older girls walk past them, arm in arm as they talked and laughed. The girls glanced back at Charity. Their steps slowed and they stared pointedly at her. Then they turned again to each other, giggled, opened the door to the schoolhouse, went inside and shut the door firmly behind them.

Charity clutched Joe's leg.

As he stared at the closed door, he heard a sudden outbreak of squealing inside the schoolroom. He turned to Charity. 'You gotta go in, Charity,' he said quietly. 'You got some learnin' to do.'

She didn't move.

He bent down to her. 'Now you listen to me,' he said, his face serious. 'You're a smart gal, and you'll enjoy learnin' the things Miss O'Brien can teach you. I'm hopin' you'll make friends, too, and maybe you will; maybe you won't. But it doesn't really matter if you don't – you're in school for the learnin', not for the friend-makin'. You gotta remember, you're as good as anyone else in the room. Promise me you're gonna learn real well, even if other things ain't right.'

She stared into the clear blue eyes that gazed at her, encouraging her. 'I promise, Joe,' she said, her face solemn.

The door opened again and Miss O'Brien came out,

holding a hand bell in one hand and tucking her crisp white blouse more firmly into her ankle-length grey skirt with the other. She glanced at Charity, hesitated, then raised the bell and rang it. Then she went back into the schoolhouse, leaving the door slightly ajar.

'School's startin',' Joe said. He handed her the schoolbag he'd been carrying and gave her a slight push forward. 'See you tonight.' He gave her a reassuring smile, thrust his hands into the pockets of his jeans and turned away.

As he looked ahead of him, the smile left his face and a lump came into his throat.

His head down, he walked briskly up the path, trying to erase from his mind the look in Miss O'Brien's eyes when she'd stared at Charity, who'd looked so small and so helpless, and struggling to blank from his memory the cruel note in the two girls' laughter.

Charity looked at the schoolhouse door, and hesitated. Then she walked slowly forward, pushed the door open wider and took a few steps into the schoolroom. Hovering in front of the water pail that stood on a low bench just inside the door, she looked nervously around.

The talking abruptly stopped. All eyes turned towards her.

She stared anxiously back at the other pupils, each of whom was sitting at an individual dark wood bench made of hand-planed boards, the boys on one side of the room and the girls on the other.

The benches stood in rows that spanned the room, one row behind the other, with a wide gap down the middle of the room and a narrower gap between the end of each row and the wall. Every bench had a back to it, and a shelf sticking out from the back, which made a table for the pupil sitting behind. A potbelly stove stood in one of the corners at the back of the room, and a hickory switch and a brush made of broom corn in the other.

Clutching her lunch pail and schoolbag with both hands, Charity turned to Miss O'Brien. She was standing at the side of her desk, staring at her, unsmiling. Her gaze rose above Miss O'Brien's shoulder to the wall behind her. Smooth boards, painted black, covered most of the wall. She took a step to the side to see past Miss O'Brien and saw that under the painted boards there was a small trough full of short white sticks, and a single block of wood around which had been nailed a piece of woolly sheepskin.

Her eyes returned to Miss O'Brien's face.

'I take it you're Charity Walker.' Miss O'Brien's voice was icy.

Charity nodded.

'The bench next to Adeline hasn't been taken by anyone,' Miss O'Brien said coldly. 'You can sit there.' She pointed halfway down the room to an empty bench next to a fair-haired girl. 'It's your third year here so you know the school's routine, Adeline. I'd like you to look after Charity Walker and tell her what she needs to know.'

Adeline jumped up from her seat, her slate falling to the floor with a loud bang. 'I'm not lookin' after any heathen Chinee, Miss O'Brien!' she exclaimed. 'Ma and Pa wouldn't like it.'

'None of our folks would,' a boy with brown hair called from the back of the class. 'We don't want no Chinamen here.'

Shouting and stamping their feet, the rest of the class showed their support for Adeline and the brown-haired boy.

Charity hugged her bag and lunch pail more tightly.

'Silence!' Miss O'Brien exclaimed, and she rapped on her

desk with her ruler. The class fell quiet, their anger heavy in the air.

'I'm American,' Charity said, her voice just above a whisper.

The pupils broke into jeers and laughter, and they banged their slates on their tables.

Miss O'Brien took a step forward. The class instantly settled.

'Such behaviour will not be tolerated,' she said slowly and distinctly. 'I understand your concerns, class, but you must understand this. The law in Wyoming Territory says that children must go to school from seven years of age to fourteen. I'm therefore unable to send Charity Walker away from our school.'

There was a low rumble of anger from the class.

'I cannot, however, force you to welcome her and include her in your activities,' she went on, 'and if she feels she would be more comfortable leaving the school right now ...' She paused and looked down at Charity, who stood at her side. 'I would not consider it my duty to force her to remain.'

'We don't want you here so why don't you go?' the boy at the back yelled out.

'If you wish to leave, Charity Walker, I will not stop you. The door you came through is the door you can leave by,' Miss O'Brien said, her face cold. 'Well?'

Biting her lip, Charity looked around the room at the large posters that had been stuck on all the walls, at the globe on one corner of Miss O'Brien's desk and at the three thick books on the other. She looked at the schoolbooks that had been placed on the children's desks next to their slates, ready for the learning to start, and she looked back up at Miss O'Brien.

'I wanna learn,' she said bluntly. 'I'm gonna stay.'

Charity sat on her bench and stared with tired eyes at the First Reader, which lay open on the desk in front of her. Her first school day was drawing to an end, and it hadn't been an easy day.

No one had shown her the school routine so she'd had to watch the others and do what they did. She'd sat on her own all day, having been given a bench with the aisle on one side and an empty seat on the other, and at intervals throughout the day, the girl behind her had stuck her toe up through Charity's seat to make her jump.

When morning recess had come and the other pupils had gone outside, she'd been told to stay in and clean the blackboard. And during the afternoon recess, she'd been given the task of brushing the chalk dust from the board eraser. For the whole hour they'd been given for lunch, she'd sat by herself in the corner of the yard, eating her bread and butter while the other children played something called Uncle John.

No one had asked her to join in.

No one had spoken to her at all throughout the day. She hadn't made a single friend, and she knew she wouldn't be making any as no one wanted to be friends with her.

But she didn't mind. Joe was her friend so she didn't need anyone else. Like Joe said, you didn't need a friend in school to learn. She was going to learn so much that she'd soon be put into the Second Reader group, and Joe would be real proud of her.

The girl behind her pushed her toe against Charity's leg again.

Looking up from her book, Charity turned towards the two windows set in the wooden wall. A thin layer of dust veiled the glass and hid the outside world from sight.

She closed her eyes and saw in her mind the white pebble-strewn plain that stretched from Carter to the distant horizon, and she gave an inward sigh. If only she were out there now, running in freedom with Joe, running away from hate.

'Charity Walker!' Miss O'Brien's voice cut sharply through her thoughts.

She opened her eyes.

Hostility hung in the air and pressed heavily on her.

She swallowed the lump that rose in her throat. 'I'm gonna learn,' she whispered to herself, and she turned her eyes back to her book.

'Girl!'

Charity stopped abruptly, halfway across Main Street on her way to the livery stable, her school bag and empty lunch pail hanging from her hands. She glanced to her left and saw that there was a Chinese girl standing in the middle of the road, staring up the street at her.

She turned slightly towards the girl and looked at her in wide-eyed amazement. She'd never seen another Chinese girl before.

'Girl!' the Chinese girl called again.

Charity frowned.

The girl looked like a real Chinese girl must look, she thought, with her baggy blue trousers and a white cotton shirt hanging outside them. She, too, seemed to be about seven, though it was hard to see under her pointed hat. And it looked as if her eyes were the same shape as her own – like almonds was how Joe described them.

Charity looked down at the ground, blinked a couple of times, then stared back at Main Street. The girl was still there, standing just down from the place where Second Street crossed over Main Street.

She backed slightly towards the livery stable, and then stopped. 'What d'you want?' she called to the Chinese girl.

The girl smiled at her. A wide smile, just like hers. 'I come here. I learn shop keep. I likee you friend. You China girl.'

Charity vigorously shook her head. 'I'm American,' she said firmly. 'I'm not a China girl.'

The Chinese girl's face fell. 'You no likee me be friend?'

Charity shook her head. 'We can't be friends. I'm American.'

'You China girl,' the Chinese girl repeated, her voice accusing.

'I'm not,' Charity said, and she glared at her.

There was a movement behind the girl. Charity looked beyond her and saw a boy of about Joe's age running up to the girl. He reached the girl and said something to her. Charity could tell he was angry with the girl, but the few words she heard, she couldn't understand so she didn't know what he was angry about.

The Chinese boy finished talking, and stood still, waiting.

'Me go.' The smile gone from the girl's face, she spun round, and she and the boy went down Main Street and disappeared into the new general mercantile store.

The girl had two black braids like she did, Charity noticed. And the boy had one black braid behind his head. Just one quite long braid.

'I'm not a Chinese girl,' she told herself as she turned away. 'I'm not.'

She took a couple of steps towards the livery stable and saw Joe standing in the entrance, staring towards her.

She paused, glanced down Main Street again, looked back at Joe, then, clutching her bag and pail tightly, turned from the stable and started to run into Second Street and back to the house as fast as she could.

* * *

35

Joe saw anguish in Charity's eyes before she turned from him.

A bolt of alarm shot through him, though he didn't quite know what he feared.

Dropping the bridle he'd been holding, he ran at full speed out of the stable, along Second Street and across the barren ground separating the town from the miners' houses, gradually closing the gap between them, but unable to catch up with Charity before she reached the back of the house.

He saw her pull open the door of her outside bedroom and throw herself into the room. Seconds later, he flung himself through the open doorway after her.

She'd dropped her school things on the floor and was standing on her bed, pulling a pair of scissors from the sewing basket on the shelf above the bed. She twisted slightly, grabbed one of her plaits and raised the scissors to it.

'No!' he yelled, leaping on to the bed and snatching the scissors from her. He rounded on her. 'What d'you think you're doin'?'

She raised a tear-stained face to him. 'I'm an American girl,' she cried, defiance in her voice. 'I wanna look like American girl. I'm not Chinese, Joe. I'm not.'

And she fell against his chest, her body wracked by huge sobs.

Wordlessly, he put his arms around her and held her tightly.

Chapter Five

Later that evening, Joe and Charity sat in front of the house, caught in the warm glow of the amber light that fell from the kerosene lamp which they'd hung on the outside wall to keep darkness at bay.

'You feelin' better, Charity?' Joe asked after a while.

Rubbing her eyes with exhaustion, she nodded.

'You gotta go to bed now,' he said. 'Promise me there'll be no more attemptin' to cut your hair like that.'

'I promise,' she whispered. 'I'm sorry.'

He leaned forward, his elbows on his knees, his chin resting on his hands, and glanced at her, a frown on his face.

'I still don't understand why you wanted to do it,' he said.

'Black braids make me look like a Chinese girl. I wanna look American.'

'But American girls have long hair, and they wear their hair in braids, too, don't they? And some have black hair,' he said. 'It's not just Chinese girls.'

'But American girls got American faces.'

'You ain't gonna cut your eyes, are you?' he asked, sitting upright in sudden fear.

She shook her head.

'That's okay, then,' he said, relaxing. 'You're real cute as you are, Charity; you don't wanna change a thing. And when you think some more, I reckon you'll be glad you didn't cut your hair. That'd really give those girls at school somethin' to laugh about. How many American girls have got short hair? Just think about it.'

'I'm sorry,' she whispered again.

He looked thoughtfully at her. 'You know, the kids in

school were mean to you today, and so was Miss O'Brien,' he said slowly. 'But you stayed on. You showed 'em you're better than them. I'm mighty proud of you for that.'

She raised her eyes to him. 'Are you, Joe?' Her voice lifted in hope.

'I sure am.' He paused. 'Not many kids your age – or any age – would've stayed on all day like you did, with them bein' nasty like they were. That makes you a special person, Charity, and you aren't ever to forget that.'

A tentative smile flickered across her lips.

'But even special people gotta have friends,' he went on. 'The Chinese gal from the mercantile wants to be your friend, so why not be friends with her? It won't make you into a Chinese girl, but it'll make you into a girl with a friend.'

'I don't want to. And anyway, a Chinese boy came out and made her go back into the store. I guess he didn't want her to be friends with an American girl.'

'That'll be her brother.'

'And I've already got a friend – you're my friend, Joe.'

He grinned at her. 'That's right – we're real good friends, you and me.' He paused. For a moment the only sound was the rhythmic beat of the steam pumps in the mines. 'But I won't always be here, you know,' he went on, and he threw her a quick glance. 'When I'm old enough, I'm gonna go off and be a cowboy, like I always said. I'll still be your friend, but I won't be livin' here, seein' you every day – I'll be drivin' cattle out on the range.'

Her eyes opened wide and she stared at him in alarm. 'Don't go away. I don't want you to.' She put her thumb in her mouth.

He shrugged. 'Things gotta change. They've already started changin'. You're in school now, and you've got chores to do before and after school, and I'm workin' days for Mr Culpepper.' He gave her a wry smile. 'I never found that gold I was pannin' for, and as we can't go down to the river in the day any more, I guess I never will. Things'll keep on changin', and then one day I'll be gone. You need more friends than just me,' he said bluntly, sitting back in his chair. 'And that's the truth.'

She took her thumb from her mouth. 'I want you to stay.' Her mouth set in a determined line.

He looked at her, his face serious. 'That's not gonna happen, Charity. I'm gonna leave as soon as I can after I've turned seventeen, and that's only three years away. When you're not tired like you are now, you oughta think about what I've been sayin'. But you must get off to bed now – you look fair moon-eyed.'

She made a move to get up.

'Hey, I almost forgot,' he said, putting his hand to his head. 'I've got somethin' for you.'

'What's that?' She sat back down and stared at him, her lips parting in sudden excitement.

'It's somethin' I was gonna give you this mornin', but I forgot. And I almost forgot it now.' He reached into his pocket, took out a tiny object and held it out to her.

She leaned close to it and saw that it was a small wooden figure. She looked up at him questioningly.

'Here, take it,' he said, shaking the figure towards her.

Hesitantly, she took it.

She glanced at him again, and then her eyes dropped to the shape that lay on the palm of her hand. It was made of wood and had been painted gold. Black stripes had been painted on top of the gold.

She peered at it. 'What is it?'

'I reckon it's a tiger. They're strong, fierce animals and they eat people. I learnt about them in school but I've never seen one – we don't have tigers in Wyoming Territory. It's yours.

39

I meant to give it back to you sooner. I found it yesterday when I was lookin' out some school things to give you.'

She screwed up her face in puzzlement. 'What d'you mean, it's mine?'

'It belonged to your ma, Charity.' He heard her catch her breath in a gasp, and saw her look swiftly down at the golden tiger again. 'That makes it yours.' An expression of wonder spread across her face as she gazed at the wooden tiger, and his voice died away.

'My ma's?' she whispered, and she ran her fingers across the black and gold tiger. 'My ma touched this tiger.'

He saw that her eyes were filling with tears.

'Sure,' he said awkwardly, changing his position in his chair. 'It's all we've got of hers. When I found you, you were all done up in a shawl and rags. The tiger was pinned on the shawl, holdin' it closed to keep you warm. I reckon she loved you, your ma.'

'You got my shawl, too?' she asked, looking up at him, the tears trickling down her cheeks.

He shook his head. 'Ma wrapped you in the shawl every day when you were little. When it wore out, she threw it away. But I kept the tiger. I meant to give it to you before, but I kinda forgot about it till I found it last night. But I think that's a good thing. This is the right time to give it to you.'

'D'you think so?'

'Yup. Your ma must've been strong like a tiger, walkin' so far like that, and in bare feet, too, tryin' to find a place where you'd be safe. The way you stuck it out at the school today, you showed 'em you're strong like a tiger, too. Your ma would've been proud of you today, like I am.'

She stared up at him, her dark brown eyes shining. 'Are you, Joe?'

He gave her a broad smile. 'Yes, I am. Today you showed 'em all you're a little golden tiger.'

Chapter Six

Later the following afternoon, having made sure that the freshly-greased wheel would spin on its axle, Joe straightened up and wiped the sweat from his forehead with the back of his arm. Only two more wheels to go. With luck, he'd get them all done before Seth Culpepper returned from his buying trip.

His boss had gone out early that morning, cock-a-hoop at the bargain price he expected to pay for a wagon, double harness, and pair of horses that not only would drive double or single, but were also accustomed to the saddle. And if he got them for what he wanted to pay, and came back and found all the wheels greased, he might be of a mind to let Joe go a bit early that evening.

He certainly hoped things would go his boss's way, he thought as he put his full weight behind the heavy wheel and started rolling it slowly towards the far wall. He'd been anxious about Charity all day, her first day at school having gone so badly, and he was looking forward to getting home and hearing how things had gone on her second day.

The strident chime of a hammer striking iron broke into his thoughts, swiftly followed by the sibilant hiss of a red-hot iron being dipped into water. He glanced over his shoulder towards the blacksmith's barn, a low open-sided structure attached to the livery stable, its split-log roof supported by unpeeled upright logs, and saw that the blacksmith had started working again, and the hearth was glowing red in the heart of the smithy, throwing out a heat of burning intensity.

No wonder he was hot, Joe thought, and he wiped his

brow again. Then he bent down to the wheel once more and continued rolling it forward.

'Joe!'

Charity's voice came from outside the livery stable.

His hands on the wheel, he stopped pushing and glanced at her. She was standing a little way back from the entrance, her lunch pail in one hand and her school bag in the other, with the afternoon sun pouring down on her. She was alone, as far as he could see.

'I'm workin', Charity. This is not a good time,' he called, and he finished pushing the greased wheel to the far wall, carefully leaned it beneath the saddles, boots and long strips of leather which hung from pegs that stood proud of the wall, picked up a piece of rag and wiped the grease from his hands, and went outside to her.

The sudden bright light stung his eyes after the semi-darkness inside the stable, and he rubbed them. 'I oughta get on,' he told her. 'But you can tell me quickly, were the other kids any friendlier today?'

Her face was solemn. 'A nasty girl pulled off my bonnet and jumped on my lunch pail. I don't like them and I don't wanna be friends with them. And I don't like Miss O'Brien. She's mean. I had to do chores in the recesses again. But I don't need friends. I'm learnin' things in school and I like learnin'.'

A wave of relief ran through him. 'That's the spirit, gal.' He paused. 'So you're not thinkin' of tryin' to cut your hair again or doin' anythin' stupid like that?'

She giggled and shook her head.

He grinned at her. 'In that case, I'd better get on with my work. Mr Culpepper will be back at any time and I don't want him thinkin' I don't work if he's not here. When I get home, you can tell me some of those things you learnt today.'

She opened her mouth to speak.

'When I get home, I said,' he cut in hastily. 'I've gotta work now. And you've got chores to do at home.'

'I'm gonna do the ironin',' she said, 'and anythin' else your ma's got for me, and then I'm gonna do my lessons for tomorrow. Bye, Joe.' Smiling at him, she waved her lunch pail in his direction, then went down to Second Street and turned into it.

He stood and watched until she was out of sight, and then he turned to go back into the livery.

As he did so, out of the corner of his eye, he saw a movement lower down on Main Street, and he glanced towards it. The Chinese girl from the general mercantile was leaning against one of the wooden posts that supported the covered porch in front of the barber's shop on the other side of the mercantile, and was staring in his direction.

She must have been watching for Charity to leave school, he guessed. So she obviously hadn't given up on her, despite her brother pulling her away the day before.

Feeling a wave of pity for the girl, and for how lonely she looked standing there on her own, he nodded in her direction. Although she was probably too far away to see it, he gave her a brief smile.

He realised at once that he'd been wrong – she must have seen him smile as she promptly straightened up, put her hand to the peaked straw hat she was wearing and took a few steps towards him.

Then she stopped abruptly and looked behind her.

Moving slightly into the road so that he could see beyond the girl, he saw that her brother, who must have come from somewhere lower down in the town, was shouting at his sister in their own language, his voice pitched high in anger.

The girl had her back to him so he couldn't see her face,

but disappointment and frustration radiated from her body. As Joe stood watching, her brother grabbed her by the arm, pushed her into the store and went in after her. He heard the faint sound of the wind chimes above the entrance wildly hitting each other.

He stared for a minute or two at the spot where the girl had been, then turned and went back into the stable.

The girl's brother was about his age, he knew. He'd asked Seth Culpepper about the Chinese family, thinking the girl could be a friend for Charity, and Seth had told him that the boy was the son of Chen Sing, who owned the general mercantile, and that he worked for his father. He'd come over from China a few years before with his father, but his mother had stayed behind in China.

He also knew from Seth that the boy's sister was Charity's age. Her mother was a China woman that Chen Sing had wed in California – a sort of second wife – and brought with him to Carter. It seemed to make sense for the boy's sister and Charity to be friends, but obviously the boy didn't agree, Joe thought ruefully as he went back to the last two wheels that needed his attention.

Dragging the next wheel to be greased away from the heat sent out by the furnace, he balanced it in the column of sunshine that fell through the open entrance, picked up the tin of grease, and started working.

A shadow fell across the wheel, slicing the light in two.

He looked up. The Chinese girl's brother was standing in the middle of the entrance, his arms folded, his expression hostile beneath the wide brim of his peaked hat.

Joe put down the grease, again wiped his hands on the oily rag and took a couple of steps towards the Chinese boy. 'If it's Mr Culpepper you want, he's not back yet. But if it's somethin' I can help you with, I'd be happy to do so.'

'I not come see Mr Culpepper. I come see you.'

'Me? Why?'

Chen Sing's son put his hand on his chest. 'My name is Chen Fai. I brother of Su Lin. I come to tell you I not wish Su Lin to speak to girl with Chinese face. I not like this.'

'I can't see why not! Your sister looks real lonely to me and there aren't any other Chinese girls in Carter for her to be friends with.'

'I not wish this. That is enough.'

'In my way of thinkin', Chen Fai, it isn't. One day I'm gonna leave Carter and Charity will be alone. Although she's been brought up like an American, to the whites she's Chinese and increasingly they won't speak to her. It's a minin' town so I reckon you can figure out why. I want her to have a friend when I'm gone, and since she's got Chinese blood in her veins, and she looks Chinese, I think it'd be good for her to be friends with your sister.'

Chen Fai shook his head. 'I not think so, and Su Lin do what I say. Chinese girls and boys learn duty to family come first, and girls must obey father and brother. This is Chinese way. Su Lin is good Chinese girl, modest and virtuous. I watch girl with Chinese face. She speak like American girl, wear clothes of American girl, is loud like American girl. Yeah, she look Chinese, but she not Chinese. I think her mother is woman without reputation. Su Lin not make good marriage if she friend of girl like this.'

'But don't you think it's important for Su Lin to have a friend?'

'Is more important make good marriage. Su Lin stay in house and learn things a woman must know. Honourable father's second wife teach her sewing, looking after house, ways to respect honourable ancestors. These things make Su Lin good wife one day, and she not bring shame on ancestors.'

Joe raised his hands in a gesture of helplessness. 'But she's still a child – she's only seven. A seven-year-old should have a friend.'

'Family of Su Lin is her friend. Tell girl with Chinese face to stay away from Su Lin.'

'She has a name,' Joe said quietly. 'Her name is Charity.'

'I not want to know name of girl. They are not ever friends. That is my wish.' Chen Fai turned sharply and moved away from the entrance, and Joe heard his footsteps echo on the boardwalk as he made his way down Main Street to the mercantile.

Angrily, Joe turned back to the wheel.

Maybe not now, he thought in intense frustration, but one day they'd be friends if he had any say in the matter. He'd have to let things be for the moment, though. Charity was being treated badly at school, and there was only so much hostility a girl of her age could take. But the day would come when she and Su Lin would be friends; he'd make certain of that.

Seth Culpepper stood in the doorway and stared around the livery stable. His gaze took in the row of greased wagon wheels lined up against the sidewall; the harness he'd left on the bench when he'd gone out that morning, which had been broken then but had obviously since been mended and hung up on the peg outside the nearest stall; the bridles and stirrups that gleamed in the way that they hadn't when he'd left, and the large heap of dirty straw just inside the livery door, which told him that the stalls had been mucked out and the horses brought in and grained.

He beamed at Joe, who'd paused when he'd seen him come in and was leaning on the handle of the broom. 'I can see you done good today, son,' he said, nodding in satisfaction. 'Yup, very good, I'd say. I reckon you've done more than enough for one day and can take yourself off home now.'

Joe grinned at him. 'From the look on your face, I'm guessing the deal went well.'

Seth beamed. 'You're guessin' right! But like I told you this mornin', I knew it was gonna go well. I dreamed of pigs last night, and my good wife told me it meant I was gonna strike lucky today. And whatever Eliza says is always right – or so she tells me.'

Both of them laughed.

'But whether or not a man dreams of pigs,' Seth went on, 'I can tell you it's payin' cash that gets you a good deal every time. Just you remember that, Joe, for when you're older and out there dealin' and bargainin'.' He clapped his hands together. 'Now be off with you, son.'

'Okay, then.' Joe started to move away, then hesitated.

'What is it?' Seth asked.

'You know I told you I wanted Charity to make friends with that Chinese girl?'

Seth nodded. 'Sure do. And as I recall, I said I didn't think it likely to happen. The Chinee don't like the white townsfolk any more than the white townsfolk like the Chinee.'

'I'm afraid you're right. The girl's brother made it clear this afternoon that he wasn't gonna allow the girls to be friends.'

'You mean Chen Fai's bin up here?' Seth asked in surprise.

'That's right. But how d'you know his name?'

'All Carter business people have gotta meet at times. Young though he is, Chen Fai's smart, and he's one of the few Chinese here to speak English.'

'You said he'd been in America for a while so that's not really surprisin'.'

'Yup, he and Chen Sing stayed in San Francisco for a few years before goin' to work on some land-reclaimin' project or other in the Sacramento area, doin' things like buildin' ditches and canals. But a lot of the Chinee who've been here for a while won't talk anythin' but Chinese. Not Chen Fai, though. He wants to do business with us so he's learnin' the lingo. Probably wants to be able to get one over on us – I've noticed his English disappear at convenient times.' He laughed, and then went on more seriously. 'It's a shame they don't all make the same effort. Look at Chen Fai's pa, Chen Sing – he doesn't know a word of English. If the Chinee tried to fit in more, folk might not be so set against them.'

'Why, that's the longest speech I've ever heard you make,' Joe remarked with a grin.

Seth laughed again. 'Maybe it is, but I kinda like Chen Fai. In some ways he's not unlike you: you're similar in age and both of you are real hard workers. So you talked to him, did you?'

'We didn't exactly talk,' Joe said, with a wry smile. 'He glared at me, thumped his chest, pointed at me, told me what was gonna be as far as he was concerned, and then left.'

Seth chuckled. 'That sounds about his way of doin' things.'

'Oh, and his sister's name is Su Lin. He told me that. And he's got his mind set against her bein' friends with Charity, which is mean of him. Charity's a good kid.'

Seth ran his fingers slowly down his grey moustache. 'But she's not Chinese, is she, for all she's got a Chinese face? And she's not American, is she, for all she sounds it? You can sorta see why none of them want her. The Chinee have got their ways, like we've got ours, and they wanna keep to their ways and not pick up ours. And the whites are watchin' the price of coal drop lower than ever and fearin' they may lose their jobs to the Chinee, so they don't want them here. Don't be too hard on any of them, Joe, you gotta understand both sides.'

'I do. I've been hearin' the whites' side often enough at home. And Chen Fai certainly got the Chinese view across today.'

'You've got a good head on your shoulders, lad. Charity's a lucky gal to be livin' with your family.' Seth started to walk into the stable. 'I'd get off home now if I were you, before I change my mind. And don't worry about Charity. She may be caught in the middle, but she ain't gonna come to no harm. Not here in Carter.'

Chapter Seven

One year later
September, 1876

Dusk was gathering over the town as Joe left the stable and made his way along Second Street, out across the open stretch of ground that led to the miners' houses and past the shacks recently built by the company.

As he neared his house, he saw that the back door was open, and also the door to Charity's outside bedroom. She must be doing her schoolwork, he thought, and decided to go round to the front of the house to avoid disturbing her. He'd just started heading for the front of the line of miners' houses when the door to Charity's room suddenly opened wider, and Sam came rushing out of her room, head down, clutching a pile of clothes in one arm and carrying a large bag in his other hand. Charity followed close behind him, screaming at him.

Frowning, Joe stopped abruptly and stared at them both.

'You stop!' Charity screamed as Sam sped between the vegetable patch and the privy on his way to the open ground. 'You can't take them. They're mine.'

Joe could see tears streaming down her cheeks as she chased after Sam, and he could hear fear in her voice.

He started to run towards them at the same moment as Martha came hurrying out of the house.

'Now you stop that, Sam,' she shouted, walking quickly after him and Charity.

His back to Martha, Sam stopped running, threw the clothes and the bag on to the dirt-covered ground and kicked them away from him. Then he glanced back at his mother.

Joe stopped and stared at Sam, open-mouthed. There was a large bruise on the side of Sam's face.

'Get back into the house, Ma,' Sam shouted, pointing towards the house. 'There's more of her stuff in there and I'm gonna be bringin' it out, whether you like it or not. Look at this!' He tapped his injured cheek. 'This is what the men think of me for havin' one of them in my home. Well, she don't belong here, and I want her out.'

Joe started towards them again.

Charity ducked under Sam's arm and tried to run round him to her clothes, but he caught her by the arm and pulled her away from them. Bending down to her, he stared hard into her face.

'Now you listen real good. We're miners here. And we're miners who're gettin' less money every week 'cos of you Chinee,' Joe heard him say as he got closer. He saw Charity open her mouth to speak. 'And don't say you're American, 'cos you ain't,' Sam snapped. 'It's bad enough to have to work alongside you lot all day – then I have to come home and find one of you in my house. And the men sure as hell wonder why I'm bein' so weak as to let it happen. So I'm not; you're gonna go.'

'Leave her be, Sam,' Martha called, coming up and standing behind Charity. 'She don't deserve that.'

'She's gotta go,' Sam repeated, straightening up.

'She's not gonna go anywhere,' Joe said, coming up to them.

Sam spun round and saw him.

'Now why ain't I surprised that you're ridin' in to her rescue?' Sam sneered, releasing Charity's arm and taking a few steps towards Joe. 'Oh, yeah!' he exclaimed, tapping the side of his head with his hand. 'It's 'cos you ain't a miner. You play around all day long in the livery stable, so you don't know what it's like to work for hour after hour in the dust and the dirt, workin' harder than you've ever worked before, diggin' out more coal than ever before, but takin' home less money than ever before. I do, and so does Pa. And so does every miner in Carter. And this is a miner's house so you don't get the right to speak.'

'This is my house, Sam, mine and Hiram's, and I'll be the one who says who gets to speak or not,' Martha said, her voice cold. 'And I'm sayin' I don't wanna hear from you again. I'm real sorry the miners are takin' their anger out on you, but Charity stays.'

Sam took a step towards Martha, the bruise livid against his face, which was white with anger. 'I reckon if it was Joe gettin' slugged, you'd be throwin' her things out real fast.'

'Will you take Charity in, please, Ma?' Joe cut in. 'I'm guessin' she's got schoolwork to do.'

Martha hesitated.

'Please, Ma,' he repeated.

She stared intently at him, and then nodded. 'Pick up your things and come in with me, Charity, gal,' she said, turning to go back into the house.

Charity glanced nervously from Sam to Joe, then ran to her clothes and started gathering them up.

'You can leave your bag, Charity,' Joe said, with a smile. 'I'll bring that. You don't wanna carry too many things at once or you'll drop them and they'll get even dirtier than they've already got.'

Her arms full, she stared at Sam, and then, clutching her clothes to her chest, ran after Martha.

'So what's all this about, Sam?' Joe asked when Charity had gone into the house and closed the door behind her.

'I would've thought I'd made that obvious, if the other miners haven't. No yellow-skinned person should be given a place to live by a white, and certainly not by a white minin' family.'

'But you hardly ever see Charity. You're in the mine from mornin' to night, and in the town for most of the time you're not workin'. Apart from when she sits with us for meals, all you ever see of her are the things she's done to help Ma.'

'But I know she's there, don't I, and so do the men. And as I reckon Ma can manage without her help now, I want her out.'

'Isn't it for Ma to decide about the help she needs, and as she said, it's up to her who lives in her house?'

'But she won't tell her to leave, will she? And that's because of you,' sneered Sam.

'And what's that supposed to mean?'

'What it says. You've always been her favourite, and you know it. I can see myself in Joe,' he said, raising the pitch of his voice to imitate his mother. 'You're always on about green fields, and it makes Ma think back to the ranch and go soft on you. Whereas me, I've worked since I was old enough to go down the mine, and I work long hours, like Pa. And I give most of my wages to Ma, such as they are these days, but does she know I'm here? No, sir; she does not. She's too busy lookin' at you and doin' what you want.'

'I could say the same about you and Pa. You work together in the mine and that makes you real close, but I won't say that as it'd make me sound as ridiculous as you,' Joe said, and he started to turn away.

'Ridiculous, am I?' Sam said icily, stepping closer to Joe. 'Well, I don't think so. And I don't think you do either. But if you *are* blind like that, and so blind that you don't know what's goin' on in the town you live in, come down to the mine for a day and feel the eyes of the white miners borin' into you, wonderin' why you're givin' a home to one of the people who's makin' them suffer. How d'you think it makes me feel to know that the men I work alongside are thinkin' hatefully about my family and me? If the gal leaves, they'll go back to seein' me as one of them.' He gestured with the upturned palms of his hands. 'That's all I want, Joe.'

'And where's she meant to go?'

'Have you looked at the town recently?' Sam asked in mock amazement. 'South of Second Street to the railroad is Chinatown. The whites hardly go there except to get to the railroad and mine. It stinks of Chinee food; their high-pitched voices are all you hear; baggy trousers, straw hats and long bamboo poles with things hangin' from them are all you see. And this is America! Let her go and live with one of the Celestials who've moved in. That's where she belongs.'

'She's eight. What d'you think would happen to her?'

'The Chinese family who've got the mercantile have got a gal. She can live there. I'm sure they'd give her sufficient work for her to pay her way.'

'I've told you they don't want anythin' to do with her, and I told you why.'

Sam shrugged. 'I don't really care. I just want her out.'

Joe shook his head. 'You never used to be like this Sam,' he said quietly. 'It's like I don't know you any more.'

Sam's expression softened, and he gave Joe a wry smile. 'But you've never really known me, Joe, have you? Look at us – I'm five years older than you. I've always liked bein' in town, but first you were too young to come out with me, and then all you wanted to do was play in the river, lookin' for gold. So we never did many brother-type things together.

And we did none at all from the moment you found that Chinese gal – you were always either mindin' her for Ma or doin' some of Ma's chores.'

'I guess all that's true,' Joe said slowly. 'But we can still be friends, can't we? We're always gonna be brothers.'

'Brothers, are we?' Sam gave a dry laugh. 'Well, I reckon that depends on what bein' brotherly means to you. Look at it through my eyes. Most of the day, I'm in the mine, feelin' the hate of the men around me. I doubt they'll be thumpin' me again 'cos I gave as good as I got, but you could put an end to any risk of that. Ma would send her away if you agreed, but we both know you're not gonna do that. So maybe you'll understand why you don't seem real brotherly to me.'

'I'm mighty sorry you feel that way, but there's nothin' I can do about it. Apart from the fact that Ma appreciates havin' help in the house, I feel responsible for Charity.'

'Another person wouldn't. They'd find her a home in Chinatown and leave her there, whether she liked it or not. But that's 'cos another person doesn't feel the need to be high-minded. But that's you, Joe, isn't it? So high-minded that you'd put a Celestial ahead of your own family.'

'You make it sound real easy to kick Charity out of the place that's always been her home, but it isn't.'

'Is that so? Well, from where I'm standin', it is real easy. And the fact you're not doin' it, tells me what you think about me. Maybe one day, I'll have the chance to show you what I think about you. I sure hope so.'

Pushing past Joe, Sam headed for town.

Chapter Eight

One year and seven months later
March, 1878

Charity burst into the living room clutching her lunch pail, her face alive with excitement.

The palpable tension in the room hit her hard, and she stopped short. The excitement left her face and she looked around, questioningly.

Joe was standing in the middle of the room, his face sullen, and his hands deep in his jeans' pockets.

Her back to the sink, Martha was staring at Joe, her arms folded. Stacked up behind her was a pile of plates waiting to be put out on the table. Still covered in pit-dirt, Hiram sat at the table in the middle of the room, rolling himself a cigarette. Sam lounged against the rear wall, his eyes on Joe.

Biting back the words she'd been about to say, Charity pushed the door shut behind her and stayed where she was.

Joe glanced across at her. His face brightened and he smiled at her.

'You seemed real pleased with yourself when you came in, Charity,' he said. 'What've you got to tell us?'

She opened her mouth, looked at Martha, saw that Martha's gaze was still on Joe, and closed her mouth again.

'We'll hear what Charity's gotta say later, Joe,' Hiram said firmly. 'It's what you're tellin' us now that we wanna hear. Isn't that right, Ma? You've told us you're leavin', but that's all you've said so far.'

Charity glanced again at Martha. She was still staring fixedly at Joe, unspeaking.

'We wanna hear why you're leavin' and not stayin' on here to help,' Hiram went on. 'Sam and I work from dawn till dusk, but no matter how hard we work, with coal down to eighty cents a ton, we're not bringin' home what we used to, and with the prices in the company store as high as they are, that's makin' life mighty difficult. We've needed the money you've been givin' us; isn't that so, Ma?'

Still Martha didn't speak.

'At seventeen, you're a man. Most men would stick around and give their ma as much as they could each week,' Hiram continued. 'They'd wanna help their family out. Families pull together in hard times. But perhaps you don't see yourself as part of this family.'

'What kind of dumb thing to say is that?' Joe said quietly.

'Well, I for one have no complaints that he's leavin',' Sam cut in. He strolled across to the table and sat down next to Hiram. 'Think about it, Pa. He ain't much use in a minin' town if he won't go down the mines. And what he brings in from Culpepper's ain't worth the havin'. With him gone, it'll be one less mouth to feed. That's what I'm thinkin'.'

'I'm not walkin' out on this family, like you're tryin' to say,' Joe said, rounding angrily on his father and brother. 'As a drover, I'll be makin' money and goin' places where there's nowhere to spend it, and I'm gonna be sendin' money back home whenever I can. You can think about that, Sam.'

Sam laughed derisively. 'If you're anythin' like the drovers I've met, you'll spend every last dollar on whiskey and women. The first thing they do when they hit town with a buck in their pocket is head for the saloon and get all roistered up. We'll see none of your wages. Yup, whiskey, women and cards, is where it'll go. There'll be nothin' left over for your family. Or to pay for Charity's keep.'

'Charity pays her way and has done for a while now,' Joe retorted, sharply. 'She's a good gal. She's always cleanin' the house, doin' the washin' and ironin' and cookin'. I know everyone's gotta work hard in a place like Carter, but not many ten-year-olds work as hard as she does.'

'We know that, Joe,' Hiram said.

'And when she's in school, she works hard, too. And when she's not in school, she's always lookin' out for jobs she can get in town. And when she finds work, she gives every cent to Ma.'

'Well, she would, wouldn't she,' Sam countered, 'if she's as smart as you always say she is? She knows she's got somewhere to live for as long as she helps Ma and contributes. She'd hardly be dumb enough to risk gettin' thrown out on to the street for complainin' about havin' to work too hard, would she? No one else around here would be loco enough to take her in. Except maybe the Chinamen who take on the gals for the *tong*.'

'I don't mind workin' hard,' Charity cut in. 'Really I don't.' She looked anxiously at Martha.

''Course you don't,' Sam said, with a scornful laugh. 'It's all just hunky-dory.'

Joe looked from Charity to Martha. 'She couldn't work any harder than she does, and any more willingly. Say it fair, Ma?'

Martha glanced at Charity. 'She's a good worker, I'll say that for her,' she said, her tone grudging.

'And I'll be able to give you more money in future,' Charity burst out. 'I've got a regular job. That's what I was gonna tell you. I'm gonna work in Ah Lee's bakery three times a week – just for a couple of hours after school. I'll be cleanin' up in the back, and helpin' with the pastries and things like that. I won't be servin' people 'cos I can't speak Chinese. But Ah Lee knows a few words of English so he can tell me what to do. I know I didn't wanna work in Chinatown or do anythin' to help the Chinese, but it means I can give you money each week.'

'Aren't we a good little China gal,' Sam said with a sneer.

'Hobble your lip, Sam.' Martha turned to Charity and gave her a slight smile. 'I can't say it won't be welcome. Joe's right – you're a good gal, Charity.' She turned her attention back to Joe. 'So when are you off, then, son? Your clothes'll have to be washed before you go.'

'And that's all you're gonna say, Ma?' Sam exclaimed in surprise. '"When are you off then, son?"'

Martha glanced at Sam and Hiram, and then she looked back at Joe. Her face softened.

'I always knew he'd leave us one day,' she said, her eyes on Joe's face. 'He's like me – he doesn't belong here. He belongs where there's green fields and fresh air. I knew he'd never go down the mines. Not just 'cos he said he wouldn't, but 'cos of the way he's been since he was born. I remember what he was like on the ranch.'

'What're you talkin' about?' Sam said with a scornful laugh. 'He wasn't even six when we left the ranch! I was eleven. I did more there than he ever did.'

'And you hated every minute of it. Your brother had a real way with the animals, and he was always followin' his uncle around, helpin' with whatever they'd let him help with. If your pa hadn't been bitten real bad by the gold-prospectin' bug, we'd still be in Savery and Joe would be runnin' the ranch by now. Not you, Sam – you'd have long gone from there.'

'Maybe not.' Sam's voice was sullen.

'I'm tellin' you, you would've gone. You always hankered after a place with more people and with more town-like things to do. You didn't wanna get on your horse and ride into town – you wanted to be livin' in that town. Your pa, too. I'm not sayin' your pa would've chosen to end up in a minin' town like this – I know he wouldn't've done – but he liked bein' around people, not animals, and he preferred life in a town to life on a ranch. And you did, too. Not Joe, though, and I'm glad he's gonna do what I know's in his blood to do.'

'Bein' a cowboy's not exactly ranchin',' Sam said caustically.

Hiram nodded. 'Sam's right, Joe.'

Joe shrugged his shoulders. 'That's as maybe. But from when I first started listenin' to the cowboys as they passed through Carter on their way back home after months on the trail, and hearin' their stories about life in the open and all the different places they'd seen, I've felt a real yen to lead that life, too. Their adventures fair set my blood on fire.'

'If it's adventures you wanna hear about, I'll tell you about some of the things that've happened in the mines,' Sam said dryly. 'That'd really set your blood on fire.'

'Now you leave him be, Sam. So when are you plannin' on goin', Joe?' Martha asked again.

'As soon as I can.'

Charity gasped.

'A couple of weeks ago,' Joe went on, his voice shaking slightly, 'a guy called Monty Taylor stopped by the livery for a new harness. He mentioned he'd soon be bossin' a herd of cattle up the trail to an Indian reservation in Montana, startin' out from south of Cheyenne, and I told him I'd be interested in bein' taken on. I've just gotten a Western Union wire from him, offerin' me a job as trail hand for the summer. If I want it, I've gotta join them in Cheyenne in a couple of weeks.'

'Cheyenne's almost the other side of Wyoming. It's quite a ride from here,' Hiram remarked.

Joe nodded. 'I've talked to folk, and I reckon I can do it in eight days. Mr Culpepper's givin' me a horse and an ordinary Texas saddle, the kind that cowboys use. It would've cost me sixty bucks. It's mighty generous of him, but he says I've earned it.'

Hiram shrugged his shoulders and stood up. 'Well, you've obviously decided what you're gonna do, so there's nothin' more to be said.' He turned away from Joe. 'Sam and I will get cleaned up, Martha, and then we can all eat.'

Joe took a step towards him. 'I've gotta do this, Pa, even though it tears at me to be leavin' you all. Right now, I can't even bear to think about it. I don't know how it'll turn out, but I wanna give it a try for a few years—'

'Years!' Charity's cry of distress cut through his words. 'Years?'

She dropped her lunch pail, flung the front door open and ran from the house.

'But you always knew I'd go at some point, didn't you?' Joe said, sitting next to Charity at the top of the short gravelly slope that led down to the river. 'I kept tellin' you, didn't I?'

She nodded, her face pale.

In silence, both stared at the water.

'I suppose hearin' someone tell you somethin' is one thing; knowin' it's gonna happen, and happen real soon, is another. I'm right, aren't I?' he said at last.

'I guess so.' Her eyes remained on the river.

'I know that 'cos I know how I feel. I've talked so long about leavin', but now it's really happenin', and I'm gonna get on a horse mighty soon and ride away from you and my family, well, it ain't gonna be easy. I'm gonna miss you all somethin' bad,' he added a few minutes later, breaking the silence that had fallen again.

She turned to him, her face accusing. 'If you don't go, you won't have to miss us.'

He smiled at her. 'Yup, that's true. But I *am* goin',' he said gently. 'Inside me I know I've gotta go, even though it's tough to leave.'

'I'll miss you, Joe. I won't have any friends. Mr and Mrs Oakland don't even talk to me now. If they see me comin' out of the house, they go back inside and I know they're waitin' till I've gone. No one in Carter will talk to me.'

'You'd have a friend if you'd let yourself get to know the girl from the mercantile, like I've been suggestin' for years. I can see you're not gonna make friends among the white girls. They've always been unneighbourly to you, and that's not likely to change, not now there're even more Chinamen in Carter.'

'I don't like havin' so many Chinamen here, either.' She stuck out her lower lip.

He suppressed a smile. 'Have you thought that Su Lin might be lonely? Most of the Chinamen's wives seem to be back in China. Su Lin's ma is the only Chinese wife in Carter, and Su Lin's still the only Chinese kid here.'

'Oh, no, you're wrong, Joe. Some of the wives *are* here. I've seen them in the buildin' at the bottom of Main Street near the railroad,' she said earnestly.

He shifted awkwardly. 'You mean in the *tong*,' he said. 'They're no one's wives, Charity; they've been brought in as company for the Chinamen. You keep away from them. Ma would tell you the same. Nope, you're Su Lin's only hope of havin' a friend. Don't you think you've held out for long enough?'

'Maybe, maybe not,' she said flatly. She folded her arms.

'A kind person would make friends with her,' he went on. 'I know you're a kind person, so why don't you go into the general mercantile and talk to her? She and her family live in the rooms behind the store, like a lot of the other Chinese shopkeepers. Their bedrooms are above the store. It's only the ones who don't have shops who live in the shacks the company's built between us and Second Street.'

She stared at him, frowning. 'How d'you know where Chinamen live?'

'Mr Culpepper told me. He's gotten into the habit of goin' along to the mercantile in the evenin's from time to time, and if there's a game of cards in one of the back rooms, he joins in. He likes somethin' called *fan-tan*. Apparently, it's about guessin' the number of buttons under a cup. He can talk to Chen Fai, but he can't understand the others and they can't understand him. That doesn't seem to matter, though. He said they sit around tables, smokin' water pipes, and they understand all they need to.'

'Why does he go there?'

Joe shrugged. 'I guess he must like them. He doesn't tell people in Carter, though, and you mustn't either. He said Carter townsfolk wouldn't like it, and he might lose some business if folk found out.'

'I'm Carter townsfolk, too.'

He stared at her thoughtfully for a few minutes. 'I can't force you to do anythin' you don't want, Charity. I hope you'll mind me and make a friend of Su Lin, but whether you do or not is up to you. I like to think of you havin' someone to talk to when I'm gone, but that's me bein' selfish, I guess. I don't like to think of you bein' alone.'

'Then don't leave me alone,' she said bluntly. 'You said you might be gone for years. Don't go, Joe. Please, don't.' A sob caught in her throat.

He turned slightly to face her. 'Yup, it could be years. I'm not gonna lie to you about that. This drive will last roughly two and a half months from its start to the delivery at the end, and when it finishes, I'll be at the top of Montana Territory. That's a long way away. I'm keen to see the place, and also to see a bit more of Wyoming, so I thought I'd probably try to get on one of the fall round-ups.'

'But you could come back after that, couldn't you?'

He shook his head. 'I'm afraid not. Wherever the fall drive ends, it'll be a real long way from Carter, and with winter about to set in, I'll immediately have to find somewhere to stay where I can work through the winter months.'

She stared at him. A tear trickled down her cheek.

'Won't I ever see you again?' she asked, her voice a frightened whisper.

'Sure you will,' he said, and he laughed reassuringly. 'You and the family are here, aren't you? But I'm never again gonna live in Carter – I'll never live in any minin' town again. No, sir. Every day I'm drivin' them cattle, I'm gonna be keepin' my eyes open for a place where I'd be happy to settle. One day I'll find it, and then you can all come and live with me. I'd like that.'

Her face broke into a broad smile. 'You promise to let me come, too?'

'I sure do,' he said, his voice warm. 'I found you, didn't I? I didn't leave you behind by the river and go back home on my own. Like I've said before, that makes me responsible for you. 'Course you might choose to stay on here, but that'd be up to you.'

'I wouldn't wanna stay here, Joe,' she said eagerly, wiping her eyes with the back of her hands.

He smiled at her. 'That's what you think now, but in a few years you could think differently. You'll be older by then and you might not wanna move to a place that's far away. You might have a special friend here and wanna stay near your friend.'

She started to speak, but he put his finger gently to her lips.

'I don't mean the Chinese girl. I mean that someone might be courtin' you. I reckon you're gonna be real pretty, Charity, and if I'm away for years, by the time I come back you might be wed. You might even be a ma. Just think of that!'

She put her hand in front of her mouth, and giggled.

'That just sort of came out,' he said slowly. 'But when I think about it, I suppose it's not impossible,' he added with a wry smile.

'I'll marry you, Joe, and I'll always look after your house for you. I'll keep it clean and make you cookies every day.'

He laughed. 'A smart gal like you can do a lot better for yourself than someone like me. And now we'd better get back.'

He stood up and wiped the dust from the seat of his jeans. Charity stayed where she was. She pulled her knees up to her chin and hugged them to her.

He looked down at her, and a wave of emotion came over him. 'I'll come back and see you again, Charity,' he said gravely. 'I promise. But now,' he added, forcing a cheerful note into his voice, 'I want you to practise smilin'. I want a smile on your face when I ride off, 'cos that's how I wanna remember you.'

Joe went wearily back into the house. Martha was sitting at the table. She glanced round at the sound of his steps.

'She stopped cryin' yet?' she asked.

'Just about,' he said, sitting down opposite her. 'But she

wants to stay out there a bit longer.' He looked at the empty chairs by the range. 'Where's Pa and Sam?'

'In town.'

'Figures.' He paused. 'I meant what I said, Ma; I'll send you money from wherever I am, and one day I may even have a place of my own that you can come to if you wanna leave Carter. I know you'd like to live on a ranch again.'

Martha nodded. 'I believe you mean that, son, but it's easy to say now. We'll just have to wait and see what happens.'

He leaned across the table towards her. 'Before I leave, I want you to promise me somethin'. It's about Charity. She's a good kid. She helps you all she can, and it's not because she's afear'd of bein' thrown out.'

She gestured dismissively. 'I know that. The gal's got a kind heart.'

'She's earned her right to be here, and I want you to promise you'll never let Pa and Sam turn her out, and that you'll never do anythin' to make her feel she's gotta go. I want her here when I return, unless she's wed, of course. And if she's wed, I want it to be 'cos that's what she wanted and not 'cos she thought you all wanted her out. You owe it to her. Promise me she'll always have a home here.'

'For my part, she will. And your pa's too soft to force anyone out. But I can't answer for Sam.'

'Promise me you'll not let him throw her out,' he repeated, his voice hardening.

She stared at his face, at the set of his jaw. Her lips tightened into a thin line. 'I promise you'll find her here when you get back, unless she's gotten wed; and if she *has* gotten wed, that it'll have been her choice to have done so.'

He nodded in satisfaction, and sat back.

'But that means you gotta come back, Joe.'

Chapter Nine

The midday sun beat down on the hard mud track that snaked across a plain scored by horses' hoofs and the wheels of the many covered wagons that had carried the early pioneers along the trail in the years before the railroad had opened up an alternative way of making the long journey from east to west.

Joe reined his horse to a halt, stretched himself and made an effort to pull his sweat-slicked shirt away from his skin.

Leaning forward against the pommel, he stared across the clumps of wind-bitten sagebrush, the once-green foliage crowned with small yellow and purple flowers that had been silvered by the bright light of the sun, to the mass of wooden houses lying in the distance – to Cheyenne, the town where his new life was about to begin.

Wisps of white smoke rose from the many stovepipes and drifted slowly up to meet the low white clouds that were floating idly across the wide blue sky, and there they dissolved.

As he sat staring at the sprawl of houses and shops ahead of him, the strains of the life and activity in the town were carried to him on the back of a gentle breeze. Not a single mine chimney, he thought, and no sound of a mine pump.

Excitement, flattened by eight days of hard riding, rose again within him.

On a sudden impulse, he twisted in his saddle and looked back down the track he'd ridden – a track that had led him across rivers and streams and miles of emptiness, that had brought him far from Carter Town, which now lay hidden beyond a horizon hazed deep blue by shadowy mountains.

All of a sudden it hit him with force that he was a long, long way from his home, and from the life he'd always known and the sense of security it had given him without his realising it. He was now alone in a way that he'd never been before, and whatever happened in the future, nothing would ever be the same again.

From the moment he'd packed his saddlebags and headed east, a part of him had realised this. He'd known that he'd be a different person when next he saw his family, and that they would be different, too. Time wouldn't stand still for them while it allowed him to grow from a boy to a man, and they would never again appear to him in the way that they were now lodged in his mind.

He'd known all that when he'd left Carter, but he hadn't really felt it. But now, on the threshold of his new life, he felt it deeply. His family were far from him, and soon they'd be still further away. And not just his family, but Charity, too, with her wide happy smile and her funny childish ways.

A wave of anguish swept through him, the force of it taking him by surprise. A lump came to his throat, and he felt momentarily winded by the powerful sense of loss that engulfed him.

He sat still in the saddle, breathing deeply.

He knew he'd done the right thing in grabbing with both hands the chance to live the life he'd long yearned for. But vivid memories of what he'd left behind for an unknown future crowded fast and furiously into his mind, stabbing him sharply, and he couldn't do anything for a moment or two but stare back at the way he'd come, his vision blurred.

At last, drained of emotion he turned again to face Cheyenne. Then, pressuring the horse's flank with his left heel, he started to gallop towards the future he'd chosen.

Chapter Ten

Charity stood on the sun-bleached boardwalk and stared up at the sign above the entrance to the wood-frame shop. On it written in large letters she read the words 'General Mercantile Store'. Nervously nibbling her lip, and frantically hoping that Chen Fai wouldn't be in the store, she lowered her eyes to the entrance, drew in a deep breath and took a step forward.

The flurry of air caused the slender wind chimes hanging above the doorway to jingle, and she winced.

She took another step forward and found herself inside the store. The wind chimes jangled furiously behind her. In a sudden panic at being in a place where whites seldom went, she turned and ran out of the shop and back to the dusty track, and stopped.

Her heart beating fast, she anxiously glanced along Main Street in both directions.

The only person close to her was a Chinaman wearing a coarse cotton knee-length jacket over baggy blue pants, and a peaked straw hat on his head. His eyes on the ground, he was coming from the direction of the railroad, a large piece of raw meat hanging from one end of a long branch balanced across his right shoulder, and a sack from the other.

There was no one else around.

With a sigh of relief that she hadn't been seen going in or out of the Chinese store by any of the Carter townsfolk, and that Chen Fai hadn't come out to see who'd disturbed the wind chimes, she turned and went back to the entrance.

She stared at the doorway. She was going to have to go through it again if she wanted that letter. And she did.

A scroll hung from either side of the doorway, with Chinese letters on each and words under them written in English. 'Ten thousand customers constantly arriving', she read on one scroll. 'Profit coming in like rushing waters', she read on the other.

Swallowing the sudden desire to giggle, she peered through the open doorway into the dimly lit interior. The wind chimes lightly tinkled. She took a step back.

'You not go,' she heard a voice say from within. 'Please honour my father's unworthy store with your presence.'

Frowning slightly, Charity stared into the store, squinting as she did so.

The Chinese girl emerged from the gloom and stood facing her, her hands flat together in front of her as if in prayer, her neck bent in a slight bow.

Charity stared at her. 'How can I?' she asked, a smile playing across her lips. 'This is a small shop and there are already ten thousand customers in it.'

The girl unfolded her hands, put them in front of her mouth and giggled. 'Unworthy self can welcome ten thousand and one customers to humble mercantile. You come in.' She backed into the shop, her eyes inviting Charity to enter.

Charity slowly followed her, the sound of her boots on the wooden planks echoing loudly in her ears; then she stopped and looked around.

A small potbellied stove stood to her right, just inside the store. A number of wooden barrels and kegs were clustered between the stove and a long sawn-plank counter that ran from the front of the shop to the rear, parallel with the sidewall. A similar counter ran the length of the store on the opposite side.

Halfway along the right-hand counter stood a small pair

of scales. She'd seen scales like that before. Joe had once pointed some out to her when they'd been in a store in the whites' section of town, and she knew they were for weighing gold dust. At the far end of the counter, there was a boxed area marked out with a grille. A chair had been placed behind the grille.

In the middle of both of the counters, a coal-oil lamp threw out a pungent cloud of oily smoke that almost hid from sight the items piled at the far end of the shelves that lined the walls on both sides of the store.

All of the shelves looked as if they were about to collapse beneath the weight of the goods on them, Charity thought. She'd never seen such a jumble of items for sale – groceries of every kind, cured fish, wheels of cheese, canned goods, soap, coal oil, hairpins, lengths of cloth, bundles of Goodwin's miners' candles, and far more things than she could take in at a single glance.

She sniffed the air. A strange, aromatic smell seemed to be coming from the counter on the left-hand side of the store. Curious, she went across and stared at the assortment of small bags and boxes spread out across the top of the counter. The smell was definitely coming from the packages, but she couldn't read the unfamiliar squiggles on them so she didn't know what was inside them.

She picked up two of the bags closest to her, sniffed them, pulled an expression of distaste and put them down again, then she turned back to the store, and to Su Lin, who was hovering nearby, watching her.

'What's that?' she asked Su Lin, indicating the grille at the end of the right-hand counter.

'People who likee send letter, give letter and money to honourable brother. Honourable brother pay man to take letter to train or stagecoach. Another people send letter back here to unworthy store.'

Charity nodded. She glanced around the store again, and then looked back at the girl. Her eyes now more accustomed to the lack of light, she saw that the girl was wearing a short dark blue quilted jacket over loose pale blue cotton trousers. Joe was right – the Chinese girl looked about ten, too, when you got up close to her.

Su Lin wriggled uncomfortably under Charity's stare. 'Name of this unworthy girl is Su Lin,' she said.

Charity frowned. 'I know your name, but I don't know why you keep sayin' that you're unworthy and your store's unworthy? Why don't you just say, My name is Su Lin, and just say store, not unworthy store?'

Su Lin looked at her in surprise. She slipped each hand into the opposite sleeve and shrugged slightly. 'Is Chinese way,' she said. 'I Chinese.' She hesitated. 'You also Chinese.'

'I'm an American girl,' Charity said firmly.

Su Lin shrugged her shoulders again, and smiled. 'You not likee, but you Chinese girl. You got Chinese face. You got Chinese *mama* and *baba*.'

Charity glared at her. 'You've got a letter for me,' she said sharply. 'Ah Lee told me so last night when I was leavin' the bakery. Your brother told him it was here. Give me my letter, please, so I can go.'

Su Lin didn't move. 'Big brother not want us be friends. But I want us be friends. I learn good English so we able to talk,' she said, a shy smile on her face. 'Big Brother teach me so I able to help in shop.'

'Well, *I* don't want us to be friends. My letter, please.'

Su Lin's face fell. She went across to the far end of the right-hand counter, took something from the pile of papers in the area behind the grille and brought it back to Charity.

'I likee us be friends. If you also likee, you come see me again,' she said, holding out the letter.

'I said I don't wanna be friends. I didn't come to see you – I came for my letter,' Charity said curtly, and she snatched it from Su Lin.

She looked down at the letter, and excitement welled up inside her. For a long moment, she stared hard at it, unable to move.

Then she ran her fingers across the words directing the letter to General Mercantile Store, Carter Town, and looked up at Su Lin with wonder in her eyes. 'This is the first letter I've ever had,' she found herself saying, impelled by something outside her to share the moment.

Su Lin nodded her understanding, and smiled. 'I not yet have letter. But honourable parents soon go home to China. When they in China, they send letter and I send letter back. You bring letter here and I send letter back.' She indicated Charity's letter. 'Letter come from who?'

'From Joe. He went away three weeks ago.'

'Joe is man in livery stable? Is big like Chen Fai. But man Joe is not big brother. He not have Chinese face.'

Charity shook her head. 'Joe's my friend. He found me.'

'He found you? I not understand.' Su Lin looked at her in friendly curiosity.

The warmth of the friendship on offer reached out to Charity and touched her. A tightness grew in her throat, and she swallowed hard. She opened her mouth to explain what had happened ten years earlier, and then she stopped. She was an American girl, not Chinese; she shouldn't be talking to a Chinese person. Carter townsfolk weren't friends with the Chinese.

She shook her head and took a step back from Su Lin. 'I don't wanna talk to you. I'm an American girl. I'm gonna go home and read my letter now. Thank you.'

Trying not to see the disappointment that filled the eyes that were the same shape as her own, she turned away and went quickly to the door.

'*M goi*,' she heard Su Lin call after her. '*Zoi jin.*'

She stopped and turned round.

Su Lin was standing in the middle of the empty shop, a lonely figure. Silence hung in the air around her.

'What do those words mean?' Charity asked, feeling the need to say something to remove the sadness from Su Lin's eyes, and the loneliness.

'*M goi* mean thank you. And *zoi jin* mean goodbye,' Su Lin said quietly.

Charity stared at her, hesitating, wondering whether she ought to say something else out of kindness. Then she shook herself inwardly. I'm an American girl, she told herself firmly, and she started to go out through the doorway.

'Goodbye,' she called over her shoulder as she left the store.

The moment she was in the street, she started to run as fast as she could down Main Street to Second Street, and along Second Street, past the row of miners' houses, and out across the open ground to the place by the river where she and Joe used to sit.

But no matter how fast she ran, she couldn't outrun the expression in Su Lin's eyes as once again her offer of friendship had been thrown back in her face. It was there at her side, keeping pace with her every step.

Dear Charity, she read, sitting on the edge of the gully.

It's lucky for me that you're a smart girl who knows her letters as it means I can write to you. The further I got from home, the bigger the lump in my throat whenever I thought

75

of you all. And then it hit me that with you being able to read so well, I could write to you from wherever I was and keep in touch with you all while I'm gone.

If you pass on my news to Ma, Pa and Sam, then none of you will need to wonder what I'm doing because you'll know. And I'll feel close to you all, even though I'm far away.

So, Charity, I'm guessing you finally did what I've long been asking you to do – gone into the mercantile and spoken to the girl there. If you hadn't, you wouldn't be reading this. Maybe it was her brother you spoke to, but I hope it was Su Lin.

In the rush of setting out for Cheyenne, I forgot to tell you that Mr Culpepper told me that Su Lin's folks are going back to China for a visit. I reckon I've been gone from Carter long enough now for you to have started to understand what real loneliness feels like, and you'll be able to imagine how Su Lin will feel when her folks have left. If for no other reason than kindness, I hope you'll give yourself a chance to get to know her. That would make me mighty pleased.

I'm wondering if you'd like to know a bit about the outfit I'm with. In case you do, I thought I'd tell you. We've around three thousand head of cattle, and four mules for the chuck wagon. The chuck wagon carries our flour, bacon, beans, medical supplies and just about everything else. We've also got a well-stocked remuda. That's the name for the spare horses. When our horse is tired, we change to another.

The actual drive begins tomorrow – yup, that's excitement you can feel rising up from the paper. We'll be aiming for about twenty miles each day for the first couple of days. That's going some, but you've got to get cows far from their home as fast as you can. They've got a homing instinct, and you don't want them trying to get back to their ranch. After a couple of days, they'll have got into the rhythm of the drive and should handle well, so we'll be dropping to fifteen miles a day. We have to go slowly and give them time to graze well else they'll be worn out and skinny by the time we get to Montana and they won't fetch much of a price.

I hope you're impressed by what I've already learnt, and we haven't even left the delivery point south of Cheyenne yet.

One last thing before I sign off. I heard tell it's possible to get letters while you're on the trail. I'd very much like to hear from you, Charity, and to learn how they are at home. You don't have to write if you're busy, though. I know Ma keeps adding to your chores and you've got schoolwork to do, and the bakery. It's just if you do have a moment, I'd sure appreciate a letter from time to time.

In case you want to write, if we're heading towards a town where we'll be stocking up on supplies and I'll be able to pick up any mail, I'll let you know in advance.

Our first stop will be Casper, but we'll have left Casper before you've got this letter and had time to reply, so the first place to write to would be Buffalo. It'll take eight or nine days to get to Buffalo from Casper because of the cows. If you just write to me care of Monty Taylor's drive, it'll find me. If you want to, that is.

Your friend,

Joe

Clutching the letter to her chest in excitement, Charity jumped up and ran as fast as she could back to the house.

'I got a letter from Joe,' she screamed as she bolted through the doorway. She came to a halt in the middle of the room, panting hard. She stared at Martha with joy in her eyes.

Clutching a serving spoon to her chest, Martha took a step towards her, a sense of wonder spreading over her face.

'I'll read it to you,' Charity said. 'And then I'm gonna write to him.'

Chapter Eleven

Charity came into the front room from the corridor and saw Martha standing in the open doorway, leaning against one of the wooden supports. She was staring in the direction of the river.

'What're you doin'?' she asked curiously.

Martha didn't move, but continued to stand there, silent.

Clutching the piece of paper she was carrying, Charity crossed to the doorway and squeezed between Martha and the doorpost. 'What're you lookin' at?' she asked, following the line of Martha's gaze. 'It's gettin' dark. And it's cold.'

'Everythin' and nothin',' Martha replied, her eyes fixed on some distant point, seemingly searching for something hidden in the darkness that was falling fast as smoky grey clouds wrapped themselves tightly around the moon.

Charity stared ahead for a moment or two, puzzled, then she inched back and glanced to her right. The bathtub was on the floor in front of the sink. It was full of dirty water, with a layer of black grime and coal splinters floating on the surface. She stared at the tub, her eyes widening in surprise. Joe's ma always got rid of the dirty water as soon as Sam and Joe's pa had washed themselves after their day in the mine, so why was it still there?

Her brow creased in bewilderment.

Moving closer to Martha's side again, she glanced up at her. 'What d'you mean, everythin' and nothin'? I don't understand.'

Martha looked down at her. 'I was thinkin' about Joe. He's only been gone for about three weeks, but it feels much longer. I'm glad he's gonna be writin' to us, and tellin' how he's gettin' on.' She glanced at the letter in Charity's hand. 'That's for Joe, I guess.'

Charity beamed at her. 'I'm gonna send it tomorrow. I'll go to the mercantile when I leave the bakery.' Martha nodded. 'But what's the everythin' and nothin' you're lookin' at? I wanna look at it, too.'

'The past,' Martha said with a dry laugh, and she turned back to the night.

The clouds slowly unravelled and drifted away from the pale moon, and the rock-hard ground took on a cold, silvery sheen in the light of the unscarfed moon. 'I was thinkin' about what it used to be like when we lived on the ranch. You would've liked it there,' she said, and she smiled at Charity.

Charity smiled happily back up at her.

'There were green hills and cows everywhere you looked,' Martha went on, turning back to the darkness, her voice taking on a dreamy tone. 'And at certain times of the year, there were wild flowers all around you. There wasn't a slagheap to be seen, not anywhere. And no black smoke driftin' endlessly over the town, coverin' everythin' with dirt. When you stepped out on to the veranda that ran round the ranch house, you breathed clean air, and all you could hear was birds singin', cattle lowin', and the sounds of horses bein' ridden and ranch hands goin' about their daily chores. Never the endless beat of a mine pump and the dull thud of metal bangin' on rock.'

'Did you look after the cows when you lived on the ranch?'

Martha laughed. 'Not me; that was a man's job. The men worked real hard. But so did the women, only in a different way. Not only did we take care of our family, we also looked after all of the ranch hands. They had to be fed, too.

And we made and mended all the clothin', cooked the food, raised the children, looked after anyone who was sick.'

'But you mend the clothes now, and when that piece of rock fell from the mine roof and hit Sam on the head, you looked after him till he was better.'

'You're right; I do a lot of that now, too. But the ranch was a much nicer place to do it in. And we women had ranchin' skills, too. We knew how to fire a gun, use a brandin' iron, and herd cattle or sheep to pasture. It was a good life. And Joe thought that, too, even though he was only knee high to a grasshopper when we left. Not Sam, though. That was never gonna be the life for Sam.'

'Why did you leave?'

'I met Hiram, didn't I? He was passin' through the nearby town, lookin' for work. Oh, you should've seen him, Charity, before life had been knocked out of him! He was a real good-lookin' man with a ready laugh, and he had a carin' way about him which made a woman melt. Everyone liked him. All the unwed girls set their caps at him, but it was me he turned to. Believe it or not, folk used to think me pretty.' She reached up and tucked her hair more firmly under her day bonnet.

Charity smiled up at her. 'You're pretty now.'

Martha put her hand to her cheek and gave a short laugh. 'I think not. But it was different then, and we were wed. He needed a job so he came to live and work on the family ranch. But he was a restless dreamer, and he was like a fish out of water there. He just didn't take to tendin' animals, growin' crops and ridin' the range all day.'

'Why not?'

'I don't really know. Maybe there wasn't enough excitement in it, always bein' with the same few people every day, and doin' the same thing year after year. Whatever it was, the life slowly drained out of him. The day he heard that gold had been found in the river and hills around here, he came to life again, and I wasn't the least bit surprised when he said he was gonna go prospectin'. He told the boys and me we could go with him or stay behind. I packed our bags that night and so did they, and we went with him.'

'But if you liked the ranch, why didn't you stay there?'

'One day you'll fall for someone, and then you'll understand,' Martha told her with a wry smile. 'And remember, I'd no idea I'd end up in a godforsaken place like this. If I *had* known ... and if Hiram had known where it'd end ... well, I reckon things might've been very different.' She shifted her weight to the other foot. 'Anyway, like most of those chasin' the yellow stuff, he didn't find it, and finally I made him see that he had to go down the mines to feed his family. And the way it's turned out, he's doin' the same thing this year as he did last year. Just what he was tryin' to escape from when he left the ranch.'

'Sam likes it here.'

'But Hiram's not Sam, for all they're alike in many a way. And anyway, I'm not sure how true that is of Sam these days. Sam likes livin' in a town, that's for sure, but bein' a miner's not turnin' out the way he thought it'd be. Things in the mine have changed for the worse since he started, and it's gotten to be a real hard life now. Sam doesn't smile that much these days. As for Hiram, he hates each day. Many a man would've left their family by now and struck out on their own, but not Hiram. He's a better man than many; I'll say that for him.'

'Why don't you go back to the ranch then?'

'Too much time's passed. My brothers and their families have been runnin' it for years, and we lost contact long ago. If we just turned up, we'd need rooms they probably don't have, and we'd be extra mouths to feed that hadn't earned the food put into them. It's too late to go back. And anyway, Sam likes Carter, and whatever Hiram thinks of minin', at least he's on the edge of a town, and I reckon that's still where he'd rather be than on a ranch.'

'You could ask him, maybe.'

'No point. I know the answer. We could've found a good patch of land near water years ago, staked a claim and become homesteaders. You can stake a hundred and sixty acres under the law. I once suggested that, but Sam and Hiram wouldn't hear of it. Joe wanted to, though.' She paused. 'I don't know why I'm tellin' you all this – you're only ten. Maybe it's that I'm feelin' a mite bit lonely. Folk around here aren't as friendly as they used to be; in fact, some have gotten downright rude. Or maybe it's 'cos you're not family that I can say to you what I couldn't say to the family.'

Joe's parting words leapt into Martha's head, reverberating loud and clear in the still of the night, just as if he were standing next to her.

'Remember your promise,' he had said as he was leaving. 'This family's all that Charity's got. The whites won't accept her as one of them 'cos she looks Chinese, and the Chinese won't accept her 'cos she's been brought up American. I'm trustin' you to do your best for her while I'm gone. Make sure she knows she belongs.'

Her conscience pricked her sharply.

'I know you're not family, Charity,' she added quietly, 'but you come pretty close.'

And she fell silent. A cloak of darkness slowly fell upon the earth again as coal-grey clouds once more curled themselves around the face of the moon.

Standing quietly at Martha's side, Charity stared ahead

with her. 'I still don't know what we're lookin' at,' she said after several minutes.

'I don't know about you, Charity gal, but I'm lookin' ahead at year after year of this, and I feel like I'm bein' buried alive.'

Chapter Twelve

Tightly holding her letter to Joe, Charity stared at the entrance in front of her, at the scrolls on either side, at the Chinese wind chimes above the door. She fingered the coins Martha had given her, then took a deep breath and went in. The chimes rung loudly in her wake.

Two Chinamen were coming towards her on their way out of the store, each of them clad in a coarse cotton knee-length jacket, baggy trousers and a peaked straw hat. Each man carried a rolled-up length of material under his arm. She stopped just inside the entrance and stood back to give them room to go out.

They glanced curiously at her as they passed, their eyes travelling swiftly from her face to her dress. Unsmiling, they gave her a slight nod. She nodded back. The long black pigtails hanging behind them almost reached to the waist, she noticed, as they went through the doorway. She heard one of them say something to the other and their laughter followed them on to the street.

Looking back along the shop, she saw that Su Lin was at the far end of the left-hand counter, rolling up a bale of material, and hadn't yet seen her. Charity walked towards her, making her booted feet sound loud on the floor to let Su Lin know she was there.

Su Lin looked up, and her face broke out into a smile of pleasure. Leaving the material where it was, she skirted the end of the counter and hurried up to Charity, the palms of her hands pressed together. Reaching her, she gave her a small bow.

'I hear chimes. Think chimes say men leave,' she said with

a laugh. 'I not see you. I very pleased you visit unworthy self today. I likee see you.' She beamed at Charity.

'I've not come to see you,' Charity said stiffly. 'I've come to send a letter to Joe; that's all.'

She saw Su Lin's face fall, and she felt a stab of guilt.

She opened her mouth to say something friendlier, something that wasn't being unkind to Su Lin in the way that the children in her school were unkind to her. It wasn't Su Lin's fault she was Chinese.

'I'm not—' she started. The curtain that covered the doorway at the far end of the shop rustled with sudden movement. Her heart skipped a beat. She stopped mid-sentence and stared past Su Lin to the doorway.

Chen Fai was standing there, holding the curtain to one side, his dark eyes fixed on her. She instantly dropped her gaze to the floor in front of him, and to his feet. His flat black shoes were embroidered with a jumble of colour over the place where his toes must be.

He stood in silence, unmoving.

Gathering courage, Charity raised her eyes from his feet to his black trousers, and up to his yellow tunic made of shiny material, and to his head. He wasn't wearing the peaked straw hat that most of the Carter Chinamen wore, she saw in surprise; he was wearing a small black cap that fitted on the top of his head.

She looked back at his face. He had a nice face, she thought. And then their eyes met. Open hostility shone from the depths of his dark, dark eyes, and she felt a sudden panic.

He released his hold on the curtain and let it fall back into place as he came forward and stood half in front of Su Lin.

'Su Lin,' he said. And not taking his eyes from Charity's face, he spoke to Su Lin in their language.

Stepping to the side to have a better view of Su Lin,

86

Charity saw her turn without a word when Chen Fai had finished speaking and go across to the curtained doorway, her eyes on the shop floor. She moved the curtain aside and disappeared into the back of the store. Then once again, the curtain closed off the back room.

In the few moments that the curtain had been drawn back, an aroma, strange to Charity, had drifted into the store. She sniffed.

'What's that smell?' she asked without thinking.

Surprise registered on Chen Fai's face. 'Roast duck and ginger,' he said tersely.

She nodded her thanks.

He stared at her, frowning. Feeling the heaviness of his gaze on her face, she stood very still.

'I tell Su Lin to help honourable father's second wife with the cooking,' he said at last, his voice cold. 'I say to her I serve you.'

Charity bit her lip.

'What you want?' he asked shortly. 'I tell Joe Walker I not wish you to be friends with Su Lin. You collect letter yesterday, Su Lin tell me. So why you come here today?'

Charity glanced at the grilled area, then at Chen Fai. She held her letter out to him.

'I've written a letter to Joe. For when he's in Buffalo. I wanna post it.'

He took the letter from her, and looked at it. 'Cost for stamp is forty-nine cents.'

She took the coins from her pocket, counted them out and handed them to him.

'Now you leave,' he said. Holding the letter in one of his hands, he slid each hand into the opposite sleeve of his tunic. 'You not come again unless you must send letter. You not talk to Su Lin, and she not talk to you. I forbid it.'

Charity stared at him in surprise. 'I don't wanna be friends with Su Lin. It's Joe who wants me to be her friend. Why don't *you* want that, too?'

'You got Chinese face, but you American girl,' he said bluntly.

Charity nodded. 'I know. But why don't you want us to be friends if Joe does?'

'Joe Walker not know Chinese way of things. Su Lin is good Chinese girl, you not. You go now.'

Charity shifted from one foot to the other.

'Maybe Su Lin's unhappy she's not got a friend,' she ventured.

'Chinese girl respect parents and obey wishes of parents and brother,' he said stiffly.

'Maybe her ma wants us to be friends.'

'Honourable father's second wife must obey wishes of son. That also is Chinese way. You go now,' he repeated. He slipped the hand holding the letter out from the sleeve and pointed towards the entrance.

Charity followed the line of his finger with her gaze, hesitated a moment, then looked back at him.

'Why've you got a braid?' she blurted out.

A look of amazement crossed his face. 'Why you ask?'

She shrugged. 'I wanna know. All the Chinamen in Carter have got one. Why?'

'Honourable father tell me it from when Manchu conquerors capture China in 1644 and make themselves rulers of all China. It become crime for Chinese man to cut hair. He has head chopped off if he cut hair.'

She pulled a face. 'But that was years ago!'

'You not understand – you not proper Chinese person. People who come from China to Gold Mountain—'

'Where's Gold Mountain? Joe's pa used to pan for gold.'

'Here.' He indicated around them. 'Gold Mountain is Chinese name for America. China people who come to America not think they stay here for ever. They think they go back to China one day so they must keep queue. The name for this braid, as you call it, is queue.'

'But no one in America would chop off your head, so you could cut it off if you wanted.'

A look of shock crossed his face. 'I not do that. If no queue, Chinese man must wander forever from land of his ancestors. Cannot return to China without queue, which is sign of respect and obedience to emperor,' he said, his voice grave. 'Now you leave.'

'What about Chinese girls? Must they keep their hair long or not be able to go back to China either?'

'Girls not matter. They not important in China like men. Go!' he said firmly, and he again pointed to the doorway leading to Main Street.

Not moving, she stared at him for a moment in thought.

'Annie wouldn't let me work in her restaurant,' she said at last. 'She said I was a Chinese girl and if she took on a Chinese girl, the whites would stop eatin' there. And the American girls in my school look at my face and say I'm Chinese so they don't wanna be friends with me.'

He shrugged his shoulders. 'I very sorry, but you find friend in other place, not in General Mercantile Store.'

Biting her lip, Charity glanced beyond Chen Fai to the squiggly writing on the tins that lined the shelves on the wall behind him, and to the grille, and to the curtained doorway through which Mr Culpepper must walk when he went to play games in the rooms behind the store – the rooms where Su Lin and her ma and pa must now be sitting – and she looked back at Chen Fai.

'I look like Su Lin,' she said, her voice taking on a

stubborn note. 'I'm a good girl, too. I always do what Joe and Joe's ma and pa say.'

He gave a short dismissive laugh. 'You not taught to be Chinese like Su Lin. You not behave like modest Chinese girl. You not know how to cook Chinese way. You not understand important festivals and how to look after ancestors. Chinese family has much respect for honourable ancestors. Is very important daughter never bring shame on them.'

Charity screwed up her forehead. 'What're ancestors?'

He thought for a moment. 'The people we come from. All the people who come before us in our family: people living; people not living. I explain well, do I?'

She nodded. She stared at him, anxiety clouding her face. 'Ma died when I was a very little baby. Joe found me down by the river and he kept me. I don't have ancestors.'

'I know this,' he said. 'Mr Culpepper tell me when I ask. Years ago I see Su Lin want to be friends with you, and I ask Mr Culpepper to tell me about you. Is not good to be without ancestors, not for Chinese girl. You go now.'

Her face fell.

He paused a moment, then added more gently, 'Is not what face looks like – is what is inside head.' He touched his forehead with her letter for Joe, and then he slid his hands again into his sleeves. 'The way you talk to me now, to older man worthy of respect, show you very American in head. I think also you have mother who not have reputation. If you friends with Su Lin, is very bad for Su Lin, so I not let this happen. You leave now. You only come to store if you have letter to send. If letter come for you again, I bring it to you at bakery.'

His face impassive, he raised his eyes and stared above her head towards the doorway. She saw dismissal in the angle of his chin. A sob rose in her throat, and she turned and ran from the store.

Why did she suddenly feel like crying, she asked herself as she hurried along the boardwalk, struggling to hold back her tears. After all, it wasn't as if she wanted to be friends with Su Lin; she didn't. So it didn't matter that her brother had forbidden it. She slipped her hand into her pocket and tightened her fingers around the little golden tiger. Her ma wouldn't have cried for no reason, and she was going to be strong like her ma.

Nearing the line of miners' houses, her steps slowed.

What would Su Lin be doing now, she wondered. Would Chen Fai be scolding her for smiling at that American girl? And if he was, would Su Lin be arguing that she should be allowed to have a friend, and that Charity was the only possible friend she could have, even if she was American in her head?

No, she wouldn't, Charity thought in a rush. Su Lin was a good Chinese girl like Chen Fai said. She wouldn't argue with her brother; she'd obey him. She wouldn't try to be her friend again.

She swallowed hard.

What would have happened if it had been someone like Chen Fai panning for gold that day and not Joe, she suddenly thought. She knew that Chinamen looked for gold, too; Joe's pa had told her that. He'd said they'd seen several Chinese prospectors in the time between leaving the ranch and ending up in Carter. Would she now have ancestors if a Chinese man had found her? Or would he have left her in the open to die, thinking bad things about her ma?

As she approached the Walker house, she saw a row of pails lined up outside the front door, and she speeded up her steps. She'd forgotten that she'd told Joe's ma she'd take the letter to the store, then come straight back and go to the well for the water, and because of talking to Su Lin's brother, she'd been longer than she'd expected.

She ran up to the first two pails, picked them up and hurried to the well that lay further down the line of houses. She'd have to be quick as she had the Saturday baking to do after she'd filled the pails, and then she'd been asked to dig up some vegetables from the small patch at the back of the house and clean them.

She had a heap of chores to do that day, but she was glad she did.

All of a sudden, as she'd left the general mercantile, she'd felt lonely. Really, really lonely. She'd never felt like that before.

She reached the well, raised the heavy arm of the pump, and brought it down hard. Was Joe feeling lonely, too, she wondered.

Chapter Thirteen

The rays of the late afternoon sun were lengthening across the town, painting the weathered grey houses with a sheen of gold that started to fade almost as soon as the last brush stroke had been drawn. As the sun dropped lower, shadows slid from behind the wooden tables and benches in Ah Lee's bakery, and from beneath the large china bowls and baking trays that stood on ledges around the walls of the room. Slowly the shadows met and merged into a veil of dark grey that settled over the back room.

Charity untied her apron, pulled it off, went across to the wall hooks and hung it up. Calling goodbye to Ah Lee, she went out through the front of the shop and on to Main Street. Pausing on the boardwalk, she waited while a Chinese vegetable seller passed by in front of her and slowly made his way down the street, a basket of vegetables balanced on each end of the bamboo pole he carried across his shoulders, then she ran to the other side of the road, hurried past the mercantile store, turned into Second Street and started walking down the centre of the track.

'Charity Walker.' A loud whisper came from somewhere on her left.

She stopped in surprise and looked round. That had been Su Lin's voice without a doubt.

And then she saw her. Half-hidden by shadow, Su Lin was pressing close against the side of one of the houses opening out on to Second Street. She was holding a bucket in her hand and looking anxiously towards her.

Charity took an involuntary step in Su Lin's direction.

Su Lin moved at the same time. She inched forward,

peered round the corner of the house, looking back towards Main Street, and then ran across the road to Charity.

They stood for a moment, wordlessly facing each other, Charity staring at Su Lin in amazement, Su Lin looking back at her, a tenuous smile on her lips.

Su Lin's pail was empty, Charity noticed, glancing down. She looked back at Su Lin's face, at the hope in her eyes, then she impulsively beckoned Su Lin to follow her, and she spun round and started running past the miners' shacks and out across the open ground to the gully.

The clunking of the pail behind her told her that Su Lin was keeping up.

Reaching the top of the gully, they scrambled down the short slope to the water's edge, their feet sliding on the loose gravel. When they were almost at the bottom, Charity sat down and hugged her knees to her chin. She glanced up at Su Lin who was standing hovering next to her, and tapped the piece of ground beside her.

Su Lin dropped the pail to the ground and sat down next to Charity. She looked at the way Charity was sitting, and pulled her knees up in imitation.

'We're okay here. No one will see us,' Charity said. 'Especially your brother. He'd be real angry if he knew you'd spoken to me. He said we mustn't be friends.' She gave a sideways glance at Su Lin. 'I thought you were a good Chinese girl. Your brother told me you were.'

Su Lin put her hand in front of her mouth and giggled. 'I good Chinese girl. And I want to be friend of you.'

Charity frowned. 'How can you be a good Chinese girl if you're not doin' what Chen Fai said? He said good Chinese girls obey their brothers.'

'Big brother very good brother. He want only what is

best for humble self. But humble self think it is best to have friend. I not have friend.'

She looked hopefully at Charity.

'I haven't got a friend, either; not now Joe's gone,' Charity said, her face serious. 'Your brother said I'm not a good Chinese girl 'cos I've got no ancestors. He doesn't like me and he said we can't be friends.'

With a sigh of hopelessness, Charity stared at the river, her eyes reflecting the golden glints on the surface of the water that was slowly deepening a dark blue-brown beneath a sky burnished gold by the light of the dying sun.

'I likee you, and I likee you be friend,' Su Lin said firmly, and she smiled tentatively at Charity.

The warmth of Su Lin's friendship crept around Charity, and a glow of happiness swept through her.

Loneliness, her daily companion since Joe had left, walked away.

Her face broke out into a wide smile. 'And I likee—' She stopped abruptly and burst out laughing.

Su Lin wrinkled her forehead and looked at her questioningly.

'I was gonna say, "and I likee you",' Charity went on. She gave a peal of laughter and covered her mouth with her hand. 'But that's Chinese American. You gotta say, "And I *like* you". It's *like*, not likee. Okay?'

'I like you to be my friend,' Su Lin said, and she giggled.

Charity nodded in satisfaction. 'Now you sound like an American girl.' Both girls laughed, and turned again to look at the water.

'I was found near here,' Charity said suddenly. She pointed to her left, in the direction of the place where the plank bridge spanned the river. 'You can't see it from down here, but it was over there.'

Su Lin followed Charity's gaze. 'Big brother tell me Joe Walker find you. That mean what?'

'That's what it means – he found me,' Charity told her. 'I was lyin' on the ground next to the water, and Joe found me and took me home. He'd seen my ma fall off the bridge. I was a real little baby, one or two days old. My ma was next to me, but she was dead.'

'I very sad for you,' Su Lin said, her face grave.

'Me, too. When I was growin' up, Joe used to take me to the place where he found me, and then we'd go to where my ma's buried. Joe's pa and Sam buried her just outside the cemetery. It's where the Chinese cemetery is now. Sam's Joe's older brother, but he's not very nice. And the Chinese cemetery's not very nice. Whenever we go there, Joe clears the weeds and pieces of rock from the patch of ground in front of the bit of wood that says Charity's ma. We don't know her name, see.'

Su Lin's face clouded. 'Bones of Chinamen must go to family in China after five years. This always happen. Friends of dead person dig up bones, scrape bones clean, put bones inside can, and send can to China. *Tong* people sometimes do this.'

Charity thought for a moment, and then shrugged her shoulders. 'We don't know where my ma's family is, so there's nowhere to send her bones.' She cleared some of the gravel from the ground next to her and drew a face in the sand. 'I've been wonderin' recently what my ma was like. I think she'd've been a very nice ma.'

Su Lin nodded. 'I also think she a very nice ma. You a very nice girl.'

Charity smiled broadly at her. 'One day, we'll go to the bridge together and I'll show you where I was found, and then I'll take you to Ma's grave.'

'I likee ... I like that.'

'Not tonight, though, it's too late, and I must go home now. I always help with the cookin' when I get back from the bakery.' She paused, frowning. 'Say, how come you were able to leave the store like this?'

'Big brother go to barber. He have front of head shaved and queue braided. Then he meet friends in *tong*.'

'You mentioned the *tong* before. I know where the *tong* building is, but not what it is.'

'*Tong* mean meeting hall. Is club for Chinamen. *Dai lou* – big brother – is not back to store till later. *Baba* work in store, but not many customers so *Baba* say I not need be in shop. *Mama* is in kitchen and she not need me help. I know you leave bakery soon so I tell *Mama* I go to well. I go out back door and wait see you come in Second Street. When I see you, I call you.'

Charity nodded. 'I'm real pleased you did. To tell you the truth, I've been feelin' a mite bit lonely since Joe left. I'm glad I've got a friend now. And you're gonna be lonely, too, aren't you?' Charity went on, her face becoming sympathetic. 'Your ma and pa are goin' back to China, aren't they?'

'They go in one week.'

'Why are they goin'?'

'To see first wife of *Baba*. She is mother of Big Brother, and *Baba* always send money to family in China and to village. Parents of *Baba* grow old. First wife look after old parents of *Baba*, but first wife now is ill. *Baba* take many gifts for family and they visit graves of ancestors.'

'I see.'

'*Baba* also go China for wife for Big Brother,' Su Lin went on. 'Is no China woman with reputation in Carter.'

Charity straightened up and stared at Su Lin in surprise.

'Chen Fai's gonna get wed?' she exclaimed. 'Does that mean he'll go back to China? If he does, it'll be easier for us to meet.'

Su Lin shook her head. 'He not marry yet. First wife of *Baba* and go-between arrange marriage. They already find girl for him. She live near village of *Baba*. She poor, but family have good reputation, and she work hard. Is important Chinese woman work hard.'

'But what if Chen Fai doesn't like her?'

'Reputation of family and hard work is more important. Is also important that year, month, day and hour of birth of girl and *dai lou* match. This is very important. Go-between already do all this. When *Baba* go back, he agree bride-price.'

'So, will Chen Fai go back and marry her?'

Su Lin nodded. 'Then he bring her here. Chinese wife always live with family of husband. But wedding not happen yet. Girl is very young. Girl is age of you and me.'

'But Chen Fai's about the same age as Joe!'

'Is good if man is older than wife. But wedding not happen while girl is very young. When *Baba* agree bride-price, girl move to house of first wife. She work for first wife until old enough to marry. When is old enough, *dai lou* go to China, marry girl and bring her here to America.'

Charity frowned in amazement. 'That's different from what happens here. I'm glad I'm American.' She thought about it for a moment. 'When she's livin' here with you, I won't be your only friend.'

'But I not live with *Baba* and *Mama* when I marry – I must live with family of husband. So I not live long with wife of *dai lou*.'

Charity thought for a moment. 'But right now, when your folks leave, you'll be lonely, won't you?'

'I not be very lonely. I got a friend now.' She smiled happily at Charity. 'And *dai lou* is good big brother. He look after me. He look after store when *Mama* and *Baba* go to China so I not work in store: I look after house and cook food.'

'Is *dai lou* another name for Chen Fai?'

Su Lin shook her head and giggled. '*Dai lou* is Chinese word for big brother. Does not show respect if little sister call older brother or sister by name. *Baba* say families in China often call children First Sister, Second Sister, Third Sister. Also Big Sister and Big Brother. It show importance in family.'

'Whatever you say about him, your *dai lou* scares me,' Charity said. 'He's always angry. I don't like him.'

'He good big brother,' Su Lin repeated.

'How long will your ma and pa be away?'

Su Lin shrugged. 'They not know. Maybe some months. Is long journey to China.' She paused. 'When *Mama* and *Baba* away, *dai lou* not able to watch me all day. If I not in house, he think I get water from well. We meet again soon?' She smiled happily at Charity.

'Of course; we're friends, aren't we? But it won't be easy. I'm only allowed to go into the store when I've got a letter to send.'

'I watch for you leave bakery and come out like today. I bring pail with me.'

'That'll be good,' Charity said. 'Come on; let's go!'

They scrambled to their feet, climbed up the slope and stood at the top, facing each other.

'I'm glad we're friends now, Su Lin,' Charity said with a shy smile.

'I very pleased, too, Charity.'

'Don't forget to go to the well,' Charity said, indicating

the pail which Su Lin was gripping with both hands, 'or your folks will wonder what you've been doin'.'

'I get water on way back to store. Chinese well is behind herb store.'

Motionless, they stood smiling at each other.

'Well, I guess I'd better go now,' Charity said at last, reluctance in her voice. 'That's my house over there.' She pointed to the line of miners' houses in the distance, then looked back at Su Lin. 'Bye, then,' she said.

As she turned and ran across the plain to her house, inside she was singing.

Chapter Fourteen

One month later
Late June, 1878

Joe jumped out of the saddle, stretched himself, and then headed for the chuck wagon. He collected two coffees and a couple of doughnuts, took them over to Ethan Grey, gave him one of the mugs and a doughnut, and sat down next to him.

Ethan glanced at him. 'You've done well for a new boy, Joe. I've bin watchin' you the last few days. You've picked up real quick the way of trailin' the cattle so they don't know you're herdin' them and makin' them go in the direction they're meant to be headin'. It takes some new trail hands a lot longer to get the touch.'

'I appreciate you sayin' that, Ethan.'

'I'm only speakin' as I find it. Monty will've seen it, too. And like me, he'll have seen you swimmin' that horse of yours.' He paused a moment. 'No offence meant, but you don't wanna get into the water too quickly. Some of the streams have hidden bogs and quicksands. If we're not careful, we could lose horses, cattle, and even men. You don't wanna be one of those who gets sucked under.'

Joe nodded. 'I'll remember, and go more cautiously.'

'That's good to hear.' He gave Joe a slow grin. 'I'm kinda gettin' used to havin' you as a trail partner, and I wouldn't wanna lose you on our first drive together.'

Joe laughed. 'I'll make sure you don't.'

Ethan bit into the doughnut. 'He makes a good mug of coffee, our cook, and these bear signs of his are the best I've ever had on a drive.'

'Bear signs?'

'That's doughnuts to you greenhorns,' Ethan said with a smile. 'But to get back to work. We'll soon reach the North Platte, and we're gonna be the lead horses over the river. Like I said, Monty must've seen your horse swimmin'. When we've finished our coffee, we'll go ahead to the river and check that the cattle and wagon will be able to get across. If they won't, the boss will have to find a better place to ford it.'

Joe nodded. 'Makes sense for us to lead. Our day mounts are the best swimmers.' He took a drink of his coffee, leaned back against the tree trunk, pulled his hat over his face and closed his eyes. 'I could've done with more than a couple hours' sleep last night.'

'Yup; third watch ain't the best. Just when you've fallen asleep, it's one o'clock and time to go on your watch, and by the time it's three-thirty, it's too close to mornin' to get back to sleep. You're lucky to have gotten as much as two hours.' He glanced at Joe and gave him a sideways smile. 'When you bin doin' this a mite bit longer, you'll find you can sleep on your watch. Your night horse will know the distance to keep from the cattle, and it'll just keep goin' round and round while you sleep pretty in the saddle.'

Joe opened his eyes, raised the brim of his hat and grinned at him. 'Not if you're my watch partner, I won't. Your singin's enough to set the cattle stampedin'. We're meant to be makin' a noise that tells the cows a friend is watchin' over them. But if I was cattle hearin' you in full voice, I'd think the sound was comin' from the devil himself. If you wanna be kind to the cows, whistle rather than sing. That way they and their stomachs will stay content.' He then threw back his head and laughed.

Ethan chuckled. 'You just keep laughin',' he said cheerfully.

'Make the most of it – you might not feel much like laughin'
by the time we get to the other side of the river. There's bin
an east wind in the night so the water could be high, and it's
gonna be bitter cold as the snows haven't long melted.' He
finished his coffee, stood up and looked around. 'I reckon the
herd's about to get movin'. We'll set off now.'

Joe got up, took Ethan's mug from him, returned the
mugs to the chuck wagon and hurried across to the horses,
where Ethan was waiting.

'Hold the reins hard when we get close to the water,'
Ethan said, putting his foot into the stirrup and pulling
himself up into the saddle. 'The horses will smell water and
you don't want them runnin' away with you. And try and
keep your saddle blanket dry. Like the boss said – if you
look after your horse and equipment, they'll serve you well.'

'I'll remember,' Joe said.

Sitting low in the saddle, Ethan set off at a fast trot, and
then broke into a canter.

Joe swung himself into the saddle and headed after Ethan
at speed, and side by side they galloped towards the river.

The flanks of their horses were steaming and their coats
glossy and slick with sweat by the time they reached the
damp earth bordering the river. Pulling up their mounts,
they sat and stared at the water, a wide band of gold in the
late morning sun.

Joe smiled to himself.

'What's so funny?' Ethan asked, glancing at him.

'Nothing. I was just thinkin'. Well, rememberin', more like.'

'Rememberin' what?'

'When I was pannin' for gold 'bout ten years ago, I heard
someone call out and then fall off the bridge soon after. It
turned out to be a China woman, who'd had a baby not
long before. She was dead when I got to her so I took the

baby home, and Ma and Pa kept her. I don't know why I just thought of the girl, with this river being much bigger and faster, but I did. Maybe it was the golden colour of the water; I don't know.'

'Not many whites would keep a China woman in their house. Leastways not these days, they wouldn't.'

Joe shrugged. 'I don't know you well yet, but from what I've seen of you, I'm guessin' you might've done the same if the choice had been that or seein' her put out to die.'

'Maybe.'

'Anyway, Charity's real useful now – that's her name. She more than earns her keep. Yup, you'd've done the same, Ethan.'

'I guess we'll never know. Right, let's get across. I reckon we'll be able to ford it here.'

Joe nodded. Slipping their feet from the stirrups, they jumped down into the soft mud at the water's edge, discarded their saddles and boots, mounted their horses again and rode into the river, Joe leading the way.

'Holy snakes, you're right – it *is* cold!' he shouted as the horse went deeper into the water. 'It's fair freezin'.'

'Release the reins,' Ethan yelled to him. 'A swimmin' horse likes to be at liberty. There's no need to touch the reins.'

Glancing across at Ethan, Joe saw that he'd buried one hand in the horse's mane and was gently slapping its neck with the other, and he did the same.

Their horses swimming strongly, they reached the opposite shore without mishap, jumped to the ground and let the animals roll on their backs in the sand and the grass.

Joe stripped off his shirt, stretched out his arms and stared up at the sun as droplets of water trickled in rivulets down his bare chest. 'That's better,' he said in satisfaction. 'The sun's warmin' me up real nice.'

'I wouldn't bother,' Ethan said dryly. 'The herd's in sight; we're gonna have to get back across the river sharpish. And then we'll be goin' from one side to the other till all the cows are across. Let's go.'

They mounted their horses again and reached the opposite bank just as the front of the herd was arriving.

Following Ethan's lead, Joe positioned himself facing the water. His horse snorting and pawing impatiently at the soft earth, he sat on its back and waited as the first three hundred cattle were cut from the herd and driven to the water's edge.

'Off we go now, Joe,' Ethan called. 'They'll take the lead from us. The dumb brutes aren't exactly social, but they'll follow a leader.'

Joe nodded, signalled the horse with his heels and moved into the water. Then he leaned forward, put his hands on the horse's mane and neck, and let the horse swim at its pace.

Lowing loudly, the cattle followed both him and Ethan, urged into the water by the drovers, who rode behind the cattle as far as midstream. By then the cows were swimming, and the drovers could return to the shore for the next three hundred.

Two hours later, with all of the cows having crossed in batches of three or four hundred, Joe again stood bare-chested in the sun, drying out as four of the cowboys counted the cattle.

By the time the counting had been done and a number agreed by all, it was too late in the day to drive any further, and the trail boss ordered the herd to be left to graze in a large circle, with half of the outfit watching them at a time. Then he rode off to scout for a patch of ground sufficiently elevated to pick up any breeze, and with the dry grass on which cows liked to bed for the night.

Since it wasn't their turn to go on first watch, Joe threw one of his pair of blankets to the ground and sat down on it. 'I'm gonna write to that Chinese girl I was telling you about,' he told Ethan. 'Ma will be wantin' to hear what I'm doin'.'

Dear Charity,

I'm writing now even though my first letter may not have reached you yet, and I don't know for sure if you'll write back. But seeing the North Platte River this morning made me think back to the day I found you, and I had a powerful urge to write again.

I'm still more sore than I thought a man could be. Maybe not as sore as in the first few days, but it's bad enough. And my hands hurt from holding the reins all day, and the insides of my legs are raw where the saddle flaps keep rubbing against them. Come sundown, I'm numb after sitting on a hard leather saddle for hour after hour without a break. You'd laugh if you saw the way I walk when I get off my horse – it's like I'm made of wood. But, like I say, it's not as bad as it was so I guess my skin's gotten tougher.

In the short time I've been on the trail, I've seen places so different from Carter you wouldn't believe. I'm not one for words, so I can't describe real well what it's like to open your eyes in the morning and see the sun come up. And there's grass all around you, sweet green grass – at least there is in the part we're in now.

And it's not just the grass that's beautiful to see. When I look back as I ride along, and see the cattle all strung out, with the sun flashing on their horns, that's a sight to be seen, too.

Being out here on the range is reminding me of being on

the ranch all those years ago, and how much I loved the life. Tell Ma I've been thinking about those days, will you?

I'm satisfied with the spare horses I picked from the remuda, and especially with the horse Mr Culpepper gave me. He's good in the water. The horse of my trail partner, Ethan Grey, is also a strong swimmer and we were chosen to lead the cattle across the river today. The water was so cold it pained me when it hit my skin and I yelled like a baby. Tell that to Ma, will you? She'll laugh.

Ethan is a few years older than I am and he's been droving for several years. In some ways he reminds me of Mr Culpepper even though he's younger. Just like Mr Culpepper taught me about horses and livery, Ethan's teaching me about driving cattle. I struck lucky getting him as a partner on my first drive.

When we get to Casper, which'll be soon, we'll be camping outside the town for the night. We had a month's supplies when we left Cheyenne, but we've used some and we'll re-stock at Casper. I'll send this letter to you from there. After Casper, our next stop will be Buffalo. Maybe I'll find a letter from you there. I'd like that. I'm missing home more than I thought I would – or rather, I'm missing the people. But I don't regret coming on this drive; not for one minute.

If you don't want to write, Charity, that's fine – I know you're busy. But if you're able to write, the place to write to after Buffalo is Columbus. That's in Montana Territory, not Wyoming. It'll be the first time ever I've left Wyoming, and that's exciting.

> *Your friend,*
> *Joe*

Chapter Fifteen

Dear Joe,

We were all wondering what you were doing, so we were
real happy when we got your letters from Cheyenne and
Casper. Your ma said to thank you for writing. She was
crying when I read them to her. She said she wasn't, but
she was. I also read your letters to your pa and Sam. Sam
acts like he doesn't want to know what you're doing, but I
can tell he does.

I laughed when I read how funnily you walked when
you got off the horse, and so did your ma and pa.
Mr Culpepper laughed, too. He said he's missing you
something bad. He told me the man he hired in your place
is no good at all, and he's now doing the work of two men.
The man doesn't know it, but Mr Culpepper is looking for
someone else.

You'll be in Buffalo now so you'll have read my first
letter. This is my second, and I think you'll be very happy
when you read my news. I can't wait a minute longer to
tell you what it is.

I think you might already have guessed.

You know I told you I met Su Lin when I went to collect
the first letter you sent me? Well, I saw her again when I
went to send the letter to Buffalo. And I saw her brother,
too. Su Lin was friendly, but her brother was mean. He
made Su Lin go into the back of the store and then told
me to keep away unless I had a letter to send. That's mean,
isn't it? He knows she wants to be friends with me. She
said he's a good brother, but I don't think he is.

But that's not what will make you happy to hear (I'm

starting to laugh with happiness as I write this). I've got more to tell you.

Joe let the hand holding the letter fall to his side. Leaning back against the wheel of the wagon, he gazed up at the clear blue sky. Charity's words could mean only one thing. 'Good on you, gal,' he murmured into the air, and he smiled to himself in satisfaction.

Turning back to her letter, he read the details of their meeting, paused a moment, and then read on.

Su Lin speaks in a strange way, and so does Chen Fai. They can't say any word with an r in properly. Instead of an r, they say an ell. I can say words like friend and very, so I'm not a Chinese girl, but they can't. But even though Su Lin sounds funny when she speaks, I like her.

Now that her folks are in China, it's easier to meet, and I've seen her several times. But we have to be careful as your ma's starting to look at me in a funny way. I reckon she's beginning to wonder why I'm later coming back from the bakery these days. I'm going to have to think of a reason why that would be. Su Lin has her empty bucket, but there's no point in me having a bucket, too, as our well is too close to the house.

I don't think your ma would go loco if she knew about Su Lin, but your pa and Sam might. They're always saying real nasty things about Chinamen.

It's almost a week later now. The big news is that your ma now knows Su Lin and I are friends. Mrs Oakland saw us going down to the gully one day when she was coming back from town, and she told your ma. She's a real nosy neighbour, and so's Mr Oakland. I used to think they were nice, but I don't now. Your ma doesn't either as, unless they want to stir up trouble and tell tales, they ignore her whenever they see her.

When I got home, your ma told me she knew about me and Su Lin. I was shaking all over about what your pa and Sam would say, but she said she wasn't going to tell them as they'd got enough worries at work without having more. She told me it was okay for us to be friends as long as I did my chores and we carried on hiding like we've been doing. She thinks it's better people don't know about us as it might make them think even worse of me than they do now. But that doesn't make sense. The whites think I'm Chinese so it's just like me being friendly with another Chinese girl, isn't it?

I asked her why everyone's so angry with the Chinese. She said it's still about the low price the company pays for coal. When I saw Mr Culpepper, I asked him why Chinamen didn't want more money like the whites did, and he said it was because whatever the company paid, it was much more than they'd get in China.

And he told me that another thing was also making the white miners angry. The whites think the Chinese miners are being given better rooms in the mines. I think he means the rooms where the miners dig out the coal. If the Chinese are given the easiest rooms, they can dig out more coal and so make more money. That can't be right, can it? The superintendent is white, and whites don't like the Chinese, so why would he help them?

I don't understand it real well, Joe. I wish you were here to explain it all.

But I understand the Chinese not liking me – they think I'm American, and they know I don't have ancestors. They can see I'm not a good Chinese girl like Su Lin. Except

*she's a bad Chinese girl as she doesn't obey her brother,
and is friends with me.*

*Did you know that Chen is their last name? The Chinese
put their last name first and their first name last. That's
why it's Chen Sing and Chen Fai. That's funny, isn't it? I
found that out when I asked Su Lin why she didn't just call
her brother Chen. She laughed real loud and told me why.
So I asked why she didn't call him Fai. She said it's not
polite to use his name as he's older than she is. It's better
to call him by his position in the family. I don't know what
you'd call me if we did that in America, Walker Joe. (I'm
giggling now.)*

*You were right, Joe. I like having a friend. Especially
now you've gone away. I'm glad you made me go into Su
Lin's store.*

*I hope you can read my letters easily. Miss O'Brien is
still a mean woman, but she saw I was trying extra hard
with my writing, and when the other kids were outside, she
helped me.*

I'm sending this to Columbus, Montana, like you said.
> *From your friend,*
> *Charity*

'I wrote to Joe and told him we were friends,' Charity told
Su Lin a few days later when they were sitting in the gully.

'I not tell *dai lou*,' Su Lin said. 'He be very angry I not
obey him.'

'I'm glad you're not obeyin' him,' Charity said happily.
'I'm not lonely any more. Oh!' she suddenly exclaimed, and
she thrust her hand into the pocket of her pinafore. 'I've got
somethin' to show you. I bring it every time we meet, and
then forget to show you. I almost forgot again.'

She pulled out her hand and opened her palm. On it lay

the small golden tiger, with black stripes painted across the gold.

Su Lin leaned across and took it from her. 'It a tiger,' she said, smiling as she turned it over and studied it. 'I see tigers in pictures.'

'I know that – Joe told me. It was my ma's. It was on the shawl wrapped round me when I was found. It's the only thing I've got of her. There are no tigers in Wyoming, so she must've brought it with her when she came from China. It means she liked tigers, don't you think?'

'I not think so,' Su Lin said slowly. 'We born in same year, you and me.'

'So what?' Charity asked, a trace of impatience in her voice. 'We already figured that out.'

'So like me, you are born in Year of the Dragon. This is tiger not dragon, so this is for Chinese ma, not you.'

'What're you talkin' about?'

'Every year is year of an animal. You and me are Dragons. Dragons very impatient people. Rush into things where should wait, and get into trouble. That's you and me.' Su Lin giggled. 'Dragons never give up – if want something, go after it till get it. That's also you and me.'

'You're right about that bein' us,' Charity said. 'You wanted us to be friends, and then so did I, and now we are. So why's it a tiger brooch, not a dragon brooch?'

'Think your Chinese ma born in Year of the Tiger.'

'What are people born in the Year of the Tiger like?'

'They stubborn people.'

Charity nodded vigorously. 'That'll be Ma all right. What about Joe? He's seven years older than me.'

Su Lin shrugged her shoulders. 'Depend on date is born. Maybe Year of the Rooster. Rooster is very good match for Dragon,' she added solemnly.

'And Chen Fai?'

Su Lin giggled. 'He is born in Year of the Horse. Girl he marry is born in Year of the Rabbit. Rabbit is good match with Horse. And Dragon is good match with Horse, too.'

'How d'you know all this?' Charity asked, staring at Su Lin in amazement.

'When go-between find wife or husband for son or daughter, must look first at year of birth to see if is good match. Is very important.'

'So in China, your go-between looked for a Rabbit for Chen Fai. That's very funny.' Charity burst out laughing.

'Sheep is better, but go-between not find Sheep. But Rabbit is good,' Su Lin said lightly. 'Is Chinese way. You and me, Charity, we must not marry man who is Ox or Dog,' she added, her voice suddenly serious.

'I'll marry who I want. I'm not gonna ask every man I meet if he's a Dog or an Ox.' She burst out laughing again.

Su Lin stared at her for a moment, then laughed with her. But her laughter died away almost at once, and she looked at Charity, her expression grave. 'But you must do this, Charity. One day you marry Chinese boy.'

Charity glanced at her. 'No, I won't. I'm American, aren't I? It's real interestin', all this, but it's nothin' to do with me.'

Smiling, she tilted her face to the sun.

Su Lin stared at her, anxiety on her face. Then she, too, looked up at the sun, but her face was still worried.

Chapter Sixteen

Two months later
Mid-September, 1878

'I thought I'd never get away,' Charity said, panting heavily as she half-slid down the slope to the water. She threw herself on to the ground next to Su Lin and pulled her jacket tightly around her. 'I had to help Joe's ma dig up the last of the turnips and carrots. The ground was real hard and it took us ages.'

Su Lin turned to her, concern on her face. 'I also very worried I not able to come.'

'Why, what's the matter?' Charity asked in sudden alarm. 'You're lookin' panicky.'

'I very worried,' Su Lin repeated, her voice shaking. 'Yesterday, I forget to fill pail with water when I go home. Where is water for washing dishes, *dai lou* ask me last night. He hold up empty pail and he turn it like this.' She turned her bucket upside down. 'No water is in there, he say. And then he tell me he see me go from store with bucket so there should be water inside bucket.'

Charity's hand flew to her mouth in alarm. 'What did you tell him?'

'I say many people wait at well, so I come back, and I forget to go out again later.'

'Did he believe you?'

Su Lin nodded. 'I think so. But I must be careful in next few days. We okay now as *dai lou* is in store with customers, but I think he watch me in next days when I go to well. Maybe is better not meet for little time. It make me very sad to say this, but is better not meet for five days than not meet again forever.'

'You're right.' Charity paused. 'Maybe we should think of somethin' else to explain you bein' out, but I don't know what.'

They fell silent, and stared at the water flowing a little way down from them.

'I do hope we think of somethin' soon,' Charity said with a loud sigh. 'Now I'm back at school, I need to see a friendly face after being treated so horribly all day.'

'Is Miss O'Brien still mean woman to you?'

'Yes, but maybe not always. A couple of times when I was on my own in the schoolroom, tryin' to work out a sum, she came and helped me, but she's nasty when the other kids are around. I asked Joe's ma if she could be scared of them tellin' their folks if she was nice to me, and she said that maybe she was as she could lose her job.' Charity shrugged her shoulders. 'But they're silly girls and boys and I don't wanna think about them. Let's think of another excuse to get you out of the store.'

They thought hard for a few minutes.

'I'll keep thinking,' Su Lin said at last. 'But next few days are very busy for Chinese family so I not able to think until after busy days.'

'How come you're so busy?'

Su Lin beamed at her. 'Is Autumn Moon Festival. Is very nice festival. Festival is in middle of month when moon is full. Family is together and all eat mooncakes.'

'Mooncakes! What are they? I've never had one.'

'Small round cakes. Round shape mean family is complete and together.' Su Lin smiled happily.

'But your family's not complete, is it? Your folks are in China so there's only you and your brother.'

'It not matter. Celebrate festival in China, too. *Baba* and *Mama* think of us when eat mooncakes, so we are together inside head.' She tapped her head. 'We say thank you for harvest and we stare up at moon and make a wish. But we not tell anyone our wish. Is very nice festival.'

'If you say so.'

'It is. Every year when I am little, *Baba* tell me story of festival. It start many years ago when China businessman offer small round cakes at time of full moon to emperor who has great victory. Emperor point the cakes to the moon, smile and say, I like to invite the toad to enjoy the *hú* cake.'

Charity opened her mouth to speak.

'You want to ask why he invite toad to eat cake, and not other animal,' Su Lin cut in quickly. 'I ask *Baba* and *dai lou* that. They not know, but is still very nice story. But I not yet finish story. Emperor share cakes with ministers, and after that, people everywhere in China eat *hú* cakes, and they start calling them mooncakes. That is story. There is good story for every Chinese festival.'

Charity grinned at her. 'What're you gonna wish for?'

'I not tell you or it not come true,' Su Lin said gravely.

'You could wish for a good reason to come out of the store to meet me,' Charity suggested, and they both laughed.

'If you are with us at family festival dinner, Charity, what is one thing you wish for?'

Charity thought for a moment. 'I'd pretend I didn't know how to count and I'd wish for two things. I'd wish for Joe to come home soon. He's been gone for almost four months now, and I still miss him bein' around. And I'd wish for Miss O'Brien to be a kind teacher all of the time.'

'You shouldn't have told me your wishes,' Su Lin said, wagging her finger at her. 'Must be secret wishes.'

'I didn't wish them, though, did I? I only said I *would* wish for them. There's a difference. So you can tell me what you *might* wish for, Su Lin. It can still come true because you've not wished it for real.'

Su Lin stretched out her legs and studied her slippered feet.

'I'm listenin',' Charity prompted.

Su Lin took a deep breath. 'Now *Baba* and *Mama* have found wife for *dai lou*, when they back in Carter they may look for husband for me. Not to marry now – I too young – but for when am older. In China, girl is often betrothed very young. If I make wish – but I not make wish now,' she added quickly, 'I make wish they not look for husband yet.'

Charity reached across and squeezed Su Lin's hand. 'If I was with you at the festival meal, I might make three wishes, not two,' Charity said. She stared up at the wide blue sky above them. 'Did you hear me, spirits above? I *might* make three wishes, I said.' She looked back at Su Lin. 'For my third wish, I *might* wish they don't look for a husband for you yet too.'

Su Lin nodded. 'They very good wishes.'

'I'm so glad I'm American,' Charity said with an exaggerated sigh of relief. 'I'm only ten and I don't want to think about husbands till I'm all grown up. American girls don't have to.' She paused. 'Does Chen Fai mind—'

'Does Chen Fai mind what?' Chen Fai's voice came from the top of the gully.

They gasped aloud. Glancing at each other in panic, they scrambled to their feet and gazed up the slope in horror.

Legs astride, his arms folded, Chen Fai stood on the ridge, staring down at them, his face cold, unsmiling.

'Come up here,' he called, his voice like shards of ice. 'Now.'

Their hearts racing with alarm, they clambered up the gully wall, gravel sliding beneath their feet and rattling noisily down to the water's edge. When they reached the top of the slope, they stood side by side and faced Chen Fai, each of them white with fear.

His face expressionless, he looked first at Su Lin, and then at Charity. His gaze returned to Su Lin.

Charity threw Su Lin a quick glance. She'd slid her hands into opposite sleeves and was standing before her brother, her head bowed in subjection. Biting her lip, Charity looked back at Chen Fai. 'It was my fault,' she said. 'I made her be friends with me.'

He glanced at her. 'It is fault of Su Lin alone that she disobey brother.' He paused. 'And not once only. She disobey brother for many months. I know this.'

Charity caught her breath. She turned to Su Lin, who'd looked up sharply and was staring at her brother in surprise. Su Lin threw her a quick glance. Their eyes met briefly, then both turned back to Chen Fai, their mouths falling open, and bewilderment spreading across their faces.

Su Lin said something to Chen Fai in rapid Chinese.

'We speak in American,' he told her. 'Charity Walker not understand our language.'

'If you know we've been meetin',' Charity exclaimed, 'how come you didn't say anythin'?'

His glance enveloped them both. 'I know for some time, Charity Walker. I wait and hope Little Sister tell me she is friend of Charity Walker, but she not say.'

Su Lin bowed her head again.

'I still don't see why you didn't tell us before now that you knew,' Charity replied, her brow creasing in puzzlement.

'In China, Chinese brother tell sister what to do. Sister must not question, but must obey. If sister not obey, brother lose face,' he said slowly, 'so it is very bad if sister disobey. But I live here a long time now and I know American way is different. I see happiness on face of American girls when they walk in town and talk with friends.' His gaze went to Su Lin's bowed head. Charity saw his eyes soften. 'For a long time, I not see happiness on Little Sister's face. I see only a sad girl wanting a friend – a girl wanting the only other Chinese girl in Carter to be her friend.'

'I'm American,' Charity cut in.

'When Little Sister is become friend with Charity,' he went on, ignoring Charity's interruption, his eyes still on Su Lin, 'I see happiness on her face, and I see happiness also on Charity Walker's face. I think I must be little bit American now, but I not want to see happiness go.'

Su Lin spoke in rapid Chinese and bowed three times to her brother. He turned to Charity.

'I watch you, Charity Walker, and I see you are good girl. You work hard, and you are polite to older people and full of respect.' He gave her a slight smile. 'This respect you show in American way, not Chinese way, but I see it. I think weather soon gets colder, and we have rain in Carter and then much snow. You not be able to sit with Su Lin by river, not till end of winter, which is many months from now. I come today to invite you to be our guest at Autumn Moon Festival.'

Su Lin exclaimed aloud.

A look of delight spread across Charity's face as she stared at Chen Fai. Then she and Su Lin turned to each other, their eyes shining. She looked back at Chen Fai in excitement, and opened her mouth to thank him.

He raised his hand to stop her from speaking. 'Before you say you come to our house or you not come, there is something I must say to you. It is very important.'

The seriousness in his voice was reflected in his face.

Charity frowned in sudden apprehension. She glanced quickly at Su Lin, but Su Lin was staring at her brother, uncertainty on her face. Charity looked back at Chen Fai.

'If you come to General Mercantile as our guest,' Chen Fai began, 'Chinese people will see you visit and white people will hear about this. You have Chinese blood, but you see yourself as American first, and then Chinese. And you hope American folk see this, too.'

He paused, and she nodded slowly.

'Going into home of Chinese people is different thing from working in Chinese bakery. If you go into Chinese home, it show closeness with Chinese family and Chinese way of life. If you show this, Americans and Chinese both see you as a Chinese girl with American ways. Chinese first, and then American.'

Charity bit her lip and stared at him. 'Does this matter?' she asked hesitantly.

Chen Fai nodded and gave her a rueful smile. 'It matter very much, Charity, as you not want this. I think you climb a tree to hunt a fish, but you wish folk to see you as American, not Chinese. So you must now make very big decision.'

'What decision?'

'American people are not allowed to marry Chinese people. It is the law. If you are seen as Chinese girl, you cannot marry American man. If you do this, American whites can kill you.'

Charity gasped. She put her hand to her mouth and stared in alarm at Chen Fai.

'So if you want American husband one day,' he went on, his tone gentle, 'you must keep far away from Chinese people, and hope white folk see your American ways and clothes, and think of you as American.'

'And if I come to your house ...?' Her voice trailed off.

He gave a slight shrug. 'You be seen as Chinese girl with American ways. You wed Chinese man; never American man. I sorry to say this, but is very important you choose now what you want to be: American or Chinese.'

Charity stared at him in dismay. 'I don't know what to do. Joe would know, but he's not here. I'll write and ask him.'

'I think it better then,' Chen Fai said quietly, 'that you not meet Su Lin till Joe tell you what to do. Is good to ask older man who is true friend to give advice, and is virtuous and modest to accept this advice. When Joe tells you what to do, you tell us. But until then, no Su Lin and no Autumn Moon Festival. This is very serious thing you must decide. You understand, Charity?'

She nodded slowly.

'Su Lin, you come now. We go home,' he said, and he turned and started to make his way back across the open ground towards the town, with Su Lin following in his wake. Every few paces, she slowed and looked back towards Charity, a wistful, lingering smile on her face. Then she'd speed up her steps to catch up with her brother.

Standing on the edge of the gully, Charity watched them go further and further away from her, taking with them their warmth and their friendship.

Chill air gathered around her, and she grew as cold inside as out.

'Wait!' she suddenly shouted.

They stopped walking and looked back at her.

She picked up her skirts and ran as fast as she could across the ground towards them, the heels of her boots kicking up dirt behind her.

'What time shall I come to your house?' she said when she reached them, panting heavily and covered in dust. 'You forgot to say.'

Chapter Seventeen

One month later
October, 1878

Still holding the letter he'd collected from the nearby town earlier that day, Joe stood up, walked across to the door of the bunkhouse on the Montana ranch where he was going to be working for the winter months, repairing and maintaining the ranch buildings and equipment, tugged open the wooden door and stepped out into the yard.

The raw night air filled his lungs and he inhaled deeply.

He paused for a moment, listening to the rustling of leaves, the creaking of boughs bending noisily beneath the wind, the plaintive yelps of hungry coyotes, and looking around him at the mountains that marked the boundary of the ranch. They stood like dark sentinels in the night, illuminated from moment to moment by the cold white touch of the restless moon, which then moved on, leaving them again in shadow, ever-watchful over the land that lay beneath their silent gaze.

A gust of pine-scented wind whistled past him and stung his ears. He pulled up his collar, thrust his hands deep into the pockets of his thick coat and strolled forward into the gathering darkness, gazing up from time to time at the endless night sky – a sky that had never ceased to fill him with awe from the very first moment he'd stood alone on the vast Wyoming prairie and felt the infinity above.

He hugged his jacket more tightly around him. The snow would come early this year, they'd been saying in town, and from the bite in the wind he was sure they were right. And he kind of hoped they were. Snow on a Montana ranch, with its sweep of fields and pastures flanked by forested slopes and mountain peaks, was going to be very different from the snow that collected at the sides of the streets in a mining town: snow that lay in heaps of yellowing slush that slowly turned black from the fragments of slate and coal-dust embedded within it.

Drifts of clean snow on a Montana ranch would be the perfect end to his first six months away from home. And what a time it had been! He had learnt so much, seen so much – it had worked out better than in his wildest dreams, and the future promised to be just as good.

Monty Taylor had turned out to be the ideal boss for a man to have on his first drive, and he'd leapt at the chance of joining Monty's outfit again the following spring. This time, they'd be starting out in Texas, and driving the cattle all the way across Indian Territory to Dodge City. Once again, it was going to be a long drive – so long that it wouldn't end till a little before fall – and it was going to be a much harder drive. But there were a lot of things about droving he didn't yet know, that he may well need to know in the future, and as Ethan Grey was going to be his trail partner again, he'd got a good chance of learning those things.

As soon as the snows had melted, he and Ethan would head for Texas to be in at the very start of the drive.

By the time he'd reached Cheyenne last May, most of the pre-drive work had been done. But not so with the next drive, and he was greatly looking forward to riding the range with the other drovers, helping them to round up the scattered cattle, select the best of the bunch, and rope, brand and castrate most of the male cattle. Then they'd have to dehorn them and check for any infections. All that was going to be new to him, but by the time he'd worked through every stage, he'd have a real good idea of how to do what had to be done if he ever decided to go into cattle ranching.

In the meantime, he was having a good winter in Montana, and that was thanks to Ethan.

Having done other fall round-ups ending in Montana, Ethan knew the ranch and had arranged to work there again. As soon as they'd reached Montana, and their herd, in good form being full of grass and water, had been inspected by the agents, found satisfactory, and the count agreed and delivery effected, Ethan had headed straight for the ranch, taking Joe with him.

Ethan had known that the owners would need to hire a couple of extra hands for the work to be done before spring, and he'd suggested Joe for the job. Rating Ethan highly, they'd taken Joe on.

Being on a ranch once more was another reminder to Joe of how much he'd liked the life on a ranch as a young boy, and he was becoming increasingly determined to have that life again one day. But the land he was going to walk tall on, and the air he would breathe, would be his; he wouldn't be working it for anyone but himself. Of that he was decided. He'd enjoy a few more years as a cowboy, learning as much as he could and earning money while he did so, but one day he'd strike out on his own.

For that to happen, though, he'd need a stake. And that was another reason to stay droving for a few more years.

He had a lot to thank Ethan for. Had he been forced to find work over the winter in one of the nearby cattle towns, like many of the other drovers, he would have had to spend some of the money he'd earned on food, clothing and livery, and he might also have spent some of it on gambling and women.

But out in the mountains as he was, unable to get into town once the snows had come, he'd have something left over at the end of winter from what he'd earned on the drive, and that was despite having sent money back home whenever he'd gotten his wages, and he'd also still have a large part of what he'd have earned on the ranch. Some of that he'd send back to his ma before they headed for Texas, but the rest he'd keep for the ranch he was going to own one day.

But all that belonged to the future, he thought, his fingers tightening around the letter in his pocket. What was happening in Carter in the present was what he ought to be thinking about.

Turning, he walked back to the bunkhouse, closed the door behind him, hung his jacket on the hook by the door, took the letter from his pocket, and went across to his narrow bunk and sat down. Leaning forward, his elbows on his knees, he stared again at the letter. He suddenly felt a long way from Charity, from his family and from everyone in Carter. And come spring, when he was down south in Texas, he'd be even further away.

Uncertainty rose as he scanned again the words written on the page. Anxiety, too, and a trace of fear. They came not from the things that Charity had said, but from the things she hadn't.

He knew her well enough to know what a wrench it must have been to have had to let go of her determination to see herself, and be seen by the world, as an American first and foremost. How it must have hurt. She'd made light of it in her letter, but that didn't fool him – he could feel her anguish between every line.

Deep down, he'd always known the day would come when she'd have to accept that she'd always be Chinese in the eyes of the world, and it was paining him to feel that he might have let her down by allowing her to cling too long to a desire for something he knew she could never have. And it wasn't just that he'd allowed her to live in hope – he'd actually encouraged it.

He should have prepared her for the reality she'd have to face, and he was angry with himself that he hadn't.

Her bright, cheerful face sprang to his mind, her eyes shining with a little girl's enthusiasm for everything, and he smiled sadly to himself. Not even the cruel taunts of the other kids in her school, the meanness of Miss O'Brien, the open hostility of the Carter whites, had stopped her from desperately wanting to be seen as one of them. No wonder he hadn't been brave enough to be the person to inflict the blow that would wipe the joy from her face.

But that was weakness on his part; he should have been stronger than that.

He'd been kidding himself that in encouraging a friendship with Su Lin, which would end the loneliness she'd be bound to feel after he'd gone, he'd done enough. Of course he hadn't.

And if he was truly honest, he'd been thinking about himself and how awful he'd feel if he knew she was totally without friends. He hadn't given a moment's thought to the effect her friendship with Su Lin would have on the way she'd be seen by both the whites and the Chinese in Carter. If he hadn't been so wrapped up in his own plans, he might have given real thought as to what would be best for Charity's future.

It had taken Chen Fai to do what he, Joe, ought to have done.

Young though Charity was, Chen Fai was right to have made her face the reality of her birth in the way that he had, and to see that being brought up by Americans didn't automatically make her American. At most, having an American home gave her a degree of protection from white hostility, but she would always be classed as Chinese in the places that had power over her life.

Chen Fai had seen that, and he'd forced her to think with both her heart and her head and come to a decision. Life was never going to be easy for her, but just maybe Chen Fai had helped her to make it that little bit easier. From the moment she'd made her choice, she'd known her identity.

Joe stood up, went across to the window and glanced through it. His features were sent back to him by the blackness outside. He leaned closer to the pane and peered into the night, his breath misting the glass.

Ethan and the other hired hands were out there in the distant town that was hidden beyond the hills, too far away for the glow of the lamps of the town to soften with amber the black of night. They'd be making the most of one of the last chances to get into town before snow rendered the trails impassable, and they wouldn't be back till after sunup. He'd ridden into town with them, intending to have some fun and stay the night, found Charity's letter, read it, and immediately climbed on to his horse and headed back for the ranch.

The night wind rattled the window, and he turned back into the semi-darkness of the room.

Yes, Chen Fai had got the right idea, he thought, going across to his bed. But it was a mite bit strong for him to bring up the subject of husbands with Charity when she was still only a child. He was right, of course, that Charity one day would have to marry a Chinese man, but she was still much too young to be thinking about husbands.

He knew from Seth Culpepper that Chinese girls became

affianced at a younger age, and he also knew from Charity that the Chen family was making the final arrangements in China for the wife who'd been found for Chen Fai – a girl of Charity's age. But Charity wasn't Chinese in the way the Chens were, and she never would be. And that wasn't the way things were done in America.

Chen Fai should keep his mind on his own future wife, and leave the worrying about Charity's future to him.

Chapter Eighteen

*Five and a half months later
Early April, 1879*

The first rays of the sun had started to scatter the early morning mists as Charity reached the General Mercantile Store. She hurried straight through to the rear of the shop, pushed aside the curtain and went into the back room.

At the sight of Chen Fai standing by the centre table, holding a large structure made of red silk and kindling sticks, she stopped short. She glanced at Su Lin, who was standing next to him. Then her focus went to the object in Chen Fai's hands. Her face broke out into a smile and she went up to him.

'It's a kite, isn't it?' she said, lightly fingering the red silk which had been pulled taut over the wooden frame. 'What's it for?'

'Kite is part of very important festival for Chinese people,' Chen Fai said, his face solemn. 'Today is *Cing-ming Zit*, Chinese name for Festival of Pure Brightness. This is day we sweep graves of our ancestors. It may be most important of all festivals. This is why we ask you to come to us this morning. Today you come see how we celebrate our ancestors and show respect for them.'

She took a step back. 'But I haven't got any ancestors.'

'You Chinese girl, Charity,' Su Lin said. 'Must learn what Chinese do. One day you sweep graves of ancestors of husband.' She beamed at Charity. '*Dai lou* has willow branch for you. We sweep graves with willow branch and this send away evil spirits that hide near graves. We like you

129

come to cemetery and sweep graves with us and put gifts for ancestors. You come?'

Charity shrugged. 'I guess so. That must be why all the Chinatown shops are still closed – everyone's gonna be sweepin'.' She paused, and frowned. 'But most Chinamen haven't got people buried in Carter, have they? Their ancestors are in China, so there can't be many graves here to sweep.'

Chen Fai nodded. 'Grave markers stand for grave of ancestor. Family in China sweep grave with ancestor in. Here in Carter we sweep in front of grave marker. All Chinamen go to cemetery today, and then have meal as family. We eat cold food at meal. We not cook on Festival of Pure Brightness. You come back here and eat with us.'

'You will come with us, yes?' Su Lin repeated, her voice pleading.

'Okay.'

'Give willow branch over there to Charity,' Chen Fai told Su Lin. 'We each have willow branch, Charity. First we sweep graves of Chen family; then we sweep grave of your family. Su Lin say you have Chinese mother in cemetery. Today we celebrate Chen ancestors, and we celebrate ancestor of Charity,' he added, and he smiled.

Charity's heart jumped. She stared at him, the blood draining from her cheeks.

'My ma *is* there,' she whispered, clutching the branch to her chest. 'But you said she hadn't got a reputation.'

'I think I wrong,' he said quietly. 'I not know what happened to your ma, Charity, but I know many bad things happen to women who come in boats from China to Gold Mountain. It is not fault of women; it is fault of bad men. I know this. I think your ma is very nice woman as you very good girl. You are her reputation, and she deserve to have honour and respect from us. Is good day today – is day of happiness that we help the dead by driving out wicked spirits, and is day of sadness they not with us any longer.'

Tears filled her eyes and rolled down her cheeks.

'So, we go to cemetery now?' he asked gently.

She nodded, wiping her eyes with the back of her hand.

'Come then. You bring basket, Su Lin; Charity bring willow branches, and I carry kite.'

Using his shoulders, he pushed away the curtain separating the back room from the shop, stood aside to let Charity and Su Lin pass in front of him through the doorway, and then followed them through the empty shop and out into Main Street. Joining the straggle of Chinese men who were making their way along the street, laden with kites, food and willow branches, they headed towards the piece of wasteland on the outskirts of Carter Town where the Chinese had set up a graveyard next to the town cemetery after being forbidden to bury their dead with the whites.

When they reached the cemetery, they went first to the patches of ground where small wooden markers indicated the members of the Chen family. Chen Fai and Su Lin took their branches from Charity, and began to sweep in front of the graves. Charity stood for a few minutes, watching how they did it, then she went to Su Lin's side and started sweeping next to her.

When all of the graves had been swept, she stood back as Su Lin and Chen Fai carefully set bean-curd cakes, rice dumplings and an orange on each grave, then lit incense sticks and wax candles and placed them around each grave marker.

When the last grave had been honoured, Chen Fai straightened up. 'We go now to your mother's grave,

Charity,' he said. 'We sweep there and leave her gifts of food. We then fly kite in honour of all of our ancestors. You show us her grave.'

Her eyes filling again, she turned and led them to the patch of stony ground at the far edge of the cemetery where her mother lay.

'Charity!'

Sam's voice reached her from outside the general mercantile.

Still holding aside the curtain as she went to follow Su Lin and Chen Fai into the room at the back of the store, she stopped.

'Charity!' she heard him shout again, a note of panic in his voice. 'I saw you go in there just now. Pa's hurt. You gotta come.'

She exclaimed sharply, dropped the willow branches, spun round and sped back through the shop and out on to the boardwalk.

Sam was standing in front of the store, covered in coal dust.

'Ma wants you,' he said, drawing his breath in jagged gasps. 'There's bin an accident in the mine. Pa's hurt real bad. You gotta come.' He turned and ran towards Second Street.

Picking up her skirts, Charity raced after him, her heart beating fast, desperately wishing Joe was there.

'Sit down, Charity,' Martha said, her voice tired. 'You've not stopped since you got back. And I think I'll do the same. Hiram's in bed. His leg's splinted and bandaged, and he's got the remains of a bottle of whisky on the table next to him. There's nothin' more we can do for him right now.'

She sat down at the table opposite Sam. Charity went and sat next to her. 'You can tell us now what happened, Sam,' Martha said. 'Your pa's always so careful.'

'It happened when he was lettin' a loaded car out of the room we'd been workin' in. We'd gotten a good room for once, so we'd been diggin' extra hard to get out as much coal as we could in the time we had. We'd only gotten the room 'cos the Chinee weren't workin' today. The white teams never get the good rooms now. We reckon the Chinee pay the foreman for them,' he added bitterly.

'Get on with the tellin', Sam,' Martha said impatiently.

'Well, it was near the end of the shift. Pa was real tired after workin' so hard all day, and I guess he must've bin careless about the rope. I feel real bad about that, Ma,' Sam said, despair in his voice. 'I told him to stand back; I said I'd deal with the loaded car instead of him, but he said no, it was his turn. He never lets me take his turn.' He put his hand to his head in anguish. 'I should've tried harder.' His voice broke.

'Don't blame yourself, Sam. Your pa's a stubborn man,' Martha said. 'When he's set on somethin', he's gonna do it and there's no stoppin' him. So how'd he catch his leg, then?'

'It was the coil of rope. You let the car down by a rope. The rope's coiled twice around the prop, and then whoever's lettin' the car down holds the loose end. That was Pa. Somehow or other his leg caught in the coil while he was lettin' the car down, and it was trapped between the car and the prop. He'll've bin careless 'cos he was tired.'

'Your poor pa!' Martha exclaimed. 'That must've hurt real bad. He didn't deserve that, whatever tomfool things he's done in the past.'

'Oh, it hurt all right. You should've heard him as they

tried to free his leg. It fair broke my heart. Well, you saw how torn and mangled it was between his knee and his ankle. We didn't need the doc to tell us his bones were broken in a dozen places.' He paused. 'You're not to worry, Ma. Doc did a real good job of puttin' his leg back together. Sure, Pa's not a young man and his bones won't knit as readily as they would in a younger man, but you heard the doc – he don't think Pa's gonna lose his leg.'

'It'll be awhile afore he can walk on it, though, and I'm guessin' he'll never be able to go down the mine again,' Martha said. 'He may not have liked minin', but I reckon he'll like bein' helpless even less, and watchin' you earn and not him. And what about our house?' She sat up sharply. 'Without his money, it'll be harder to pay the rent and with your pa not workin' in the mines, the company might throw us out. What'll we do then?'

'You can rest easy about the money, Ma. I'm gonna work extra hard to make up for what Pa's not able to bring in. And there are no worries about the house – I'm in the mines, too, aren't I, so we're entitled to a house.'

She gave him a tired smile. 'You're a good son, Sam, and I'm grateful to you, but I don't want the next mangled leg to be yours. You might not be as lucky as your pa about keepin' it. And I'd forgotten when I spoke that we've got Joe's money now, and that means we'll manage.'

Charity leaned forward, her eyes hopeful. 'You know the herb store next to the laundry, the one run by a Chinese doctor? All the Chinamen go there when they're ill. I could ask Chen Fai to get us some herbs that'd make bad legs better. I reckon they'd have herbs for that – they've got them for everythin' you can think of.'

Sam thumped the wooden table in anger. 'Don't you let Chinaman Doc near him, or any of his so-called medicine.

134

If it wasn't for those heathen rice-eaters, Pa would be goin' down the mine tomorrow, not lyin' sick in bed.'

'I don't know, Sam,' Martha said slowly. 'It might be worth a try. I'm thinkin' of that time when Caroline Oakland's baby wouldn't stop cryin'. It cried for more than two days – we could hear it through the walls – and she became real fearful for it. Jeb got the white doc in and the doc said the baby would settle down. But it kept right on cryin'. Real early on the third mornin', Jeb had had enough and he sent for Chinaman Doc. The Chinaman went to the house, looked at the baby, said it was colic, rubbed a kind of peppermint oil around the baby's mouth and navel, and it stopped cryin' at once. He said the baby would be all right, and it was.'

'What are you sayin'?' Sam asked testily.

'That if the Chinee have got somethin' that'll take away pain and ease your pa, then maybe we should ask for it.'

'I ain't askin' them for anythin',' Sam said stubbornly. 'And you ain't either. What's more, with what's happenin' in the mines, I've bin wonderin' again lately why Charity's still livin' here. We're a minin' family and yet we're—'

'One moment, Sam,' Martha said, hastily interrupting him. She turned to Charity. 'We'll need more water, gal. I want you to go to the well and fill four pails. You'll find some pails by the door.'

Glancing nervously at Sam, Charity swiftly got up and went to the door. She picked up two of the pails, opened the door and went out.

Martha leaned forward. 'Now you listen to me, Sam,' she began. 'Charity's stayin' with us.'

'She isn't really with us, though, is she? She's always with her Chinese friends,' he said, his voice a sneer. 'I'm thinkin' she'd do better to move in with them. The whites in the mines are wonderin' aloud when I'm near them why the Walkers are puttin' a roof over the head of one of the Chinee. They don't like it. The Chinese are takin' the food right out of our mouths, yet we're givin' food to one of them. It's not right.'

'We're not givin' Charity anythin', as you put it,' she said sharply. 'She's paid for her place in this house. She's gone out and found work from the moment she could, and she hands over everythin' she earns.'

Sam opened his mouth to speak. 'But—'

Martha cut through him. 'There's no but, Sam. Apart from anythin' else, three men make a lot of work, especially when two of them go down the mines, and many's the time over the years I've been real grateful for her help. Are you suggestin' that now, with your pa unable to lift a bucket to help me or himself, and with the extra chores caused by him bein' ill, I should get rid of Charity and do all the work myself?'

Sam shifted in his seat. 'I can see it wouldn't be easy, but—'

'Charity stays. She stays for reasons I already said, and she stays 'cos I promised Joe. The last thing he made me promise was that she'd always have a home with us. I'm gonna stick to my promise, and you'll have to accept it.'

'Joe's bin gone a year. Things are changin' real fast around here and it's not like it used to be. There's reason enough to forget such a promise.'

'That so?' she said, her tone sarcastic. 'It'd be real good for Joe to quit his job, would it? He'd come home like a shot if he thought Charity wasn't with us, and you know it. Is that what you really want – Joe back here, mad angry, and no longer able to give us much money? He's doin' a lot better where he is than he'd do at Culpepper's. No, I reckon—'

The door opened and Charity came in, a heavy bucket in each of her hands. She put the buckets on to the floor in front of the sink, glanced from Sam to Martha, and went back to the door for the last pails.

'I'll fill these,' she said, 'and then do anythin' else you've got.' And she started to go through the doorway.

'You do that, gal,' Martha called after her. 'And first thing tomorrow, you can go to the mercantile and ask Chen Fai to get us those herbs you were talkin' about.'

Chapter Nineteen

Fifteen months later
July, 1880

Dear Charity,
Thank you for your letters – you can't know how much I look forward to receiving them.

I'm sorry I've not written back for so long. It's been a hard drive with little time for writing. By the time we've bedded the cattle at night and bunked down ourselves, we're fair exhausted and we've still got a watch to do before sunup. Ethan once said I'd be so tired that I'd learn to fall asleep in the saddle while my horse kept right on circling around the herd, and he was right. But more about the drive later.

Firstly, I was mighty relieved to learn that Pa's leg was doing well, but I'm sorry he's out of sorts for much of the time. That's not like him. I'm sure that when he accepts it's better to walk with a stick than not walk at all, he'll return to his old self.

You know I'm counting on you to tell me if you think I should come home, don't you? The drive ends in about six weeks, and I'd planned to go up to Ogallala and work out the winter months on one of the ranches there, but I could return to Carter instead.

The way I figure it at the moment, though, is that Pa's over the worst, and the money I'm sending home is more useful than me being there, an extra mouth for Ma to feed, more clothes to wash and all that. And I'm not sure what I could do that's not already being done. I know you real well, Charity, and I know you'll be doing everything you can to help with Pa.

But if you think I should come back, I'm sure I could work for Seth again. He always said he'd find a place for me if I returned. I'm trusting you to tell me what's best to do.

So to get back to the drive. Like I said, it's a difficult drive, but on the whole I'm enjoying it. Riding sixteen to eighteen hours a day in the Texas heat isn't easy, not for us and not for the cows. We do early and late drives to avoid the midday sun, and we often let the cattle lie down and rest for an hour or more, but even so, by mid-afternoon they're restless. It's hard on our horses, too, and we have to change mounts four times a day so they don't get exhausted.

The terrain we've been crossing is also a challenge. One day we're driving through a canyon, and the next across a low mountain range. It's interesting land, but not easy for droving, and it certainly isn't land I'd want to settle in. With the dry air and scorching sun, the earth's as hot and tired as we are, and there's dust everywhere. When you look back, you see clouds of dust for twenty miles. I've had to wear a bandanna over the lower part of my face for most of the drive.

As you can imagine, water's a problem. Not long ago, we drove across a wide open mesa for days without finding so much as a single drop of water. A few times at first, we were able to dig a well, but our mounts got the water, not us. Washing was the first thing we gave up, despite the heat. I won't describe what we smelt like, or how dirty we were.

After three days of no water, we began to be afear'd. The cattle wouldn't graze any longer or lie down – they just wanted to move on. They were becoming harder to control, and started milling all over the place, not seeming to know where they were going. And they were lowing *something awful. We'd never seen them like that, and then it hit us – they were going blind.*

That shocked us to the core. We knew we had to get them to water real soon or they'd not get their sight back. We'd no idea how much further we'd have to go to find water, but we knew we'd passed a lake several days earlier, and we turned round and went back. After a couple of days, you could see from the way the cows started moving that instinct was telling them there was water ahead.

When they reached the lake, they waded in till the water covered their flanks, and just stood and moaned a while, drinking little. Then they came out and lay down, and then went back and drank some more. And when they'd done with the water, they grazed. Seeing them recover like that was a real good feeling. Needless to say, we took a different route out of there.

We've seen Indians, but as I told you we'd be crossing Indian Territory, that won't be a surprise. The boss paid the local tribes a toll of ten cents a head for the right to cross their land, and we went through without any trouble.

One of the hardest things we've had to do so far was get the cattle across a large creek. I know that doesn't sound that hard, but remember we're driving half-wild Texas Longhorn cattle, and they can be real contrary and stampede at nothing. Also they're stubborn beasts.

We'd got them across two large rivers and a number of small creeks, and each crossing had gone okay, except for the last small creek when they'd got a bit bogged down. Not long after being mired like that, we reached a large creek, and they must have remembered what happened before because the moment they put their hoofs on the soft earth at the water's edge, that was as far as they would go.

It took us almost three whole days to get them across.

But by the end of those days, I'd picked up a skill I'd never expected to learn on a drive, and it could come in real useful in the future.

Because we just couldn't get the cows into the water, and because there was a slight risk of them getting mired again, the boss said we'd have to make a bridge. No one had heard of that happening before, and we thought we'd never be able to build one. But we did.

We got a load of brush from the trees and piled it from one side of the creek to the other to make a foundation. Then we cut down cottonwood logs, put them on top of the brush, filled every chink and gap with sod and dirt and pounded it down real hard. And we had a mighty fine bridge.

But the cattle had never seen a bridge before, and refused point blank to go over it. The remuda crossed without a problem, but not those cows. In the end, we gave up for the day, settled down for the night and let the cattle graze. We figured that if we waited till the sun was high the following day, the cows would be well grazed and sleepy, and they'd just walk across.

We figured without their stubbornness, and we had to spend another night on the wrong side of the river.

It was looking as if we were going to be spending a third night there, when one of the drovers had a bang-up idea. He suggested finding a cow and a calf, roping the calf around its neck and pulling it on to the bridge. If we dragged it across the bridge, he said, and tightened the rope all the time, it'd keep on bellowing, and nothing stirs range cattle as much as the bellowing of a calf, so the cow and the rest of the herd would surely go after it.

It worked. They were so eager to get to the calf they didn't know if they were walking on a bridge or on land.

Building that bridge taught me how to build a house, if

ever I wanted, or at least a soddie. But like I said before, I won't be building it in Texas or in Indian Territory. They aren't the sort of places I want to live. It's still green fields and rolling hills for me.

You've probably guessed I'm seriously thinking about setting up a ranch of my own one day. But not for a while – I've more things to learn, and I'll need more money than I've got at the moment. But that's the way my thoughts are going.

I'd better stop now. It's almost time for my watch. Ethan and I are on the first watch tonight.

But before I finish, I just want to say I'm glad that Chen Sing is letting you carry on going to their home. I'd been worried that when he got back from China, he might stop you visiting, but not so, I see. Their ways are different from ours, but they seem good people, and Chen Fai has shown himself to be a good friend to you. I've not forgotten that thing about your ma's grave.

I feel sorry for him having to take a woman he doesn't know for a wife. I wouldn't like that at all.

Don't ever stop writing to me, Charity, will you? Your letters make me feel close to home, and I'm interested in everything you say about the Chinese way of doing things. I should tell you more often than I do that I get a real warm feeling when the boss hands me a letter from you.

But it's not just getting news from home that makes me appreciate your letters – it's more than that. You know I've always felt a person should have friends. Seth Culpepper's my friend. So is Ethan Grey. And so are you, Charity. You're a very special friend. I can talk to you about anything and everything, and I know you'll listen.

I hope you'll always feel you can say the same about me.
                    Your good friend,
                    Joe

Chapter Twenty

Charity paused in her reading aloud and glanced across at Hiram. He'd leaned forward in his chair and was staring ahead in the direction of the river.

'You want me to stop readin' now?' she asked, making a move as if to fold up the newspaper.

He didn't reply.

'I'll stop if you want,' she repeated.

There was still no reply.

She glanced down at *The Carter Miner* and bit her lip, wondering whether to continue. 'What're you thinkin' about?' she asked after a few minutes' silence.

'What I'm always thinkin' about is that I shoulda kept pannin',' he said, his eyes fixed on the view in front of him. 'If I had, I might've been walkin' tall like a man, not bent over and leanin' on a stick, about to start a job that's usually done by boys, which will hardly give me enough to put food into the mouths of my family.'

'No, you wouldn't,' Martha called out to them, coming to the open doorway. 'You'd've been dead in the ground and so would we,' she said, wiping her hands on her apron. 'You weren't ever gonna find gold in that water, Hiram, and you know it. Because you knew it and because you're a good man, you stepped into the cage and went down the shaft.'

'Maybe,' he said.

'There's no maybe about it,' she said bluntly. 'If he's stopped listenin' to what's in the paper, Charity, you might

143

as well take it back to the superintendent.' She went back into the house.

'I've not finished listenin', woman,' Hiram called after her. The front door closed. He turned to look at the view ahead. 'I was just thinkin',' he said. 'Not just about pannin', but about those mountains there.'

'What about them?' Charity asked.

'When you're deep under the ground from mornin' to night, it's easy to miss what's around you. I always thought those crags across from Carter were just ugly grey rocks. But I bin lookin' at them day after day while sittin' here, and I now know that grey is only one of the colours. D'you know, gal, they go from grey to lilac in the mornin', then they're pink like a wild rose in the middle of the day, and then real green? And I never knew that till now. I can see why Joe took you there at times.'

'I can't remember much about it except standin' on the rock and lookin' out at the plain. Joe would point things out to me, and also things around Carter, but I can't remember what they were.' She paused. 'I miss Joe bein' around.'

He nodded. 'Me, too.'

She glanced at Hiram, sudden hope in her eyes. 'You think he'll come back soon?'

He slowly shook his head. 'Nope; I don't. And it's more help to us, him doin' what he's doin' wherever that is. He was right about that. I don't reckon he'll be back for some time, if he comes back at all.'

Her hope faded. A lump rose in her throat, and she looked quickly down at the newspaper on her lap.

'You don't need him any more,' he went on, glancing at her downcast profile. 'You've got other friends now. That Chinese lot.'

'But they're not Joe,' she said.

'And nor will Joe be the Joe you knew when he left, gal,' he said gently. 'He was a lad of seventeen when he rode off. He's twenty-one now, and he'll be older still when he finally does get back. He's a grown man.'

'I know that.'

'I'm not sure you do. His letters are tellin' you that it's not an easy life, drivin' cattle thousands of miles in every weather, over every kind of terrain, but I can tell you're still thinkin' of him as that boy you knew. You're imaginin' he'll come back and start climbin' the rocks with you again. Well, he won't. You must let go of that dream, 'cos that's all it is – a dream.'

She stared at the ground, her mouth setting in a stubborn line. 'I know he's all grown up,' she said, 'but I can tell from his letters he's still Joe.'

Hiram shrugged his shoulders. 'Think on this, then. He's not the only one who's grown up – you are, too. You're fourteen now, and you've finished school and are lookin' to pick up more work. Pretty soon, you'd not have time to climb the rocks with Joe, if he came back and that's what he wanted to do.'

'I'm gonna ask Annie if she'll let me wait tables. I'd like that. I know she said I couldn't before, but I'm older now.'

'You'd be wastin' your time,' he said flatly. 'It wasn't your age that was the problem – it was the colour of your skin. And you bein' yellow's an even bigger problem today than it used to be. Stick to Chinatown. Ask Ah Lee for more hours in the bakery or ask Chen Fai for a job. You must know the store well enough by now – you go there whenever you've got a spare minute.'

'Okay. I'll ask Ah Lee, then,' she said, her voice despondent. Frowning at the ground, she kicked the pebbles with the heel of her boots.

He threw her a quick glance. 'You know, gal, sometimes

everythin' can seem real terrible for a while. But as time goes by, you see it ain't as bad as you thought, and there's even good in it.'

'What's good about not bein' able to do what you wanna do 'cos your skin's the wrong colour? And not seein' someone you wanna see?'

'That's what you'll have to find out for yourself. Like I found out the rocks are not just grey. And the bits of short grass you see among the sand and the gravel aren't just a dried up yellow. In the mornin' they're more like grey; later on in the mornin', they're a real bright green; in the afternoon they're yellowy green, and when the sun's gone down, they're a sorta purple.'

She stared at him, puzzled.

He smiled at her. 'The accident made my world seem black. But it gave me time to look around, and that's bin good for me. Things ain't so black now.'

She frowned. 'But how could never seein' Joe again be good for me?'

'If he was here, you might get to rely on him again, and that wouldn't be good 'cos even if he came back, he wouldn't stay. From real little, he's said he'll never live in Carter. He'd leave one day, and then you'd be upset all over again. He's now made a life for himself that isn't in Carter and doesn't include you. Now you've gotta make a life for yourself that doesn't include Joe. You've gotta stop dreamin' about the past and look to the future.'

'I'm gonna carry on writin' to him,' she said sullenly. 'He likes gettin' my letters; he said so.'

'And we wouldn't want you to stop. We're grateful that you're lettin' him know what's goin' on here. Which reminds me, you'll tell him that Sam's walkin' out with the superintendent's daughter, won't you?'

She nodded.

'And another good thing that's come out of my accident is that Joe and Sam have had the chance to show me what fine men they've become. Joe's never stopped sendin' us money, and I appreciate that. And look at what Sam's done for me! He's worked real hard to put extra money on the table to cover what I've not been able to earn. To be honest, I'd had growin' concerns about him, seein' him so eaten up with hate as he was.' He paused. 'I'm sorry to be sayin' that to you, gal, but you know what I mean.'

'He's never liked me,' she said bluntly.

Hiram nodded. 'It's not you; it's the Chinese generally he don't like. But he's bin worse since Joe left to have a fine time who knows where, while he's strugglin' daily with the fallin' price of coal, and I'd been worried about him. Not that Sam would wanna do what Joe's doin'; he wouldn't. But it can't be easy, knowin' his brother's miles away from the problems here in Carter.'

'Is Sam jealous of Joe?'

'I reckon he might be. But it's understandable. Minin's not gone the way Sam thought it'd go – it's not gone the way any of us thought it'd go – and with Joe obviously happy about what he's doin' ... Well, like I say, it's not easy. But I was wrong to worry about Sam: he's proved a good son to me.'

'Is that 'cos he's got you the job of breaker?'

'In part. He knew I needed work – a man can't sit in a chair all day and look at the hills – and being a breaker's about the only thing I could do in the mine with my leg as it is. All I'll have to do is sit on a wooden seat above the chute and remove the slate from the coal. Then break the coal into pieces and put the pieces into sizes. It was Sam pushin' for me day after day that made them finally agree to take me on and not look for a lad. It's given me a lift, I can tell you, knowin' I'll be bringin' home wages once more, little though it'll be.'

'Why d'you wanna go in the mine again? I thought you didn't like it.'

'Havin' a job is a matter of pride. And it's about keepin' our house. We tried to hide it, but I reckon Sam saw his ma and me beginnin' to fret about losin' the house if he wed Phebe and moved out – I can't see that gal wanting to live with us – and I reckon that's why he ain't wed before now. But now I'm workin' for the company again, we've gotta right to stay on in the house. So the accident's shown me I've two fine sons, and that's done me a power of good. And you, too, Charity,' he added warmly. 'You've shown what a good heart you've got. Don't think we don't appreciate you, 'cos we do.'

She blushed. 'I guess.'

'Anyway.' He sat back in his chair and smiled at her. 'I've done enough talkin' for now. Why don't you read me some more?'

She smiled back at him, lifted the paper and started to scan the columns for what might be of interest. Then she stiffened. Frowning, she stared hard at the paper, her face growing pale.

He sat upright. 'What is it, Charity?' he asked in alarm. 'What've you read?' He leaned across and caught her by the arm. 'Tell me, gal; it's not about Joe?'

She shook her head. 'It's not Joe – it's about Chinese people,' she said, squinting at the print. Biting her thumbnail, she looked at Hiram. 'I don't understand it real well.'

'Read it aloud,' he said impatiently. 'I may not be much for readin' words that are written down, but I can understand well enough when I hear them spoken.'

148

'It's about somethin' called the Chinese Exclusion – I think that's what it says, exclusion; yes – it's about somethin' called the Chinese Exclusion Act. Exclusion means stoppin' someone from doin' somethin', doesn't it?'

He nodded. 'I expect you're right, gal. It'll be stoppin' the Chinese from doin' somethin'. What's it say?'

Stumbling over some of the words, she read the column aloud to him. When she'd finished, she looked at him anxiously. 'What's it mean?'

He shrugged. 'What we already know: Americans don't like the Chinese and they're tryin' to stop them comin' here. They're not gonna let any skilled or unskilled Chinese labourers into the country for ten years, and they're certainly not gonna let anyone in who might work in the mines. If they try to come in and they're caught, they'll be put into prison or sent back to China. Yup, keepin' the Chinese out – that's what it's all about.'

'It says here that merchants, students, teachers, diplomats, and tourists are exempted,' she read out. She lowered the newspaper and stared at Hiram. 'That means the Act doesn't apply to them, doesn't it?'

'I guess so. Yup, merchants and the others on the list can still come in. That's what it'll mean.'

'Chen Fai's a merchant.' She stared down at the paper again. 'It says any Chinaman who leaves America must get a certificate for re-entry before he leaves if he intends to come back. Also, Chinese immigrants can't ever become American citizens.' Her face brightened. 'If Chen Fai gets that certificate, he'll be all right, won't he? He's gonna go to China in a few years to get wed and then bring his wife back. And Chen Sing's a merchant, too. He and his wife are goin' with Chen Fai. They'll all get that certificate and be able to come back, won't they?'

Hiram rubbed his jaw thoughtfully. 'I don't know, Charity. They're merchants all right, but I'd be surprised if the Act meant merchants like them. There are lots of small merchants like the Chens all over the place. If they were all allowed to go in and out, the Act would be pretty useless.'

Her face fell.

'And even if Chen Fai did manage to get a re-entry certificate, and one for his wife, too, if that's the way it'll be done, I'm not so sure they'd let him back in, certificate or not. The whites want rid of the Chinese, and the way I see it, anyone who goes to China thinkin' he'll be allowed back in 'cos he's got a piece of paper might just be takin' the bait like a bass, and that could be the last he sees of America.'

She stared at him, her eyes opening wide in anxiety.

'So what d'you think Chen Fai will do?'

'If I had to say,' he said slowly, 'I'd say he'll not be goin' back to China. Leastways, not for ten years.'

'Maybe he'll go to San Francisco to find a wife then,' she said. 'There's a real big Chinatown there. He used to live there, you know. He and his pa came from a place in Canton I can't pronounce, and that's where they landed. They were there for a bit, and then they went on a riverboat to Sacramento, and that's where Chen Sing met Su Lin's ma.' She paused and glanced again at the newspaper. 'I wonder what he'll do,' she said after a moment or two.

Chapter Twenty-One

One month later
August, 1882

'What do you want?' Sam pushed Martha aside and faced Chen Fai, who stood on the doorstep. A hand on the wooden jamb on either side of the door, Sam glared at Chen Fai. 'We don't want your sort here.'

With each of his hands in the opposite sleeve of his red brocade tunic, Chen Fai tried to look above Sam's arm to Martha, who was hovering behind Sam, her eyes anxious.

'I come to ask Charity to go for a walk with me tomorrow, Mrs Walker,' he said, raising his voice slightly to reach her, 'and I bring you this.' He took one of his hands from the sleeve it was in, and held out a slender package.

'What d'you think you're playin' at, comin' here like this?' Sam exclaimed angrily. 'And if you think bringin' us things is gonna make you welcome, you're wrong.'

'Move out of the way, Sam,' Martha said, and she pushed one of his arms aside.

Scowling, he moved slightly to let her through.

She took the package from Chen Fai and opened it. 'Oh my, it's the new yellow cotton Charity was tellin' me about last week!' she exclaimed in surprise. Her face broke into a smile. 'She told me it'd suit me and I should get some. She must have told you, too. Thank you, Chen Fai; it's a very kind thought, but there's no need to do this.' She wrapped the paper loosely back around the material and held the parcel out to him.

He shook his head, took a step back and gave a little

bow. 'It's my wish to give this to you,' he said, a trace of awkwardness in his voice. 'It's Chinese custom to give gifts to show respect to other person.' He hesitated. 'Gift is given by one family to another when one family wants to make arrangement with other family.'

'I see,' Martha said slowly, looking down at the material in her hands. She glanced behind her into the room. Charity was nowhere to be seen, but Hiram was coming towards her, leaning heavily on his stick.

She turned back to Chen Fai. 'I see,' she repeated.

He gave her a half smile. 'In China, one family does not talk to another about these things. It is someone else who talks for them and who takes gifts to woman's family. But we are in America now, and we can do things in American way, I think, and I come to ask Charity if she like to walk with me. A short walk,' he added. 'You'll see us walk from your chairs there.' He indicated the two wooden chairs outside the house.

Martha nodded. 'And the American way is that Charity will answer for herself.'

He nodded. 'This is what I expect. I hope she agree.'

Martha hesitated a moment. 'To speak plainly, Chen Fai, I think I can see where this is leadin'. When we read about that new Act, we saw at once how it might affect you. You do know, though, that in America, girls don't get affianced as young as I hear they do in China? I'm sayin' this in a general way,' she added quickly, 'not meanin' anyone in particular. But in a general way, they don't; and they don't get wed as young, either. Charity's only fourteen, and she's been brought up in the American way.'

'I mean only to go for walk tomorrow,' Chen Fai said with a smile. 'I like her to see me as her friend, not only as Su Lin's brother. This is all I like for now.'

'I understand. And for what it matters, we don't agree with what the law said.' She fingered the yellow cotton, then turned to Hiram. 'What d'you say, Hiram?'

'I say he should take her back to Chinatown with him right now and stay there. We don't want any Celestials here,' Sam cut in.

'Like your ma told Chen Fai, that's rather up to Charity, don't you think, Sam?' Hiram said quietly. 'It's not up to any of us, and it certainly isn't up to you. We'll let the girl decide for herself.' He turned slightly. 'Charity!' he called. 'Leave whatever you're doin' and come here at once.'

A moment later, Charity came from the corridor into the sitting room, a threaded needle in one hand and her pinafore in the other.

'Chen Fai!' she exclaimed, catching a glimpse of him beyond Martha and Hiram.

She hesitated, then went slowly up to the group at the doorway. Hiram and Martha moved aside to let her through, and she found herself facing Chen Fai. 'What're you doin' here?' she asked awkwardly. She caught her breath. 'Is Su Lin all right?' she asked in sudden alarm.

'It's not about Su Lin,' Hiram said. 'He asked if he can go for a walk with you tomorrow, Charity.'

She glanced at Hiram and then turned back to Chen Fai. 'And what did you tell him?' she asked, her eyes on Chen Fai's face.

'We made sure he was only talkin' about walkin' where we could see you,' Hiram told her. 'And we reminded him of your age. That said, we told him it was for you to answer. You must do what you want, gal.'

'Tomorrow's my day for cleaning the bedrooms,' she said, glancing at Hiram. 'And I help with the lunch, and then go to the bakery.'

'I reckon you could fit in a walk if you wanted after you've done the bedrooms. Maybe you could leave off helpin' with the lunch for once. Don't you think, Martha?'

'If that's what you want, Hiram,' Martha said, a trifle stiffly.

'I suggest you go outside and tell Chen Fai if you wanna go for that walk or not. It's up to you.' He gave Charity a gentle push, and she found herself outside the house. The front door clicked shut behind her.

'You needn't look like that, Martha. She ain't a servant, tied to us till her last breath,' they heard Hiram say. 'And as for you, Sam: you've got yourself a gal. Charity's got a right to look to her future, too. And her future's never gonna be with the whites. Think about it, this is the best thing for her.' A moment later, they heard a bedroom door slam shut, and then there was silence.

She and Chen Fai stared at each other for a moment, the sudden lack of ease between them tangible.

Then he gave her a slight smile. 'I ask only to go for a walk, and talk a little, maybe,' he said.

'Why? I seen you lots of times. I've been friends with Su Lin for years and you often talk to us.'

'Maybe I want to talk to you by yourself. I like you begin to see me as your friend, not just as Su Lin's big brother.'

She stared at him thoughtfully, biting her lower lip. 'Is that 'cos you think Joe's not comin' back and I might need someone to look after me like Joe used to? Is that it? Or is it about you not goin' to China? You aren't, are you? Joe's pa said that even if they agree you're a merchant and give you a paper sayin' you can come back, they might not let you back in.'

'For the first thing you say, I will look after you if Joe is here or if Joe is not here, and if you not want to walk with me, I still look after you,' Chen Fai said simply. 'You are good friend to Su Lin. And you are good girl, Charity, and worthy of respect.'

She gave him a sly smile. 'Even if my Chinese ma has a reputation?'

He grinned at her. 'That is so.' He paused. 'For the second thing you say: no, I not go back to China. Not ever, I think. I not wed girl they choose to be my wife. I think like Mr Walker – I not be allowed back here, even if I have certificate. And even if I allowed come back, wife not be able to come here, too. I not want wife in China and me here.' His smile broadened. 'I live in America for most of my life and I become too American for that.'

'I'm sorry,' she said quietly.

'Be more sorry for girl in China. She expect in a few years to bathe in pomelo leaves before her wedding, to sit in family's rice-drying tray while female relatives comb her hair and braid it into style for married woman. She expect to lie on ground before family's ancestral tablets, and before parents, who she know she never see again. She expect to be taken by palanquin to her wedding and have banquet after it. But this now not happen.'

Charity's eyes widened with sympathy for the girl. 'She must be so disappointed.'

'I sorry for her, too. And is more bad. Arrangement is now made and bride price paid, so Chinese people see girl as wife to me, and she is not now able to marry another person. Chinese wife live with family of husband so she must live as servant to honourable mother. I am able to see this is not nice for girl.'

'You see that because you're a nice person, Chen Fai,' Charity said gravely.

A pale pink hue spread across his cheeks. 'I'm glad you

think I'm nice, Charity.' He hesitated. 'In China, unmarried man and woman must not be alone together, must not talk together. This mean I must not speak to you like this, and walk with you, even if American family watch us. It is very bad for reputation of woman. I tell you this long time ago when I not want you to be friend of Su Lin.'

'I remember,' she said, and she pulled her single braid over her shoulder and started sucking the tip of it.

Smiling, he gently separated her hand from her hair.

'But we are not in China now. In China, unmarried Chinese girl is not seen outside home by people who are not family, but we not easily able to live here if Su Lin never come out of room behind store. So Su Lin do like an American girl and she come out. Chinese people in America understand this and it not harm her reputation. If we do one thing different from in China, we also can do another thing different. Do you agree?'

She shifted her weight from one foot to another. 'I guess.'

'So I like to walk with you, Charity. You want to come with me to river over there tomorrow?'

He pointed towards the river.

She looked up at the dark eyes that gazed at her with warmth and hope, at the mouth that smiled a smile which reached the eyes, at the face she'd grown to know so well since she'd met Su Lin, at the man Su Lin called a good brother and who'd never shown her anything but kindness.

She took a deep breath. 'Sure,' she said. 'Why not?'

Chapter Twenty-Two

Three weeks later
September, 1882

Sitting in the back of the chuck wagon, a mug of coffee next to him, Joe finished reading the letter for a second time. He let the hand holding the letter rest on his knee, and pulled his hat low over his face to protect him from the glare of the unforgiving sun.

It was good news about his pa and the breaker's job. It must have been difficult for him to have had to be supported by his sons for all that time, and not been able to contribute to the home himself. His pa would feel much better about himself now that he was back at work.

And Sam was walking out with someone, was he? That really brought home to him how long he'd been gone and the changes he must expect to find when he returned. He tried to picture the superintendent's daughter, but beyond the fact she was blonde, he couldn't see her at all in his head, having always kept as far away from the mines as he could.

As for the new Act stopping the Chinese from going in and out of America – he raised his hat slightly and glanced again at the letter – and then Chen Fai asking Charity to go walking with him ... Well, it was no great surprise. He'd long realised that at some point, the Chinamen in Carter would stop seeing her as too American in her ways, and start seeing her for what she was – a sweet young Chinese girl.

And one of only two Chinese girls in Carter.

But she was a Chinese girl with an American family to support her, and she was never gonna end up in a crib or a sporting house like so many of the girls shipped over from China. And nor would she become a thing to be used by men in a railroad camp, which was probably what had happened to her mother. When Charity was old enough, she'd be someone's wife. He'd make sure of that, and the folk in Carter knew it. He may not be there to keep an eye on her interests in person, but he knew his ma and pa would be looking out for her.

So why did he feel so empty inside, he wondered, as if a bit of him had fallen away.

Frowning, he scanned the letter again. He'd write in his next letter that she shouldn't spend too much time alone with a man of Chen Fai's age, he decided. Maybe that was what was disturbing him. He and Chen Fai were similar in age, and he knew how he and the other drovers spent the evenings in the towns they passed through, with the women they met.

Not that Chen Fai would be thinking of anything casual like that, of course.

In everything he'd done, he'd shown respect for Charity. He had a home and a business, and he'd want a wife and a son who could take over that business one day. Calling on Charity as he'd done showed that he was thinking about her as a wife.

And Chen Sing must have agreed to his son visiting Charity. He knew enough about Chinese ways by now to know that Chen Fai would never have knocked at the Walker house that day if Chen Sing hadn't given him permission to do so. Chen Sing, too, would be looking at the future.

But he was sure that when Charity agreed to walk with Chen Fai, she was too young to have been thinking about such things. It was Chen Fai's kindness to her that will have been foremost in her mind, contrasting as it did with the way in which the Carter townsfolk treated her. But hopefully, she wouldn't one day confuse her gratitude for the Chen family's friendship with the way in which someone should feel about the person they were going to spend their life with. Such a mistake could cause her great unhappiness.

Then he mentally shook his head and smiled inwardly – he was getting way ahead of himself, thinking of Charity as someone's wife. He took off his hat, smoothed down his hair, put the hat back on and pulled the brim into position. How she would laugh at him if she could see into his mind, he thought as he jumped from the rear of the wagon. She was still only a child, and as far as she was concerned, she and Chen Fai were going for a walk, and that's all there was to it.

But it was time he went back to Carter for a visit, he decided as he walked across the sun-baked ground to join Ethan. He wasn't sure when he'd be able to get there, though, as by the time the drive had ended, it'd be too late to get to Wyoming before the snow set in, and he'd already signed for the round-up the following spring. But after that, he'd keep his eyes open for a drive that finished within striking distance of Carter, and when he found one, he'd go and see Charity and his family. He'd find work in Carter for the winter months, which'd give him time to see how his folks were getting on, check that they'd got what they needed, catch up with Charity and Sam, and then leave again in the spring.

It'd be interesting to see what Charity looked like now she was more than four years older, he mused. She probably still had that wide, happy smile of hers, but would just be a bit taller.

A wave of warmth spread through him as he remembered the trusting way in which she used to slip her little hand into his larger one, and how they'd stand side by side on the craggy peaks overlooking Carter.

Yup, he'd go back as soon as he could. After all, he was responsible for her.

Chapter Twenty-Three

Two and a half years later
Early March, 1885

The knocking was loud on the door.

Charity paused in scraping the mud from the carrots and turnips they'd bought at the company store the evening before, and glanced towards the door in surprise. It wouldn't be Chen Fai, she thought, dipping her hands into the jug of water next to her and wiping them dry on a rag.

With the hatred of the whites for the Chinese getting worse with each passing month, Chen Fai had long ago stopped coming to the Walkers' house.

The moment he'd heard she was looking to work more hours in the town, he'd given her a job in the store, and they'd been able to relax and get to know each other away from the eyes of the white community.

The knocking sounded again with increased urgency.

She smoothed down her pinafore, and moved swiftly across to the door.

'It's all right, Charity; I'll get the door,' Martha called to her, hurrying into the room. 'Finish the carrots before you leave for work if you can – we'll need them this evenin'.'

She went back to the bowl of vegetables and picked up the knife as Martha opened the door.

'Why, Eliza Culpepper!' Martha exclaimed, seeing the woman standing on the doorstep, her breath a cloud of white vapour in the raw morning air. 'This sure is a surprise!

Come on in and sit down. You look real cold, and fair worn out, if I might say.' She stood aside to let her into the room. 'Here; give me your coat and I'll hang it up.'

'Thank you, Martha,' Eliza said.

'You can bring us some milk and biscuits, Charity,' Martha told her, going across to the table. 'And then you can leave for work. I'll finish the vegetables later.'

Charity dried her hands again.

'Oh, no,' Eliza said quickly, glancing anxiously at Charity as she sat down. 'I need the gal's help, Martha. It's Seth; he's ill.'

Martha gave an exclamation of dismay. She leaned across the table and took hold of Eliza's hand. 'Oh, Eliza. I sure am sorry to hear it.'

Tears sprang to Eliza's eyes.

'What's the matter with him?' Martha asked gently. 'Seth's a good man, and whatever's wrong with him, if there's anythin' we can do to help, we'll do it. Hiram will say the same when he gets back from the mine.'

'I'm grateful for your willingness, Martha; it's mighty neighbourly of you,' Eliza said, her voice shaking. 'I confess, I've never been so afear'd. We were sitting at home at the end of the day, like we've been able to do more often recently, now one of the lads is living at the stable, and Seth got up from his chair to go for some water, and fell to the floor. Just like that. Without any warning. He was all bent over, holding his chest real tight, and I could tell from his face that something powerful was paining him.'

'Oh, dear God, Eliza!'

'Curled up like a babe, he was, saying his chest hurt something bad. I'm telling you, he couldn't breathe, and I feared for his life. I sent Greg for the miners' doc – Greg's the new stable lad. Waiting for the doc felt the longest wait

I've ever had. Seth was blue around the mouth by the time he arrived.'

'And what did Doc say?'

'That Seth had probably gotten ill because of anxiety. You know how he frets about the lads not running the stable properly if he's not watching them.'

Martha nodded. 'I know it's gotten to be a worry with him.'

'It's all the different boys he's had working for him. They aren't hard workers like your Joe was. Joe had the right instincts about dealing with horses as well as with folk. These days, Seth always feels he needs to check that the lads've done what they should've done.' Her voice broke.

Martha tightened her grip on Eliza's hand. 'He's gonna be all right, though, isn't he?'

'The doc said so, but only if he rests. He'll be laid up for quite a while. Poor Seth – he's an active man and he'll hate that. And this is the time the livery's starting to get busy.' She broke down in tears, freed her hand from Martha's, dug into her pocket and pulled out a handkerchief. 'You should see him, Martha,' she sobbed. 'He looks so grey and so ill, just lying there.'

'Don't you fret so, Eliza. The doctor knows what he's doin' – he's had to deal with enough minin' accidents and illnesses. And you know he's an honest man – he'd tell you straight out if he thought Seth wasn't gonna make it.'

Eliza nodded. 'I know that,' she said, and she wiped her eyes.

'D'you want Charity to get some herbs like Chinaman Doc gave us for Hiram after his accident? Is that it? She'd do that; wouldn't you, gal?' She turned to Charity.

Charity took a step forward. 'You know I would.'

Eliza blew her nose. Her eyes watering again, she stared

at Martha. 'It's not that, though I reckon those herbs might help. Chen Fai would get them if I asked, and I think I'll do that. I expect Joe told you that Seth drops by the mercantile in the evenings from time to time. But no, it's not that.' She wiped her eyes again. 'It's bigger than that and I sure hate asking, especially with you so busy helping Phebe and Sam with the baby.'

'What is it, then?' Martha asked, her forehead creasing in anxiety.

Eliza took a deep breath. 'Seth's not gonna be able to rest just by staying in bed – he's gotta rest in his mind, too. And that won't happen if he's fretting all the time about what's going on in the stable.'

'I reckon I can see where this is goin', Eliza.'

Her eyes red-rimmed, Eliza stared into Martha's face. 'None of the lads Seth's taken on since the day Joe left could run the stable for more than a week or two. And Greg's only just started. It'll go to ruin, and you know Seth – the stable's his life. If he didn't have that to look forward to …' She pulled out her handkerchief and blew her nose again.

'You want us to ask Joe to come back to Carter and run the stable for Seth till he's back on his feet?' Martha asked gently. 'Is that it?'

Eliza nodded. 'If Joe was running it, Seth'd be able to relax and he'd get better. If we had sons, they'd do it; but we haven't. Your Joe was like a son to him. It'd be for a month or two. Six at the most – probably till the fall. With the snow flying less and starting to melt, someone must soon get down to ordering supplies for the rest of the year, and there are horses to buy and equipment to mend. But it's not Seth asking; it's me. I know it's a lot to ask—'

Martha shook her head. 'It's not a lot to ask, Eliza,' she interrupted. 'Helpin' each other is what neighbours do. Of course, I can't answer for Joe,' she went on, 'but Seth's been a real good friend to him and I'm sure Joe will come back if he can. The snow's still thick on the high ground, but if I know my Joe, he'll find a way of gettin' through to Carter as fast as he can.' She turned to Charity. 'Where's Joe been spendin' the winter months? He won't have moved from there yet.'

'In Kansas. On a cattle ranch just outside Ellsworth.'

'Then you go and send a letter to Ellsworth right now, gal. Let Joe know what's happened as briefly as possible and ask him to come home. A soon as you've written it, take it to the mercantile and tell them it's got to get off sharpish.'

'I'll do it right now,' Charity said, and she hurried out of the room.

'You don't know what your kindness means to me, Martha,' Eliza said with a watery smile, and she squeezed Martha's hand in gratitude.

'Oh, but I do. I still remember what Seth's kindness meant to Joe when Seth gave him a horse and a fine saddle so he could ride off and be a cowboy. That was a generous thing Seth did, and I know Joe will be glad of a chance to say thank you in a way that's not just sayin' it with words.'

'You're making more of what Seth did than it was.'

'No, I'm not. We felt your kindness to us then, and you're gonna feel ours to you now. No matter how old Joe's got, nor how many years it is since he left Carter, I know the way he'll think when he gets that letter. He'll wanna help Seth more than he'll wanna go on the spring round-up.' She vigorously nodded her head.

Eliza's eyes filled with tears again. 'I don't know what to say.'

'There's nothin' to say,' Martha said with a warm smile. 'You just dry those eyes.'

Eliza put the handkerchief to her eyes again. 'I must get back to Seth,' she said, standing up and straightening her bonnet.

Martha got up and went across to fetch Eliza's coat.

'Joe will probably wanna live here, havin' been away so long,' Eliza said as she tightened the ribbons under her chin, 'so Greg will continue to sleep at the stable and keep an eye on the horses at night. But Joe can use the other room in the back for whenever he wants.'

'I'll tell him that. Now, you be sure to give Seth our best wishes, won't you?' Martha said, helping Eliza on with her coat

'I will,' she said, nodding. She paused. 'Joe's been long gone, Martha, and maybe it doesn't suit him to leave off what he's doing at the moment, or maybe the weather's still bad where he is. If that's so, we'll understand, and you're not to feel regretful if you have to tell us he can't come. Happen what may, we're not gonna forget you tried to help us, and for that we'll always be grateful.'

'You think on this, Eliza Culpepper,' Martha said. 'You might just be doin' us a favour, too. It's been seven long years since we last saw Joe, and recently I've had a powerful hankerin' to see him again.'

'As any ma would.'

'And Hiram's of a mind to see him, too, though he'd never say as much. I know Joe'll never stay in Carter as he's got no future here, but we wanna see the man he's become, and you've given us a good reason to ask him to come home, so the gratitude isn't all on one side.'

'But there *is* a future for Joe in Carter, Martha,' Eliza said, pausing at the door. 'If he comes back to the town, you can tell him that if he decides he'd like to stay in Carter after all, he can carry on at the stable with Seth, and the stable will be his one day, along with our house behind it. He'd never have to choose between leaving Carter or going down the mines.'

Martha drew in a sharp breath. She grasped Eliza by the hand, her eyes telling Eliza what she was too overcome to say.

Eliza shrugged. 'Like I say, we've no sons. Joe's always been special to Seth and me. And he always will be, even if he's not able to return.'

Chapter Twenty-Four

Less than an hour had passed after Eliza's leaving when Charity left the house, a letter in her hand, and hurried across the ground between the miners' houses and town holding her skirts high enough to keep them out of the piles of yellowing snow mixed with pit-dust. As soon as she reached the boardwalk, she half-ran to the mercantile store, trying to avoid sliding in the layer of watery slush that coated the slippery boards.

'Why are you here now, Charity? You not work till later,' Chen Fai asked in surprise as she ran into the store, a discordant jangle of wind chimes following in her wake. She came to a stop in front of him, and struggled to catch her breath. 'But I'm very pleased to see you,' he added quickly, putting down the pen with which he'd been marking dried apricots at fifteen cents a pound.

'It's not work, Chen Fai,' she said when she could breathe more easily. 'I've gotta send a letter. It's a letter to Joe, askin' him to come back.' She waved her letter at him.

He saw the excitement that radiated from her eyes, and felt a wave of panic shoot through him. 'To Joe?' he echoed, his voice hollow.

She nodded vigorously. 'Yup. Isn't that a surprise? I can't believe I'm finally gonna see him again. I wonder what he looks like. He'll be back very soon, I hope. Well, maybe not that soon – he's a long way away at the moment. He's in Kansas.' She beamed at Chen Fai.

In spite of the warmth of her smile, he felt cold.

He stared hard at her face, at the expression in her eyes, and the fear he'd been trying to smother for so long broke through and filled his mind with dread.

'Don't look so worried,' she said, laughing. 'I'm not gonna ask to work fewer hours – Joe will have things to do, too.' She hugged herself. 'But just the thought of bein' able to spend some time with him again, and of being able to tell him what I want to without havin' to write it in a letter – I reckon it'll soon be like he never left.'

She paused for breath, and looked around her, her happiness lighting up the store.

A piece of paper fell to the floor from the counter, unnoticed. 'But he did leave,' he said flatly. 'And you are asking him to come back to Carter now?'

'Not me – it's Eliza Culpepper. I guess you'll have already heard that Seth's ill. Well, they want Joe to come back and run the livery stable till Seth's fit enough to run it himself again. As you may have guessed,' she said with a giggle, 'I'm real excited at the thought of seein' Joe again. It's been a long time.'

'I'm very happy for you,' he said, his smile not quite reaching his eyes. He went round the end of the counter, came up to her and took the letter from her. 'I send this to Joe now,' he said. He stood a moment, staring down at Joe's name, then he looked back at her. 'You like Joe very much,' he said quietly. 'I think you feel about him like you would feel about a big brother.'

She stared at him, startled. 'No, I don't!' she exclaimed. 'He's my friend. But he's not like a brother and never has been. No, I've never thought of him like that.' She frowned slightly. 'And I'm sure he's never thought of me as bein' like a sister to him.' She looked back at Chen Fai, her eyes questioning, then her face cleared and she smiled. 'No, Joe's a friend; that's all. Big brothers are like you are to Su Lin. You're a good brother to her.'

'Thank you,' he said solemnly. He paused. 'You are

very good friend of Su Lin, and we do many family things together, you, me and Su Lin. Maybe you think about me as if I am a big brother to you, too.' He paused. 'Do you?' he asked. His gaze returned to the letter to Joe.

Hearing the awkwardness in his voice, and suddenly conscious that they were alone in the store, she felt a strange sensation spread through her. Her heart seemed to stop beating, stilled by a sudden awareness she couldn't put into words. Slowly she shook her head. 'No,' she said. 'Not at all.'

'You think of me in same way as you think of Joe?' His eyes were still on the letter.

She shook her head again. 'No; I don't.'

He raised his eyes from the letter to stare into her face.

At the expression that flooded his gaze, she drew in her breath, and held it.

'When I am in room on my own, Charity, I think of many ways to say this. Is very strange for me to be saying this. In China, this is for go-between to say. But we in America now and there is no go-between. Su Lin is in back room with honourable father's second wife, and honourable father is in *tong*. So we now alone. Maybe now is good time to say something I wait long time to say.'

She gulped. Staring up at him, her lips parted slightly.

'I very happy if you will be my wife, Charity,' he said. 'Will you?'

A formless thought flooded her mind, and panic rose within her. She tried to reach out and grasp the thought, but it was too vague, too insubstantial for her to take hold of it and give it shape, and slowly it faded, taking her panic with it.

She looked up into the warm brown eyes of Chen Fai, the man who'd shown her nothing but kindness from the moment he'd discovered her friendship with Su Lin, the man who'd increasingly tried to protect her from the taunts of the whites and who could be trusted to keep her safe, the man who was offering her a home where she'd be welcome for the rest of her life, and where she wouldn't cause them to be shunned by their community.

'I guess so,' she said, and she gave him a shy smile.

Chapter Twenty-Five

Two weeks later
Late March, 1885

'Ethan,' Joe called, hurrying across to Ethan, who was brushing his saddle blanket. 'I've gotta go back to Carter, and I've gotta go real soon.'

Ethan stood still, brush in hand, and stared at Joe in surprise. 'How come? I thought we were gonna head to San Antonio as soon as the snows had melted, and then ride the Chisholm Trail to Caldwell. We've already been taken on for the drive.'

'And that would still be my plan if I hadn't just gotten this letter.' He held up the piece of paper in his hand. 'I reckon it's the shortest letter Charity's ever written. They're askin' me to get back home as fast as I can. You remember the man I told you about, Seth Culpepper, the man who owns the livery stable where I used to work?'

'The one who gave you your first horse and saddle?'

'Yup; that's the one. Well, he's laid up and will be a while. He was always real good to me, and now it's my turn to help him by runnin' the stable till he's back on his feet and able to work again. That won't be till the fall, they reckon.'

'It's nice of you to be willin' to go back just like that.'

'Not really, it isn't. He's been a good friend to me. And to tell you the truth, I've been thinkin' for some time now that I oughta go home. It's seven years since I left.' He paused a moment. 'And I've also been thinkin' that maybe my next drive oughta be my last.'

Ethan stared ruefully at him. 'Well, I can't say I'm

surprised. You've bin seemin' restless recently. Seven years atop a horse from the time the sun comes up till it goes down at night, and workin' through all the winter months on one ranch after another – I guess that's about long enough for most men.'

Joe nodded. 'You're right about me feelin' restless. I reckon I'm about ready to settle down.'

Ethan nodded slowly. 'That's good thinkin', Joe. You've always said you wanted a ranch, but a drover's life's a real hard life, and if you let it, it'll use up all your strength, and you won't be left with enough to set up on your own. You're stoppin' at the right time.'

'That's my way of lookin' at it, too.'

'And, of course, with your brother married and him a pa now, it's not surprisin' you're thinkin' about gettin' yourself a wife, too,' Ethan added with a wry smile.

'Who's said anythin' about a wife?' Joe exclaimed.

Ethan grinned at him. 'You didn't need to. I seen the way the gals in town look at you, and the way you look back at them. But you ain't gonna find the right gal for you if you're always on the move. I didn't, and you won't.' He paused. 'So when are you settin' off?'

'Right now, if you'll oblige me by explainin' what's happened to the ranch foreman. I've over a month of hard riding ahead of me, and it's not gonna be an easy journey.'

Ethan nodded. 'I'll tell him,' he said, 'and I'll get you an extra blanket for the nights. You'll need it – it'll be real cold sleepin' beneath the stars when the sun's gone down.' He started to turn away.

'Wait a minute, Ethan,' Joe said quickly.

Ethan turned back to him. 'What's up?'

'I know I'm gonna see you again, but I just wanna say how grateful I am that I had you for a trail partner when

I started out, and that we've always been able to work together since then. Luck was on my side the day I met you. You've been a good friend: you've taught me what I needed to know; you've seen that we've had interestin' drives led by foremen who knew what they were doin' and you've always found us somewhere to work over winter that was real congenial. I appreciate that.'

Ethan gestured for Joe to stop.

'Not till I've finished,' Joe said, smiling. 'I owe you a lot, Ethan. I've now seen enough and listened to enough people to know there are a lot of drovers who aren't as lucky as I've been and who've had it mighty hard. Many have had to work long hours for little more than food and clothin'. I've had a better experience than that, and that's thanks to you.'

Ethan shrugged. 'There's a lot of men drivin' cows who haven't got your skill or education, and I guess many of those are the ones who're linin' the bottom of the barrel. Same can be said of any job.'

'True, but my greenness of youth has long since passed and I can see that this is a more difficult job than many. That I've had such a swell time of it is thanks to you.' He smiled at Ethan. 'That's what I wanted to say, and now I've said it.'

'You sure did,' Ethan drawled. 'And I thank you.' He paused. 'But to go back to now, I'll not expect to see you till after winter, and if you don't make it back for the spring round-up, or for any other, you be sure to keep in touch.'

'You bet I will.'

'Drop a line to me in Caldwell, and I'll let you know where I'll be after that. After all, one day you might need someone who knows about horses and cattle to help you out on that ranch of yours.' He grinned at Joe, raised his hand in a slight wave, and turned away.

'You're gonna have to learn to sleep real quiet then,' Joe called after him, laughing. 'I don't wanna have to deal nightly with a stampede of frightened cows.'

Ethan stopped walking and turned back to Joe. He gave him a slow smile. 'Stay safe, my friend,' he said, and he turned away again and continued walking.

Chapter Twenty-Six

Early May, 1885

Light on sleep after weeks of heavy riding, Joe's tired gaze swept across the plain that was frosted lilac in the chill of the dying day, to Carter Town. His weary eyes traced the charcoal-grey outline of the roofs and the jagged shapes of the rocky peaks behind them, shadowy structures that reached up and slowly dissolved into the darkening sky.

His first glimpse of the town for more than seven years.

As he sat there, his mind went back to the many times he'd wandered across the plain as a lad – sometimes alone, sometimes with Charity – and a wave of strong emotion ran through him. His family was out there among that haze of grey wooden houses, and he was going to be seeing them soon. And suddenly that felt very strange.

Chilled to the bone at having taken to the saddle as soon as dawn had begun to streak the leaden sky with bands of yellow-grey light, and at having ridden hard all day, as he'd done each day since he'd left the ranch, he hugged his arms around himself to bring heat to his body as he stared at the town ahead.

Then he turned slightly to the right. His eyes followed the indistinct line of the gully carved out by the river, the view broken at intervals by the row of miners' houses with their stovepipe chimneys. Day after day, he'd panned for gold in that water, he remembered, his heart brim-full with the hope of the young. It may have been years ago, but it was as alive in his mind as if it had been yesterday.

Beneath the red bandanna wrapped around the lower part of his face for warmth, he smiled.

He really ought to complete his journey before he got much colder, he thought, but sitting there in the deep silence of the gathering darkness, gazing across the plain as its mantle deepened into a purplish hue, he felt a strange reluctance to move.

It was nervousness, he knew. There would be many changes in Carter that he already knew about, but there were sure to be others he didn't.

The letters he'd gotten from Charity had kept Carter vivid in his mind, but they would have told only a part of what had happened over the years, just as his letters had merely skimmed the surface of his life. The lad of seventeen, who'd cinched his horse and ridden away from the town to become a cowboy, was a very different person from the man who was returning. So, too, there would have been significant changes in the town and, more importantly, in those he was about to meet again.

And that was a daunting thought.

The wind changed direction and he shivered. He'd forgotten how cold the spring evenings could be.

His ma and pa would show signs of age, and in addition his pa would show the effects of his mining accident. Sam would probably still be Sam. Becoming the head of a family of his own, and renting his own house, might have mellowed him a bit, and he'd like to think it would have done, but he wasn't about to wager any money on it.

And as for Charity … well, she'd still be a young girl, although not quite as young as when he'd left, and she'd be taller, for sure.

He grinned to himself as he pictured the wide beam that would spread across her face when she opened the door and saw him standing there, and the outpouring of excitement that would follow. Seeing her again was going to be one of the best things about coming home.

A sudden longing to complete his journey swept away his nervousness. He clapped his gloved hands together to bring some warmth back into them, gathered the reins and pressured the horse's flanks with the heels of his brown leather boots. As the horse eagerly picked up pace, he urged it faster and faster until soon he was galloping hell-bent across the mottled ground that lay between him and his family.

And then he was back in Carter.

With his harness slung over one shoulder, his leather saddle bag over the other, and the brim of his Stetson hooding his eyes against the cold, Joe pulled the bandanna down from his face, knocked on the door of the wooden house and took a step back.

In his mind's eye, he pictured Charity's expression when she opened the door. He could almost touch the excitement he felt.

From inside the house, he heard steps coming towards the door. The door started to open. His face broke out into a smile. The door opened wider. Caught in shadow, a slight figure stood in the doorway.

It wasn't Charity; it was his mother.

He felt the sharp stab of disappointment.

His smile faded slightly and he stood motionless as his mother stared at him, one hand on the door, the other on its wooden frame.

As he felt her questioning gaze on his face – the face of a man, not a boy; a face shadowed by the brim of a hat and several days' growth of beard – a huge surge of love swept through him for the woman in front of him, her dark brown hair now streaked with grey, her face etched with lines of worry that hadn't been there the last time he'd seen her.

His smile broadened again.

She blinked a couple of times. Then her face cleared and broke out into a smile of pure joy.

'Joe.' His name was a long low sigh of delight. She brought her hands together in front of her mouth. 'You're my Joe.'

Love filled her face, and with a cry, she stepped forward into the arms he'd opened wide for her. His arms closed around her and he hugged her tightly.

Still embracing her, he stepped into the house, pushed the door shut behind him with the heel of his boot, hugged her more tightly and then dropped his arms. Slipping the leather bag off his shoulder, he let it fall to the floor and threw the harness on top of it. Then he took off his hat, hung it on a peg by the door and turned to his mother.

'That's better,' he said. 'Now let's have a look at you, Ma.' He put a hand on each of her shoulders and held her at arms' length. 'Why, I do believe you look just the same as on the day when I left, if not a bit younger.'

Laughing, she moved back. 'I see you've picked up a real sweet way of talkin',' she said, tucking some loose grey hairs into the bun that hung low on the back of her head. 'It don't fool me, though. The years have left their mark on me, just like they have on your pa.' She nodded towards the chair in the corner of the room near the potbelly stove.

Joe turned from his mother and saw Hiram. He had risen to his feet and was leaning on his stick, smiling at him, silent tears rolling down his cheeks.

He took a step towards him. 'Pa,' he said, and he

stopped, his voice catching in his throat as he saw the stance of the man whose back had been straight when he'd left and whose face had been free of the damage wrought by pain.

'Your pa's leg's never really healed,' Martha said quietly. 'That's the mine for you; not that we're complainin' – at least they've taken him on again. That's Sam's doin'. It's more than's happened to some who've had accidents.'

In a moment, Joe was at his father's side, his arms around him. 'I missed you, Pa,' he said, emotion cracking his voice. 'I sure missed both you and Ma.'

Hiram pulled back and stared up into Joe's face, tracing his features with eyes full of tears. 'There was a time I thought I'd never see you again, son,' he said, shaking his head. 'They were dark days, indeed.'

'Well, you were wrong, weren't you? I'm here now, aren't I?' Joe said. 'Here, sit down. I'll help you.' And he helped Hiram back into his chair.

'You both sit down while I finish gettin' the dinner ready. You'll be fair hungry, I reckon, after all that ridin', Joe.'

He grinned at her. 'You reckon aright,' he said, and he sat down opposite his father. He glanced towards the corridor leading to the bedrooms. 'I didn't expect to see Sam here now as I know he's got a place of his own, but where's Charity? I figured she'd be in by now, helpin' with the dinner.'

'She'll be back real soon,' Martha called, coming out of the store-closet. 'She still does a few hours for Ah Lee, as well as her hours in the mercantile. But I expect you know that.'

'She always was a hardworkin' kid,' Joe remarked. 'But she still found time to write and I'll always be grateful to her for that. I've never felt as far from you as I was at times 'cos I've always known what's goin' on. Like Sam gettin' wed. And now a pa, too!' He laughed. 'I really can't see him as anyone's pa. D'you see much of him these days?'

'Rather more than we'd expected,' Hiram said dryly. 'He's got a house further down the row in the new houses and he stops by most nights on his way back home. Wants us to think it's to talk about minin' things, but your ma and I reckon it's to cut down on the amount of time he has to spend with that wife of his. She's got a sharp tongue on her, has Phebe.'

'And a real cheerless way of lookin' at things,' Martha called. 'We didn't see that at first. When she started walkin' out with Sam, she seemed a pleasant enough gal. If he'd kept walkin' a mite bit longer, he might've seen the other side of her before it was too late.'

Joe glanced round at her. 'I'm pickin' up that you and Pa don't like her.'

'I wouldn't put it as strong as that,' Martha said, taking some flapjacks from a stoneware storage jar and putting them on to a dish. 'We don't really know the gal.'

Hiram shrugged. 'Like your ma says, we don't know her. We've not seen enough of her to know one way or the other. They hardly ever came here when they were walkin' out together so we didn't get to know her afore they wed, and nothin' much has changed since.'

'Only time we see her is when she wants somethin',' Martha said, going across to Joe and pulling a stool to the side of his chair. 'She's here fast enough when she's run out of food, or when she wants us to mind the boy, or when she wants help with the washin', but that's about it.' She put the plate of flapjacks and a glass of milk on to the stool. 'Dinner isn't quite ready. You get that down you while you're waitin'.'

'Thanks, Ma.' He took a flapjack, and bit into it. 'My,

these are tasty. I'd forgotten what a good cook you are.' He took another bite. 'Phebe can't have been the only gal around,' he went on, 'so how come Sam married her? Sam was a good-lookin' lad, and I'm guessin' he's the same as a man, so surely he could have had his pick.'

Hiram leaned back. 'And that's what he had. She's a real pretty gal, I'll say that for her. One look at her blonde hair and blue eyes, and Sam was actin' like a lovesick pup. But after a few months, he started to see that Phebe had quite a tongue on her and was given to complainin', and she suddenly stopped lookin' quite so pretty to him. He told me he was fair worn out by the naggin' and he was gonna stop callin' on her. After all, they hadn't got an understandin' in so many words.'

'And if he'd limited himself to walkin' and talkin', he could've done just that,' Martha said, bitterness in her voice.

Hiram shrugged. 'Your ma's right. By the time he'd seen beyond the pretty face, it was too late, and he did the only thing he could – he wed her before her pa had time to load his rifle.'

'Let that be a lesson to you, Joe,' Martha said sharply. 'Sam should've kept his trousers done up.'

He laughed. 'I'll remember that, Ma.' He shifted his position. 'I must say, I never thought I'd find myself feelin' sorry for Sam, but listenin' to you both, I do.'

'Changin' the subject, does Seth know you're here?' Hiram asked as Martha went back to the kitchen area, pulled out a drawer and started taking out some cutlery.

Joe nodded. 'I looked in at the stable before comin' here, and I left my horse and bedroll there. The stable lad's gonna wipe him down, grain him and find him a clean bed to lie in. After that, he's gonna take a message across to Seth, tellin' him I'll be callin' on him first thing tomorrow. Or second thing rather,' he said, ruefully rubbing his hand across his chin. 'I reckon my first visit's gotta be to the barber's to get my face shaven. It wasn't easy to shave myself on the ride from Ellsworth.'

'Seth'll be mighty pleased to see you. And Eliza, too,' Martha said, carrying the cutlery and plates across to the table. 'There's a room at the back of the livery for you to use if you need to stop there the night, but there'll always be a meal for you here and a bed. You must do whatever's best for you, lad.'

'Best for me is stayin' with my ma and pa and gettin' to know them again,' Joe said, smiling at Martha and Hiram. 'I'm sure there'll be times when I stretch out in the back room at the stable, but for as long as I'm home, home is where I wanna sleep whenever possible.'

Martha beamed at him. 'After Sam wed, I moved Charity into the room you used to share with Sam, but you must have your room back.'

'Leave Charity where she is, Ma. I'll take her old room. It's still cold at nights, and it will be for a while yet. She'll be warmer inside the house. And also, I'll have to be at the stable on bad nights, keepin' a watchful eye on the horses – we may well have some more storms and late snow blizzards. Nope; you leave Charity where she is. I prefer to think of her bein' inside the house.'

'Well, I will, if you're happy with that,' Martha said, starting to put the cutlery around the table. 'She's a lucky gal.'

'I guess you won't have heard yet, Joe!' Hiram suddenly exclaimed.

'Heard what?'

'That Charity's gettin' wed. Chen Fai offered for her a few

weeks ago, just after she wrote to you. Not that we were surprised – he set his little black cap at her the moment he knew he wouldn't be able to marry that gal of his in China. He either had to go huntin' in one of the other towns around here that's fillin' up with the Chinee, or marry Charity. He's got big ideas for the store, and he obviously wants a wife real bad, and a son to take over the store one day.'

'But we were a bit surprised he offered for Charity when he did,' Martha said, looking up, 'even though they'd been walkin' out for years.' She straightened up. 'Your pa and I think he might have been pushed into it by the arrival of Ah Lee's son. He's just moved into Carter, and like Chen Fai, he could be thinkin' about gettin' himself a wife. And we figure Chen Fai might have thought that, too.'

'But isn't she a bit young to think of marryin'?' Joe asked in surprise. 'I know I've been gone a bit, but she's still not much more than a kid.'

'She's seventeen now – same age as you were when you rode off,' Martha said dryly. 'You were old enough to know what you wanted, and so is she. Chen Fai seems a kind, gentle sort of man, and I'm sure he'll always be good to her.'

'Your ma's right about the man,' Hiram said. He grinned at Martha. 'And it's nothin' to do with the fact that he gives us presents and smiles and bows to us real nice. At least, he used to when he was able to come by here.'

Martha made a noise of impatience. 'You're bein' silly, Hiram Walker. I don't take note of things like that. I like him; that's all. And it makes sense, him and Charity gettin' wed. She's gotta marry someone and it means she'll stay in Carter and we'll be able to watch her babes grow up. I've gotten used to her bein' here and I wouldn't want to see her go miles away.'

'I like him, too,' Hiram said. 'But I don't underestimate him. For all his kindly ways, I reckon there's a streak of iron runnin' down the centre of the man, and I don't think I'd wanna cross him. Mind you, havin' a streak of iron's not a bad thing these days. You have to be tough to keep a Chinese business going in a town where they hate the Chinee.'

Martha stood still and stared at him in surprise. 'I don't know why you should think like that about him; he's never been anythin' but kind and helpful to us.'

'You're right about that. But when you sit for long stretches of time, as I did afore I returned to the mine, you get to watchin' people, and you see things you'd never've seen if you'd bin workin' every hour of the day. From the moment it was clear Chen Fai had intentions towards Charity, I've been watchin' him. I'm fond of the gal and I wouldn't wanna see her wed to the wrong man.'

'Nor would I,' Martha retorted. 'But I believe he genuinely likes her.'

'So do I. And things bein' as they are in Carter today, I figure he's the right man to be at her side. I'm just sayin' that I wouldn't wanna be the person who tried to cross him.'

'I know she won't be goin' far, but I guess you'll miss her when she's no longer livin' here,' Joe said. 'Both of you will. She helps you with the chores, Ma, and I know she still reads to you whenever she can, Pa.'

Martha stopped laying the table, and stared at Joe. 'To speak true, I'm glad she's gonna leave here and live at the mercantile.'

'How come?' Joe asked in surprise. 'She's a great help to you.'

'The whites don't like us havin' a China woman in the house. They've been making that very clear for years now,

185

and the more Chinee who settle here, the worse it gets. Most whites don't speak to us any more, and that includes the Oaklands next door. They all wanna see the Chinee driven out of Carter, and us after them. I just worry where it'll end. When Charity moves out, I reckon I'll feel more comfortable goin' into the town than I do now. But you're right; I've got used to her help, and I'm gonna miss it.'

'I know Chinese wives live with their husband's family,' Joe said, 'and they often don't see their own family again. But despite her blood, she's more American than Chinese, and I'm sure she'll come back and give you a hand from time to time.'

'I don't want her to,' Martha said bluntly. 'Like you said, she's not so Chinese she'll let herself be cut off from the people that brought her up, and she's told me she'll come back and help. But it's better for us if she doesn't.'

'I didn't know things had gotten so bad between the whites and the Chinese,' Joe said slowly.

'Well, they have,' Martha said, putting the plates down on the table.

'When's the weddin'?' he asked after a few minutes.

Martha shrugged. 'You'll have to ask Charity that. She hasn't told us yet. I don't know if they've even decided. And I don't know where they'll wed. There's a Chinese priest in Carter now, but there's no temple in town, or joss-house, which is what Charity said they call their church. They use the *tong* for anythin' to do with religion, and for just about everythin' else it seems, so I guess it'll happen there. Chen Sing had a wife when he arrived in Carter, so we've never had a Chinese weddin' here. And if there had been one,' she added, 'I still wouldn't know how they went about it as the whites would've kept far away.'

Joe shook his head. 'I'm findin' it real hard to think of little Charity gettin' wed.'

Martha raised her eyebrows slightly, then went across to the sink, picked up an earthenware pitcher, felt the temperature of the water inside with her finger, and poured some of the water into a bowl in the sink. 'There's some water to wash in,' she said. 'I'll fill the tub after we've eaten and you can have a bath then.'

'Thanks, Ma.' He paused. 'Learnin' about Charity's a bit of a surprise, I must confess. But at least I already know just about all the other changes I'm gonna find in Carter.'

'Don't be too sure about that. You've been gone a long time, Joe. Readin' about it is one thing; seein' it for yourself is another.'

'There were two mines when I left, and now there're four, so I'm expectin' the town to be bigger and dirtier. And I imagine that means even more work for the Marshal.'

'You're right about the size. But it's not just the whites' part of town that's grown; Chinatown's bigger too. And I don't know if Charity told you, but the whites have gotten themselves a club and it's stirrin' up hatred in town. It's one of the reasons why things have gotten worse. But you've plenty of time to catch up, son. Come and wash while the water's still warm, and then sit at the table. You, too, Hiram. The meal's ready and we can start eatin'.'

'What about Charity?' Joe asked, getting up.

'She'll be home any minute. Just put your things against the back wall, out of the way, will you?'

Joe helped Hiram to his feet and they went to the sink. When they'd finished washing, Hiram sat down at the table while Joe went and picked up his bag and harness from the floor and carried them to the back of the room. Just as he reached the rear wall, he heard a sound outside the front door. He felt a surge of excitement. Dropping his things on the floor, he spun round to face the door.

It swung open, and Charity entered, a rush of cold air blowing in with her.

'It sure is chilly this evenin',' she said, hastily pushing the door shut behind her. 'I'm beginnin' to think it'll never be hot again.' She pulled off her coat, hung it on the peg next to the door, turned to face the room, a smile on her face – and saw Joe.

Her breath caught in her throat, and her smile faded.

Her arms fell to her sides and she took a few steps towards him. Then she stopped walking, put her hands to her mouth and stared at him in wonder, her dark eyes drinking him in.

'Oh, Joe,' she said, her voice a whisper that escaped between her fingers. 'You're back.'

He stood there, unable to move, his eyes on her face.

'Why, you're beautiful, Charity,' he said at last, his voice coming from somewhere far away from him. 'Real beautiful.'

Chapter Twenty-Seven

His hand on his mug of coffee, Joe leaned against the back of his chair and stared across the table at Charity, who was sitting at the other end. 'You must be tired,' he said. 'You should've done what Ma and Pa did, gone to bed.'

She smiled at him. 'No point. I wouldn't be able to sleep, not now you're here again.' She glanced at him shyly. 'Every time I wrote to you, I tried to picture what you'd look like, bein' older and workin' real hard. But in my head you always looked like you did when you left. Maybe a bit taller. But now I don't have to imagine you any more because I can see you.'

'I'm afraid it's not a pretty sight,' he said ruefully, running his hand through his sun-streaked brown hair. 'I gotta get to the barber first thing in the mornin' to have my hair cut and this beard shaved off.'

'But your eyes are the same. They're the bluest eyes I've ever seen. And they look even bluer now you've got such a brown face.'

'Are you tryin' to tell me you think of saddle leather when you look at me?' he asked with a grin.

She giggled.

'You look all grown-up, Charity,' he said, his voice smiling at her. 'But you've still got that real cute way of laughin'.'

A blush spread over her cheeks, and she took a sip of her coffee. 'I knew you'd come home when you got my letter.' She stopped and looked at him, her face suddenly anxious. 'Or don't you feel like it's home any more, now you've been gone for so long? Your ma said you might prefer to live at the stable on your own.'

He looked around the room, then his gaze returned to her. 'Nope, this still feels like home. Bein' on the move all the time – out on the range in the summer; on someone's ranch over winter – you're never long enough in any one place to pick up any feelin' for it. And anyway, it was like a part of me was still in Carter, even though it wasn't, 'cos I always knew what was goin' on in the house and the town. I appreciated your letters more than I can say, Charity.'

'I'm glad,' she said. 'I liked writin' to you. It made me feel you were still close by.'

Their eyes met. They stared at each other for a long moment, the length of the table between them, then Charity dropped her eyes and took another sip of her coffee.

Joe glanced towards the windows. 'If it wasn't so cold, we could've sat outside on our chairs like we used to do at times when you were little.' He turned back to look at her. 'Or perhaps you're too grown up now,' he said. He gave an awkward laugh. 'You kinda take my breath away. I was expectin' a little girl with a round face and a big wide smile. I wasn't expectin' you as you are now, all grown up and lookin' lovely. I don't really know how to talk to you any more.'

'You're doin' real well,' she said quietly.

'I'm glad.'

They smiled at each other.

'I'll never be too grown up to sit outside with you,' she said, breaking the silence that had fallen upon them. 'I'd've liked that, too. D'you remember the day I started school and came home and almost cut off my braids?' She pulled a face. 'And we sat outside and talked after that?'

He laughed. 'I certainly do – I had a shock that day.'

'You gave me this. Look.' She put her hand into her pinafore pocket and pulled out the wooden brooch. Leaning across the table, she showed it to him. 'I always keep my golden tiger with me. It reminds me of my ma, and it reminds me of you. You saved my life, Joe.' She closed her hand over the brooch and put it back in her pocket. 'I'm never gonna forget that.'

'You're makin' more of it than it was,' he said, awkwardness in his voice.

'No, I'm not – it's the truth. Like you said, I've grown up. I now know what would've happened to me if your folks had left me at the railway office that day – the railway people would've taken me out of town and left me somewhere in the open to die. Chen Fai told me. Your ma and pa knew that, so they kept me. But they only kept me because you begged them to.'

He nodded slowly. 'That's as may be. But they've never regretted their decision. Not for so much as one day in the past seventeen years. None of us have, and that's also the truth.'

She pushed her empty mug away from her. 'You were only here for ten of those years, Joe, so you don't know what it's like in Carter now, with the whites hatin' the Chinese like they do. I know you haven't regretted takin' me in, and I know your pa hasn't.'

'And nor has ma,' he said quickly.

'Maybe she has; maybe she hasn't. Maybe regret is the wrong word. I believe she's grown fond of me in her own way and I'm certain she's never wished that she and your pa had left me to die—not at all. But at the same time, she's real unhappy. She feels the whites' meanness more than your pa. I've heard Sam tell your ma that the miners see your pa workin' real hard, anxious to keep his job, and they leave him alone. Your ma reckons they look at his leg and figure he's had his punishment. And he's so tired all of the time he wouldn't notice anythin', anyway. But they turn away from your ma; no one talks to her now. Nope, I'm sure that whatever she now feels about me, she's got some regret that you ever found me, and I don't blame her. And Sam certainly has – he hates me.'

Joe straightened up. 'I'm sure you're wrong about that. I know you've never been close to Sam, him bein' much older and already down the mine at the time you were growin' up, but that don't mean he hates you.'

'He does,' she said bluntly. 'Not me as a person – after all, he doesn't know me – but he hates all the Chinese, and I'm Chinese. Like all the whites, he's afear'd for his job. I'm not blind – I can see the miners workin' harder each year and takin' home less.'

Joe sat back in his chair and stared at her. 'Why, Charity; you just said somethin' I've never heard you say before – you said, "I'm Chinese".' There was a tinge of sadness in the smile he gave her. 'The little girl I knew always insisted she was American.'

A slow smile spread across her face. 'And I'll always be American in my head, Joe, and in my heart, even though I'm gonna have to do some things the Chinese way in future. But to the whites, I'll always be Chinese. Chen Fai made me see that. And not just see it, accept it.'

'He's been a good friend to you,' Joe said. He paused. 'But when I used to say you should have another friend apart from me, I was thinkin' more about Su Lin than her brother,' he added with a wry grin.

She smiled. 'You were right about Su Lin, and you were right about me needin' a friend. I'll always stay friends with Su Lin, even when she's wed. They're lookin' for a husband for her now, but it'll be someone in Carter so she'll carry on livin' here, which I'm pleased about. I'd miss her if she moved away. It might even be Ah Lee's son. He used to work for Ah Lee's brother in San Francisco, but he's just moved to Carter to live with his folks.'

He smiled. 'Well, you've got two friends now that I'm back; three, if you count Chen Fai.'

She laughed. 'You're right; I have. But you'll be goin' away again, and then it'll be only two.'

He looked at her in surprise. 'What makes you say that? You heard Ma tell me at dinner that I'll have Seth's livery one day if I want it. And his house, too. Don't you think I'd stay here if I had a business of my own?'

She shook her head. 'No, I don't. For as long as I can remember, you've wanted to live somewhere else. You've always wanted wide open spaces and green fields, somewhere with clean air, where you can't hear a mine pump.'

'But I'd get to ride outside the town each day if I worked at the stable. Horses need regular exercise.'

She stared at him, disbelief on her face. 'Are you sayin' you don't think you'd get restless being tied to a business that keeps you in a town – a minin' town at that, with dirt and coal-dust everywhere? Because I think you would. You'll stay until Seth's well enough to start runnin' the stable again, and then you'll leave.'

'You might be right; I don't know,' he said, staring into his coffee. Then he looked across the table at her and smiled. 'I don't know about Su Lin, but there's definitely gonna be at least one weddin' in Carter from what I hear. Ma and Pa tell me you're gettin' married.'

Her eyes widened in surprise. 'I didn't think you knew,' she said, and she gave an embarrassed laugh.

'You're gonna wed Chen Fai, aren't you?'

She bit her lip. 'I guess so.'

He stared at her, frowning slightly. 'Pa said you accepted his offer a few weeks ago. That's right, isn't it?'

She nodded.

'It's what you want, isn't it?'

She nodded again. 'Of course. He's a good man.' She stood up. 'I should go to bed now. It's late.' She started to turn away.

He rose quickly to his feet and moved to stand between her and the corridor.

She stopped.

Glancing up at him in sudden nervousness, at the strong planes of his face that was only inches away from hers, a sudden heat rose within her at the physical closeness of the man himself. This was no longer the laughing young Joe of her dreams, but a Joe made of flesh and blood; a Joe who was lean and beautiful, with eyes as deep blue as the summer sky; a Joe who carried the wildness of the open range with him, whose movements spoke of power and strength.

Every muscle in her body tightened.

She dragged her eyes from his face and stared down at the pine floorboards.

'A good man, is he?' she heard him say, his voice low. 'Well, I guess that's a reason to marry someone. But me, if I was about to get wed, I'd wanna be able to say somethin' more than that she was a good woman. Is there anythin' more you can say about him, Charity?'

She looked back up into his face, and a shiver ran down her spine.

'Good night, Joe,' she said, and she took a step back. 'I'm tired.'

They stood for a moment, each gazing at the other. Then she turned away from him, took a kerosene lamp from the shelf on the wall, went to her bedroom and closed the door firmly behind her. Putting the lamp on the bedside table, she lay down on the bed in which Joe used to sleep, and stared at the ceiling, her eyes wide open.

Chapter Twenty-Eight

'So this is where you are!' Sam's voice reverberated throughout the livery.

Joe looked up from the metal bit he'd been polishing, dropped the bit on to the pile of newly cleaned equipment on the ground next to his stool, and stood up. 'Where else would I be?' he asked, smiling broadly as he went across to the entrance to where Sam was standing, a dark silhouette framed by the bright morning light that fell through the open entrance.

'Do I hug you, brother, or shake your hand?' Joe asked, pulling off his leather gloves.

Leaning slightly back, Sam put up his hands, his palms facing Joe. 'We'll take that as done.'

Joe shrugged his shoulders and took a step back into the stable.

'Ma wants to know if you're eatin' with them this evenin'. She didn't know if you'd be through here in time. She can save the meal for you, but she hopes you'll be there. And she wants me there, too. I sure can tell you're back,' he added, a note of malice creeping into his voice. 'Pa tells me that Ma ain't stopped smilin' since you got home. I've been here for all the time you've bin gone, supportin' them, but that don't count.'

'I'm sure that's not true,' Joe said with a smile. 'But about tonight, I'm eatin' with Seth and Eliza. I was gonna walk across and tell Ma. There're things I've gotta talk about with Seth.'

Sam nodded. 'Yup; she thought you'd say that. And she said if you couldn't be there tonight, what about tomorrow?'

'Tomorrow would be good.'

'I'll tell her.' Sam turned and started to walk away.

'Hey, Sam,' Joe called after him.

Sam stopped where he was and turned. 'Yeah?'

'Is that all you've gotta say after seven years – are you comin' to dinner? There's nothin' else you wanna say?'

Sam visibly thought for a moment. 'Nope; I guess not.'

'Not even to ask how it's been with me? Or to tell me you've got a wife and a child? Ma tells me your boy's name's Thomas.'

'Yup, Thomas it is. But as you already seem to know all there is to know, there's nothin' for me to add, except maybe that your Celestial's gonna be wed. Oh, but I expect you know that, too.' He came back towards Joe, feigned sorrow on his face. 'It must be a real disappointment for you, brother, to come back home when she's all grown up and ripe for the takin', and find you're not gonna be able to use her in the only way a China woman should be used by a white. But if it's the thought of Celestials that keeps you awake at night, I'm sure you'll find what you want at the *tong*. Or maybe Su Lin will open her legs for you – after all, she's got yellow skin, too.'

Joe's fingers tightened into two fists.

Sam glanced pointedly at Joe's hands. 'You wanna hit me, Joe?' he said, and he laughed and held his arms open wide. 'Go on, then. Marshal McGregor might have somethin' to say about it, but at least you'll know you behaved like a man and defended that Chinee's honour. What's more, I'll stand stock-still so you won't be able to miss. And I'll even promise not to hit you back. Can't say better than that.'

Grinning at Joe, he moved closer and stood facing him, his arms hanging loosely at his sides.

Shaking his head, Joe relaxed his fingers. 'You'd like

that, I'm sure. I'm real sorry to say this as I'd be happy to oblige, but I'm gonna hold off. I'm here to help Seth, and I can't do that from jail. And there's Ma and Pa to think of, too. They matter; you don't.' He took his gloves from the pockets of his jeans and put them back on. 'The last seven years haven't been good to you, Sam. I don't recognise you any longer.'

Turning away from his brother, he went across to his stool and bent to pick up the cleaning rag, the weight of Sam's dislike pressing heavily against his back.

Lying on the narrow bed in the room at the rear of the stable, his fingers locked behind his head, Joe listened to one of the horses kicking the wooden wall of its stall. A moment later another horse whinnied. He lay still, listening to them, waiting for them to settle before going across to have his dinner with Seth and Eliza.

The way they were kicking and moving around, it was as if something had rattled them, he thought, but he might be wrong – he didn't yet know their characters and habits. Once he'd spoken to Seth and learnt everything about those particular horses and their daily routine, he'd probably discover he'd disturbed them by doing things differently that evening from the way in which they were usually done.

Another noise reached him, a noise that didn't sound like a restless horse, and he felt a sudden sense of unease. Somewhere in the livery barn, something wooden scraped against the floorboards. He sat up fast, his eyes narrowing. That wasn't a horse – that was a person!

He swung himself off the bed, hurriedly pulled on his buckskin jacket, grabbed a kerosene lamp, opened the door and went out.

'Stay where you are, Greg,' he called to the stable lad as

he passed his room, and he walked quickly along the narrow corridor, past the door to the tack room, past the horses' stalls and out into the barn itself. Standing in the middle of it, he held up his lamp and moved it slowly around the room.

A figure stepped out of the shadows to meet him.

'Chen Fai!' he exclaimed, lowering the lamp. 'What in tarnation are you doin' here?'

Chen Fai put his hands together and gave a slight bow. 'I come through door at side of stable.'

'That might be how you got in here, but it sure isn't why.'

Chen Fai straightened up and slid his hands into the opposite sleeves of his tunic. 'Charity tell me you return, Joe Walker. I come to welcome return of man who is good friend of Charity.' He paused a moment, then gave another little bow. 'Charity do this humble man great honour when she agree be wife.'

Joe threw back his head and laughed. 'Pull the other leg, Chen Fai! Ten or eleven years ago, the first time you came here, you were speakin' the American lingo better than that. So you're going backwards, are you, even though you've been talkin' English with Charity for the best part of seven years?' He laughed again. 'I think not. And what's more, I reckon you're a long way from considerin' yourself a humble man. But it was a mighty good performance, and I applaud you for it.' He put the lamp on a stool and clapped his hands.

Chen Fai smiled broadly. 'You see through me, Joe Walker. I act as white people think a Chinaman should act. White people feel themselves better than the Chinaman if the Chinaman bows and is humble, and that makes white people feel very happy.'

Joe looked at him in surprise. 'But why d'you need me to feel happy?'

Chen Fai looked at him in mock amazement. 'Now *you* are putting on a performance. You must know it is very important to Charity that you are happy for me to take her as my wife. If you are not happy about this, whatever she already say, she will not agree to marry me.'

Joe shrugged. 'The way I see it, it's up to Charity what she does. She's known you for long enough to know what you're like, and if she feels you're the right man for her, then that's good enough for me.'

'Thank you, Joe Walker,' Chen Fai said. 'This is no act. You must allow me to show my gratitude in the Chinese way.' He bowed low, then straightened up. 'If the man who is like a brother to Charity is happy to see me wed her, then I am very pleased.'

Joe held up his hand in protest. 'Hey, stop there! You've got that wrong. Not the bit about me bein' happy, but the like a brother thing. Charity's never looked on me as a brother, just as I've never looked on her as a sister. She's never been seen as a member of the family in any way at all. We're her friends, and she's ours. As her friend – and the friend who found her – I feel responsible for her. But it ends there.'

Chen Fai looked at him in surprise. 'I think my English is now not good enough to understand. I do not see the difference between being a responsible friend and being like a brother. Why does it matter if she thinks of you as a brother? A brother is also a friend, is he not?'

Joe stared at him. 'I don't really know,' he said slowly. 'But they're not the same.'

'I think there is no difference,' Chen Fai said steadily. 'You are like her brother, Joe Walker – a brother who is also her friend. Not every brother is also a friend.' He smiled at Joe – a smile that didn't quite reach his eyes. 'And I also shall think of you as my brother when Charity is my wife.'

Their eyes met.

Joe shrugged dismissively. 'Think what you want. I've gotta go now; it's late. I suggest you leave the way you came.'

Giving him a slight nod, Chen Fai turned and made his way across the stable to the side door. A moment later, Joe heard the door close behind him. He picked up the lamp, went across to the door, took the key from the hook on the wall and locked the door. Then he returned the key to its place and went back along the hallway towards his room.

When he reached the door to the stable lad's room, he knocked, opened it and put his head inside. 'It was someone to speak to me, Greg, but it wasn't important. The horses seem to have settled now so I'm gettin' off to Mr Culpepper's. If you need me, come and get me. I've locked the side door so there shouldn't be any more visitors. Goodnight.'

As he went through the rear door and made his way across the yard, past the outhouse and the corral, he found himself thinking about his instinctive objection to being thought of as like a brother to Charity. It was a compliment more than anything else, so why was he so against being seen as such, he thought, and he shook his head in bewilderment.

Standing outside the livery stable, Chen Fai heard the sound of the key locking the door behind him. Head down, he turned into Main Street and began walking down to the general mercantile store.

The nebulous fear that had haunted him from the moment that Charity had told him they were asking Joe to return, that had kept him awake night after night since he'd heard her words and seen the look in her eyes, was still at his back. His visit to Joe Walker had done nothing to diminish it. If anything, it was stronger than ever.

But his patience towards Charity over the past few years deserved to be rewarded, and the respect and consideration he'd shown her. So, too, the strong love he'd come to feel for her—a love that had grown so powerful that his body now ached for her, day and night.

He could think of no greater happiness than being her husband. And nothing – and no one – must be allowed to come between him and the thing he wished for most of all.

Chapter Twenty-Nine

'So it's just us again, with Ma and Pa gone to bed and Sam back at his place,' Joe remarked. He leaned back and stretched his legs out under the table. 'I thought Sam real quiet at dinner. I know I've only been back two days so I don't really know what he's like these days, but as I recall, he used to talk non-stop about the mines and what the guys had said and done. But not tonight. And not about much else, either – not even about his son. I hate sayin' this, and I hate feelin' this way, but I don't seem to know him any more.'

'I imagine goin' down a mine year after year can do that to a person,' Charity said, putting a mug of coffee in front of Joe and sitting down with her coffee at the other side of the table. 'When you're young, you think it's gonna be one way. Years later, you find it's very different. It must change a person.'

He nodded slowly. 'You could be right.' He paused. 'He didn't speak to you at all, I couldn't help noticin'.'

Charity shrugged dismissively. 'He's a white miner; I'm Chinese. I understand that. But I'd rather talk about you, Joe; not Sam. I know what you told your folks, but how are you really findin' it? You must have found many things different, and I can't see how you can feel as settled as you say you do.'

He thought for a moment. 'In some ways, I do,' he said slowly. 'It's not as different as it might have been, thanks to your letters. It's the people who're different. Like Sam. And Ma and Pa have changed. I know it's not to be wondered at, seein' the length of time I've been gone, but I wasn't ready for the way they've gotten.'

'Your pa's lookin' better now you're home,' Charity said. 'The improvement began when the company took him back, even though the work tires him, but now you're here, he's really tryin' to get back to bein' the man he was. He can't, of course, but it helps him if he tries. It's good you've come home, Joe.'

He nodded. 'I think so, too; and I'm thinkin' I should've come back sooner. It's not just Pa's leg that got broken – it's somethin' inside him, too. And Ma's greyer now and more tired, and her face is lined like it never used to be. I can't see any trace of the happy young woman who'd take me by the hand when I was real young and run out with me into the fields, laughin'.'

'She didn't want you to return, you know. Sure she wanted to see you, but she also wanted to know you were free of Carter, and as long as you stayed away, you were. I figure that in a way, if you were free of Carter, then so was she. I've grown to understand your ma. If you'd stayed here, you might have lost sight of that happy young woman a whole lot sooner.'

Joe nodded slowly. 'It's clever of you to see it like that, Charity, and I reckon you might be right. Even before I left, she was gettin' harder to find. I just didn't wanna see that.'

'But at least Carter's how you thought it'd be,' she said with a smile.

'To look at, yes. But I hadn't expected the new mines to be so close to the stores. It means some of the new streets are real windin', and not in blocks like the older streets.'

'The Chinese like that. Crooked streets make it harder for evil spirits to find the people they're searchin' for,' she said.

He laughed. 'Is that true?'
'It sure is.'

They smiled at each other across the table.

'One of the new things I don't like is the white men's club,' Joe went on. 'There's a tension in the air I haven't felt before, and accordin' to both Seth and Ma, the club's responsible.'

'The tension's always been there. Any Chinaman will tell you that.'

He frowned. 'The mines have a lot to answer for.'

Charity shook her head. 'It's not only the mines – it's the Chinese, too. They keep themselves to themselves, and don't try to fit in. They wear traditional clothes, have traditional hairstyles, eat only Chinese food, and very few of them try to learn the language. I'm sure they wouldn't be disliked as much if they copied Chen Fai and learned the American way of doin' things.'

He shook his head. 'You'll not hear me blamin' the Chinese. That'd be like blamin' you, and I'd never do that. And anyway, I'd never blame them for somethin' that's not their fault. Yup, they're wrong to turn their back on everythin' American when they're livin' here, I grant you, but it's where they've come from that's made them the way they are.'

She looked at him in surprise. 'What d'you mean?'

'On that first drive to Montana, I met some drovers who'd spent time in San Francisco, the port where the Chinese used to land and where a lot of them still live.'

'I know. Chen Sing arrived there with Chen Fai, who was seven at the time.'

Joe nodded. 'So Seth told me. I asked the men what they knew about China, and they said they'd heard that life was real hard there. The Chinese had to work all day on someone else's land, had little to eat—'

She cut in. 'Chen Fai said they had a bowl of watery rice

gruel or a millet cake each day, if they were lucky. People were always hungry and had swollen bellies.'

Joe smiled at her. 'So what we heard tallies. And they had to pay taxes to the person who owned the land, even though they earned very little, and even if the crops had been destroyed by floods or drought. It's hardly surprisin' they wanted to leave.'

She nodded. 'That's why Chen Sing came. He heard there was gold here, and came to get a better life for himself and his family. Apparently, he just rolled up his blanket and mattin' one mornin', told Chen Fai to do the same, packed a basket of possessions and set off for Hong Kong. They picked up a ship there and went to San Francisco. Lots of Chinese did that.'

'Does Chen Fai remember much about the journey?'

She nodded. 'It lasted for two awful months. The ship was crowded and the Chinese had to live below the decks in narrow bunks, three above each other. He said the men couldn't stand up straight, and you couldn't get away from the smell of whale-oil lanterns and unwashed bodies, and even worse. The food and water were dirty and people were sick all the time.'

'It sounds real bad.'

'He and Chen Sing would've been treated better if Chen Sing had been a sojourner, which means he'd have promised to return to his village one day, but he wasn't. He intended to send money back to his wife and village, but he was never gonna go back for more than a visit. He still sends money back.'

'I've always thought him a good man. Of course, I only know about him from Seth, but Seth's a sound judge of a person.'

'They were all expected to send money back. Any man

who wasn't wed was made to take a wife before he left,' she said. 'That was so he'd always send money home, and also so he might leave behind a son. Or a daughter if he was unlucky – sons are more important.'

Joe sat back. 'So like I said, you can't blame them for leavin' China, and you can't blame them for takin' whatever the company pays. Whatever they earn in Wyoming, it's gotta be ten times what they'd earn in China. It's makin' the whites work for the same small amount that's causin' the problem. The whites clearly don't understand why the Chinese won't make a fuss, and they're resentful.'

She shrugged. 'But no one's tryin' to understand anyone else.'

'Thinkin about it,' Joe said slowly. 'You've been here in Carter, and I've been out on the range, but we've both been learnin' the same things. That's real strange, but I kinda like it,' he added with a smile.

'Me, too.' She paused, and then looked at him curiously. 'But why did you want to learn about the Chinese?'

He shook his head. 'I don't really know. I guess it was because you were learnin' about the Chinese way of life from Chen Fai and Su Lin, and I knew I'd see you again one day, and wanted to be able to talk about Chinese things with the little girl I expected to find.' He gave her a slow smile. 'And then I came back and found you as you are now. Nothing had prepared me for that.'

She stared at him across the table.

'Or me for the grown-up Joe,' she said quietly.

A slender figure, stark against the night sky, Charity stood at the tip of the tapering light that flowed from the open doorway behind her, and stared into the darkness ahead.

From time to time, the moon broke through the thick

bands of slate-grey cloud that drifted across its face, and a swathe of pale moonlight slid out across the barren waste, outlining in ice-cold white the ridges of the gully, and sheening with silver the rock-hard ground. And then once again, the clouds regrouped themselves and plunged the world back into darkness.

Joe leaned against the doorpost, watching Charity.

'How come you're out there, Charity?' he finally called to her. 'It's the middle of the night and it's cold. You oughta go back to bed.'

She didn't move.

He put his jacket on, turned the collar up against the cold, walked up to her side and stood next to her.

'You shouldn't be out here now,' he said, glancing at her profile.

She didn't reply, but continued to stare ahead, hugging her thick coat around her nightdress.

He followed the direction of her gaze. 'What are we lookin' at?' he asked after a moment or two. 'I'm seein' only blackness, and occasional patches of moonlight on the ground.'

He saw her smile, but still she didn't reply.

'Well?' he repeated.

'I asked your ma that same question a few days after you'd left,' she said. 'It was late like it is now, and she was standin' in the doorway, lookin' towards the river, but you couldn't see the water for darkness. Like you can't now.'

She turned to him. The side of his face gleamed gold in the light thrown from the house. She caught her breath, and stared at him, a strange sensation running through her. Her skin tightened.

She looked quickly away and forced her focus back to the darkness.

'And what did Ma say?' Joe prompted.

She heard the friendly smile in his voice.

'Somethin' I didn't understand then, but I think I do now,' she said slowly. Unwilling to look at him again, she kept her gaze fixed ahead. 'Or at least, I'm closer to understandin' it.'

He frowned slightly. 'You're startin' to worry me. What did she say?'

'That she was lookin' at the years ahead of her, and she felt like she was bein' buried alive.'

'Look at me, Charity,' he said, turning to face her.

She pulled her coat tighter around her.

'Look at me and tell me truly – is that how you feel about your future? That you're bein' buried alive?'

She didn't move.

'Please, Charity; answer me. Are you plannin' on doin' somethin' you don't want to do real bad, somethin' that will affect the rest of your life?'

She glanced at him. 'You gave me my life, Joe, but if I make a mistake, it's *my* mistake, not yours.' She turned to look back at the darkness.

He stood for a few minutes in silence.

'Is marryin' Chen Fai the mistake you're talkin' about?' he asked. 'Are you thinkin' you shouldn't have agreed to this, and that in marryin' him, you'll be buryin' yourself alive?'

She turned sharply, took a step back and stared at him, her face in shadow. 'No, Joe; I'm not. Chen Fai is a good man. I'm doin' what I must do. Doin' what you must do isn't makin' a mistake. I said, *if* I make a mistake; not that I was makin' one.'

'Doin' what you must do,' he repeated, a note of concern in his voice. 'I've heard about the Chinese sense of duty. Are you gettin' wed out of a sense of duty? But if so, why? Why d'you owe a duty to anyone but yourself and the folks who raised you?'

Shaking her head, she turned away. 'That's not what I'm doin'.'

'But you said you're doin' what you must. What else could that mean?'

She thought for a moment. 'Maybe must is not the right word, like regret wasn't. I'm doin' what's best for everyone. It's best for Chen Fai, who cares for me and wants a wife and son. It's best for Sam and his wife. Sam's always resented me, and now he's angry, too, about what the whites are doin' to your ma and pa because I'm livin' here.'

'But that's not your fault.'

'It doesn't matter whose fault it is – it's there. With Carter as it is today, he shouldn't have to see a Chinese person when he goes to his home. It's not good for him, and it's not good for Phebe to be wed to a man so full of hate. And it's best for your ma and pa, too. When I leave your house, the Carter townsfolk will be nice to them again.'

'And what's best for Charity?'

She stared at him. 'It's best for me to know I'm not hurtin' the people I care for by bein' with them. The way to do this is by marryin'. And if I want to get wed, it must be to a Chinese man.'

'I realise that,' he said quietly.

'Chen Fai's a good man,' she went on. 'A man who can think kindly about a woman like the woman my ma must have been forced to become, is a good man. Over the years I've gotten to know him well, and there's no Chinaman I'd rather wed than him.'

He thought for a moment. 'And is it best for me, too, that you wed him? In your list, you left me out.'

She nodded. 'Yes, it's best for you, too, Joe. And in your heart you know this is true. You've felt responsible for me since the day you found me, even though many people wouldn't have done. But when I marry Chen Fai, that responsibility will end – he'll take it from you and you'll be free.'

She started to turn from him. He caught her arm. Their eyes met, and held for a moment. She took a step back, and pulled her arm away from him.

'You're makin' it sound like being responsible for you was a burden,' he said awkwardly. 'It never was; and it never could be.'

She gave him a sad smile. 'It may not have felt it, but it will have weighed. And it would also weigh on the woman you'll one day wed. By marryin' Chen Fai, I'm liftin' that weight from you, and just as you gave me life seventeen years ago, I shall be freein' you to live a full life. So, yes, Joe; for me to marry Chen Fai is best for you, too.'

He stared hard into her face. 'You always were a smart gal, Charity, and you've just proved you can reason well. But you said you felt like you were being buried alive. That's feelin', not reasonin'. Would a real smart gal ignore what she felt in her heart?'

Her eyes filled with an emotion he couldn't fathom, and he frowned slightly, trying to understand her.

She shivered and looked up at the sky. 'You were right, Joe – it's gotten very cold. I'm goin' in now.'

With her hand touching the place on her arm where moments before his hand had been, she walked steadily back through the column of light and into the house.

Slowly, he followed her up the path. Reaching the open doorway, he paused and watched her cross the room and turn into the corridor. A moment later he heard her bedroom door close. Then he went inside the house, shut the front door, threw his jacket on to the back of the chair and walked across to the corridor.

As he made his way along the corridor to the back door, he heard her moving around on the other side of her bedroom wall, and his steps faltered.

The face of the lovely woman she'd become filled his mind – lovely inside, as he'd always known, and now as lovely outside; breathtakingly so. And a sudden powerful longing shot down the length of his body and settled into an ache that throbbed low in his stomach.

'Oh, no!' he cried out inwardly. 'Oh, no!'

His body churning with emotion, he half-ran through the back door, pulled opened his bedroom door, went inside and slammed the door shut.

Leaning back against the door, the wood chill against the burning heat of his skin, he turned his head to the left, and stared at the sawn-plank wall that separated him from Charity.

'Oh, no!' he cried again in despair. 'This can't be.' He put his hands to his head, and let out a low shuddering sigh of anguish.

Chapter Thirty

Joe nodded goodnight to the miner with whom he'd been walking from the town, opened the door to his house and went in. Hiram was sitting by the range, staring towards the door. Joe saw his face light up as he entered.

He hung his bag up by the door. 'Hi, Pa,' he said. 'I left earlier today. I wondered if I'd catch you up comin' back from the mine.'

'You came close; I've not been long back.'

'Dinner won't be ready for a while,' Martha said, coming from the corridor with a heap of bed covers in her arms. 'I'll get you some water to wash in. Then sit yourself down and talk to your pa, and I'll get you somethin' to drink.' She dropped the bed clothes into one of the tubs standing against the back wall and went across to the sink.

'If it's okay with you and pa, I'll wash my hands and then go on down to Sam's house before I have that drink and talk,' he said. 'I've been feelin' pretty bad about the way things are with Sam. And his wife stayed home last night as the child was sleeping so I haven't met them yet.'

'You and Sam certainly didn't seem to have much to say to each other,' Hiram said.

'I doubt we exchanged more than a few words. I've seen hide nor hair of him since I got here. The way I figure it, we need to clear the air. Thought I could go down to his house now, meet his wife and son, and have a drink with him. If he's not yet back, I'll wait for him, if his wife don't mind.'

Hiram nodded. 'You're doin' the right thing, son. Sam's not a happy man right now; I reckon he could use a good brother.'

'His house is third from the end of the row of new

houses,' Martha said, as Joe went over to the bowl of water she'd poured for him. 'And if he wants you to stay and eat with them, you do that, too.'

'I can't see that wife of his suggestin' that!' Hiram exclaimed. 'It's as likely as seein' a hog fly.'

'Maybe we shouldn't be quite so hard on Phebe,' Martha said shortly. 'Sam can't be the easiest man to live with, the way he is now.'

'I'll be off then.' Joe wiped his hands dry, put his hat back on, went out of the house and pulled the door closed behind him.

Turning right, he walked down the line of miners' houses, past the well and along to the newer buildings that had been added to the far end of the row, their wood yet to turn from pine-yellow to a weather-worn grey, until he reached Sam's house. He knocked at the door.

The door opened a crack and a blonde woman peered through the gap.

Joe stood still as clear blue eyes travelled down the length of him. The door opened slightly wider. He tipped his hat to her. 'Howdy, ma'am.'

She pulled the door wide open. 'I'm guessin' you must be Joe.'

'And I'm guessin' you must be my sister-in-law,' he said with a smile. 'Thought it was high time I met you.'

She stepped back, her hand still on the door. 'And met Sam's boy, I'll warrant. You'd better come in, you won't see him from out there. He's asleep now, but you can have a look at him. You won't want me to wake him, though – he's gotten his pa's way of bawlin' for what he wants.'

'Actually, it was in my mind to get to know you, but I'd like to see the boy as well,' Joe said, taking off his hat as he followed her into the room. 'And Sam, too, if he's at home.'

Her face clouded. 'You'll have to settle for me and the boy. Sam won't be back till I'm puttin' the dinner on the table, if then. It'll be a drink with the men first, then stoppin' by at your folks. We come last on the list.'

Joe made a sympathetic noise.

'He's over there,' she said, indicating a wooden crib that stood in the corner of the room, not far from the range. 'His name's Thomas, though I expect you already know that.'

Joe went across, leaned over the bed, and stared at the child who was lying on his stomach, fast asleep. 'How old is he?' he asked.

'Eleven months.'

He straightened up. 'He looks a fine boy. Charity didn't say much about him in her letters.'

Her mouth tightened. 'That don't surprise me – the Chinese think only about themselves. You should hear Sam goin' on about them. He can tell you what they get up to, bribin' the foremen and all that. Sam knows all about it. They don't care about makin' things harder for the whites.'

Swallowing the impulse to give her a sharp retort, he forced a smile to his face.

'Changin' the subject, ma'am, it's you I'd like to hear about, not the mines,' he said, and he sat down at the table. He raised his hands slightly. 'I hope I'm not givin' any offence by makin' myself at home like this, sittin' down without an invitation.'

'Not by sittin' down, you're not, but you will be if you keep on callin' me ma'am. My name's Phebe. But I'll wager you already know that,' she added, and sat down opposite him.

'You're right; I do.' He sat back in his chair and looked across the table at her. 'So tell me about yourself, Phebe.'

'Why d'you wanna hear about me? There's nothin' interestin' about me.'

214

'There is to Sam – he married you. And there is to me – you're family now. Charity was able to tell me what was goin' on with Ma and Pa, but I didn't hear much about you and Sam. I'd like to catch up with what I've missed.'

'I guess you already know all there is to know. I'm sure your folks couldn't wait to give you the details about us gettin' wed – the detail that's in the crib over there.'

Joe followed her gaze. He gave a wry grin. 'You're right about me catchin' up with that bit fairly soon.'

Relaxing a little, she laughed.

'My folks weren't best pleased, either,' she went on. 'Pa's a mine superintendent and they'd expected me to find myself someone who was at least at his level, if not higher. Or maybe someone who owned a shop.' She put her hand to the fair hair caught in a thick knot at the nape of her neck. 'I was always considered real pretty, you see.'

'And you still are a good-lookin' woman, Phebe.'

'Instead, I'm wed to an ordinary miner, livin' in a shack, and I've got a baby,' she went on as if he hadn't spoken. 'Sam works hard all day, but there's not much money to live on. But he's not the only one who works hard – I do, too. But no matter how hard I work, there's always somethin' else to do. It's not surprisin' that every day I look a bit uglier. I sure thought I'd get a better life for myself than this.' She looked around her.

'I can see at a glance why Sam fell for you. What I don't understand is, what did you see in that ornery brother of mine?'

She laughed. 'He was a man, not a boy, and a fine-lookin' man at that. And I guess that's why I wasn't enough of a lady not to get myself where I am today.'

'Sam's a lucky guy,' Joe said with a smile. 'And I mean that. I know it's not easy bein' a miner these days, but I know from watchin' my ma that it's not easy bein' a miner's wife, either.' He paused. 'What about your folks? Can they help you some?'

She shook her head. 'They're disappointed in me and in the way I'm livin' now, and they keep away as much as they can, which won't be hard for them – they're movin' back east. So no, my folks won't be helpin' me lighten my chores.'

'I'm sure Ma would help you. She could show you ways of makin' things easier.'

'She's already fair sick of seein' me at her door as it is; I can tell,' she said with a dry laugh. 'I've never had to cook and keep home before. I don't know how to do it and I'm always runnin' out of things. With the snow there's been, I've not wanted to take Thomas out, and it's been easier to ask your ma if she can let me have what I need.'

'I'm sure you're wrong about Ma. I know her and I know she'll wanna help. What's more, she'll be lonely when Charity moves out, which I'm guessin' isn't far off. She doesn't realise it yet, but she's gonna miss her bein' around. You're family now, and she'll be glad she's got you nearby.'

Her face darkened. 'I'm lookin' forward to that China woman movin' out and I hope she stays put in Chinatown,' she said sharply. 'Sam's full of hate for her and all the Chinee. And it angers him mightily that we have to shop in the company store. Thanks to the Chinee, we get little enough money as it is, and havin' to give what we've got back to the company sticks in the throat.'

'That must be difficult for you, Phebe,' Joe said quietly.

She nodded. 'It is. I hate seein' him like he's gettin'. I know I complain about the life I've got, being wed to a miner, but Sam's a good man at heart. You won't know it 'cos you weren't here, but he had to work real hard to persuade the company to take your pa back on. Sam knew what it was doin' to your pa, not bein' able to provide for his family, and he wouldn't give up till he'd got that job for him. Like I say, there's a lot of good in Sam. It's just not so easy to see it these days under all the hate.'

Joe nodded. 'I know Pa appreciates what Sam did for him.'

'Most of all, it's the Chinese thing. It's eatin' Sam up and I hear him soundin' meaner about them each day. It's all he ever talks about: He wasn't like that when he started courtin' me, and I want that old Sam back. But it's not gonna happen as long as he's got a Celestial in his face everywhere he turns, and above all in his home.'

'I understand,' Joe said slowly. 'I really do. And I've got sympathy for what you're sayin'.'

Phebe leaned forward. 'Then tell her to go, will you? She'll listen to you, as she'll want to please you. She owes her life to you, after all.'

He stood up. 'Charity will marry when she's ready and not when I say. She's a strong-minded gal and she'll do what she wants. But I *will* have a word with her,' he added, 'and see if I can help.'

'Thanks, Joe,' Phebe said, getting up and going to the door. She opened it. 'I'm sorry you've missed Sam. I expect he'll be sorry, too, that he's missed you. But I've enjoyed talkin' to you, and I hope you'll visit again.'

'You can bet I will,' he said with a smile. 'I've enjoyed talkin' to you, too, Phebe. You're a fine addition to the family. Just make sure you ask Ma for help. There's many a time she's needed help herself, and whatever she might say, she won't mind how often you go to her. She found it real difficult herself before Charity came along, and she won't have forgotten that.' He grinned at her. 'And if she has, you tell me and I'll remind her.'

He put his Stetson back on, tipped the brim to her and went out.

'Thank you, Joe,' he heard her call after him as he started walking towards his house.

Without looking back, he raised his hand in a wave, and he heard the door click shut.

The rhythmic thud of the pumps beat time with his steps as he walked back up the line of houses, the acrid stench of coal strong in the air. Glancing up at the sky, he saw that darkness was edging closer as the last bands of orange, rose and violet melded into the purple shades of night.

How different it was from the nights on the range when he'd sat low in the saddle surrounded by the silence found when a person was far from a town; a silence broken only by the cry of an owl, the yelp of a coyote or by the lowing of cattle; a silence you could almost reach out and touch; a silence that let you hear the beat of your heart.

And how different from the nights when he and the other drovers had watched the sun drop slowly behind the mountains, casting shadows that lengthened and threw into shade the ground where their horses stood and their cows grazed. Or the nights when the sun plunged at speed behind the vast horizon, reddening the sky, reddening the earth, and finally covering the land with a thick all-consuming blackness.

How he missed the loveliness of those nights, their wild emptiness and the taste of air that was sweet on his tongue, and how he missed the peace of mind he'd had at those times; a peace of mind that seemed to have deserted him since his return to Carter.

No, not since his return to Carter – it was since the moment he'd set eyes again on Charity.

From that moment on, he'd been struggling not to think

about her in the way that he kept on wanting to do. She could never be his. Chinese and whites were forbidden to marry, so he was wasting his thoughts on what he couldn't have, and he knew he must stop.

But it was a mighty big struggle, and he appeared to be losing the battle.

Chapter Thirty-One

Mid-April, 1885

As soon as Charity came out of Ah Lee's bakery, she saw Su Lin standing on the boardwalk in front of the mercantile, staring towards her, her face shining with excitement.

Charity hurried across the road.

'I was watching for you, Charity,' Su Lin said as soon as Charity reached her.

'I could see that. And I could also see you were excited about somethin'. So tell – what's so excitin'?'

'You will hear soon,' Su Lin said with a wide smile. 'Follow me.' She turned and went into the shop, with Charity close behind.

Chen Fai was at the far end of the store, studying some bales of red and yellow material that were spread out on the counter in front of him. He looked up as they came in, and smiled broadly. Su Lin glanced round at Charity, giggled happily, and then led the way down the shop to her brother.

'It's big and wonderful news that Su Lin has to tell you,' Chen Fai said, and Charity heard pride in his voice. 'And there is something for you to think about, too, Charity,' he added.

Charity smiled at Su Lin. 'I'm guessin' what this is about, Su Lin,' she said. 'And I'll wager you know what I'm thinkin'. So, am I right?'

Su Lin giggled again. She clasped her hands together in front of her face. 'I think you guess right, Charity. I'm to be wed. I'm to marry son of Ah Lee. His name is Ah Lee Don. I am very happy. He is born in the Year of the Rooster; like

Joe Walker. This is a very good year for a person born in Year of the Dragon, which is you and me.'

'I'm so happy for you!' Charity exclaimed, and she hugged Su Lin. 'His father is a good man, and from what I've seen of the son, he's a good man, too.'

Su Lin nodded. 'I also think so. I have seen him in street and I think he has a fine face.' She paused, her face suddenly anxious. 'I hope future mother-in-law is kind woman. I not know her. It is custom in China for mother-in-law not to like wife of son, and son must agree with what mother say, even if mother is wrong. Chinese girls in China expect this, but I am not real Chinese girl – I never been to China – and I know I will be unhappy if mother-in-law is not kind to me.'

Charity glanced towards Chen Fai. His eyes met hers, and he gave her a slight smile.

She put her arm round Su Lin's shoulders. 'Chen Fai knows this. He won't let you be unhappy. You're not goin' to another village – you'll be livin' here in Carter, across the street from your family. And Ah Lee's son has lived a long time in America so he'll know American ways. That makes everythin' different.'

'I think so, too,' Su Lin said, her face brightening again.

'When are you gonna wed him?'

'*Dai lou* talked with Chinaman Doc. He looked at our horoscopes and found a date for the wedding. Late in June is very good date, so maybe then.' She glanced at Chen Fai. 'But *dai lou* must speak with you first.'

Charity looked at Su Lin in surprise, and then at Chen Fai. At the look in the eyes that met hers, her stomach gave a sudden lurch. Her arm fell from Su Lin's shoulders. 'What do you want to speak to me about?' she asked, trying to hide her nervousness. 'Is it about Su Lin's weddin'?'

'In a way, yes,' he said. 'Wait; I come round to you.' He put down the bale of red silk he'd been holding, walked round the end of the counter and went up to her.

She wasn't the only one feeling concerned, she realised, looking at Chen Fai's face as he approached her; he, too, seemed uneasy.

He glanced at Su Lin. 'Su Lin, you will please go now and help honourable father's second wife with the cooking.' He turned back to Charity. 'Su Lin and I are now going to talk in American to each other at all times. It will help Su Lin not to forget it when she live with Ah Lee Don's family. If she speaks very well before she goes there, she not forget it.'

He paused and waited until Su Lin had pushed aside the curtain and disappeared into the back room. Charity saw him take a deep breath.

'What's this about?' she asked, her voice shaking.

He cleared his throat. 'As Su Lin tell you, she can marry at end of June. This is good date for Su Lin and Ah Lee Don. Is good date for you and me, too, but honourable father not want us to wed in same month as Su Lin. It is also his wish that our wedding is first.'

'Are you sayin' you want us to marry at the end of June and Su Lin a month later?'

He shook his head. 'That is not possible. You remember, a month later is Ghost Month. This is most dangerous time of year as ghosts of our ancestors visit us, and evil spirits come among us and try to capture our souls.'

'I'd forgotten it was that month.'

'It is,' he said, nodding. 'From first day of month, when Gates of Hell open and hungry ghosts come out into world, to last day of month, we have ceremonies, hoping ghosts not cause us harm. We cannot do many things in Hungry

Ghost Month, like travel or swim in the river or start a business. Or have wedding,' he added.

She stared at him. 'So Su Lin can't marry then.'

'That is so. If we wed in June, Su Lin not wed until September or October. Chinaman Doc will say what is better date. But that is far away, and Ah Lee want wedding sooner.'

She bit her lip. 'So what d'you suggest?'

He cleared his throat. 'It is also my wish that Su Lin marry very soon after you and me, Charity. You are good friends with Su Lin. You share many thoughts with her, and you tell her all you do.' He gave her a wry smile. 'Is more comfortable for me if wife not have very good friend in house where she starts life with friend's brother.'

Charity felt a slow blush spread across her chest and up over her cheeks.

She looked down at the floor.

'I think it very good idea if Su Lin is wed in June,' he went on, 'and if you and me marry in May.' He paused. 'If you agree, I ask Chinaman Doc to find good date in May.' He paused again. 'What you say to this?'

Gazing down at the floor, she struggled to suppress the panic rising within her. 'It's April now,' she said, her voice little more than a whisper. 'May sounds very soon.'

'Look at me, Charity,' he said quietly.

She raised her eyes to his face.

'May sounds very soon, as you put it, but is not really so soon. I think we know each other well. It is three years since I first knock on door of Walker house and ask you to walk out with me. And you have worked here many months. It is now four weeks since you do me great honour of agreeing to marry me. I think there is no reason to wait longer.'

'I guess not.'

'And I not wish to wait longer. For much of the time that we are friends, we are alone together. This is American way, not Chinese way. But I behave always in Chinese way. When we are alone, I never touch you. This is because I respect you, Charity; you are woman with reputation.' He stared into her face and she saw love shining in the depths of his dark eyes, and hunger. 'It is not that I not wish to touch you, to hold you close to me, because I do.' His voice broke with emotion. 'For many months, I wish very much to hold you. For me, waiting until May will feel very long time.'

She tensed, and felt her breath drain from her body. 'I should be happy to wed you in May, Chen Fai,' she said quietly.

His face broke out into a smile of delight.

A wave of guilt for the flatness she felt shot through her. 'So that's decided, then,' she said, forcing a note of brightness into her voice. 'Now I must think about what to wear.'

'I already think about that for you,' he said happily. 'You are Chinese girl marrying Chinese man, so you must dress like person you are. Here. You look at this.' He turned and rushed across to the place where he'd been standing when they'd come in. He picked up the bale of red silk and held it out to her. 'This is finest material.'

She stared at it, and then looked questioningly at him.

'I order this for you. You wear this on day of wedding – a Chinese bride wears red. It make lovely *chang-fu*. *Chang-fu* is long dress that hang from shoulder to ankle. Honourable father's second wife make *chang-fu*, and Su Lin embroider yellow dragon and phoenix on it. And Su Lin help you learn Chinese customs for wedding day.'

'It's beautiful, Chen Fai,' she said, lightly touching the material. 'I'm real grateful to you.'

'Red and yellow are colours of happiness and good fortune. This is what I wish for us, Charity. I do my best to be good husband to you.' He paused, and gave her a half smile. 'I hear Su Lin tell you her fear about mother of Ah Lee Don. Honourable mother is in China so you not serve her. Honourable father's second wife is happy you come here. She is long time in America and will follow American way and be kind mother-in-law.'

'Well, that's a relief.' She forced a laugh.

He looked at her anxiously. 'You have pale face,' he said. 'We decide important things this morning, and you must rest now. You go back to Walker house and not work today. Su Lin look after shop with me. I tell her she marry in June and then I think there are wedding things she want to talk about with me, and we can do this when in store together.'

'If you're sure,' she said. She put her hand to her forehead. 'I do have a bit of a headache.'

'I see you tomorrow,' he said with a warm smile. 'You go now.'

She smiled and turned from him. Holding in check her desire to run out of the store as fast as she could, she forced herself to walk steadily through the shop, out on to Main Street and along the boardwalk to Second Street.

Her inner tension slowly faded as she walked.

But why had she felt such tension, she thought in bewilderment. Why was she suddenly so panicked in there? And why did she now feel as if she'd escaped and was free? The mercantile was a shop, after all, not a prison, and she'd been there with the man she'd agreed to marry.

She'd long realised where her friendship with Chen Fai would end, and she hadn't fought it. In fact, by continuing to walk out with him, she'd actually encouraged his expectation. So why, oh why, had she suddenly felt as if she was being smothered? And when did that feeling start?

Being buried alive was how she'd described it to Joe.

Yet as she'd told Joe, there was no Chinaman she'd rather marry than Chen Fai. And she did want to get wed. Even so, she'd suddenly felt trapped.

She couldn't make sense of it all.

Reaching the door to the house, she paused a moment, stood still and gazed up at the sky. The clouds that were drifting from east to west across the wide blue emptiness slowly formed themselves into a shape – the shape of a face. A smile rose to her lips as she traced the features, lingering longingly, lovingly, on each one of them. It was a face she knew real well.

But it wasn't the face of Chen Fai.

And suddenly it all made sense.

Chapter Thirty-Two

'It's gettin' dark. We've done the horses, so I think we'll pack up for the night. Everyone else seems to have done so,' Joe told Greg, as he finished filling the water trough outside the livery stable. 'Then I'll get off home. You can take tomorrow afternoon and evening off—you've earned some time to yourself. I reckon I'll—'

A scream shattered the silence of the evening. It was followed by loud, angry shouting and the sound of a number of people moving around at the bottom of town.

'What's goin' on?' Greg exclaimed, turning to Joe, alarm on his face.

'No idea, but it ain't gonna be good.' Joe threw the can to the ground and ran into the stable, closely followed by Greg. 'Somethin's happenin' in Chinatown. Pull the doors closed, Greg, and latch them. I'm gonna see what's goin' on. I'll go out through the side door. Lock it after me, and don't open any of the doors till I get back.' He lifted his Winchester from the hook by the side door. 'You hear me now?'

Greg nodded vigorously. 'Yes, boss.'

'Good lad.' Joe tugged open the door, ran out into Second Street and headed down the centre of Main Street towards the *tong*, his rifle hanging from his hand.

Ahead of him, he saw that there were a number of white miners milling around in front of the *tong*, shouting angrily as they jostled each other. Swerving slightly, he headed directly for them. As he neared the group, he saw they were crowding around someone on the ground, and seemed to be kicking that person.

He looked swiftly at both sides of the street – not a single Chinaman could be seen, but he could feel their eyes on him.

He heard one of the crowd shout something extra loudly. There was a jeer of enthusiastic support from the others, followed by more forceful kicking.

Joe tightened his grip on the butt of his rifle.

'Get me some rope, and I'll hang him!' a voice shouted from the heart of the mob. A voice Joe knew well.

Shock winded him.

For a second, his steps faltered, then he rushed headlong towards the group.

'Sam!' he yelled. 'Don't do it!'

Sam spun round and faced him. Pushing through the mob, he came towards Joe, his eyes wild with hate.

'Why, if it isn't my yeller-lovin' brother,' he shouted mockingly, and he grinned back over his shoulder at the men behind him. 'You're just in time, Joe, to see what we're gonna do to the people stealin' the food from our mouths. Startin' with the priest. We're gonna string him up, and show the rest of the cheatin' Chinee what'll happen if they don't get outa Carter right now.' Turning his back on Joe, he faced the crowd. 'We're takin' our town back, aren't we, boys?'

'And about time, too,' someone shouted to a chorus of agreement.

'Now where's that rope?' Sam yelled, holding out his hand.

One of the breaker boys rushed forward with a length of rope 'Here, Sam.'

Sam took it and tugged at it as if to test its strength. 'That'll do,' he said. 'You all stand aside.'

He moved to the sidewalk nearest to him, raised his arm

and swung the rope up over the cross beam at the end of the wooden awning. Catching the end of the rope, he quickly looped it and secured the loop with several wrapping turns. Then he tightened the knot, stood back and let the noose hang down.

'I reckon that'll do,' he said, satisfaction in his voice, turning back to the miners. 'Now bring me that stinkin' priest.'

The men started dragging the priest towards Sam.

Joe took a step forward. Trying not show the nervousness he felt in the face of an angry crowd that looked out of control and set on having blood, he raised his rifle and levelled it at the group. 'I wouldn't go any further if I were you,' he said steadily, 'Or that'll be the last thing you do today or any day. My advice is that you let him go real fast, and don't make any sudden movements. Right now, my gun finger's mighty twitchy.'

'You dry up, you son of a bitch,' growled one of the miners, pushing forward. 'Like Sam said, we're takin' our town back. If you don't like it, you can leave with the Chinee. Come on, lads; let's finish this.'

Joe heard the priest cry out in pain as the miners resumed pulling him along the dusty ground.

He raised his rifle higher, and cocked the hammer.

The men dragging the priest stopped where they were. They edged slightly back and glanced at Sam.

'He's all talk. He won't do a thing,' jeered Sam, moving forward. 'Come on, then. We're gonna teach them heathens a lesson they won't forget.'

Several of the men looked anxiously towards Joe, and then at each other. One or two dropped their hold on the priest and stepped back into the crowd. But the rest firmed their hold on him and began again to pull him to Sam.

The priest cried out again in agony. He was close enough now for Joe to see that he was covered in blood.

He raised his rifle a fraction.

'I advise you men to listen to Joe if you wanna see the day out,' a voice drawled from behind him.

A wave of relief shot through Joe.

He glanced quickly over his shoulder and saw Marshal McGregor standing in front of the alley running between one of the Chinese laundries and Chinaman Doc's herb shop. The Marshal's rifle was aimed squarely at the crowd.

Thank God his was no longer the only gun, he thought, and he turned back to face the angry miners.

In a burst of rowdy defiance, three or four miners pushed the priest the remaining short distance to Sam's feet, and left him there, bruised and bleeding. Throwing a triumphant glance at Joe, Sam started to reach down to the priest.

Joe and the Marshal fired above the heads of the mob at exactly the same moment.

As the rifle fire sprayed into the air, Sam let go of the priest and straightened up. The other miners hastily moved back.

'Now you've shown us how easily fine upstandin' people can be transformed into a mob of wild beasts,' the Marshal said, walking towards them, his gun still trained on them, 'I reckon you should go back to your homes and become those fine upstandin' people again. I'm gonna take the priest back into the *tong*, and then I'm gonna go up to the saloon and have me a drink. Any of you who wanna join me for one before you go home are welcome. But this ain't what we do here,' he added, indicating the hanging noose with the barrel of his rifle. 'Leastways, not on my watch.'

Their heads down and with an air of embarrassment, the crowd started moving in small groups up Main Street and past Second Street to the saloon that lay just beyond the livery stable and blacksmiths.

Joe heard one of the men shout out to Sam as he passed him, his voice bitter; 'You wanna keep that little brother of yours in check, Sam.'

Joe saw the rage on his brother's face.

'I'll help you get him inside,' Joe said, turning to Marshal McGregor. 'He looks hurt real bad.'

The Marshal shook his head. 'I reckon I can manage him myself. I'll send someone for Chinaman Doc – though I'm guessin' he's already seen what's gone on – then I'll cut the rope down. I suggest you take that brother of yours back to his house.' He glanced towards Sam, who was standing alone on the emptying street, his face white with anger and humiliation. 'The priest's got a lot to thank you for,' the Marshal said, looking back at Joe. 'That was a brave thing you did, standin' up to the mob like that. One gun wouldn't've got you far if they'd turned on you.'

Joe nodded. 'Don't I know it?'

Slinging the rifle over his shoulder, the Marshal walked down to the priest who lay without moving in the dust.

Sam watched motionless as the Marshal helped the priest to his feet, and half-carried, half-dragged him towards the *tong*. When the *tong* doors had closed behind them, he turned away and walked across to Joe.

Joe eyed him warily.

'You think you've won, don't you?' Sam sneered, his face inches from Joe's, hostility and hatred burning in the depths of his eyes. 'Well, you haven't. Yeah, this time maybe, but this won't be the last time. Oh, no. You made me look a fool today, goin' against me like that in front of the men I work with, and you my brother, too, and I'm not gonna forget that. Not ever.'

Pushing past Joe, he made his way up Main Street.

When he reached Second Street, he turned to go along it, paused and looked back down at Joe, who was standing watching him. 'Not ever, Joe,' he yelled down the street. 'You can count on that.'

Chapter Thirty-Three

The following day, as the grey light of dawn broke up the leaden hue of night, Charity finally abandoned her attempt to lose herself in the oblivion of sleep and rose from her bed, stiff with cold and inner torment.

Trying not to make any noise, she went across to the table in the corner of her room, poured some water from the stoneware pitcher into a bowl, and swiftly washed herself. Then she slipped her corset on top of her undershirt, laced it up, pulled her unbleached muslin petticoats over her head, and dropped her brown poplin overdress on top of the petticoats. When she'd buttoned the dress bodice from its tight-fitting waist to her throat, she plaited her hair into a single black braid, swung it over her shoulder and left the room.

The ever-present smell of bad eggs that came from the coke in the iron stove hit her as soon as she went from the corridor into the chill main room. She glanced at the stove and hesitated, wondering whether to light it before she went out.

But by the time she'd emptied the ash pan, piled torn paper on to the grate, covered the paper with a thin layer of coal, waited for blue flames to appear, and then heaped on the rest of the coal, the town would be alive with miners heading for their shift and with shopkeepers readying their stores for the coming day. The wells in town, too, would be busy, as Chinese laundry workers would have started hauling water to the washtubs in the three laundries in Chinatown.

With so much going on, she wouldn't be able to find

anywhere to be alone, but she desperately needed solitude if she was going to think clearly about the feelings that had struck her with such force the day before. The thought of seeing Chen Fai again, with her mind still in such a state of confusion, filled her with alarm and she knew that she had to get far from the Walkers' house as soon as she could, and from the room in which she'd tossed and turned all night, acutely conscious at every wakeful moment of Joe lying close to her, separated from her by no more than a thin wooden wall.

She turned from the stove, pulled her coat from its hook and put it on. Then she opened the door, stepped outside, quietly closed the door and headed for the river.

If she walked fast enough for long enough, she thought, speeding up, she might be able to leave behind her the thoughts that had plagued her throughout the night, thoughts that would have filled Joe with shock and discomfort if he'd been able to see into her mind and, even worse, been able to see the effect they were having on her body.

And last night wasn't the first night she'd had such thoughts, if she was being brutally truthful with herself – they were the same thoughts she'd been struggling to suppress since the night of Joe's return.

The moment she'd got home that night and seen the grown-up Joe for the first time, seen the qualities she'd loved about the younger Joe shining out of the striking blue eyes of a tall man, whose body was lean and taut, whose skin gleamed gold in the soft amber glow of the lamp, who moved with latent strength and power, her insides had somersaulted in sudden violence, and from that moment on, there'd been a sensation low in her stomach that she'd never felt before.

But such thoughts about an American man were forbidden to her, a Chinese woman, and she'd struggled to stop thinking that way about someone who could never, ever be anything more to her than a friend. And she'd almost convinced herself she was winning the battle. But the way she'd felt in the store the day before, and the thoughts that had raged in her mind throughout the sleepless night, showed her that she'd struggled in vain.

Her feelings for Joe had deepened with each passing day. And forbidden or not, she yearned for his touch with a powerful longing.

But he must never know.

Why, oh why, couldn't she feel like this about Chen Fai, she agonised as she went past the miners' houses and past the well. He deserved her love for all the years of kindness he'd shown her, and nothing would have made her happier than to have been able to feel about him as she felt about Joe.

Reaching the river, she followed the gully away from Carter and towards the open plain. From time to time, she glanced down at the water and watched the morning vapour, a milky-white cloud that hovered above the water's surface, gradually start its upward drift, stealthily unveiling the river, coal-black in the chill light of dawn.

When she came to the spot where Joe had been panning for gold when he'd first heard the sound of her mother's approach, she paused. Because of Joe, she was alive. What kind of gratitude was it to let herself think about him in a way that was unseemly and unvirtuous for any girl, American or Chinese?

Instead of dreaming of what she could never have, she should list all the good things she had in life and be satisfied with those, something Miss O'Brien had regularly ordered her class to do. Well, she'd do that, she resolved, and she started walking again.

She'd begin with the Walker family. They'd never been anything but kind to her, and they still were, despite the hostility of the Carter townsfolk. Even though their former friends had long been shunning them, they'd never reproached her or said she should leave.

And Sam. He hated her, yes. But only once had he ever tried to throw her out. And he'd never taken a hand to her, and had never told his folks she must go, and made it a choice between him or her – a choice that would have seen her cast out for sure. So for all his harsh words, there must be some goodness deep within him.

And the kindness of Chen Fai was another thing she should be thankful for. He deserved better than to be planning on taking as a wife a woman whose heart, unknown to him, had been given to someone else and who couldn't get it back. What a way to repay him for everything she owed him!

And Su Lin. Her friendship with Su Lin was precious. Looking back, she couldn't imagine how she'd have got through the last few years without the happiness their friendship had brought her.

And Joe. He was the very best thing in her life; yet she was letting herself think about him in a sinful way.

Full of anger at her weak self and at the wrongfulness of her thoughts, she left the river and headed out across the wind-bitten desert, the soles of her boots crunching noisily whenever they landed on a patch of dull yellow sand or earthy white dust. A tumbleweed rolled across her path, and she kicked it away, her eyes still on the horizon, a distant grey-white backcloth, broken here and there by the shapes of flat-topped buttes and spires of rock.

'Charity! What in tarnation are you doin' out here at this time?'

She gasped.

As if from nowhere, Joe stood before her, his hat low over his eyes and his thick brown jacket done up to his throat, its fur-lined collar turned up against the cold. A coil of rope hung from one of his gloved hands.

'Joe!' she exclaimed.

He inched up the brim of his hat and she saw him stare hard at her, his eyes seeming to seek the recesses of her mind, the places where emotions she'd no right to feel lay hidden.

Her heart started racing.

'Well, I guess we've established that we know who we are,' he murmured, his breath a column of silvery mist. 'I'm now interested in why you're out here at this early hour.'

'I could say the same to you,' she said, and she managed a smile.

He shrugged. 'That's easy for me to answer.' He held up the rope. 'There was some trouble in town last night and I stayed at the livery. Bein' awake early, I thought I'd bag me a wild horse. The terrain gets rockier the further out you get and there are springs of fresh water if you know where to look, and that's where you find wild horses – they're drawn by the scent of the water.'

Her heart jumped in alarm. 'What sort of trouble? And why d'you want another horse? Are you leavin' again?'

'Just some nastiness between the miners and the Chinese priest,' he said dismissively. 'The fault was the miners'. And nope, I'm not goin' anywhere right now. Havin' spent some of the past seven winters breakin' in horses, I figured on findin' me a horse to break in here so I can sell it and bring in a few extra bucks for Seth.' He paused. 'And bein' out here on my own gives me time to think. Okay, it's your turn now. Why aren't you at home?'

Her eyes dropped from the face that was smiling down at her, warm and friendly and forbidden, and she focused on a horned toad which was scuttling in short bursts across a small patch of green where a few hopeful shoots had broken through the gravelly soil and were yet to be seared by the heat of the sun.

'Well?' he asked again after a moment or two.

She looked up at him. 'I felt like a walk. I'm indoors all day and I wanted some fresh air. It's late when I finish work, and I go straight back and help with the supper. After that it's dark. So it's either come out now or not at all.' She glanced back in the direction of the river, and then turned again to him. 'Once I'd started idly walkin', I just seemed to carry on.'

'It didn't look like idle walkin' to me. You seemed to be walkin' with real purpose.'

She attempted to laugh. 'I was tryin' to get to some air that didn't stink of coal, but I seem to have come further than I meant to. I must get back.' She made a move to go back.

'Don't go,' he said quietly, and he reached out to stop her.

At the touch of his hand on her arm, she stood still, her eyes on the ground, her heart beating fast, the warmth of his gaze filling her with heat. Slowly, she raised her eyes to his face. For a long moment, their eyes locked.

Words rose and caught in her throat.

She felt a sudden powerful longing to tell him the way she felt, to unburden herself and perhaps find some peace. But the words lay heavily inside her, held back by fear.

'Charity.' His voice was so low she hardly heard him.

Her gaze travelled across his face, lingering on his

features, one by one. Instinctively, she started to raise her hand to his cheek, wanting to touch his skin, but she caught herself in time, and let her hand fall to her side. Inwardly, she shook herself at how close she'd come to doing something that would've made him uncomfortable. 'I must go now,' she said quickly, 'or I'll be late for work.' She started to turn away.

'No!' He caught her arms and pulled her to him. 'There's somethin' I've gotta say. I can't not say it any longer.'

'Don't say anythin', Joe,' she whispered. She drew back. 'You mustn't.'

'I have to,' he cried, a note of desperation in his voice. 'I can't hold it in any more. From the moment I saw you again, there's been an emptiness inside me. It ain't the sort of emptiness that can be filled with food, and it ain't the sort of emptiness that can be filled by family time or by havin' a drink with friends. It's a different sort of emptiness, and I think you feel it inside you, too.'

He paused, waiting.

Her unspoken words hung in the air between them.

'Well, aren't you wantin' to know what could fill this emptiness of ours?' he said with a wry smile. 'A woman always wants to know that sort of thing.'

She shook her head. 'No, Joe; I don't. I already know.' She stared up into his face. 'You're right, I feel that emptiness, too. And I know that nothin' can fill it. Not walks in the mornin'; not workin' hard every minute of the day; not sleep. Definitely, not sleep. That sort of emptiness is keepin' me awake, night after night.'

He dropped his arms and gestured despair. 'Is it so wrong to feel as we feel?'

'Yes, it is.' She pulled up the sleeve of her jacket and held out her bare arm. 'Look at my skin, Joe,' she cried. 'It's yellow.' She pulled her sleeve down again. 'I've got yellow skin and you're white. American law says it *is* wrong to feel the way we do, and they could put us in prison for it, or even hang us for it. You mustn't say anythin' more. Words that are spoken aloud can't be taken back.' She took a step away from him. 'I'm goin' home now.'

She spun round, and felt a hand on each arm again. She stiffened. Gently he pulled her back against his chest. Through his thick jacket, she could feel his heart racing, and she could feel his strength. In a moment of weakness and yearning, she let herself relax and lean back. His arms tightened around her and she felt the sigh of joy that ran through his body.

Then he turned her to face him and angled her face to look up into his.

She ought to leave at once, she knew, but she couldn't move.

Rooted to the spot, she stared up into deep blue eyes flecked with burnished gold; eyes that were alive with emotion – turbulent, forbidden emotion – and she knew she couldn't stop her hunger for him from pouring out of her gaze.

'Charity,' she heard him whisper, his voice hoarse.

Then his lips were on hers, hard and desperate, an explosion of love and need.

His heat spread through her body. Her mouth moving eagerly beneath his, she slid her arms around his back and pressed the length of her body tight against his, getting as close to him as she could. She felt his hardness.

With a frightened gasp, she pulled away and put her hands to her cheeks. 'We mustn't do this. I'm not allowed to think of you in a man and woman kind of way. Much as I want to – and I do want to, Joe,' she cried, gazing despairingly up at him. 'I really do. But I mustn't.' She pulled her coat tighter around her. 'We've gotta forget today.'

He held out his hands in a gesture of despair. 'But I feel the same about you, Charity. I love you. You know I do.'

A sad smile played across her lips. 'And I love you, Joe, very much, and that's why it stops here. What kind of love would it be if I let you break the law and risk bein' hanged?' She paused. 'And what kind of woman would I be if I took the chance of the same happenin' to me as happened to my ma?'

He shook his head. 'Oh, Charity,' he said quietly. 'You know that would never happen. I'd make it all right.'

She looked up at him, hopelessness in her eyes. 'But you couldn't, Joe; the law makes it impossible. You must never touch me again. Not so long ago, a riot against the Chinese got out of hand in Denver, and a Chinese laundryman was dragged down the street with a rope round his neck, and then kicked and beaten to death by a mob of whites. And you said there was trouble in Carter last night. I don't know what sort of trouble it was, but I can imagine. With the mood the whites are in, we'd be lynched if folk found out there was anythin' between us.'

'What happened in Carter last night won't happen again. Carter folk are not like that,' he said firmly. 'And the Marshal's got everythin' in hand.'

'I hope you're right, but I don't wanna take a chance on findin' out you're wrong.'

He took a step towards her. 'Suppose I choose to take the risk rather than live without you?'

She stepped back, tears brimming in her eyes. 'I won't let you. Today was the first and the last time. I'm gonna work hard to love Chen Fai. He deserves no less – he's a good and honourable man. I know somethin's changed between you and me – it obviously has – but I also know that nothin's changed because we've stopped now and everythin's still as it was. We've always been good friends, and we still are. But we're no more than friends.'

'Charity.' He stared at her, his face distraught.

'Nothing lies between us, and it never will,' she repeated, her voice shaking. 'I'm cold now and I'm gonna go back, and I'm goin' alone. You've got a horse to find.'

She turned and walked quickly across the ground in the direction of the river, forcing herself not to look round, his anguish and despair cutting into her back.

Reaching the river, she turned left, leaving the line of his sight, and followed the river in the direction of Carter. Letting her tears fall unchecked, she struck out across the open ground to the well and made her way along the line of miners' houses to the Walkers' house.

Standing a little way back from the group of women at the well who were pointedly ignoring her, an empty pail in each of her hands, Martha watched Charity pass close by. Charity didn't see her, but she saw Charity, and she saw the tears streaming down her cheeks. Standing there in growing disquiet, she gazed after her until she'd disappeared into the house.

One by one, the other women filled their pails and returned to their houses, taking with them their laughter and chatter and contempt, and leaving her with silence. Finally, left on her own, she moved across to the pump and pulled down hard on the pump arm. As she did so, she saw Joe walk by a short distance away, a length of rope in his hand. Even from afar, she could see agitation and desperation on his face.

A frisson of fear ran through her.

She'd known the moment would come, and she'd been dreading it. But she hadn't known how she could stop it.

She'd seen the eyes of them both on the night that Joe returned. They'd looked at each other in the way she knew she'd looked at Hiram the first time she'd seen him, and from that moment on she'd been terrified of the day they gave in to their feelings.

And now it looked as if that day might have come.

Her buckets full, she walked slowly back to her house, her heart heavy.

When she'd gone to bed on the night of Joe's return, tense and ill at ease, she hadn't known what to do for the best, and she still didn't know. But the time had come when she must think of something, and she must do so fast.

She reached the front door and stared at it. 'Oh, my son,' she whispered. Then, ashen-faced, she pushed the door open and stepped over the threshold.

Chapter Thirty-Four

A distant cock was crowing when Charity quietly pulled the back door shut behind her. She paused a moment and glanced at the door to the bedroom where she used to sleep, the room where Joe now slept.

The room was empty, she knew. She'd heard Joe go out earlier.

First he'd come into the house from outside, lit the stove, waited a while for it to heat up and then made some coffee. She'd heard the chair scrape back as he'd sat down, and she'd wondered whether he'd sit a while when he finished his drink or go straight to the stable. But soon after that, she'd heard him walk past her room, open the back door and go out.

It was what he'd done every day for the past two weeks since the morning they'd met on the plain.

And that morning, as with every one of those other mornings, his footsteps had slowed as he'd passed her bedroom door. She'd heard his hesitation, felt it through the wall. She'd clutched her quilt to her chin. A throb of desire pulsing low in her stomach, she'd lain there, longing for him to open the door, willing it to stay shut.

It had stayed shut.

He'd continued along the corridor, leaving her in her bed, unable to move and in despair at her wantonness, her cheeks wet with tears of disappointment in herself.

Their time apart clearly hadn't helped him control his feelings any more than it had helped her, she'd realised. Thoughts of him had filled her mind from morning till night. And her yearning for him had built up inside her.

She'd known this was happening and had resolved to talk to him as soon as she could in an attempt to get things back to where they used to be. But there hadn't been a single moment in which to do so. For the past two weeks, Joe had left the house every morning before anyone else was up, and had returned each night well after dark, when it was far too late to sit down and eat with them, and after a few words with his parents, he'd gone straight to bed.

Hearing his steps falter again as he'd passed her room that morning, she'd realised that this couldn't continue, and she'd decided to go to the stable and talk to him. Greg would be there, too, but Greg would never tell the Carter townsfolk that she and Joe had been talking together, she was sure. And even if he did, everyone knew she'd been friends with Joe all her life, and they wouldn't get riled up about him speaking with her.

She'd thrown back her cover and washed and dressed at speed, anxious to get to Joe before the town filled with people. What she would say to him, she didn't know, but she'd think of something. He'd be in the middle of watering and graining the horses by the time she reached the livery, but she was certain he'd be able to break off briefly to talk with her.

She turned away from his bedroom door and started walking past the vegetable patch towards the town, its buildings bleak beneath a bank of grey cloud that hung low across the sky. The morning air was bitter-cold, and she wound her scarf more tightly around her head and thrust her hands into her coat pockets as she hurried across the open ground.

The stable was the right place in which to talk to Joe, she reassured herself as she walked. With Greg there, they wouldn't be alone in the building, so the wrong sorts of thoughts wouldn't flood her mind and distract her from what she had to say to make sure she didn't lose him.

She caught her breath. Why did she think she could lose Joe?

The law might stop them from ever being more to each other than friends, but he would always be her friend. One day he, too, would wed, and then, married to other people and living in different cultures, they'd obviously lose some of their closeness – that was only to be expected – but they would still be friends. Law or no law, they had a bond that could never be broken.

That she must never let be broken.

She turned into Second Street and hurried along on the Chinatown side of the street, her eyes on the livery stable on the opposite corner, her heeled boots shattering shards of ice that littered the boardwalk. Reaching Main Street, she glanced in both directions, making sure that no one was close by in either part of the town, then stepped off the boardwalk to cross over to the stable.

'Charity!' Martha's voice came from her left.

She stopped in surprise in the middle of the road, turned and saw Martha hurrying along on the whites' side of the street. She made a move to go to her, but Martha indicated for her to stay where she was. Stepping down from the boardwalk, Martha walked across the street towards her, placing her feet with care between the ridges of hard mud that criss-crossed the centre of the track.

'What are you doin', gal, comin' over to this side of the street?' Martha asked when she reached Charity. 'When I last looked, the bakery and mercantile were in the other direction.'

'I was just goin' to say hello to Joe. I've not spoken to him for a couple of weeks, with him bein' gone real early in the mornin' and back so late each night.'

Unsmiling, Martha nodded. 'I seen that, too. He's not sat down at the table to eat with us for a while now. But what's two weeks of not speakin' to him? Before that, you'd not spoken to him for seven years.'

Charity tried to laugh. 'I know that. But now he's here, I thought I'd ask how he was settlin' down. I didn't want to write it in a letter.' She attempted a laugh again.

At the sight of the grim expression on Martha's face, she stopped.

'I don't know about Joe, but I've been wantin' to talk to you, gal,' Martha said, 'and now's as good a time as any, with the men not bein' around.'

Charity's face filled with anxiety. 'What about? Have I done somethin' wrong?' She pushed her hands further into her pockets.

'Look, Charity,' Martha began. 'You're a grown woman now and I'm not gonna beat about the bush – we both know what I'm talkin' about. You need to move out. You're gonna wed Chen Fai in May, I think you said. I sure am hopin' nothing's gonna stop that weddin' from going ahead.'

Charity bit her lip.

'I don't have to say more, do I? Joe did what he was asked when you were little, keepin' an eye on you at times and helpin' with the work I would've been doin' if I hadn't been lookin' after you. But you're not a little gal any longer, and there's no need for him to keep lookin' to see you're all right. You've got Chen Fai to do that for you now. Isn't that so?'

Charity nodded.

'And it wouldn't be proper for you and Joe, a grown man and woman, to be spendin' time together away from other folk. Isn't that also so?'

'I know it wouldn't,' Charity said, her voice low.

'I hope you do, gal. It's time Joe started thinkin' of himself. He's a fine-lookin' man with a good future and he'll find himself a woman real easy. But he won't until he takes his eyes off you and starts lookin' around him.'

Charity's heart missed a beat, and she swallowed hard. 'Joe's a friend. I've never thought of him as anythin' else. I'm gonna marry Chen Fai, aren't I?'

'Like I said, I certainly hope so. But you've got some work to do there, I rather think. The last few times I've seen Chen Fai, he's not looked a happy man. It's not just San Francisco that's got Chinese gals, you know.'

'I know.'

'So you'll know there are some in Green River and Evanston now, and that's not far away. Not many, I grant you, maybe only one or two. But how many does a man need? And Chen Fai would be a real good catch for any of them. I'm suggestin' you put a smile on your face and be real nice to him. If you wanna get wed, that is.'

'Of course I do,' Charity echoed hollowly.

'Well, I hope you do.' Martha took a step closer to her. ''Cos I'm tellin' you, gal, if Chen Fai changes his mind about marryin' you, you'll go to Green River, get a job as a domestic and live there, or you'll do what Chinese women have to do in places like the *tong* if they wanna eat. I want you out of the house, and out of Joe's life. I reckon I couldn't make that any clearer. D'you understand?' Cold grey eyes pierced her.

Charity nodded.

Martha took a step back. 'Good. You can stay till your weddin', but you'll be gone before June, married or not.'

'Okay,' Charity said quietly.

'And there's another reason why I want you out of the

house and livin' in Chinatown,' Martha went on. 'I reckon there's gonna be big trouble between the whites and the Chinamen. What happened two weeks ago is just the start, not the finish, like Hiram and Joe seem to think. The whites' club gave the Chinese miners a chance to join the club and stand up with them against Union Pacific, but they turned it down and there's real resentment about that.'

'They think it's a white man's organisation,' Charity said. 'And also they've got *tong* leaders to speak for them.'

'Whatever the reason, the whites ain't pleased. I'm hearin' more and more of them say the Chinese must go. I don't want my Joe caught in the middle, a white man lookin' to defend a Chinese woman. Who knows what could happen?'

'I wouldn't let him,' she said quickly.

'You wouldn't be able to stop him! No, he's got the chance of a good life here, thanks to Seth, and I want him free to take it. With you wed or livin' in another town, Joe would only have himself to think about. And if there *is* trouble, well Chen Fai's a good man. He knows what's happenin' in town as well as anyone else, and he'll keep you safe from harm. You'd best set your mind on keepin' him.'

She stared at Charity, whose face was pale in the morning light.

'You been a good gal, Charity,' she said, her eyes and her voice softening. 'You've worked hard and never complained, and I don't regret takin' you in, whatever you may think. What's more, I guess I've come to feel affection for you, which I sure hadn't expected.'

Charity stared at her, a sudden hope springing to her eyes.

'But things've changed now, and I gotta look to the future and think of Joe. Anythin' wrongful between you and Joe, and he'd find himself in jail real fast, or even worse. And probably you, too. I hear what's in the papers, too, you know. And there's Sam and Phebe and Thomas to think about, and Hiram. Hiram needs that job of his, and I wouldn't wanna see him lose it 'cos of a friendship that's against the law. Joe's always said you were a smart gal. So act smart and marry Chen Fai before he decides he doesn't want a woman with her mind set on someone else.'

'I don't think about Joe like that,' Charity said, her hope now gone, her voice a whisper. 'I don't.'

'Is that so, gal?' Martha gave her a wry smile. 'Then I reckon you're not quite as smart as Joe thinks. You'd do well to face what's in your heart, and work hard at overcomin' it, as it's never gonna be. If I can see it, so, too, can Chen Fai, and so can anyone with eyes in their head.' She stepped back. 'And now that I said what I came to say, I'll let you get yourself to the bakery – it's fair cold out here. As for me, I think I'll go and see how Joe's gettin' on.'

She nodded at Charity, walked briskly across to the boardwalk on the whites' side of town and turned left into Main Street. A moment later, Joe's exclamation of pleased surprise at the sight of his mother sounded from the other side of the livery wall.

Her head bowed, Charity turned away and walked slowly down Main Street in the opposite direction from the stable, and then she crossed the road and went inside the bakery.

Chapter Thirty-Five

Leaving the bakery, Charity crossed over to the general mercantile. She paused a moment in front of the entrance and stared at the scrolls on either side of the door. Then she took a deep breath and, with the words of Joe's ma earlier that morning ringing loud in her ears, went inside.

At the discordant chorus of wind chimes, Chen Fai looked up. He was standing on the customer side of the left-hand counter, arranging some packets that were on display. His face broke into a smile and he came towards her.

She unwound her scarf and took off her coat. He held out his hands and took her outdoor clothes from her, and she felt a sharp pang of guilt at how kind he was, and at how reluctant she now was to be with him.

Making a great effort, she beamed at him. His mouth curved into a smile, but an anxious fear flickered in the depths of his dark eyes, and there was a slight reserve in his manner. If Joe's ma hadn't said what she had, she might not have noticed it, she thought, but she could certainly see it now.

Panic sliced through her.

She waited until he'd returned from hanging her things in the back room, and then went closer to him. 'I hope I'm not late today,' she said, her fingers lightly running along the top of the counter.

He gestured the unimportance of time with his hand. 'This does not matter,' he said, his face still anxious, his eyes still fearful.

'It's just that I was thinkin' about the *chang-fu* for my weddin',' she added, and she saw the anxiety begin to fade.

'And I was thinkin' about the shoes I'd wear, and that it's time I asked Su Lin to tell me what happens at a Chinese weddin'.' She managed a little laugh. 'May is not so far away, after all.'

Chen Fai leaned against the counter and slid his hand along its wooden surface, coming to a stop as he reached the tips of her fingers. He glanced down at their hands as they rested on the counter, fingertip to fingertip, but kept his fingers from touching hers.

'It's wrong for a man to touch the woman he'll wed. He must not touch her in front of people before wedding, and not after, and I not touch you now. But if I was American man, I would take both your hands and squeeze them in joy. I am very happy you think about our wedding in this way, Charity.'

She stared up at him. 'I think I've probably not said the sort of things I should have said, Chen Fai. I've been thinkin' like an American woman, which is the way I've been taught to think. But when I listen to the way Su Lin speaks to you, and how she speaks to Chen Sing and her mother – to her honourable father and mother, perhaps I should say,' she added smiling, 'I know you've not been hearin' from me the things you've a right to hear, that a real Chinese woman would say to you.'

He stared at her in surprise. 'I not expect to hear anything you not say. You are American as well as Chinese. I know this and I know you will not think in every way like a Chinese woman. But this is not a problem – we live in America, not China. And I also am a little bit American now.'

'Hear me out, Chen Fai,' she said gently. 'I've been talkin' to Su Lin, and I know there's somethin' I should do to show you how I feel.' She took a step back, knelt down on the floorboards in front of him, lowered her head to the floor and lightly touched the boards with her forehead three times. Then she sat back on her heels and looked up at him. 'It will be a great honour for this unworthy person to give you a son,' she said solemnly.

'Charity,' he said, clearly overcome. At the love that flooded his eyes, she heaved an inner sigh of relief. 'I think it better we forget for one moment we are not allowed to touch,' he said, and he put out his hand to help her up. Taking both of her hands in his, he gently squeezed them, and then dropped them. 'What you say makes me very happy. But you not need to kowtow to me again. We are in America now, and this is not the way Americans do things.'

'But we are both Chinese, and this is the Chinese way of doin' such things. I want you to know I feel great respect for you. Su Lin showed me how to do this.'

'I see.' He smiled at her in amusement. 'Another Chinese custom is for wife to make shoes for mother-in-law. This shows her respect for her mother-in-law. But in my Chinese heart, I feel very sorry for honourable father's second wife if you make shoes in the same way as you sew clothes.'

She giggled. 'I think I'll skip that custom.'

'And what about Chinese custom that a wife must refer to her husband in public as the useless one? This is Chinese way of showing affection. Chinese man and wife not embarrass each other by giving compliments in public. We also do this Chinese custom?'

She laughed. 'Nope, we won't do that one, either. Americans would think I was a pretty strange woman to marry someone I thought useless.'

He laughed with her, and then his face became grave. 'I understand what you say when you kowtow to me, Charity, and I feel your respect for me. This makes me very happy.

But we are in America and you are not wife chosen by go-between. You have met man who will be husband before wedding day.'

A little surprised, she nodded. 'I know that. Why?'

'You and me, we know each other for long time. I am hoping you feel more than just great respect for me now.' His cheeks went pink. 'I am hoping that thought of doing what we must do if you are to bear me a son is something you want in here.' He placed his hand on his heart. 'I think you know what I try to say, Charity.'

She felt herself going red. 'It isn't somethin' a virtuous Chinese woman would say aloud, or a well-brought up American woman, for that matter.'

'But do you feel this?' he asked quietly. 'Since Joe Walker come back, I not know.'

'I do,' she said quickly. 'If I did not, I wouldn't marry you. I'd look for another Chinese man.'

His face broke out into a broad smile. 'Then I a very lucky, very happy man. Now, you go to Su Lin. She will remind you how to make tea. Making tea is part of the wedding celebration. You will make tea for Walker ma and pa before wedding, and for Chen parents after wedding. When honourable parents accept tea, they are saying they accept you.'

'Then I'd better learn to make it well,' she said lightly. She smiled at him and started to walk towards the back room.

'One other thing,' he called after her. She stopped and turned towards him. 'It's Chinese custom to have new bed for night of wedding,' he said. 'It's for husband to get bed, and for parents of bride to get bedding, but I get bedding, too. Sheets are red or pink, and are embroidered with dragon and phoenix in gold threads, or with flowers such as peony and magnolia. It brings good fortune on wedding night.'

'Does it?' she said. Her voice sounded hollow to her ears, and she swallowed hard.

In her head, she saw the bed. And she saw him standing next to it, waiting for her. Then she saw herself stepping forward, naked beneath her thin batiste nightdress.

An icy hand clutched her heart, and a shiver ran through her.

He laughed. 'And there's more,' he went on with a happy smile. 'No adult is to sit or rest on bridal bed before wedding. Not even the bride, as this could bring ill health. Only babies and children are allowed to sit on wedding bed. Children bless the man and woman with fertility. But we will not have this blessing. I think Sam Walker will not agree to baby son sitting on bridal bed to help bring another Chinaman into Carter.' And he laughed again.

She forced a smile to her lips, and headed quickly for the back of the store.

Pushing the curtain aside, she stepped into the Chen living room, let the curtain fall behind her, and leaned back against the wall, trembling. She closed her eyes.

'I hear *dai lou* tell you we make tea today,' she heard Su Lin say, her voice dancing with happiness. 'Is very important so we both must do this well. I have a tea set here, and we use sweet tea for what is a sweet occasion. I have longans and red dates' tea for both of us. Longans are like dragon's eyes and show wife's wish to give her husband a male child.'

Charity opened her eyes and stared at Su Lin, at her radiant face.

'I think getting son with husband will be very good,' Su Lin said giggling, and she blushed.

A powerful shudder ran the length of Charity's body.

She looked at Su Lin. Her face white, she slowly shook her head. 'I'm sorry, Su Lin, but I can't,' she said, her voice a whisper. 'I just can't.'

The smile faded from Su Lin's face. She stared at Charity, startled. Then Charity saw realisation dawn in her eyes, followed swiftly by distress.

An urge to get away from them all welled up inside her.

And a burning desire to see Joe.

She picked up her skirts. 'I'm sorry,' she cried. 'Tell Chen Fai I'm sorry, but I've gotta go.' And she half-ran across the living area, and flung herself through the back door and out to the yard. Without pausing, she sped round the side of the house, into Second Street and across the track to the livery stable.

As she rounded the corner, she saw Joe in front of the entrance, cleaning the water troughs with Greg. She came to an abrupt halt and stared at him, her breath coming fast, her arms hanging in helpless despair at her sides.

He glanced up. She saw the pleasure on his face as he realised she was there, then surprise, followed by concern. He stood up and stared at her, a brush in one hand and a rag in the other. 'Charity?' Her name was a question.

She stared back at him, unable to speak, her heart full of grief. Then with a cry of sorrow, she turned and started to run back along Second Street towards the miners' houses, oblivious to the risk of slipping in the pools of water where the ice had melted in the heat of the strengthening sun, oblivious to everything but the need to get as far away as she could from her future.

Joe turned sharply to Greg.

'Take over,' he said. 'I've gotta find out what's upset Charity.'

'But—'

'There's no but, Greg. Do as I ask.' Joe dropped the rag, threw down the brush, knocking the pail on its side, and ran after her as fast as he could.

Across the open ground she ran, past the miners' houses and out towards the river. Expecting her to head for the place where they used to sit, he ran at an angle to the right, hoping to cut her off, but she suddenly swerved to the left.

He stopped in surprise and stared after her. She was making for the bridge that spanned the river by Carter, he realised, the bridge where her mother had fallen, and which they'd crossed on the occasions he'd taken her for an afternoon's freedom in the rocky hills on the other side of the river from town.

Then he started to walk slowly after her. There was no longer any need for him to run – he knew exactly where she'd be heading, and his every instinct told him that she'd need a moment or two by herself before she felt able to talk.

Standing in the middle of the track between the mercantile and the bakery, Chen Fai stared up towards the whites' part of town, his gaze fixed on the livery stable and on the lad cleaning the trough with a brush. A pail lay on its side near the trough, its contents spilled. The brush on the ground near the pail looked as if it had been thrown down in haste.

There was no sign of Charity. Nor of Joe Walker.

Sensing Su Lin hovering behind him, he turned to her. Her eyes were clouded with anxiety, he saw.

'What did you say to Charity that make her run out?' he asked.

'I not say much,' she said, her face puzzled. 'I tell her I hear what you say, and I say I am ready to show her again the Chinese way to make tea.'

'And that's all?'

She screwed up her face in thought. 'I also say we use longans and red dates' tea for the ceremony, and I tell her longans show a wife's wish to give her husband a male child.'

And he'd just talked to Charity about the wedding bed, he realised.

A sense of loss shot through him, followed by pain, and he felt the blood drain from his face. 'And she leave then?' he asked, a tremor in his voice.

Su Lin nodded. 'She say to tell you she can't, and then she go.'

He turned back to look towards the livery stable, and stood very still.

'She is maybe ill,' Su Lin ventured after a minute or two.

'Maybe,' he said, his eyes on the stable. 'But I think it an illness that come after Joe Walker returns.'

He fell silent.

After a few minutes, Su Lin cleared her throat. He glanced at her over his shoulder. 'You go inside now, Su Lin,' he said flatly. 'I think you will not show Charity how to make tea today. And maybe not any day.'

She gasped. Quickly putting her hands together in front of her, she gave her brother a slight bow. 'I am sorry if I do wrong. I do not want to be Charity's friend any more.'

'You do nothing wrong,' he told her, and he attempted a smile. 'You are a good little sister to me, and good friend to Charity. In fact—' An idea sprang into his mind, and he paused, his heart thumping, and then turned to face her more squarely. 'In fact, I think there *is* maybe a way you can help me,' he said. He nodded slowly. 'Yes, maybe there is.'

'I will be very happy to help you,' Su Lin said, and her face brightened. 'What do you want me to do?'

'I want you still to be her friend,' he said. 'Ah! I see you are surprised by this,' he added with a wan smile. 'But this is what I want. I know Charity will not come back here today. Maybe she will go to Ah Lee tomorrow, maybe not. It would please me if you watched for her like you watched for her when you were child and wanted her to be your friend. And when you see her, I would like you to talk with her. You then tell me what she say, and I know what is inside her head.'

She gave a start, as if to speak.

He smiled reassuringly. 'You must not worry, Su Lin. I accept now that I am not in her heart, but many Chinese man and woman can say the same thing on their wedding day. They not meet before the wedding, so this is not surprising. But they live happily together after the wedding, and often with love. There is still chance for Charity and me.'

She clasped her hands together. 'Oh, that pleases me very much, *ge ge*.'

He smiled warmly at her. 'You not often call me this now you are a grown woman,' he said. 'Yes, I would like you to stay Charity's friend. We are still friends, Charity and me. One good friend does not ask another to feel what she cannot feel, and I do not ask Charity to feel what is not inside her. But to be friends is a good beginning to marriage. And maybe one day she will feel as I feel. I can wait for this. If I know what Charity is thinking now, I know if we still have a chance to find happiness together. If we have not …' He paused, and shook his head. 'But I not want to think that yet.'

'I watch for Charity,' she said eagerly.

'And it also help *you*, Su Lin. If Charity leaves Carter Town, you lose your friend. I not want this to happen, and I will try to keep your friend in Carter.'

She beamed up at him. 'I will be very happy if that happen.'

He nodded. 'You are not needed in the store for a day or two. It is more important you find Charity and speak with her, and tell me what she say. You go now to honourable father and say you do work to help me.' He smiled encouragement at her.

She bowed to him once more, and went back into the shop.

He watched her go, then turned away and stared again towards the stable.

The smile left his face.

No matter what he'd encouraged Su Lin to think, he and Charity would never marry now. Despite the fact that at some point in the past three years – he wasn't sure when – the liking he'd originally felt for Charity had deepened into love, a love that had grown so strong that it hurt, and despite the fact that to his shame, he still loved her.

But he could never marry her, not even if she begged him to take her back, something that might well happen one day.

Because of American law, she could never wed Joe, and she'd never agree to become Joe's unwed concubine. Not just because they were sure to be lynched by the whites if they ever found out about it, but because she'd never risk the same thing happening to her as had happened to her mother. Of that he was certain.

So when Joe Walker got on his horse and rode away again – which one day that restless man would do – and she found herself alone once more, she might well decide that marriage to him was better than working as a servant for a white master, or finding another Chinaman to wed, and he could easily see her coming back to him, asking him to forgive her.

But when that happened, even if he still loved her, he would not be able to take her for his wife. The shame of doing so would be too great.

It was known throughout Carter Town that he'd walked with Charity for years, that presents had been offered and accepted, and that she'd agreed to be his wife. Soon it would be known by everyone that she had turned her back on him.

A shudder ran through him at having lost face in so shameful, so humiliating a way.

Chinamen would never again look at him with envy in their eyes as he walked down the street with the beautiful woman who had chosen him out of all the Chinamen in Carter to be the father of her son. Instead of envy, there'd be pity, and the contempt given to any Chinaman who'd lost face and thus brought shame on his parents and ancestors.

To take her back after that would make him an object of even greater contempt, and heap still more shame upon his family. And this he could never allow to happen.

No, he had lost Charity forever, and where once he'd been full of dreams of a life with her, there was now only a painful, aching void, a void that had been brought about by Joe Walker.

Charity had changed towards him the day that man had returned.

Others wouldn't have noticed the change, but he'd seen it – it was in every word she'd said since then, in every look she'd given him, every movement she'd made when he was near. Before Joe had come back, she'd been content to be alone with him. And at times their arms had accidentally brushed as they'd walked together or worked side by side behind the counter, and there'd been no shudder of disgust from her.

But from the moment of Joe Walker's return, her thoughts

had been on that man. Her promise to marry him had been swept away like dust, and his wishes trampled upon.

He felt a sharp stab of self-pity. He had deserved better than that from her.

He had allowed his sister to befriend her; he had made a friend of her himself; he had never been anything but kind to her, and he had offered her a future in which she would be loved and kept safe from the hostility of the whites.

But still she had spurned him. And cruelly so. From the way she'd behaved, she'd shown him that the very thought of him as a man, of what they'd have to do to get a son, was so distasteful that she couldn't go through with the wedding.

Rage started simmering deep inside, spreading through him, gradually filling the void.

He would get his revenge on Joe Walker if it was the last thing he did. And not just on Joe – Charity must suffer, too.

A sob caught in his throat.

She must suffer for failing to love him in the way he deserved to be loved after all the years in which he'd cared for her. And she must suffer, too, for being so disregarding of his standing in the Chinese community that she'd brought shame on him and made it impossible for him ever to take her back.

He stood there trembling, unable to move, blinded by the sudden intensity of anger and hurt that blazed within him, and of overwhelming grief.

Struggling to take control of himself, he took a few deep breaths. Giving way to his feelings would stop him from thinking clearly and sensibly. He needed a mind empty of emotion if he was to find a way of making them pay for the cruel hurt they'd inflicted on him. As they must do.

Joe would get the punishment he deserved when the

whites learnt that he wanted to lie beside Charity, a Chinese woman. When he, Chen Fai, found out how Joe planned to do this, for he was certain that this was Joe's aim, he would make sure that the whites knew of Joe's unlawful intentions. And he *would* find out. Su Lin would tell him.

And Charity would pay, too. Oh, yes, she'd be made to pay.

He could easily see her coming back to him, begging his forgiveness, promising to do anything he wished in order to show the purity of her remorse. And he could easily see himself leading her on, encouraging her to prove to him that he was mistaken in thinking she found his body repugnant, and in thinking she couldn't bear to do what she'd have to do with him as his wife.

He smiled grimly to himself. There'd be only one way in which she could demonstrate the sincerity of her words, and he'd make her take that way. He'd make her lie down and open her legs for him, and then he'd sate himself.

He'd wanted this for so long, and so patiently, and he deserved it. He'd increasingly had to struggle to control himself as she'd grown into the desirable woman she'd become. So many times when they'd been alone, and he'd been thick and hard with want in his groin, he'd come close to begging her to lie beside him and so put an end to his painful ache, but he'd always managed to hold back. He'd respected her.

But no more.

Yes, he thought with quiet satisfaction; he'd sate himself, and then he'd walk away.

Only then would he be able to think about finding another wife.

Chapter Thirty-Six

Winded from running at speed out of the town, across the bridge and up to the top of the snow-frosted rock, Charity was bending over, her hands on her hips, drawing her breath in jagged gasps when Joe drew close to her.

He paused for a moment on the rock beneath hers, and watched as she gathered her breath, then straightened up and stared towards the plain, a slender figure in a dress the colour of ripe corn, her black braid lying over her shoulder, an air of deep misery engulfing her.

Then he walked slowly up the last few steps, and took his place at her side, his gaze following the direction of hers.

'It's been a long time since we stood here together, just you and me,' he said. 'And you were a mite bit smaller then,' he added, the trace of a smile in his voice.

Her eyes fixed ahead of her, she didn't speak.

'But why come up here?' he asked, glancing sideways at her. 'Why not go to the river? That's where you always used to go when you wanted to think. You'd crouch down at the water's edge, shut your eyes, screw your face up tight and think real hard.' He smiled at her. 'So hard I could almost hear the thoughts movin' around in your head.'

'Life was easy then,' she said flatly. 'It's gotten more difficult now. Just shuttin' my eyes doesn't work any longer.'

He waited, but she didn't add anything.

'I know there's a problem—' he began.

'*You* are the problem, Joe,' she said quietly, and she turned to him, her face stained with tears. 'It's you.'

He frowned. 'I don't understand.'

'It's real easy to explain.' Her voice caught. 'I was okay

with Chen Fai when we were walkin' out, and I was sort of okay when he asked me to wed him. I did hesitate a moment when he asked me – it was like I could hear you whisperin' to me from afar – but the whisperin' died away and I said yes. Marryin' Chen Fai was the obvious future for me. And then you came back, and nothin' was okay any more.'

He gestured helplessly. 'Tell me what I can do.'

She shook her head. 'There's nothin',' she said. 'I let him see today that I didn't feel about him as a wife should her husband. If I'd been brought up a real Chinese girl, I'd know that didn't matter – the most important thing would be to do my duty. My duty as a wife would be to try hard to give my husband a son, and my feelin's about what we were gonna have to do to get that son would come way behind. But I was brought up American.'

He stared at her in surprise. 'But you must have thought about that side of things in all the time you've been friendly with the man. You've been walkin' out with him for years, and you must've known he intended to offer for you. At some point since you've gotten to be a woman, you must've thought about what you'd have to do, as you put it, to get a son with him.'

'You're right, I did. And when Su Lin and I used to talk about getting wed and havin' a husband, I didn't think I'd have any problem being a wife to Chen Fai. He's a good man, and he's a good son and brother; I've seen this for myself. He's clean in his ways and he's got a pleasin' face. Also, he's smart. You can see that from the way he runs the business. And in a way, I do love him – but as a friend, and not in the way a wife should. I didn't think about bein' with him at night, what I'd have to do ...' She shuddered. 'Though even if I had, I still may not have felt about it as I do now.'

He stared at her, mystified. 'I don't understand.'

'I didn't know what I wasn't feelin', what I should've been feelin'. I didn't know what it was like to want someone so bad that it hurt. I learnt that by feelin' the way I do about you. Since you came back, I've not been able to bear the thought of touchin' his body, or him touchin' mine.'

'Oh, Charity,' he said, and he caught her hand.

She pulled her hand away. 'So I'm leavin',' she said.

'Leavin'!' He grabbed her hand again. 'You can't leave. I won't let you. I love you.'

His words echoed around the rocks and returned to them.

She gave him a sad smile. 'But there's no future for us together; not as man and wife.'

He shook his head in desperation. 'Don't say that. Out there on the plain that mornin', we admitted we loved each other. From the moment I saw you again, I've not been able to think of anythin' else but you. We're never gonna be apart again.'

'Oh, Joe,' she breathed wistfully. 'How I wish that was true. But it's not; it's impossible.'

He cupped her face in his hands and stared into her eyes, his breath hot against her cold face. 'Nothin's impossible; not when you love someone as I love you. I've always loved you. I loved you as a child who was real nice to be with. When I grew up and left home, I loved you as a friend who made sure I always felt part of my family; and now that I'm back, I love you as a man loves a woman. I've met many women in the past seven years, and I won't lie to you, I've been with some of them, but no one has ever made me feel the way you make me feel when I look at you, and I'm not leavin' you again.'

She stared up at him, her eyes open wide, questioning. 'But you have to. Whatever I feel inside, to the rest of the world I'm Chinese. There's no future for us together.'

'We're gonna have the future we want,' he said.

She took a step back. 'I don't understand.'

'We're gonna get wed, and we're gonna have a home and a family.'

'But we can't,' she said, her eyes filling with tears. 'Someone else will have to give you that family.'

'It's you I'm gonna marry,' he said firmly, and he put his arms around her and drew her close. 'At least, I'm hopin' you'll agree to be my wife.'

'No, Joe.' She raised her head and looked up into his face, her eyes full of longing. 'I love you with all my heart, and you know that. But like I said, I won't be part of anythin' that might end up with you bein' thrown into jail or killed.'

He tightened his arms around her.

'Your ma wants me gone from Carter,' she said, sinking against his chest, her voice muffled by his jacket, 'and she's right. She and your pa will do better without me. And I've broken my promise to Chen Fai, which will be seen as very bad by the Chinese. I'll never again get work in Carter so I'm gonna go to Green River and find a job.'

He put a hand on each of her arms and held her from him at arms' length. 'You're right about leavin' Carter,' he said quietly and firmly. 'But you'll be leavin' as my wife.'

'How?' Her question trembled with hope.

'For the last few days, I've been thinkin' about what we can do, and I reckon I've worked it out now.' He turned her gently to face the dusty white plain that lay to the left of the town. 'There's a whole other world out there,' he said, putting one arm round her shoulders and pointing with the other to the empty expanse ahead of them. 'Somewhere out there, we'll find a place to live, a place with real good ranchin' land.'

She glanced at him in surprise. 'But you like being a cowboy and travellin' around.'

'Yup, I did. It was a great life for the years I did it, and I learnt a heap of things that'll be of use. But even before I came back to Carter, I knew I'd gotten drovin' out of my system and I was ready to stake me a homestead and start buildin' up a ranch.'

'A homestead,' she echoed.

He pulled her to him as they stared towards the plain. 'That's right. Just think of it,' he said, his words falling over themselves in his enthusiasm. 'A hundred and sixty acres of our own! We'll head for one of the towns growin' up in the north of Wyoming, far away from the railroad and far away from minin' towns full of hate. Everyone's buildin' a new life in a town like that, and no one cares about laws they probably don't even know exist.'

She felt excitement start to build up inside her. 'D'you really think it's possible?'

'I reckon it is,' he told her, his eyes shining. 'And I'm certain my trail partner, Ethan, will join us when we've got the claim and he'll help us build it up. I know he'd like that a lot, and I know you'd like him. Ethan's someone to ride the river with – you couldn't have a better man at your side.'

'But what about the livery stable?' she asked, her face suddenly anxious. 'You'll be lettin' Mr Culpepper down.'

'The stable's not a problem. Greg's a good lad and I've been teachin' him what he needs to know about horses. I've set a routine for the stable, and he'll be able to carry on with it quite easily. Seth will know that. I've already ordered all the supplies they'll need till the fall, and by then, Seth will be able to take over. The stable will be fine, and so will Seth.'

'But you could have had it for yourself one day.'

'But I couldn't have had you, too, and I'd rather have you.'

She thought for a moment. 'Even if we settle miles away in a place where folk don't know we're breakin' the law by bein' together, we still won't be able to get wed.'

'I think we will – in a way.' He glanced up at the sky. 'It's like I can feel the touch of your ma's eyes on me, willin' me to find a way to do the right thing by you.' He looked back down at her, and a broad smile spread across his face. 'And I think I've come up with an idea. It involves the Chinese priest. The law that's stoppin' us from gettin' wed is an American law, and it's a law that's hurtin' all the Chinese. I reckon there's many a Chinaman who'd choose to live with a woman rather than live alone, if they could, even if the woman was white.'

She nodded. 'I'm sure you're right. I don't think they'd gamble as much, or use opium like they do, if they had a woman to go home to. I know they use the *tong* women, but for most of them that's because there isn't a choice.'

'And the law that's stoppin' them from goin' to China and bringin' their wives back here is an American law, and I reckon both of those laws stick in their craw. Just think of Chen Fai and the bride he was gonna have. No, there's not much love for the whites in the Chinese community, just as there isn't the other way round, and I'm thinkin' the priest might help us.'

'How do you mean?'

He took a deep breath. 'First of all, he owes me a favour as I stopped him from bein' lynched, and I reckon he'll want to clear the debt. Secondly, I can see him being persuaded to think himself outside American law when it comes to what the Chinese do among themselves, and you're one of his people. I think he might agree to marry us. If he married us, we'd have a sort of certificate, and we'd have a marriage recognised by one of our communities. It's just that it won't be a marriage in the eyes of American law. But married by the priest, you'd be as close to a lawful wife as can be. If you agree.'

He looked anxiously at her.

She bit her lip, thinking about his words. 'I do,' she said slowly, and her face broke into a radiant smile. 'Oh, Joe; yes; I do,' And she threw up her arms up to the sky and shouted, 'I do, I do, I do.'

He caught her arms and pulled her to him.

Tilting her face towards his, he cupped it in his hands. For a long moment, neither moved, each gazing deep into the eyes of the other, their hearts thudding loudly, their breaths swift and shallow.

Then she took a step closer to him. Pressing her body against his, she slid her hands under his jacket, and ran her fingers across his lean chest, flooding his body with desire.

Blood thundered in his head, in his groin. 'Oh, Charity,' he groaned, and he brought his mouth hard down on hers.

'I reckon we should plan on gettin' wed in a couple of weeks, and leave Carter straight after,' Joe said as they made their way down the side of the rocky outgrowth. 'It's Tuesday today. If we marry a week on Monday, as early in the day as the priest will do it, assuming he'll do it, and then head north at once, we should be pretty far from Carter by sundown.'

'So we're definitely goin' to the north of Wyoming, are we?' she asked, clinging to his arm.

'Yup. We'll skirt round the south of Sheridan and head for one of the valleys due east of the town. The grass there is as green as it can be, and there are acres of land just waitin' to be staked. With mountains around there's plenty of water, and you'll see fruit trees and flowers you've never seen before. Watercress grows wild along the rivers, and there are thickets of chokecherries and huckleberries just there for the pickin'.'

'It sounds perfect,' she said, her voice trembling with excitement.

'It is. When I was last that way, we passed through a small town that was just startin' up, and that's the place we'll head for. We need to be near somewhere like that so's we can get our provisions. While I was there, I saw a white man walkin' along the street with an Injun woman at his side, and no one was bothered. That's a place we can live in.'

'Where'll we sleep when we're travellin'?'

'In the wagon for the first three weeks or so as it'd be too risky to get a room. But you'll like sleepin' beneath the stars. It's a special feelin'. And we'll get the water we need from rivers and streams. Once we're far away from any minin' towns, we should be able to stop the night in a roomin'-house. It's two dollars a night for a room, and two bits extra if they bring hot water up to us.'

'How long will it take to get where we're goin'?'

'Around seven weeks, I reckon.' He grinned down at her. 'We'll do what we do when drivin' cows – we'll go as far as possible in the first few days to put as much ground as we can between us and Carter, and then we'll go at a slower pace. But we must make sure not to push the horses too far without a break, or let them get winded – it's not like on a drive where we've got *remuda* horses to swap with, and our horses will be pullin' a wagon.'

She nestled closer to him, feeling the hard muscle beneath his jacket. Every nerve in her body tingled. 'I can't wait for us to be wed, Joe,' she breathed.

He tightened his hold on her. 'Nor can I,' he said. 'I

wanna kiss you so badly right now, but it's too close to town and someone might see. But once we're away from this part of Wyoming, we'll be free to do whatever we want.'

'I'm scared,' she blurted out, glancing up at him. 'So much could go wrong.'

'Trust me, I'm scared, too. We'd be loco not to be, things bein' as they are. But if I didn't think it could work, I wouldn't suggest it. I couldn't bear it if anythin' bad happened to you.'

The bridge came in sight. Instinctively, they dropped their arms and drew apart.

'Your folks will miss you,' she said as they started walking across the bridge. 'I hate to think of them hurtin'; they've been real good to me.'

'We mustn't tell them what we're plannin' on doin',' he said quickly, alarm in his voice. 'No one must know. We'll leave them a note to find when we're gone.'

She frowned slightly. 'What if they see me gettin' my things together, and guess we're leavin'?'

He shook his head. 'They won't, not if we're real careful. We'll fetch the things we're takin' across to the stable in stages. Seth will have to know, of course, but no one else. He knows the danger we'll be in and won't say anythin'.'

'You don't think your folks would tell the Marshal if they knew, do you?'

He shook his head. 'Nope, they'd never do that, no matter how upset they were. But I don't know about Sam. And I couldn't ask Ma and Pa to keep it a secret from him – it wouldn't be right.'

'Surely Sam wouldn't tell the Marshal!' she exclaimed. 'You may not be close, but he *is* your brother.'

'The truth is, I don't know, and we can't take a chance. You didn't see the hate in Sam's eyes when I stopped the lynchin'. I know he'd never willingly see someone from his family livin' with a Chinese woman, and possibly havin' children with her, and there's a real chance he'd try to stop the weddin'.'

'D'you want me to ask the priest? It'd save you goin' into Chinatown, a white man amongst the Chinese. I've seen him in the mercantile, but I've never said much to him, but bein' Chinese ...' Her voice trailed off.

He shook his head. 'It's me he owes the favour to, so it'd better be me who asks. And you bein' Chinese could make him say no. From what you've told me in the past, a Chinaman brought up in China, which he obviously was, might think badly of a Chinese girl approachin' him in such a way. You told me unmarried girls aren't seen in public in China, and even wives walk behind their husband and don't speak out for themselves. A priest is the sort of person to cling to tradition, and he might not like our American ways.'

'That makes sense.' She stopped and stared over the side of the bridge at the patch of ground where her mother died, her eyes on the white pebbles at the water's edge. She looked back at Joe with a smile. 'I know my ma's hearin' this and I can feel her happiness.'

He grinned at her, and they continued walking, several paces apart from each other.

'I'll go to the priest tonight,' he said when they reached the other side of the bridge and turned to the left to go to the miners' houses. 'I've got a real good feelin' about this, Charity.'

Chapter Thirty-Seven

Martha glanced at Charity. 'You can put that mendin' down, gal,' she said. 'I wanna talk to you.'

Charity's mind sped back to what she and Joe had decided the day before, and her heart leapt in anxiety. She glanced nervously across the room at Martha, who was standing by the stove.

Martha gave the stew a final stir, went to the store-closet, filled a glass with milk from the pitcher that stood on a slab of stone on one of the shelves, took the glass across to Charity, and then went and sat at the other end of the table.

'That's the last thing in the pile,' she said, nodding at the camisole in Charity's hand, 'so it can wait a while. Hiram will be back soon, and maybe Sam, too, and we need to talk before then.'

Charity put down the camisole and needle, and picked up the glass. 'What about?' she asked, her hand shaking. She took a sip of milk.

'That's what I was hopin' *you* could tell *me*,' Martha said. 'Yesterday, I told you I wanted you out of our house. I know you went straight to the mercantile after that, and I thought you were plannin' on using a woman's ways to make Chen Fai believe you were keen on gettin' wed. To him, not Joe.'

Charity made a slight exclamation.

Ignoring her, Martha leaned forward, her forearms on the table. 'And that would've been the sensible thing to do. But next I hear, Eliza's tellin' me that when she dropped by the stable later that mornin', Greg said you'd turned up in a real bad state, and had then run off, and Joe had run off mighty fast after you.' She sat back in her chair. 'I've waited more than a day for you to tell me what's goin' on, and that's long enough. So you can start talkin' now.'

Charity shrugged. 'Like Greg said, I was upset.' She sighed. 'I'd realised I didn't feel about Chen Fai in the right way and didn't want to marry him, and I told him that. He was upset and so was I. That's what it was.'

Martha folded her arms and sat back. 'It sure took you long enough to find out what you didn't feel about him. Years, in fact.'

'I know, and I feel bad about that. But I can't help the way I feel, can I?' Charity took another sip of her milk, her heart hammering.

Martha stared at her thoughtfully. 'And where does Joe fit into this?' she asked at last.

Charity shook her head. 'He doesn't. He came after me to see what had happened, and that's all. He said he wanted to help, but we both know there's nothin' he can do.' She gestured helplessness. 'I'm gonna do the only thing I can – I'm leaving Carter. I was gonna tell all of you tonight.'

'Where are you movin' to?'

'Green River. And if I can't get a job there, I'll get back on the train and go further down the line to Evanston. I can't stay here. You want me out, and you're right to want that. You've given me a home for long enough, and you're sufferin' now because of that. The whites hate me, and now the Chinese will, too. They've always mistrusted me, despite the colour of my skin, and they'll think they were right to do so.'

'And Joe agreed with you goin'?' Martha's voice sounded doubtful.

'Not at first. But I persuaded him. He can now see, like I can, that I've got no choice.'

275

Martha was silent for a moment or two. 'Well, as I told you yesterday, I've come to feel affection for you, gal,' she said finally, 'and I'll be sorry to see you go, but you're doin' the right thing. I would've liked you to have stayed in Carter so I could've seen you in the street and watched your nippers grow, but that's not gonna happen now, and that saddens me.'

'I'll be sorry to leave you, too – I wouldn't be alive if it wasn't for you,' Charity said, a sudden tremble in her voice. 'But I know I'm doin' what's right. I don't like bein' the reason bad things are happenin' to you.'

Martha nodded. 'So when d'you plan on goin'?'

'Monday week, I thought. It'll give me time to sort out my things. I've been savin' for when I was wed, and I'll use some of the money to buy a train ticket. And I'll have enough to get a room for a few days while I look for work. Joe said it costs two dollars a night for a room, and two bits extra if I want hot water brought up.'

'Well, I can see you've thought this out, and that pleases me mightily, gal. You're a hard worker and reliable, and I doubt you'll find it difficult to get a job. Is there any way Hiram and I can help?'

'I don't reckon so, but I thank you for the thought.' Charity gave her a slight smile, and picked up the needle again.

Her fingers drumming quietly on the table, Martha sat watching the needle move back and forth across the hole in the camisole. 'You'll never be a good needlewoman,' she said after a few minutes, 'but you're gettin' better. At least at mendin'.'

'I'll never like sewin', but it's gotta be done.' Increasingly nervous beneath Martha's probing gaze, Charity forced a smile to her face.

The drumming stopped. 'You've obviously told Joe your plans. You gonna tell Chen Fai and Su Lin, too?'

Charity looked up from her sewing and shook her head. 'I won't be goin' into the store again. But if I see Su Lin around, I'll tell her. I'll miss her,' she added. 'I know she's gettin' wed, but I'd have liked us to stay friends and I know it won't be possible, not now I'm movin' away. And if I ever came back to see you, I know Chen Fai would forbid her to see me. She wouldn't disobey her brother again or her husband. But Chen Fai's a good man, and I've treated him badly, so I'd never reproach him for stoppin' her from meetin' me again. Everythin' that's happened is my fault.'

'Well, a part of it is, but not all. It's not your fault you're Chinese,' Martha said bluntly. Her gaze travelled around the room, then returned to Charity, whose head was again bent over her sewing. 'I wonder why I don't believe you, Charity gal,' she said slowly.

Charity looked up sharply. 'What d'you mean?' She attempted a laugh.

Martha leaned forward. 'I would've thought my meanin' obvious,' she said. 'You're real calm and you're sayin' all the right things. But the gal I've been seein' since Joe came back – since she was born, in fact – had fire in her eyes. And she's had fight in her since the day she started school. In all these years that fight has never gone out of her. Not till now, that is. Where've that fire and that fight gone, I wanna know. Are they're still there, but you're hidin' them for some reason? I'm wonderin' if there's somethin' you're not tellin' me.'

Charity stared at her. 'That fire, as you call it, has been put out. I can't keep fightin' a fight I'm never gonna win. I have to accept that or go plum loco.' She injected an air of despair into her voice. 'Joe's back in Carter now, and as he's gonna have the livery stable he'll stay here. I can't live with him – and yup, you're right; that's what I wanna do more than anythin'. But it's not gonna happen. Even if the law allowed a white and a China woman to marry, the Carter townsfolk wouldn't. So what can I do but go to another town?'

'You could try your luck with Chen Fai again.'

She vigorously shook her head. 'He wouldn't agree. And I couldn't bear to wed him. I could've done if Joe hadn't come back, but not now I know what it feels like to love someone so bad that it hurts. You once talked about feelin' as if you were bein' buried alive. Well, bein' Chen Fai's wife would bury me alive. Better almost anythin' than that.' She slumped back in her seat. 'Anyway, that's my way of thinkin'.'

'Okay, you've convinced me, I guess. If you wanna take—' There was a rap on the door and Martha stopped abruptly. She glanced at the schoolhouse clock on the wall. 'That'll be Phebe,' she said with a sigh, getting up. 'She'll want to borrow somethin' again. Not that borrow's the right word – I'll not see it back.' She went to the door and opened it. 'Come on in, Phebe,' she said, her voice resigned, and she stood back from the doorway.

Phebe stepped into the room, saw Charity and stopped. She glanced at Martha. 'I thought she'd still be at the store,' she said sharply. 'Sam would be real mad if he knew I was in the same room as her. And so would my pa.'

'Then don't tell them,' Martha said, and closed the door behind her. 'You gonna take what you want at once or sit with us a while?'

'I can't stay. I've left Thomas asleep, and he could wake at any time.'

'So what's it you need to borrow?' Martha asked, and she started to walk over to the store-closet.

Phebe gave her a wan smile. 'It's carrots,' she said, her voice apologetic. 'I thought I'd make a stew this evenin', but I found I didn't have carrots.'

Martha raised her eyebrows. 'Isn't it a bit late to start a stew for this evenin'?'

Phebe shrugged. 'Maybe. But as I was comin' back from gettin' some cans of condensed milk in town, the air smelt so sweet as I passed your house that I decided to make some myself. As soon as I'd fed Thomas and settled him, I came straight up for the carrots.'

'You've got Charity to thank for the nice smell. She did most of the work. Like she always does. But not for much longer,' she added. 'She's not marryin' Chen Fai; she's leavin' Carter.'

Phebe pulled out a chair and sat down. She glanced at Charity, and then back at Martha. 'Sam'll be pleased to hear that,' she said. 'And I am, too. I won't have to listen to Sam goin' on nightly about the Chinese. It's bad enough he's gotta work with them in the mines, with all their cheatin' ways, but he shouldn't have to know there's one of them livin' in his home, no matter how she got there.' She indicated Charity with her cool gaze.

'When I last looked, this was my home and Hiram's; Sam's home was further down the row,' Martha said tersely.

Phebe shrugged her shoulders. 'You always think of the house you were brought up in as home. No, her not marryin' that Chen man is a real good thing. If she had, she'd have stayed in Carter and kept on comin' to see you, and every time Sam saw her, he'd get all fired up again.'

'Since you recognise the feelings Sam has for the house he's always lived in, I take it you've got some sympathy with Charity havin' to move away. Or haven't you? She's been in this house since a few days old, and now she's gonna have to leave it and go to a town where she doesn't know anyone. Just because her skin's a different colour.'

Phebe looked at Charity with dislike. 'It's not my fault she's Chinese. When's she goin'?' she asked, turning back to Martha.

'Soon. But she can speak for herself, you know.'

'Maybe I don't want to speak to her.' Phebe paused. 'Can I have the carrots, then? If not, I'll get off.'

'Sure, but they'll need soakin'. You know, it's high time you quit beatin' the devil around the stump and started plantin' your vegetable patch. It isn't much of a patch, I know, but nor's ours, and you'd be surprised what we can grow, even on stony ground like this. If you plant it in spring, you'll have greens, peas, and radishes, and then plant it in summer and you'll have what you need for the winter: things like pumpkins, beans, potatoes and squash. I'm surprised your ma didn't teach you that.'

'We had a Celestial for a cook, didn't we? It was his job to put food on our plates. I'd kinda thought I'd have the same when I was wed.'

'Well, you haven't. And you and Sam have been married for long enough now for you to be thinkin' about preservin' and the like. Thomas is easier now so you've got more time. Sam does a man's work, and he needs food on his plate when he gets in. The garden's the woman's chore, and it's time you started workin' on it.'

Phebe stood up. 'I reckon I can manage without the carrots,' she said stiffly.

'Sit down, Phebe, gal,' Martha told her, her voice softening. She stood up. 'I doubt you'll want to take dried carrots back with you and start soakin' them – not this late in the day – so you can take some stew home with you.' She went over to the dresser, lifted down an earthenware crock and took it across to the stove.

'I'm obliged to you,' Phebe said. She hesitated, and then turned to Charity. 'I won't pretend I'm sorry you're goin',' she said slowly, ''cos you know I'm not. But I feel for you havin' to leave the place that's always been your home, and I hope you find a job it pleases you to do, and in a place where they like the Chinee more than Carter folk do.'

'That was real prettily spoken, Phebe,' Martha said, coming over with a crock of stew. She handed it to her with a smile. 'You're a good gal at heart.'

Phebe stood up and took the crock. 'Thank you,' she said. She nodded to Charity, turned and went to the door.

When Martha had closed the door behind her, she returned to the table and stood staring thoughtfully down at Charity, who'd resumed her mending.

'Is there anythin' you wanna add to what you said before?' she asked at last.

'Nope,' Charity said, looking up from the camisole. 'I'm leavin' on Monday week, and that's the truth.'

'This feels real good, Martha,' Hiram said, stretching his injured leg out as much as he could. 'It's a fine feelin' to be able to sit outside the house in the evenin' again. Sure, there's a chill in the air, but there's also a feel of spring, and the breeze is gettin' warmer each day.'

Martha glanced across at him and smiled. 'Sure is,' she said, and she turned slightly to look to her left. Her gaze settled on the hills opposite Carter where Charity and Joe had occasionally walked in years gone by, charcoal-grey shapes that stood proud against the darkening sky. She stared at their jagged outline, her expression thoughtful.

'Where's Charity?' Hiram asked after a while.

'Sortin' out her things for when she leaves.'

'You'll miss her help.'

'That's for sure. But I'll miss her for more than that. She never became that daughter we wanted, but nevertheless I've gotten real fond of the gal. I hadn't realised how much.'

He nodded. 'I know you have, and so have I. But we've got our Joe back now and that's gonna help.'

'But for how long?'

He looked at her in surprise. 'What d'you mean? For always, I reckon. He's gonna take over the livery stable, isn't he?'

She turned her head and stared hard at him. 'Is that what you truly think, Hiram?'

'Yeah, it is.' He frowned. 'Don't you?'

She looked back at the darkness gathering ahead. 'I don't know.'

'What d'you mean?' He twisted in his chair to face her. 'Look at me, Martha.'

She turned to him. 'I know my Joe, and I know what he's like,' she said slowly. 'I remember him when he was workin' for Seth, a lad between hay and grass, neither man nor boy. He liked the work well enough, but he still talked of leavin'. The times he was happiest was when he was out in the corral with the horses or ridin' them hard across the plain, exercisin' them for Seth.'

'I know that. So what are you sayin'?'

'That I never heard him say that if the livery stable was his, he'd never leave. Think about it, Hiram. He's always wanted the open fields. He only worked in the stable to bring in money and that was the best job for him in Carter. But it was never anythin' more than a job – it wasn't his dream.'

'So you think that first Charity will leave, and then at some point next year, when Seth's fit and well again, Joe will ride off, too? And we have to be prepared for it. Is that what you're tellin' me?'

'Maybe. To speak the truth, I'm not sure what I'm tellin' you. When Joe came back to Carter, you could see he was a man ready for a woman, and I don't mean in the passin' through town kinda way, the kind cowboys look for when they've money in their pockets – not that sorta woman. He already knew Charity was lovely inside, and when he saw her again on the night he returned, and saw how lovely she was outside, too – well, I reckon he fell for her real hard.'

'And what about Charity?'

'You only had to look at her to know it wasn't just Joe feelin' that way, and I've been scared about what could happen ever since. Whatever Charity says, I can't see the Joe I know givin' her up without a fight.'

'Can you see the Joe you know settin' up home with her without them bein' wed? You're always sayin' how like you he is. What would *you* do if you were Joe?'

She gave him a rueful smile. 'I only have to look back at what I *did* do. I wed a man I hardly knew, a man with dreams, who was full of charm and sweet-talk. I took him to the home I loved, and when he didn't like the life I wanted to live, and told me to choose between stayin' there or followin' him to some godforsaken place or other, I packed my bags, picked up the kids and followed him.'

'If he loves Charity, he'll do what's best for her,' Hiram said quietly. 'I know that, and in your heart, so do you. Them bein' killed is what could happen if they decided to do what you fear they might, but Joe would never put her in any kind of danger.'

Martha nodded. 'Not deliberately, he wouldn't. But I reckon he might just think he could get away with somethin'. I'm not too sure what that could be. But I reckon he won't just sit back and do nothin', and that's what makes me afear'd.'

Chapter Thirty-Eight

Rain fell from the sky in sheets of silken grey, gathering in the moonlight-pitted pools that formed in sunken patches of ground, overflowing into rivulets of glistening grey-black water that raced down Main Street.

Her coat drenched and the hems of her skirt and petticoats muddied, Charity ran into the livery stable and came to a stop inside the barn. She stood there, looking around for Joe as the rain hosed noisily on to the wooden roof, its insistent beat reverberating in the hollow space beneath. One of the horses whinnied. And then another.

Water ran off her coat and pooled around her feet on the wooden floor. 'Joe,' she shouted, unbuttoning her coat and moving further into the barn. She shook her coat and then squeezed the water from the end of her braid.

'Joe!' she shouted again, more loudly this time to be heard above the sounds of the rain and of the horses kicking against the wooden walls of the stalls.

He'd be somewhere nearby, she knew, and she just had to talk to him.

For the whole of the last two days, she'd been watching for a moment to ask if he'd been able to get to the priest, but to her intense frustration there hadn't been one. Martha had been up early each morning, before either of them had left their rooms, and Hiram had taken to sitting with them at night. Although clearly exhausted and hardly able to keep awake, he hadn't retired to bed until after they'd gone to their rooms.

She'd begun to despair of ever having a chance to speak alone with Joe when Phebe had hammered on the door that evening, frantically pleading for help with Thomas. He was flushed and sweating and had a bad cough, she'd said, fear on her face. Martha had thrown on her coat to go down to Sam's house, and Charity had seen her chance.

She'd told Martha she'd run into town for a chicken. If Thomas turned out to have pneumonia, she'd said, they'd need a fresh chicken, and it'd be better to get it while there were still people at work in the stores rather than have to disturb someone later at night if he took a turn for the worse. Martha had nodded her agreement, and had then hurried down to Sam's house.

She'd grabbed her coat and had run to the livery as fast as she could, heedless of the mud and the rain, fearful that Martha might not be with Thomas for long.

She glanced round the stable again, wondering where Joe could be. A moment later, she heard the back door click shut and footsteps come along the corridor towards her.

'Joe,' she called again.

'Charity!' he exclaimed as he came into the barn and saw her. His face broke out into a broad smile. 'I thought I'd imagined hearin' you call me,' he added with a laugh, and he pulled off his hat and oilcloth duster coat, slung them over a nearby stool and came across to her, bringing with him the earthy smell of damp hay and wet leather. 'What in tarnation, you're soaked!'

'It's nothin' that won't dry,' she said, laughing. The horses neighed in unison, and she glanced anxiously towards the stalls, then back at Joe. 'The horses seem restless.'

'They're always like this in a storm – you should've seen them in the corral this afternoon; they just couldn't be settled. It means we'll have thunder and lightning before the night's out. But if you think horses are noisy, you should hear cattle lowin' when there's a storm on the way. Which I hope you will hear one day,' he added, with a grin.

'Me, too,' she said, gazing up at him.

'Anyway.' He came closer, and raised his hand to brush away a cloud of tiny black flies that hovered around her damp face. 'What brings you here in weather like this? It's rainin' pitchforks.' He ran his fingers slowly down her wet hair, and she felt the touch of his love. 'Your eyes are as dark as the sky's gotten,' he said huskily. 'They're beautiful, Charity. You're beautiful.'

At the expression in his eyes, a sigh of happiness ran through her, and she moved closer to him, her face raised to his, her lips parting slightly.

He put his hand to her cheek, and trailed it lingeringly down the side of her face, and down the slender column of her throat.

Then he let his gaze fall to the line of her body beneath her dress, visible between the flaps of her open coat. 'You're so lovely,' he said softly. 'Wet or dry, with the sun on your face or when you're covered in mud, you're never anythin' but real beautiful. I wanna hold you right now and never let you go.'

'Oh, Joe.' She reached up to him and brushed her lips against his, then she stepped back. 'That's as close as I'm gonna get to you for now,' she said, laughing. 'You won't want to be covered in that mud you mentioned.'

He held out his arms at his side and grinned at her. 'Come as close as you want. I don't mind; not one little bit.'

She gave an exaggerated sigh. 'If only I could, but there isn't time. I doubt your ma will be with Phebe for long, so I must get back soon. And I've gotta get a chicken first.'

He lowered his arms. 'What's Phebe want this time?'

'Advice about Thomas. She said he wasn't well, and she and Sam were worried. It sounds like a bad cold and

286

nothin' more, but it gave me an excuse to come out and see you. Your folks have clearly decided we're not to be left alone together,' she added with an amused smile, 'so I've not yet been able to ask if you've been to the priest.'

He nodded. 'I have and it's fine. He was pleased to be able to return the favour I did him, and he was also real keen on doin' somethin' that asserted the right of the Chinese to sort things out for themselves, whatever the laws of the whites said.'

She clasped her hands together in glee.

'And he had a grand suggestion to make. We can't do it here in Carter, but we might be able to do it in Sheridan as Sheridan's a sight bigger than Carter. He said we could get a lawyer to draw up a marriage contract. We can never be wed in the eyes of American law, but with a contract, and a Chinese weddin', we'd be as wed as we can be.'

'That would be wonderful. So where and when's the weddin' gonna be?'

'In the *tong* in just over a week; on the Monday like we wanted. He'll use one of the downstairs rooms. It'll be early in the mornin', when the Carter women are doin' their washin'. He asked if we wanted food afterwards – some cake and wine perhaps, as that's a real important part of the weddin' for the Chinese – but I've told him there won't be time.'

She shrugged in dismissal. 'We don't need any food.'

'What we'll need to do is get out of town as fast as we can. I'll load the wagon the night before, and then just before sunup on the Monday, drive it out to the plain and leave it there with one of the horses. I'll ride back on the other. I've ordered the horses through some drovers I know. I'm not usin' Seth's contacts, as I don't wanna risk him bein' blamed for any part of this.'

'I'm real pleased about that. Seth mustn't be in any trouble for what we're doin'.'

He nodded. 'As soon as you've had breakfast,' he went on, 'you'll tell Ma and Pa you're goin' to the station and that you'd rather go alone. When you've said goodbye to them, go straight to the *tong*. When we leave the *tong*, you'll walk out to the plain. I'll collect the horse from the stable and ride out of town, lookin' like I'm exercisin' it. I'll hitch it to the wagon and drive the wagon to meet you when you're far enough out of town.'

'I do hope nothin' goes wrong,' she said, biting her lip anxiously. 'I keep thinkin' back to the Chinaman who was lynched in Denver, and the violence you stopped here. But for you, the priest would've been lynched.'

'It won't go wrong, Charity. By the time anyone realises you didn't get on that train and that I've gone, too, we'll be far away, and we'll not have left any sign of where we've gone.'

'Suppose the priest says somethin' to someone before the weddin' and they tell the Marshal?'

'He won't. He made a point of sayin' that neither of us should tell anyone. He knows that tensions are high and he doesn't want to risk what might happen in town if we were found out. And the Chens have friends. There'll be people in both communities who'd try to get us thrown into jail at the very least if they knew, and the priest knows that. And also he'll be encouragin' us to break American law, so they could put him in jail, too.'

'D'you think they'll come after us when they find we're gone?'

'I don't rightly know. I guess it depends on how soon they find out. The Marshal could easily round up a posse with all the anti-Chinese feelin' in town. But if they do come after us, they'll most likely think we've gone due south towards the Rockies or west to Evanston. They're likely to think we'd hide in the forests south of Evanston and then head out of Wyoming. I'd be surprised if they thought we'd stay in Wyoming Territory.'

There was a distant rumble of thunder.

'I must go,' she said quickly.

He nodded. 'We'll speak again as soon as we can.'

Turning away, she started buttoning up her coat. He caught her arm. She stopped moving and stared up at him. For a long moment, they gazed at each other, their eyes filled with a powerful yearning.

Somewhere outside, thunder rumbled again; this time closer.

As they stood there in thrall to love, a jagged bolt of lightning streaked through the stormy sky and cracked it open. A pristine white light lit up the town and fell through the stable entrance on to them.

Momentarily blinded by its shining intensity, Joe put his hands to his eyes and rubbed them.

When he opened his eyes again, Charity had gone.

Chapter Thirty-Nine

Lifting her boots high with each step to avoid kicking up more water and mud than was necessary, Charity made her way carefully across the ground which was coated with a thick layer of soft mud that had oozed from the ridges of dirt when they'd collapsed beneath the violent onslaught of the weekend's rain. Reaching Second Street, she stepped on to the damp boardwalk, and started to walk more quickly.

As soon as she turned into Main Street, she crossed over the track to the bakery side to avoid walking close to the mercantile, and with her head down, went quickly through Chinatown towards the railroad depot.

Every so often, she glanced ahead to the railroad, which ran across the end of Main Street, its metal-topped rails silvery grey in the light of the morning sun, and to the wood-frame depot that lay on the other side of the track. Going to the depot to find out the time of the trains to Green River the following Monday, which Joe's folks would expect her to be able to tell them, had been the right thing to do that morning, she thought.

When she'd told Joe's ma she was off to the station, his ma had nodded and then, on an impulse it seemed, had squeezed her lightly on the arm and stared at her with eyes full of sympathy and concern. Guilt had welled up inside her, and she'd left for town as soon after that as she was able.

'Charity!' She heard her name being called from behind by a breathless voice. 'Charity, you stop.'

She turned in surprise and saw Su Lin hurrying up to her.

'Su Lin!' she exclaimed, and she beamed at her. 'I'm so

glad to see you.' Then a thought struck her. Her smile faded and she glanced nervously over Su Lin's shoulder towards the mercantile store, but there was no sign of anyone else in the Chen family. Smiling again, she turned back to her friend.

'How did you know I'd be comin' this way at this time?' she asked, her forehead creasing in amazement.

'I did not know. I watch for you every day. I sit in the upstairs bedroom and look at Second Street. Today I see you coming.'

'Doesn't Chen Fai mind you not workin' in the store or helpin' with the cookin'?' Charity asked in surprise.

'No. He is very kind. He sees that I am very sad as I am not speaking to Charity friend for a long time, and he say I need not work for some days, not until I am happy again. But you come with me – it is not good to talk in the street.'

Beckoning to Charity to follow, she hurriedly led the way to the narrow passage between the Chinese laundry and Chinaman Doc's herb store. Halfway down the passage, Su Lin stopped and leaned back against the cold stone wall of the laundry.

'I miss you, Charity,' she said, as they huddled close in the small space, the scent of herbs and spices strong in the air. '*Dai lou* says I must wish you well, then forget you and think only of my wedding to Ah Lee Don. But I do not want to wish you well and then forget you.' Her face widened into a smile. 'I am able to remember my good friend and also think about my wedding.' She giggled. 'I am a very clever Chinese girl.'

Charity sighed. 'I miss you, too, Su Lin. Sadly, I've not been a very clever Chinese girl. I've upset everythin' and everyone, and above all your brother. Chen Fai's a good man and I'm real unhappy at hurtin' him. That he still wishes me well, after what I've done to him …' She shook her head. 'It just shows what a nice man he is. I wish him well, too, and I'd like you to tell him that.'

'He still very happy to wed you, Charity,' Su Lin said, her face suddenly earnest, her voice tinged with hope. 'Maybe there is one day a chance of this?'

Charity shook her head. 'I'm leavin' Carter. That's why I've come down here,' she said, nodding in the direction of the depot. 'I need to find the time of the train to Green River as that's where I'm goin'.'

Su Lin's face dropped. 'To Green River! When you go?'

Charity hesitated. 'I'm sure it won't hurt to tell you – next Monday.'

Su Lin drew in her breath in an audible gasp. 'Monday! You leave Carter in one week?'

Charity nodded. 'Yes, I do. Things have gotten much worse since the whites' club started up. I'm sure you know what they tried to do to the priest, led by Joe's brother. Everywhere you go there're signs sayin' the Chinese must go. The whites are set against them and anyone who has anythin' to do with them, and that means Joe's folks. They've been very kind to me and I must think of them. And now I'm gettin' nasty looks from the Chinese, too, after what happened with your brother. I'll never be able to get any more work here.'

Su Lin nodded slowly, biting her lower lip. 'I know this.'

'That's why I'm leavin'.'

'But I think Walker family will not want you to go.'

'Maybe; but they know I've no choice.' She paused a moment. 'And me bein' here isn't fair on your brother, either,' she went on. 'As long as I'm here, I'm a reminder to him and everyone else that he's lost face. I know what that means to a Chinese man,' she said quietly, 'and I very much regret causin' this. And also, me not bein' here will make it easier for him to concentrate on findin' a wife. There're more Chinese women in the towns around here than there used to be. Maybe not many, but I'm sure there're enough for him to find a suitable wife among them if he looked. Whoever it turns out to be, she'll be a lucky woman.'

Su Lin looked at her in surprise. 'If you feel this way, why you not wed *dai lou*?'

'I can't. I like him – you know I do – but I just don't feel about him the way a woman should feel about the man she's gonna marry. I guess I'm too American for that not to matter.' She hesitated. 'You know what I mean?'

Su Lin nodded. 'I understand.' She put her hand gently on Charity's arm. 'But maybe one day you will feel this way.'

Charity shook her head. 'I won't.' A look of helplessness spread across her face. 'I love Joe; that's the trouble. If Joe had never come back, everythin' might have been different. But he did come back, and from the moment I saw him again, I knew what it was to love someone in every possible way. That's why I can't wed Chen Fai.'

'I see it is a problem,' Su Lin said, her face thoughtful. 'But you are not able to marry Joe. You must marry a Chinaman. So why not *dai lou*? He will not expect you to feel what you do not feel. Is it not better to marry *dai lou* than work for lazy American woman who order you cook, you clean house, she like you wash clothes, iron, mend clothes, you fill tubs with hot water for her sit in? She like you do everything she not want to do.' Her voice rose.

Charity leaned forward and hugged her. 'Don't distress yourself, Su Lin. I'll be fine as I've got you for a friend. I'm gonna be your friend wherever I live, and you're gonna be mine. That's because you're in here, and you always will be.' She put her hand on her heart.

Tears came to Su Lin's eyes, and she started to cry.

'I do not want you go,' she sobbed. 'I very worried. White people are mean to Chinese people. You not feel much meanness in Carter because you live in Walker house and you are friend of *dai lou*, and he is respected businessman. But when you leave ... when you leave ... you all alone. No one keep you safe.' Her voice broke and she put her face in her hands.

Charity hugged her again. 'Please, don't cry, Su Lin,' she said. 'I won't come to any harm.'

'You not know this. You be all alone in strange town. I am afraid for you.' Su Lin cried harder, her shoulders heaving.

Impulsively, Charity bent her head to Su Lin's ear. 'I won't be alone,' she whispered. 'I shouldn't have told you this, and you mustn't tell anyone. But I can't bear to see you like this.'

Su Lin pulled back and stared at Charity in amazement.

'What you mean?' she asked, her voice choking.

'D'you promise you won't say anythin'?' Charity repeated.

Su Lin nodded, her tears slowing. 'I promise. What do you mean, you are not alone?' she repeated.

'I'll be with Joe. We're gonna get wed.'

Su Lin's mouth dropped open. She wiped the tears from her cheeks with the palms of her hands, and stared at Charity, fear in her eyes. 'You can't. Is not allowed. You get big trouble. White folk kill you.'

'We're gonna have a Chinese weddin'. The priest's gonna do it. He's Chinese, and so am I, so it'll be a Chinese weddin'. It's just that it won't be lawful in American eyes.'

'Oh, Charity.' Su Lin grasped her hand. 'I want to come to wedding. When is wedding?'

'Next Monday mornin'. We're leavin' Carter straight after. Much as I'd like you there,' she said, her voice full of regret, 'it's better you don't come. It might draw attention to Joe goin' into the *tong*, and me, too. I've never been there before, and if it's just us, it'll be safer.'

'But you get big trouble in Green River when folk see white husband.'

Charity moved closer again. 'We're not really goin' there. I'm just tellin' everyone that I'm gonna get a job there. Joe's thinkin' of other places we can go.'

'I am frightened for you, Charity,' Su Lin said slowly. 'But I am also joyful for you. I think you and Joe will be very happy together if you find a town where white folk like Chinese folk. But I am very sad you never be my sister.'

'Me, too.' She took a deep breath and gave Su Lin a watery smile. 'I hate to say goodbye, so I won't – not yet, anyway – but I'd better go now. If anyone sees you talkin' to the girl who brought unhappiness to a well-liked Chinese man, it could be bad for your reputation. You're gonna wed Ah Lee Don, and nothin' must stop that.'

Su Lin nodded, tears again trickling down her cheeks.

Charity leaned forward and hugged her. 'I wish you lots of boy babies,' she said, a smile in her voice.

They drew apart and stared hard at each other, as if trying to memorise every feature of the face in front of them.

Then Charity raised her hand in a wave of farewell, and turned away. Her vision misting, she walked out of the alleyway, turned right into Main Street and made her way steadily to the depot, forcing herself not to look back, not even once.

Chen Fai was standing at the end of the long counter on the left-hand side of the store, the bale of vivid red silk in front of him, when Su Lin went slowly back into the mercantile. He instantly pushed the red silk away from him, moved round the end of the counter and came towards her, his face anxious.

'I see you run down the street after Charity,' he said eagerly. 'What did she say? You think she come back to us, and want her and me to be friends again, and maybe more than this one day? I hope so. I look at red silk for your *chang-fu* and think of her.' Putting hope into the depths of his eyes, he stared at Su Lin.

She looked down at the floor, bit her lip and shook her head. 'She will not come back, *ge ge*,' she said, her voice trembling with misery. 'She is leaving Carter.'

His face dropped, registering great disappointment. 'When is she going?'

She looked up at him with red-rimmed eyes. 'On Monday morning. She go to the station today to find out time of train.'

'Train for where?'

She hesitated.

'You can tell me,' he urged. 'You know I wish her well.'

'Green River,' she said. Not wanting to see his unhappiness, she looked down at the floor again.

He stared at the top of her bowed head, his eyes narrowing speculatively.

Then his face cleared. 'To Green River!' he exclaimed in loud delight. Su Lin looked up in surprise. 'That is not far from Carter. Last year, I think to do business in Green River with Ah Wong, and then I think no. But now I will speak again to Ah Wong. Each time I visit him, I will also see Charity, and one day she might agree again to be my wife. I think that can happen.'

His eyes filled with hope.

She trembled.

'This can happen,' he repeated, smiling happily at her. 'It is possible, is it not?'

Slowly, she shook her head. 'I think not, honourable brother.'

A look of annoyance darkened his face. 'You do not know this,' he snapped. 'If she does not like the job in Green River, there is maybe still a chance for me.'

'Charity is not the only Chinese girl,' she ventured. 'You can ask a go-between to find a wife for you in one of the other towns near Carter.'

He glared at her and took a step back. 'It makes me very angry that you say this. I hope one day Charity will want me as a husband, and I wait for that. I not look for another woman.'

'I not want you to wait for something that never happen,' she said, her voice shaking.

He let a wave of anger twist his features and his voice become shrill. 'You not know that for certain. I wait for Charity, I tell you. I wait until I know for sure she never ever agree to come to me. I forbid you speak of another woman again.' And he made a move as if to go to the back room.

'She is getting wed,' she blurted out. 'To Joe Walker.'

His heart seemed to stop, and he felt sick.

He turned slowly and stared at her, his mouth falling open, no words coming out.

'You wrong. She can't,' he said at last, his voice accusing, and he shook his head in disbelief. 'She can't. He's American man. Is not allowed.'

'Priest not obey American law, and he do wedding in our *tong* on Monday morning,' she whispered, her face ashen. 'For Charity and Joe Walker, this is a real marriage: she is

Chinese; priest is Chinese. She then leave Carter with Joe.' She gasped aloud. Her hands flew to her mouth. 'I should not have told this to anyone. I promised.'

'I am not anyone,' he said impatiently. 'I'm your brother, and I'm a friend of Charity. But this cannot be – Marshal in Green River will take them to jail or whites there will lynch them! I fear for her.'

'She not really go to Green River. She not know where they go.'

'She marry Joe Walker in *tong* and then they leave Carter together. That is right? And this happen on Monday morning?'

She nodded.

His last lingering hope – a hope he thought he had buried in favour of revenge – died away. Grief rushed in, followed swiftly by jealousy.

A powerful, burning jealousy.

Joe Walker was going to have Charity for himself.

And she was willing to make herself little better than his concubine. For that she'd turned down her chance of being a lawful wife.

He felt Su Lin's eyes on him, worried, concerned. 'She ask me not to say what she is doing to anyone, so you not tell,' she said anxiously.

His relaxed his features. His hands slid into the opposite sleeves of his cornflower blue tunic, and he gave her a smile, a gentle smile that he tinged with sorrow. 'It hurts me in my heart to know I lose her, Su Lin, but I wish her well. And she needs my good wishes, I think. It is not easy to do something that is against the law.'

'So you not tell anyone?' She looked at him fearfully.

He shook his head. 'I will not tell anyone. We must forget what we know about Walker plans, and think only about our own happiness. You must think about wedding with Ah Lee Don, and because of what you tell me ...' He glanced towards the red silk, then looked back at Su Lin. 'Because of what you tell me, I know I must ask go-between to find me a wife. I am not ready to do this now, but I do this after you wed Ah Lee Don.'

Su Lin beamed at him in relief. 'I am very happy about this, *ge ge*.'

'You are right, Su Lin. Charity is a good friend, but she is not only China woman around here. I look for a woman who is a good friend, and also a good wife.' He twisted his mouth into a smile of reassurance.

'I want you to soon be happy again,' she said quietly. 'You are kind brother and good man. You deserve a nice wife.'

Chapter Forty

On Tuesday evening Chen Fai stood in the shadows cast by the closing down of day and listened hard.

Finally, he heard the sound of footsteps.

He gave a quiet sigh of relief. Pressing closer to the wooden wall of the house that stood at the end of Second Street, the last house before the stretch of ground, dotted with wooden shacks, that led to the miners' houses, he waited for the first of the miners to walk by on their way home at the end of their working day.

Hiram Walker was one of the first to pass by. Leaning heavily on his stick, his face was etched with fatigue. Joe Walker's father was alone, he noticed with relief. He'd been worrying about what he would do if Sam Walker had been at his father's side, but he'd worried in vain.

Gradually, the steady flow of pit-dirt miners who had followed Hiram in their groups of two or three, their heavy boots loud on the boardwalk, dwindled to the occasional one or two. But the miner he was waiting for had yet to reach the spot where he stood concealed.

Relaxing a little, he leaned back against the wall.

Sam Walker must have stopped at the saloon for a drink, he thought with an inward sneer of contempt. What a way for a man with a wife and son to behave. He should go straight back home to them as soon as he left the mine. A father should be with his family whenever possible.

He found himself feeling almost sorry for the fair-haired woman Sam Walker had married, even though she was a stupid woman. She had a pretty face, and would have found a better husband if she'd respected herself as a woman should do. Instead, she'd behaved like a *louh geu* with Sam Walker before she was wed, and had found herself with a child in her belly. Having shown herself to be a woman of no reputation, she was lucky Sam Walker had agreed to marry her.

And Sam Walker, too, was at fault. He had not shown her the respect that a man should show to the woman he is thinking of taking as wife.

At last he heard the sound of someone else coming along the boardwalk in his direction. Straightening up, he peered cautiously round the edge of the wall and saw a solitary figure in the darkening night, a lunch bucket in one hand and a miner's hat in the other.

He pulled back a little and smiled inwardly – his wait was almost over. Motionless he stood there, thick-veiled by shadow, waiting for Sam Walker to pass him by.

There was a flurry of air as Sam stepped off the end of the boardwalk and struck out across the open ground.

Chen Fai moved into position and started walking after him.

Sam went a few steps more, turned round and faced him. 'Oh, it's you!' he exclaimed sharply. 'I thought I heard someone. What d'you want?'

'To tell you something of interest to you, something I found out yesterday. But I think you've had a drink and you may be too drunk to understand my words, so maybe I won't tell you.' He made as if to go.

Sam grabbed Chen Fai's arm and pulled him round to face him. 'Like you said, I've had a drink. One drink. But that don't make me drunk. If I'd gotten the wages I deserve for the coal I dug today, I could've had more than one drink, and maybe then I'd be drunk, but I didn't. So if you've got somethin' to say, I'll understand it real well. So say it quickly and go.'

Chen Fai assumed an expression of concern. 'It's about your brother Joe, and Charity,' he said.

'Don't you say those two names in the same breath,' Sam snapped. 'And anyway, she's leavin' Carter, I'm delighted to say.'

'They are soon much closer than just in the same breath, as you put it,' Chen Fai said, his tone mild.

Sam stared angrily at him. 'What *are* you talkin' about? Say what you're tryin' to say in simple words.'

'You are correct that she's leaving Carter Town. But she's leaving with your brother. They will have a Chinese wedding first, Charity and Joe.'

'Joe's gonna wed her!' Sam stared at him in amazement, then he threw back his head and laughed. 'Sure she's as hot as a whorehouse on nickel night, but he'd not be so stupid as to wed her! And he wouldn't need to. The way she's followed him around all these years, he could have it for the askin'. And if it's just yellow whores he wants, he can have his fill at the *tong*. Nope, he wouldn't need to wed her.' He laughed again.

'But he is,' Chen Fai said, his face ice-cold.

The laughter stopped abruptly. Sam thrust his face closer. 'You listen real good. I don't want my brother's name in the same sentence as that … that whore. D'you hear?'

Chen Fai gave him a humourless smile. 'I do. But it is not *my* sentences you need to worry about; it is the law's. He will be doing with Charity what is forbidden by American law.'

'Why, you blam-jam, no account, yellow-skinned—' Sam raised his hand to strike Chen Fai, but Chen Fai was faster. He caught Sam's arm and held it in the air.

'No need to cuss me,' he said, his voice stony. 'I'm not the man who is going to break the law and bring shame on

302

the Walker family. I am not the man who make you lose face in front of white miners.' He dropped Sam's arm and stepped back. 'Joe Walker do this; not me.'

'Why're you tellin' me this?' Sam asked, rubbing the place where Chen Fai had gripped him.

'Because I think you want to stop this.'

Sam looked surprised. 'Why would I? In fact, the more I think about it, the more I like the idea of Joe leavin' again, and this time for good. Without him around, Ma might find some time for me. It's always bin Joe this and Joe that,' he added with a snarl, 'even though I've given her a grandson.'

'And he also may give her grandson. But the son of Joe Walker and Charity will be a child with yellow skin. I think you want to stop this because you not want half-caste child in the Walker family, a child with skin and eyes like this.' He pointed to his face. 'Is Walker mother happy to have a Chinese girl in the family, and a son with half-Chinese children? You think this will make white people in Carter Town kind to Walker family when they find out, and they *will* find out?'

Sam stared at him thoughtfully. 'You're right. If my brother had a child with a China woman, and if Carter folk ever found out, I'd never hold my head up again and no one would ever talk to Ma and Pa again. We hate you Celestials.'

'And we feel same about you,' Chen Fai said, his voice filled with hate.

Sam stared at him, his eyes narrowing. 'And what's *your* reason for wantin' to stop it, then?'

'I do not want to stop it; I want wedding to happen. That is the best thing. But I do not want them to have time together after wedding. I do not want the man who take Charity from me to find happiness with her; I want him in jail. And I not mind if Charity is in jail, too. But in a different jail.' He heard the bitterness in his voice, and was angry at himself for showing his hurt, and his jealousy.

'So if you can't have her, no one will. Is that it?' Sam asked with a sneer.

'She brings shame to me and to Chen ancestors. She should have punishment,' he said firmly.

'Then why are you talkin' to me? All you have to do if you want them caught is go to the Marshal. You speak the lingo, after all.'

'Marshal McGregor likes Joe and Charity, and I think he will not do anything. He will say he will go to *tong*, but he will not. So they will marry and get away. If I later complain about this, he will lie and say I not tell him. Whites will not believe a Chinaman against a white marshal. And anyway, they are gone from Carter by then. I not want them to have even one night together.'

'So you want me to tell the Marshal. You think because I'm white, with miner friends, who've always thought Joe looks down on them, thinkin' he's too special to go down in the dark, dangerous mines, you think the Marshal will have to act on what I say as he'd know we'd all be real mad if he didn't. Is that it?'

'Exactly.'

Sam nodded. 'Okay, I'll tell him. Not for your sake, but for ours. So when are they gonna get wed? And where?'

Chen Fai's heart leapt. 'Next Monday morning,' he replied, steadying his voice, suppressing the urge to shout out in glee. 'They must finish ceremony before Marshal goes into *tong* – it proves they plan to live together and this is what law is not allowing. If they not have ceremony, Marshal can do nothing.'

'Right,' Sam said. 'I'll do it. There'll never be a Celestial in the Walker family, not if I can help it, and it don't bother me if I never see that brother of mine again. And now I've agreed, that's you and me finished.' He turned his back on Chen Fai and continued walking towards the miners' houses.

Chen Fai watched him until he was completely out of sight, then he turned and made his way back to his store, a lightness in his step, quiet satisfaction on his face.

'So you're back, are you? You obviously stopped for a drink, even though we've no money.' Phebe's voice was sharp. 'Your dinner's ruined again.'

Sam winced. 'I had one drink; that's all. I was delayed on my way home.'

'There's always a reason, isn't there?' she said angrily. 'It's never because you preferred to stop a while in the saloon rather than come straight home to us, is it?'

'A drink helps me unwind,' he said tetchily. 'But that's not what made me late. If you hobbled your lip and stopped naggin' for a minute, woman, I could tell you what delayed me. Or rather, who delayed me.'

She folded her arms and sat down. 'So what's the story for this evenin'?'

'I've bin talkin' to Chen Fai, haven't I?'

'I very much doubt it. You hate him so why would you talk to him? And why would he wanna talk to you? He knows what you think of him.'

'Aha.' He gave her a knowing look. 'He wanted to tell me somethin' he'd found out and he asked me to do somethin' he couldn't do.' He sat down opposite her. 'Get me some food, will you, and I'll tell you what he said. I reckon it'll interest you. But you've gotta promise me not to tell anyone. D'you promise?'

'I guess so,' she said, sulkily. 'But this better not be just another excuse. Let me get your dinner first, though. It's been on too long already.' And she stood up and went across to the stove, lifted off the saucepan, piled a mass of over-boiled mutton and potatoes on to two plates and carried the plates to the table. She put one in front of him and sat down with the other.

'Be quick about it, then,' she said. 'Thomas is still pretty restless and he could wake at any time. I can't be dealin' with him and listenin' to you. So what's this big secret Chen Fai wanted to tell you?'

He picked up his knife and fork, leaned forward and told her.

Chapter Forty-One

The sun was climbing high in the steel-blue sky on the Monday morning, the first real heat of the year lying heavily on the land, when the Chinese priest came down the stairs in the *tong* between walls that were coloured with decorative paintings of pagodas, and walked across to the entrance hall, his face mottled with purplish-black bruises. His inner robe was covered by the ceremonial red outer robe that he'd wrapped around himself and fastened in the front with a gold clip in the shape of a dragon, and his braid hung down his back from beneath the soft back cap he wore.

He crossed the hall, took his place near the main door, and waited for the two people he was expecting.

Not a breath of air stirred in the streets of Carter Town.

Marshal McGregor took off his Stetson, wiped his forehead with the back of his arm, returned his hat to his head and pulled the brim low over his eyes. Smoothing down his long grey moustache, he looked around at the small group of men standing with him outside the *tong*. 'It's unusually hot for this early in the year, and I dunno about you, but I'm gettin' hotter and hotter, standin' here, listenin' to the sound of that infernal pump. We've not seen hide nor hair of them, and we've been here since early mornin'. I'm going into the *tong* now, and if the priest isn't there, we'll know they're breakin' the law some place else.'

'You want company?' one of the men asked.

'Nope, you men wait here. One of you tell the men round the back I'm goin' inside. They'll need to be on the watch in case anyone's of a mind to leave through the window.'

He pushed the front door open, walked into the *tong*, stopped at the foot of the staircase and looked around.

At a corner table to his right, one Chinaman appeared to be helping another to write Chinese characters. Further away from them, three men were studying a list of figures, and commenting on them. Apart from that, the hall was empty.

He hesitated a moment, and glanced back at the front door, wondering what to do.

At the swish of a skirt, he turned sharply. Two heavily painted Chinese women were coming down the stairs. They reached the bottom, glanced in his direction, looked at each other and raised an eyebrow in amusement. One of them said something in Chinese to the other, and they laughed. They were still laughing when they went into a room on the right of the hall.

A door on the left of the hall started to open, and he heard the sound of the priest's voice.

His heart sinking, the Marshal drew his gun from its holster and waited as the priest slowly edged out, back first, talking to the people who were coming out with him. Raising his gun, he took a step towards them and positioned himself to confront them when they emerged from the room into the hall.

The door opened wider. The priest turned as he came into the hall. At the sight of the Marshal, his gun levelled at him, he stopped and a look of bewilderment crossed his face.

'Marshal!' he exclaimed, his tone of voice questioning.

'Tell the people behind you to come out real slowly,' the Marshal said, his gun trained on the door as he waited for Charity and Joe to appear.

The priest glanced over his shoulder and said a few words in Chinese.

Two elderly Chinese men came out into the hall, shaking in visible fear, their hands pressed together, repeatedly bowing.

Relief washed through the Marshal as he saw the men, and he swallowed a grin. He lowered the gun, straightened up and swore aloud.

'Ah, Marshal. I pleased to see you,' the priest said in jovial tones, coming across to him, his gait reflecting some pain. 'But why you hold a gun in your hand?' His voice rose in exaggerated surprise. 'These two men have dispute over pit teams. We talk all morning and dispute is now solved. We solve it with words, not guns. That is one of things we do here in *tong* – we solve problems.' His voice took on a note of concern. 'But maybe you have a problem I can help with; maybe even solve. You help me not long ago, and I now very happy to help you, if you wish.' He smiled at the Marshal.

Their eyes met – the Marshal's amused; the priest's expressionless.

The Marshal threw back his head and laughed. 'Well, I reckon we got well and truly suckered. You're a wily old dog, I'll give you that. How they did it is a mystery, but I sure as hell believe that they *did* do it, and that they're long gone by now. And that's a mystery I'm guessin' you *could* solve, if you were so minded, but I'm sure you aren't, so I'm gonna save my breath and not ask.'

The priest gave him a small bow. 'Is wise decision, Marshal,' he said, a smile playing across his lips.

The Marshal tucked his gun back into its holster and started to turn away. Then he paused and looked back at the priest. 'I'm real glad I never took you up on that offer of a few hands of poker. I reckon if I had, I would've bin walkin' outa here in nothin' but my smalls!'

And laughing hard, he pushed the door open, glanced back at the priest, touched the brim of his hat to him, and went out on to the street.

At the sound of the Marshal's laughter, Chen Fai, standing in the road outside the mercantile, moved slightly towards the centre of the track and stared down the road towards the *tong*.

He saw the Marshal come out alone, and he saw that his face was wreathed in smiles.

Frowning, Chen Fai took a step or two closer to hear what the Marshal was telling his men, and heard him say that they might as well wind up the business and get off home as there were no signs of anything untoward having happened at the *tong* that day, or on any other day. And there was no one to arrest since there was no reason to think that anyone there had been party to an act that would have broken the law had it taken place.

Without vital evidence to suggest wrongdoing, the Marshal went on, his voice cheerful, they might as well disband – they'd already wasted more than enough time on a mighty hot day on what had proved to be a wild goose chase.

But before they returned to their homes and their work, he added, looking round at the group, he'd like them to join him in the saloon. He wanted to stand them to a glass of who-hit-John as a thank you for their ready willingness at all times to help him crack down on any law-breaking desperadoes that threatened the stability of Carter Town.

Then, led by the Marshall, the men walked boisterously up Main Street to the saloon, passing by Chen Fai without a glance. He turned and watched them go inside.

The doors swung shut behind them, but the sound of their laughter lingered in the air.

His face pale, Chen Fai slid his hands into the opposite sleeves and stared from afar at the Walker house. He'd been watching the house for some time now, but there'd been no sign of Joe Walker or of Charity. And nor of Sam Walker.

As soon as the Marshal and his men had gone into the saloon, he'd hurried to the station to see if Charity and Joe were waiting there – not standing together, but on the same platform – but they weren't. And they hadn't taken any train so far that morning, he'd been told when he'd gone into the depot and asked. They hadn't been at the livery stable, either, he'd found when he'd gone straight there after leaving the station. Only the stable lad had been there.

And neither of them had gone in or out of the Walker house in all of the time he'd been standing outside it.

It could mean only one thing – they'd already gone from Carter, and they'd gone together.

His plan had failed.

The numbness that had struck him the moment he'd seen the satisfaction on the Marshal's face as he'd come out of the *tong* started to lift and give way to rising anger. Anger that such a simple thing as arresting them after their wedding should have gone wrong. Anger that Joe Walker was now going to have the happiness with Charity that he should have had, that he deserved to have had.

Pent-up anger and frustration exploded within him, pounding loudly in his head. It was all Sam Walker's fault that his plan had failed, he seethed.

Sam Walker must have given the wrong message to the Marshal, straightforward message though it was. The message he'd passed on to Sam had been exactly what

Su Lin had told him, and Su Lin had learnt of their plans from Charity herself. Charity wouldn't have lied to her. She couldn't have known that Su Lin was watching out for her, with orders to tell her brother what was in her mind, and she will have spoken with honesty.

But it was his fault, too, he berated himself; yes, it was his fault, too.

He'd been a silly, silly man to trust such an important message to another person. He should have thought harder for a better way of sharing his information, a way that didn't involve anyone in the Walker family. Because of his stupidity and because of Sam Walker's stupidity, Joe Walker had got out of Carter, and had been able to take Charity with him.

Of course, it could be that Sam Walker had given the Marshal the correct message and that for some reason Joe Walker had become fearful about waiting until Monday, and had managed to persuade the priest to perform the forbidden ceremony on an earlier day. But this wasn't likely as there'd have been no reason for any sudden concern.

But however it had happened, they'd got away and would be far from Wyoming by now. And no one had any idea where they'd gone, so no one would be going after them.

Fury blazing within him, he could hardly breathe as he turned and started to walk back to the mercantile.

All those wasted years, he raged inwardly. Years when he could have looked to another town and found a wife there, but with Charity in his heart, and no reason to think she would ever turn her back on him, had chosen not to.

Charity was gravely at fault, too, in the way she'd behaved towards him. As she'd grown older, she must have known that one day he would ask her to become his wife, and she should have made him understand that she might not wish this. To have done so would have freed him before he'd lost his heart to her. But instead of such honesty, she'd agreed to wed him when he'd finally proposed marriage. That she had then betrayed him showed her to be a deceiving, ungrateful woman.

And it was also Joe Walker's fault. If Joe hadn't returned, Charity would have wed him; of that he was sure. He knew she didn't feel about him as he felt about her, but he also knew with certainty that there was no other Chinaman in Carter she would choose to wed instead of him.

But it was his own fault, too, he thought, his steps slowing. He'd blinded himself to what he'd known in his heart and had brought this pain upon himself in part. Long before the grown-up Charity had seen Joe, he'd realised that she didn't crave him in the way he craved her. Never so much as once in all the years they'd been walking out together, when they'd been alone with no one able to see them, had she seemed to struggle to control the sort of feelings and desires that a virtuous Chinese girl would not own to. Not once.

But he had been so determined that she would one day want him as he wanted her that he'd refused to see the true nature of her feelings for him – that she saw him as a friend, and appreciated his many kindnesses, but it was no more than that.

And that was why, fearful for a reason he couldn't put into words, from the moment he'd learnt that Joe Walker was returning, he'd rushed Charity into agreeing to wed him.

That had been wrong of him. It had not been fair to Charity.

But Joe and Charity had not been fair to him, he cried inwardly.

Su Lin was standing in the entrance to the mercantile when he drew near, watching him approach. Disappointment in him radiated from her eyes.

He reached the entrance, and stopped. In a moment of frightening clarity, he saw himself through her eyes, and his stomach turned over. The overwhelming sense of shame that swept through him drove out the last of his anger, and he found himself unable to move.

She took a step towards him, her face white, her eyes fixed on him. 'I watch the *tong* this morning and I see what happen. I also see you. You watch the *tong*. You wait for Marshal McGregor to arrest Joe and Charity. You tell the Marshal what I tell you.' Her voice was cold. 'You not tell the truth when you say you are friend of Charity.'

'You not understand—' he began.

'I understand,' she cut in. 'I believe what you say because I believe you good man. Today I know I am wrong. You not wish Charity well – you wish her in jail. A good man not wish a friend in jail. But you not just wish – you try to make this happen. This is a cruel thing to do. Very cruel. Charity not deserve this. Why you do this?'

Cringing inside, stung by the truth of her words, he bowed his head and placed the palms of his hands together in front of him. 'I do wrong, Su Lin; very wrong. I know this now. And I am very happy that what I try to make happen, not happen. I hope one day you are able to forgive your unworthy brother.'

He stood before her, his head still bowed.

'I look at you,' she said with scorn, 'and I not see good

brother, worthy of respect. I am a very sad and disappointed sister.'

Turning, she walked back into the store, the wind chimes ringing sonorously behind her.

He straightened up and stood on the boardwalk in front of the mercantile, alone with his shame and grief – the shame of having acted in a way that dishonoured his ancestors so, and the grief for what he would never have with Charity, and for what he'd once had with his sister, but might have lost forever.

The notes of the wind chimes died away, the same wind chimes that had told of Charity's arrival each day, but would never again tell of her coming.

He looked up above the entrance, and he saw Charity's face. She was laughing happily as she gazed down at him.

A smile flickered across his lips. He took a step forward and raised his hand to touch her cheek, to feel her warmth, to absorb her forgiveness. But her face faded into nothingness, and he found himself standing in front of the store, grasping at air.

He squeezed his eyes tight shut, trying to block from his sight his sense of his unworthiness, trying to hold back his tears of shame and regret.

There was a faint jangle, and he opened his eyes again.

Su Lin stood in the entrance. 'I find I am not able to leave you like you are now, standing here by yourself,' she said quietly.

'I very very sorry, Su Lin,' he said, and tears rolled slowly down his cheeks. 'Forgive me.'

She stepped close to him.

'You are always a good brother to me. Only once you are not. I try to think of you only as a good brother, not as a man who do a cruel thing to a kind friend. You become a sad man because of Charity and Joe Walker, and a sad man does things he not usually do. I understand this.'

'I am a very sad man, you are right; and I am a very sorry man. I want you to believe me.' His voice caught in his throat.

'I do,' she said. Her voice became warmer. 'And I forgive you. In my heart, I know Charity forgives you, too. And if she is here, she will say what I say: in Green River or Evanston, there is wife for you. You find this wife and one day you are happy man again.'

'I do this soon,' he said, nodding. 'Yes, I do this, Su Lin.'

'And now,' she said, taking his hand with a gentle smile, 'we go in, *ge ge*, and we drink tea.'

Chapter Forty-Two

Sam rushed from the saloon and heard the doors swing clamorously behind him. He stared up at the darkening sky, his face distorted with rage.

Joe had got away!

He put his hands to his head. How in tarnation could that have happened?

What could possibly have gone wrong?

How could the Marshal not have caught him? All he had to do was wait outside the *tong* till Joe and Charity came out, all glowing and happy, thinking they'd got the better of the law-abiding folk in Carter, and then arrest them. What could have been easier than that?

He spun round and headed for Second Street. He had to get home; he had to think. And he couldn't think now, not with the anger that burned inside him. And the bitter, bitter disappointment.

He'd been fizzing with excitement all day at the thought of what he was going to hear when he stopped at the saloon on his way home that evening. With every shovel of coal he'd tossed into the cart, he'd tried to imagine what must be happening on top of the ground at that very moment.

In his head, he'd seen the surprise and horror on the faces of Joe and Charity as they'd emerged from the *tong* and found the Marshal waiting with his men, and he'd seen their expressions as they'd realised they'd be spending that night in jail, and all the rest of their nights. And that they might even finish up at the end of a hangman's rope.

And that never again would they be together.

Apart from in court, they'd never see each other again.

And he'd seen in their faces their anguish as that realisation had dawned on them, and he'd felt their grief.

And it had filled him with pleasure.

Working with ferocious speed, he'd filled cart after cart with pieces of coal, tagged each with his number and sent it on its way, his thoughts in the jail and on what Joe must be thinking as he sat in his cell, far from those green fields he'd always been on about, knowing what the guards might be doing with his woman and that there wasn't a damn thing he could do about it. And knowing he'd brought it all on himself, thinking he could set himself above the law.

He turned into Second Street, tears of helpless frustration blinding his eyes. What an end to a day that had begun with such hope.

The moment he'd gone into the saloon that evening, he'd realised that the day hadn't gone as he'd planned. Instead of a crowded bar, filled with the raucous excitement of men celebrating an arrest that day, there'd been only one or two miners having a drink before heading home, and Marshal McGregor.

The Marshal had been sitting at a table facing the door, a drink in front of him. Sam could almost have sworn that he'd been waiting for him to arrive.

'Evenin', Sam,' the bartender had called to him as he'd gone in.

His steps faltering, he'd taken off his miner's hat and nodded vaguely in the bartender's direction. A chill hand had tightened itself around his heart as he'd stared round the almost deserted bar.

He'd looked back at the Marshal.

'It's powerful quiet this evenin',' he said, hovering near the Marshal's table.

'It sure is,' the Marshal agreed. 'But it wasn't at the end

of the mornin' when I stood the men to a drink after causin' them to waste half the day. It was mighty noisy then.'

'To waste half the day?' Sam echoed questioningly.

'That's what I said.' The Marshal stared up at him, his gaze steady. 'I reckon you got things wrong, Sam. We waited outside the *tong* as the sun rose higher and higher. Sweatin' like pigs we were, and not a thing to show for it. No one went in; no one came out. Nothin' went on in that buildin' that shouldn't've done.' He finished his drink and stood up. 'At least, not today it didn't,' he added with a broad smile, and tipping the brim of his hat to Sam, he'd walked out.

So somehow Joe had got away, Sam raged as he came to the open ground leading to the miners' houses. And with Charity, too. And they'd find the green fields and fresh air they wanted. And it was going to haunt him for the rest of his life, knowing Joe was free, and breeding with a woman who'd be spewing out half-yellow kids.

He reached the place where he'd learnt of Joe's wedding plans, and slowed down, scowling at the spot where Chen Fai had stood. Trust that Celestial to have got the day wrong. There could be no other explanation for what had happened – or not happened.

No one could have warned Joe and Charity in advance because he and Chen Fai were the only two who knew. Su Lin knew, too, but she was a mouse and would never disobey her brother. And Phebe, of course, but he'd heard her say often enough that she couldn't wait for Charity to be out of their lives, so she would've kept quiet.

No, that fool Chen Fai must have confused the day.

His boots pounding loudly on the hard ground, he speeded up his steps and was soon turning down the row of houses.

As he passed his folks' house, he wondered whether to stop, whether in his state of fury he'd be able to control himself while listening to their grief, for they must surely know by now that Joe and Charity had gone, and that they'd never see them again. He shook his head – he knew he couldn't. He'd wait until they'd talked themselves through it and seen it for the good thing it was.

But not as good as it would have been had Joe and the woman been thrown into jail, he thought bitterly. Anger shot through him with every step.

Reaching his house, he pushed the door open. Phebe was standing, one hand on the side of the table, the other in the pocket of her pinafore, staring towards the doorway. Behind her, he could see Thomas sitting up in his bed, his thumb in his mouth, staring towards them both.

'I heard you comin',' she said, her voice shaking. 'Your meal's ready.' She turned to the range.

He stared at her back, frowning. 'You haven't asked me,' he said sharply.

'Asked you what?' She turned slightly towards him, her eyes still on the stove.

'About what happened at the *tong* today.'

She picked up a spoon. 'What happened, then?'

He heard the tremor in her voice, and he felt suddenly cold.

'It was you,' he said slowly. 'You warned Joe or someone.' His voice rose, harsh, accusing. 'Look at me!' She turned slowly to face him. 'I can see it in your eyes.'

'You're right, Sam,' she said, her voice trembling. 'It was your folks I told. Also that you weren't gonna tell the Marshal till Monday mornin'. You knew he liked Joe and Charity and thought the laws against the Chinee unfair, so he might've warned them if you'd told him sooner. By

Monday morning, it'd be too late, and he'd have to get his men together and wait outside the *tong*. He'd have to do it – upholdin' the law's his job. That's what I told your ma and pa.'

His hands clenched into fists. 'My own wife went against me!' His face thunderous, he took a step towards her.

'Don't you wanna know why I told them?' she cried, edging back. 'Aren't you interested?'

He stopped where he was. 'No, not one bit,' he said, his eyes like splinters of ice.

'I didn't do it against you – I did it *for* you, Sam. I did it *for* you.'

'Ha! And how d'you work that one out?' he sneered, taking another step closer to her.

'Because I know you. I know you'd never have been able to live with yourself if you'd been responsible for Joe bein' arrested. I didn't want that—I wanted the old Sam back and that wouldn't have brought him back to me.'

'You've got me all wrong, honey,' he spat. 'There's nothin' I woulda liked better than to see Joe arrested.'

'No, I haven't,' she said, and she moved a shade closer to him. 'It's not 'cos of Joe you would have suffered inside, Sam; it's 'cos of your folks. If Joe had been jailed 'cos of you, you'd have felt their pain every time you saw them. They'd never have gotten over it, and nor would you.'

'You're wrong about that. The whites would've bin speakin' to them again, and they'd soon have felt real good.'

She held out her palms, indicating helplessness. 'But that'll happen anyway now that Joe and Charity have gone. The difference is, your folks will know they're free, not in jail, and they'll be happy for them. Bein' gone 'cos you're in jail or dead isn't the same as bein' gone 'cos you're on a ranch somewhere.'

He scowled. 'I know that.'

'I know you, Sam. If you'd destroyed the lives of the people you love, it would have poisoned every single day of the rest of your life. I couldn't let you do that to yourself.'

'You're talkin' rot, woman!' he exclaimed angrily.

'I don't think so. You've been jealous of Joe for so long, and hatin' the Chinee 'cos of the mines, that you can't see anythin' else. When you've had time to think real hard about what it would have done to your folks, you'll know what I say is true.'

'Breakin' the law's wrong, but it's not me that's breakin' the law; it's Joe, and he should've been punished for it.'

'Then maybe the law's wrong. Is it so dreadful to have fallen in love with a woman he's known all his life? It's his misfortune that she's Chinese. But does he really deserve to be arrested for that?'

'I think he does,' he said, glowering.

'Then think about your pa,' she said, despair in her voice. 'He's more than just your pa – you're real buddies. He was your mine partner; you can't get any closer than that. And look at you after his accident – you didn't stop till you'd got him a job as a breaker. That's 'cos you truly love him. D'you really wanna see him hurt again, and in a worse way? With you bein' the one who caused it?'

Shrugging, he slightly turned away. 'You're makin' more of it than it would've been.'

'And what about your ma?' Phebe went on. 'She helps me with what I need; not 'cos she likes me – I don't think she does – but so you'll have the best home possible. That's because she loves you. Would you really have wanted to destroy her happiness for ever?'

He glared at her. 'I know you're smarter than I am, Phebe, and better with words, but I know my folks. Sure they'd have been sad at first, but they'd have gotten over it. You're my wife and you should've kept silent like you promised. You let me down and that shows what you think of me.'

She went up to him, and stared up into his face. 'You say you think I'm smarter than you. Well, if you can't see how much I love you, then maybe you're right. It's because I love you so much that I wanted to stop somethin' from happenin' that would have destroyed all our lives. And that means Thomas's, too.'

He gave a slight start and looked down at her in surprise. Then a slow smile spread across his face. 'Why, Phebe; you just said you loved me. I can't remember when you last said that.'

'And it's not just me who loves you; so does Thomas. And your folks, and that's why they'll forgive you.' She reached up and ran her fingers lightly down his cheek. 'I'll say it again – I love you, Sam, and I want everythin' to be like it used to be when we were walkin' out together; not like it's become with all the talk of hate.'

'You want it like the early days, do you?' he said, his eyes gazing into hers. 'I seem to recall we could never wait to find ourselves a patch of real soft ground to show how much we loved each other.'

Blushing, she laughed. 'Well, aren't we the lucky ones – we've got a bed now! And I reckon Thomas is about ready to go to sleep.'

Chapter Forty-Three

Wrapping her shawl around her against morning air that had yet to feel the warmth of the sun, Phebe hurried to the Walker house and knocked on the door. It opened almost before the sound of her knock had died away.

She stepped back and laughed nervously. 'Oh, my, that was quick. You must have been standin' right behind the door.'

Martha smiled at her with tired eyes. 'Maybe I was. Maybe I was hopin' you'd stop by this mornin', and if you didn't, maybe I was gonna walk down to you.'

Phebe laughed again. 'So many maybes. But I must be quick – Thomas won't sleep for much longer.'

'We saw Sam returnin' last night, covered in coal dust. His face was black with temper, and we've been worried since. Not about Joe and Charity – we reckon they'll get where they're headin'; Joe knows what he's doin' – but about you. Did Sam figure out it was you who told us about the weddin'?'

'He didn't have to – I told him.'

Martha stared at her in surprise. 'From the mood he seemed to be in, that was a brave thing to do, gal.'

'I wanted everythin' open between us. And I'm glad I did – it turned out all right. He's still bitter about Joe not being caught – I wish I could say other, but I can't. He's never really liked him so I guess that's not to be wondered at. But he's regretful he didn't give any thought to you and his pa. I think he can see now that he let hate and jealousy take over, and he's powerful sorry he didn't think about what it would do to you if Joe was caught. He's not gone to the mine today as he wants to come up now and tell you he's sorry himself, but he's kinda scared about what you'll say.' She hesitated. 'I said you'd forgive him.'

Martha nodded. 'Which we will. You can go and tell him to come up now, and why don't the three of you come and eat with us tonight? It'll show Sam that we truly wanna put all this behind us. Everyone has the right to do somethin' loco once in their lives. He's been a good son over the years, and that's what we're gonna remember.'

A smile spread across Phebe's face. 'Thank you,' she said, her voice shaking a little. 'You forgivin' him will show him how much you think of him. I know he's done wrong ...' Her voice trailed off.

'... But everyone needs to be shown they're loved from time to time,' Martha said gently. 'That's it, isn't it? Since he came back, we've been showin' Joe how much we love him, but maybe we've rather forgotten about Sam.'

'But you've been kind to me, and that's bein' kind to Sam,' Phebe said quickly.

'It's good of you to see it that way, gal. And when we're all less tired, I'm gonna be kinder still, as you put it – I'm gonna come down and help you with the cookin'. I'll show you how it's done instead of just tellin' you. And I'll do the vegetable patch with you.'

Phebe's face lit up. 'I'd sure appreciate that.'

Martha smiled at her. 'Sam's a lucky man to have you for a wife, Phebe, and don't you forget that.'

'How d'you know? I do a heap of complainin' and I can't cook.'

Martha smiled warmly at her. ''Cos I see me in you. You could've gone back east with your folks, takin' Thomas with you, and you'd've had that easy life you keep sayin' you want. But you didn't. You don't like your life here, but you chose to stay. Long ago, I realised how much I'd hate livin' in a minin' town and bein' wed to a miner, and I could've taken the boys and gone back to the ranch. But like you, I chose to stay with my man. Sam did well for himself when he married you, Phebe gal.'

A blush of pleasure spread slowly across Phebe's face.

She pulled her shawl more tightly around her. 'I'd better get back now. Sam'll come right on up. And we'll come this evenin', then; if you're sure you've enough for three extra. Thomas is gettin' a real good appetite.'

'I'm sure, honey,' Martha said firmly. 'There'll always be enough for you. You're family, aren't you?'

She stepped forward, put her arms around Phebe, pulled her close to her and hugged her with every bit of her strength.

'Phebe came to see us the mornin' after you told her, Sam,' Martha said, putting a mug of coffee and a slice of apricot pie in front of him, and sitting down opposite him. Hiram came across to the table with a piece of pie and joined them. 'I was darnin' when she came,' she added. 'Hiram and Charity were here, too.'

Sam nodded. 'I'm sorry,' he said, looking at the table. He raised nervous eyes to his folks. 'I'm real sorry.'

'We know you are, son,' Hiram said quietly.

Sam turned to Martha. 'And you believe me, Ma, don't you?'

She smiled at him, and patted his hand. 'Yes, Sam; I do.'

He nodded again.

'Phebe didn't find it easy to break her promise to you, son, you know?' Martha went on. 'You could tell she felt mighty uncomfortable about it.'

'She told me why she did it.'

Martha leaned across the table, and stared hard at Sam. 'I sure hope you heard more than just her words; I hope you heard the love, 'cos that gal loves you. You'd become so full of hate for the Chinee that you couldn't see anythin' else. But she could, and she knows you well enough to know that if Joe had been caught, you'd never have gotten over it, not only for what it did to us, but for what it did to you.'

'Yesterday, I wouldn't've agreed, but today I'm sayin' you're right. I've bin awake all night, doin' some thinkin', and I reckon I've bin gettin' more and more jealous of Joe over the years. Minin' ain't what it used to be, and for years now, while I've been afear'd about losing my job, there's Joe doin' what he wants to do, and it's makin' him happy. I guess I wanted to wipe that happiness off his face. I don't like that about myself, but I can see it now. I'm always gonna hate the Chinee who've made me like this, but I'm gonna try and think about Joe in a kinder way.'

'I'm mighty pleased to hear that,' Hiram said. 'I know you've never bin close, you bein' five years older and different in your likin's, but you're flesh and blood, and it's good for a man to think of his brother with warmth.'

'And with Phebe as your wife, you've got a chance for a happiness of your own,' Martha said with a smile.

'If she still loves me after all the things I've done or tried to do.'

'Oh, she does,' Martha said. 'I've never been more certain of anythin'. You've got a good gal there.'

Sam nodded. 'Thanks, Ma. I reckon so, too.' And he pulled the pie towards him.

When he'd finished eating, he sat back. 'That was a fine pie,' he said, and he paused a moment. 'I'm gonna ask you both somethin' now, but you don't have to tell me. I wouldn't blame you if you didn't trust me yet. But I sure am curious to know how they got away with it, 'cos I reckon they went through with that weddin' of theirs and were long outa Carter by Monday mornin'. But, as I said, you don't have to tell me.'

Hiram and Martha glanced at each other, then back at Sam.

'We don't mind tellin' you, Sam, 'cos we do trust you,' Hiram said.

'And you know I wouldn't want the white miners knowin' my brother had wed a Celestial,' Sam added wryly.

Hiram smiled.

'It was very simple,' Martha said. 'They brought everythin' forward a day, and 'cos we knew about it, we could help. They got wed early on Sunday in the *tong*. After that, Charity came back here and said goodbye to Hiram. Then she and I took a bag of her clothes and walked to the plain. Anyone seein' us would've thought we were goin' foragin'. Joe met us out there with the wagon. I stayed on a while after they'd left, and then went back through the centre of town so no one would notice Charity wasn't with me any longer.'

Sam looked from Martha to Hiram. 'Sayin' goodbye must've been hard.'

'Charity said the hardest thing about leavin' as they'd originally planned would've been not being able to say goodbye to us to our faces,' Hiram said. 'And we would've found that difficult, too. So in a way you did us a favour, Sam; you and Phebe, too. Thanks to you, we got to say goodbye to them and wish them well.'

Martha shrugged. 'Hiram's right. But I always knew Joe would leave Carter again one day and I'd have to say goodbye at some point, and that helped, even though he'd've been able to come back, and now he won't.' She paused. 'But we believe they'll be happy on the ranch we're sure Joe will get, and that makes us content. And one day, we might even get a message from him, perhaps through Seth, tellin' us where that is. We'd know it was from him, and so would Seth, but others wouldn't.'

'I sure hope you get that message, Ma, and I really mean that,' Sam said, standing up.

'I know you do, Sam; you're a good lad at heart.' She stood up. 'And now I'm gonna get some vegetables for that stew I'm gonna do for you and your family tonight.'

Martha started to move towards the store-closet, then hesitated, turned back and walked across to Sam. Standing in front of him, she opened her arms wide.

He looked at her face, at the forgiveness and love in her eyes. A choking sob escaped him, and he stepped into her embrace.

The sun was shedding a vivid red-gold glow over the plains as Joe and Charity reached a waterhole lined with trees. As Joe brought the wagon to a halt, a flock of dark birds rose from among the leaves, wheeled around in the air above them, and then sank again to the upper branches.

He glanced at the sky. 'It'll be dark before long. There's wood for a fire and water, so I suggest we spend the night here. We no longer need to push ourselves in the way we've been doin' for the past week.'

Charity slid along the wooden seat and nestled close to him. 'That's good,' she said, smiling up at him. 'We've not had a moment to think since we left Carter.'

He put his arm round her and hugged her to him. Resting her head on his shoulder, she fell silent.

'So what are those thoughts you didn't have time to think?' Joe asked after a few minutes.

'I was thinking about our weddin',' she said dreamily. 'By goin' over it in my head, I'm hopin' to make sure I don't forget a single detail.'

'I know I won't. I'm real grateful to the priest – he gave us a weddin' that was way beyond anythin' I'd expected.'

Charity had been the first to get to the *tong*. She was wearing her best blue dress, which she often wore on Sundays. Her golden tiger was pinned to its front. Joe had arrived soon after in the leather jacket and jeans he always wore to the stable.

'You look real grand, Charity,' he'd said, his face breaking into a smile as she turned to him. 'I'm afraid I didn't dare wear fine clothes,' he'd added apologetically, glancing from Charity to the priest. 'We're not a family of churchgoers and I'd've stood out if I'd bin lookin' unusually smart. Folk know I go to the livery every day.'

'I know Chinese brides wear red,' she told the priest, 'but I didn't have a red dress.'

The priest gave a slight bow. 'Red colour is for strength, good luck and good fortune, and I think you and Joe need much good fortune. There is red cloth in the room upstairs. You wear this red cloth over dress.' He turned and moved towards the stairs. 'You come now,' he said with a smile, and he started walking up the stairs.

Hand in hand, they followed him up to the landing, glancing as they went at the paintings on the wall of social scenes in ancient China and of carefully laid-out gardens surrounding elaborate pagodas.

The priest crossed to the right, and opened a door. A strong spicy scent instantly hit them, and they noticed in surprise that cut-outs, duck-shaped and of the phoenix and dragon, had been stuck all around the doorway.

As they went into the room, they saw a deep red banner stretching from one wall to the other, with two large lighted candles flickering on a table beneath the banner. The aroma of incense rose from a censer in the middle of the table. Glancing around them, they saw that more small red cut-outs had been stuck to a large mirror at the back of the room and on all of the cupboards.

Charity looked questioningly at the priest.

'I get *tong* room ready for wedding,' he told them. 'It is custom to have double joy stickers throughout the house on wedding day and in bridal room, and to have red banner in front of houses of man and woman. This announce that joyous event take place.' He gave them a wry smile. 'I think it not a very good idea to have red banner outside Walker house today. Instead, we have banner in here.'

'Thank you,' she said, a wave of emotion rising in her.

'Chinese wedding is ceremony of ritual and custom. I bring red cloth, Charity, and you put cloth on shoulders. In China, bride also wear red veil, but we not have veil. Is no need – Joe already see your face,' he said, and he smiled at them both.

She and Joe beamed at each other.

'It is also custom for man to give woman a pair of dragon and phoenix bangles,' he went on, turning to Joe. 'She wear these during ceremony and after. Dragon and phoenix symbolise great happiness of man and wife – is perfect union. This we do today.' He slipped his hand into the fold of his outer garment and brought out two bangles. 'I give bangles to you, Joe.' He held them out to Joe, who took them. 'They are now your bangles. You now give bangles to Charity.'

Joe slipped them on to her wrist, and squeezed her hand. She smiled up at him, and with her free hand lightly touched the golden tiger.

'Come,' the priest said, walking over to the table beneath the red banner. Taking his place behind the table, he indicated that they stand on the other side, facing him. 'Wedding now begin,' he said solemnly.

At the end of the ceremony, the priest led the way down to the front door. Reaching the door, he bowed to them. 'I hope wedding bring happiness and good fortune,' he said, 'and many sons.' He straightened up.

'I'm mighty grateful to you,' Joe said. 'We couldn't have had a better start to our life together. Thank you from the bottom of my heart.'

'And from me, too,' Charity said, a lump in her throat. 'I haven't the words to tell you how I feel.' She started to slip the bangles from her wrists.

The priest had put up his hand to stop her. 'You keep bangles, Charity. I give them to Joe. Joe give them to you. They are for you now. They are symbol of marriage.' He'd slipped his hand into the fold of his robe and taken out a piece of paper. 'And I have this for you, Joe. It is written in Cantonese and in American. It says you are wed. And you *are* wed, Joe and Charity. In my Chinese heart,' he'd touched his chest, 'I know that is the truth.'

Stepping forward, he'd opened the door for them and together they'd walked out, man and wife in their hearts.

His arm still around Charity, Joe looked up at the sky. The deep blaze of red was giving way to an ever-widening band of the darkest blue. A scattering of stars had appeared on the horizon.

'If we sit here much longer we'll not be able to see to build our fire,' he said. 'We'd better get movin'.'

He jumped down and held up his hand to help Charity from the wagon.

When her feet were on the ground, he pulled her gently to him. Slowly he slid his hands down the back of her bodice and over the flare of her hips. Beneath his fingers, he felt her tremble in excited anticipation.

'I love you, wife,' he said, his eyes burning into hers with passion.

'And I love you, husband. Very much.'

Her arms closed around him.

As he bent his head towards her face, she raised herself towards him on her toes, and their mouths met in the heat of their mutual desire.

Chapter Forty-Four

Seven weeks later

At the very moment that Joe and Charity reached the top of the slope, a shaft of golden sunlight broke through the clouds that had hung low over the land they'd been driving through since leaving the last small town they'd stopped at – a town so young in age that the pine wood used to build the shops, houses and boardwalks was still yellow with newness.

Motionless, they sat on the wagon and gazed down on the lush green grass that stretched from the east to the west, and rolled back from the foot of the slope to the blue-hazed mountains that lay to the north, their snow-capped peaks agleam in the sun. A river meandered through the heart of the valley, bordered by solitary cottonwoods and willows, their leaves shimmering bronze in the shifting rays of the sun.

'It's beautiful,' Charity breathed. 'It's everything the man in town said it was, and more. And look!' She raised her hand and traced with her finger the outline of the mountain peaks, her dragon and phoenix bangles jingling loudly. Then her arm fell to her side and she turned to Joe. 'Did you see that?' she cried in excitement.

'Not really,' he said with a grin. 'What was I meant to see?'

'The peaks are shaped like the pagodas in the paintin's on the walls of the *tong*. Don't laugh, Joe, but I feel as if we were meant to find this place.'

He shook his head. 'I'm not laughin', Charity; I feel

that way, too. This is gonna be our land,' he said, his voice trembling with emotion, and he looked back ahead of him. 'It's got everythin' we need. The town's only half an hour's ride away, and the river will always be fed with water from the mountains, so even if the water level drops in the summer, it won't dry out. Those cottonwoods tell us that – they like to keep their feet wet. And there are trees enough to give us wood and shade, and as for the grass – well, you couldn't want better-looking grass than that. This is ranchin' land. This is the sort of place I used to dream of havin'.'

'And the man in the office said it's not yet been staked, so it could be ours.'

'It sure could.' He inhaled deeply. 'You can smell the freshness of the air, and you can't hear a thing except the sound of the wind and the birds. But the best thing of all,' he said turning to her, his eyes shining with love, 'it's where the two of us can live together. My life would never be complete if you weren't part of it, Charity.'

She trailed her hand across his back and leaned her head against his shoulder. 'And all I'll ever want is to be with you, Joe, mornin', noon and night. I love you.'

He swung round, took her face in his hands and brought his lips down on hers in a kiss that was both hard and tender. Then he jumped from the wagon, took a few steps down the slope and stopped. Charity climbed down from the wagon after him, and went and stood at his side.

'So,' he said, putting his arm around her shoulders and looking down at her with eyes that were ablaze with love. 'Shall we definitely do it? Shall we make this land our home?'

Her gaze travelled across the valley as she slid her arm around his waist. She slipped her free hand into the pocket of her skirt, wrapped her fingers around the small wooden tiger painted in gold with black stripes, and clutched it tightly. 'Oh, yes, Joe.'

A smile of deep happiness spread across his face.

'And I say yes, too,' he said quietly, tightening his arm around her shoulder.

The words hung in the air.

Their hearts beating fast, they looked at each other, and together they turned to face the grass-covered valley that was to be their home. Then raising their eyes, they gazed up above the mountains to the Wyoming sky, a sky that was vast and blue and empty, and waiting for them to fill it with their lives.

Thank you

For ten months, I lived in my head in Carter Town, Wyoming, in the 1870s and 1880s. Throughout those months, as I watched Joe and Charity grow into adulthood, I shared in their hopes and their dreams and their fears. And I loved every minute of those ten months.

Setting a novel in Wyoming again, a State that I came to love when I first went there for research, has been sheer pleasure, and my fervent hope is that you've enjoyed following the lives of the characters – American and Chinese – as much as I enjoyed writing about them.

If you did so, and if you have time, please do take a moment to tell me. My contact details are under my author profile, and I should love to hear from you.

If you are also able to leave a review on Amazon or a book review site such as Goodreads, or a retail outlet site, that would be tremendously kind. Not only are reviews very helpful to readers, but they provide invaluable feedback for authors from the most important of people. After all, for whom is the book written if not for you, the reader?

Happy reading!

Love,

Liz

About the Author

Liz was born in London and now lives in South Oxfordshire with her husband. After graduating from university with a Law degree, she moved to California where she led a varied life, trying her hand at everything from cocktail waitressing on Sunset Strip to working as a secretary to the CEO of a large Japanese trading company, not to mention a stint as 'resident starlet' at MGM. On returning to England, Liz completed a degree in English and taught for a number of years before developing her writing career.

Liz has written several short stories, articles for local newspapers and novellas. She is a member of the Romantic Novelists' Association. *The Road Back* won a Book of the Year Award. Her second novel *A Bargain Struck* was shortlisted for the Romantic Historical Novel of the Year Award.

Follow Liz on:
Twitter @lizharrisauthor
Facebook: https://www.facebook.com/liz.harris.52206
Web: www.lizharrisauthor.com

More Choc Lit

From Liz Harris

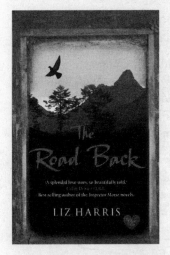

The Road Back

Winner of the 2012 Book of the Year Award from Coffee Time Romance & More

When Patricia accompanies her father, Major George Carstairs, on a trip to Ladakh, north of the Himalayas, in the early 1960s, she sees it as a chance to finally win his love. What she could never have foreseen is meeting Kalden – a local man destined by circumstances beyond his control to be a monk, but fated to be the love of her life.

Despite her father's fury, the lovers are determined to be together, but can their forbidden love survive?

'A splendid love story so beautifully told.' Colin Dexter, O.B.E. Bestselling author of the Inspector Morse series.

Visit www.choc-lit.com for more details, or simply scan barcode using your mobile phone QR reader.

A Bargain Struck

Shortlisted for the 2014 Romantic Historical Novel of the Year Award

Does a good deal make a marriage?

Widower Connor Maguire advertises for a wife to raise his young daughter, Bridget, work the homestead and bear him a son.

Ellen O'Sullivan longs for a home, a husband and a family. On paper, she is everything Connor needs in a wife. However, it soon becomes clear that Ellen has not been entirely truthful.

Will Connor be able to overlook Ellen's dishonesty and keep to his side of the bargain? Or will Bridget's resentment, the attentions of the beautiful Miss Quinn, and the arrival of an unwelcome visitor, combine to prevent the couple from starting anew?

As their personal feelings blur the boundaries of their deal, they begin to wonder if a bargain struck makes a marriage worth keeping.

Set in Wyoming in 1887, a story of a man and a woman brought together through need, not love ...

Visit www.choc-lit.com for more details, or simply scan barcode using your mobile phone QR reader.

A Western Heart

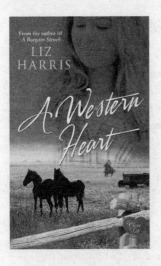

Wyoming, 1880

Rose McKinley and Will Hyde are childhood sweethearts and Rose has always assumed that one day they will wed. As a marriage will mean the merging of two successful ranches, their families certainly have no objections.

All except for Rose's sister, Cora. At seventeen, she is fair sick of being treated like a child who doesn't understand 'womanly feelings'. She has plenty of womanly feelings – and she has them for Will.

When the mysterious and handsome Mr Galloway comes to town and turns Rose's head, Cora sees an opportunity to get what she wants. Will Rose play into her sister's plot or has her heart already been won?

Visit www.choc-lit.com for more details, or simply scan barcode using your mobile phone QR reader.

Evie Undercover

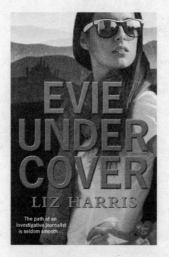

When libel lawyer, Tom Hadleigh acquires a perfect holiday home – a 14th century house that needs restoring, there's a slight problem.
The house is located in the beautiful Umbria countryside and Tom can't speak a word of Italian.

Enter Evie Shaw, masquerading as an agency temp but in reality the newest reporter for gossip magazine Pure Dirt. Unbeknown to Tom, Italian speaking Evie has been sent by her manipulative editor to write an exposé on him. And the stakes are high – Evie's job rests on her success.

But the path for the investigative journalist is seldom smooth, and it certainly never is when the subject in hand is drop-dead gorgeous.

Visit www.choc-lit.com for more details, or simply scan barcode using your mobile phone QR reader.

The Art of Deception

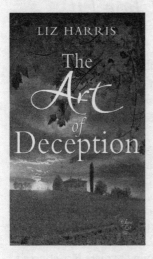

Jenny O'Connor can hardly believe her luck when she's hired to teach summer art classes in Italy. Whilst the prospect of sun, sightseeing and Italian food is hard to resist, Jenny's far more interested in her soon-to-be boss, Max Castanien. She's blamed him for a family tragedy for as long as she can remember and now she wants answers.

But as the summer draws on and she spends more time with Max, she starts to learn first hand that there's a fine line between love and hate.

Visit www.choc-lit.com for more details, or simply scan barcode using your mobile phone QR reader.

Introducing *Choc Lit*

We're an independent publisher creating
a delicious selection of fiction.
Where heroes are like chocolate – irresistible!
Quality stories with a romance at the heart.

See our selection here:
www.choc-lit.com

We'd love to hear how you enjoyed *The Lost Girl*.
Please leave a review where you purchased the novel
or visit: **www.choc-lit.com** and give your feedback.

Choc Lit novels are selected by genuine readers like yourself.
We only publish stories our Choc Lit Tasting Panel want to
see in print. Our reviews and awards speak for themselves.

Could you be a Star Selector and join our Tasting Panel?
Would you like to play a role in choosing which novels we
decide to publish? Do you enjoy reading romance novels?
Then you could be perfect for our Choc Lit Tasting Panel.

Visit here for more details …
www.choc-lit.com/join-the-choc-lit-tasting-panel

Keep in touch:
Sign up for our monthly newsletter Choc Lit Spread for
all the latest news and offers: www.spread.choc-lit.com.
Follow us on Twitter: @ChocLituk and Facebook: Choc Lit.

Or simply scan barcode using your mobile phone QR reader:

Choc Lit
Spread

Twitter

Facebook